MW01269013

The
Fragrance
of
Geraniums

A Time of Grace
Book One

For Marie ♡
With love in Christ,
Alicia G. Ruggieri

Alicia G. Ruggieri

By Alicia G. Ruggieri

A TIME OF GRACE TRILOGY:

The Fragrance of Geraniums

All Our Empty Places

A Love to Come Home To

THE REGENCY ADVENTURES OF JEMIMA SUDBURY – a middle-grade series for girls

The House of Mercy (stand-alone novel)

ISBN: 1503022056
ISBN-13: 978-1503022058

For my nana,
With much love

"In those days they shall say no more,
The fathers have eaten a sour grape,
and the children's teeth are set on edge."

Jeremiah 31:29

CHAPTER ONE

September 1934

She tucked a piece of gold behind her ear, nervously twisting the whisper-thin strands from the root to the tip. Her hands – blue veins rivering through the translucent flesh – shook so badly. She held them out from her body, willing them to stop trembling, entreating, pleading with them. But they wouldn't stop shaking, acting as independent entities, outside of Grace's control.

Desperate now, she clasped them together tighter than the knot that tethered the family cow to its post in the barn. Her knuckles turned white from the pressure. The blood began to hammer through her chest, and she tried to remind herself to breathe…

But breathing was the last thing she really was worried about at the moment.

It's now or never, Grace, she reminded herself. She tasted blood and realized that she'd clenched her jaw so hard that she'd bit the inside of her mouth without meaning to. Hastily, she ran her tongue over her teeth, just in case.

The auditorium had emptied of other students, like a lunchbox after noon. Its vast ceiling domed over the rows and rows of seats, their wood polished by so many years of parents and students sliding around on the surfaces. *In Memory of Pauline Durferts: 1912* proclaimed the gold plaque above the stage's proscenium arch. Grace couldn't see it in the dim light – Mr. Kinner only had a lamp on now – but she'd read it every time there had been a school assembly last year.

What would it be like, Grace often had wondered, *to have a school auditorium named in your honor?* She knew that she would probably never experience that, but wasn't that what secret dreams were for? Grace lived in awe of Pauline Durferts who had the auditorium named after her. Though she wished poor deceased Pauline might have had a more elegant name. Durferts Memorial Auditorium didn't swing off the tongue very prettily... nor did it look so great on the playbills. Grace shrugged. *I suppose, if you have the money to give an auditorium to the high school, it doesn't matter what your last name sounds like.*

She moved down the aisle, silently making her way up to Mr. Kinner. Beneath her blue cardigan, worn so threadbare that she could see her blouse through it in the light, Grace felt her heart clatter loudly. For a moment, she thought that the teacher might hear it. But Mr. Kinner sat with his head turned away from her, seemingly oblivious to Grace's obnoxious heartbeats as she approached him.

Flop. Grace froze in the aisle. Her eyes darted toward Mr. Kinner. He hadn't heard; his head still bent over his papers, the piano lamp sending up a glow, illuminating the man like a candle in the darkness. Relieved, Grace crouched down to examine her shoe.

Where's that elastic? Grace gritted her teeth and felt about in the darkness. Her fingers came into contact with several sticky substances on the worn floor, including a chunk of old bubblegum. She bit back her disgust and kept inching her way around in circles. *Where is that elastic?* Finally, Grace's fingers touched the rubbery strand. She gave a sigh of relief and scooped it up.

But the elastic band had broken. Not merely fallen off, but totally snapped from where she'd put it to hold her flopping sole on - and to take away some of the disgrace her shoes brought her. The hollow agony of her situation nibbled away at Grace's shaky confidence. She couldn't face Mr. Kinner with such an obviously-broken shoe. She couldn't stand to see the derision or, worse, pity smooth over his handsome college-graduate features as he took in not only her dingy plaid skirt, stockingless legs, and scrappy cardigan but also her flopping shoes. As she'd dressed this morning, she'd hoped against hope that the rubber band might mask the fact that her footwear was so... used up. But it hadn't worked after all.

In the dark, cold auditorium, Grace let one tear press its way past her iron reserve. Then she gathered up her broken dreams, folded them neatly in the drawers of her memory, and turned the key. She silently rose to her feet and turned to leave the assembly room by the same door through which she'd entered.

Flop. Flop. Grace froze again. Her shoe was giving her away! Perhaps Mr. Kinner hadn't heard. Perhaps he had immersed himself too entirely in his work to pay any mind to some miscellaneous *flop…*

"Is someone here?" The deep voice, friendly though it was, made Grace nearly choke. She heard the creak of the piano bench and knew that Mr. Kinner had twisted around to look out into the auditorium's blackness. "Hello?"

Grace forced herself to turn. She had thought that her nerves were bad before she'd broken the shoe's rubber band. Now she thought she might really, truly faint. "It's just me, sir," she squeezed out. Her hands went numb. "But I'm going now."

She turned and made it almost to the heavy double exit doors before Mr. Kinner's voice rang out again, cheerfully asking about the shocking thing Grace had actually come here to do:

"Did you want to sign up for something?"

She swallowed and faced him again. My, but the room seemed to have grown every minute she'd been there. She opened her mouth but not a syllable could find its way to her dry tongue, past her stiff teeth. There was nothing for it. She moved down the aisle clumsily, trying to prevent the flop-flopping of her shoe. When she finally reached the piano, Mr. Kinner sat sifting through the stack of papers before him. He smiled up at her. "Grace Picoletti, right?" She nodded and tasted blood in her mouth again. Consciously, she forced her teeth to relax their grip on the inside of her cheek.

"I have the sign-up forms here. Band? No, you don't play an instrument, do you? Theatre?"

He looked up at Grace, who shook her head violently, drawing a smile from him again. "No? What, then?"

Grace swallowed down the lump that felt like cancer in her throat. "Chorus," she managed to breathe out finally, but Mr. Kinner just looked confused.

He hadn't heard. She would have to try again. "Chorus," she forced her voice box to grind out. There, it was done. She felt the sweat cool on her forehead and looked numbly down at her defunct saddle shoes.

"Chorus? Oh, well, what part do you sing?"

Startled, Grace gaped up at him. What did he mean? She had no idea of singing a *part*; she only wanted to be in the chorus, standing as far to the back row as possible. "I… I don't know," she finally stuttered, sure that she looked as foolish as she felt.

Mr. Kinner smiled like he'd been eating molasses cookies, and Grace – in the midst of feeling embarrassed and awkward – found her heart skipping beats. He flipped through the music piled on the piano, selected a single sheet, and set it before him. "Well," he said, eyes on Grace, "do you know *America the Beautiful?*"

Grace nodded. Everyone knew that.

"How about if I play it, and you try to sing along? Just so we can see what your range is." He poised his long fingers expertly over the ivory keys and looked up at her, waiting for her answer.

Grace froze. Sing? In front of Mr. Kinner? Alone, without any other voices to drown hers out?

"Here, I'll get you started." Mr. Kinner tapped his foot a few times and his fingers began to run lightly over the keys, with the same kind of joy she saw her Mama feel when…

But now he was singing in that lovely caramel voice, and he expected her to follow suit! She opened her thin lips, but the notes would not emerge. Mr. Kinner looked over at her encouragingly after the first verse, and Grace tried valiantly once more.

This time, she managed a half-whisper, half-croak for the first few words. Mr. Kinner smiled – Was he making sport or did he like how she sang? Grace tried a few more lines, and Mr. Kinner's lips spread into a wide half-moon as he dropped his hands from the piano and onto his knees. "That was excellent, Grace!" he exclaimed before turning back to the piano, his shining eyes reflecting in the instrument's well-polished surface. Grace turned the color of wild strawberries, confused at the mixture of embarrassment and overpowering pleasure she felt at his compliments.

"I think I'll start you on soprano and go from there. Practice is every Friday after school." Mr. Kinner glanced at his pocket-watch, and the bench squeaked as he rose to his feet with a smile. "I've got to get going now, but you just get this permission slip signed by your parents." He handed her a sheet of mimeographed paper from one of the piles on top of the upright.

Still returning to earth, Grace nearly dropped the permission slip. She clutched at it with her sweaty fingertips. "Thank you," she breathed.

"You're welcome," he returned, grabbing his briefcase from beneath the piano. He clicked off the piano light, and darkness settled into the room, leaving only the light from the partially-open door. "Careful as you exit," he cautioned.

Grace nodded mutely, backing up, holding onto the permission slip for dear life, not paying mind to the flop of her shoe. And of course, that did it. With the sickening knowledge that she was too far gone to do anything about it, Grace stumbled backward in the aisle, clutching helplessly at the empty air. She landed flat on her back, gasping for breath, staring up at the far-off ceiling, desperately pulling her pleated skirt down from where it bunched at her waist.

Before she could regain any composure, though, Mr. Kinner knelt at her side, concern written over his smoothly-shaven face. "Whoa, there. Are you alright?" he asked, hand to her shoulder.

Grace struggled to sit up, and he helped her, holding her elbow gently. She nodded. "I'm... I'm... o-okay," she stammered and scrambled to stand, straightening her skirt and blouse. Her cheek stung where she had hit it on one of the wooden seats, but that was nothing – *nothing* – to the excruciating shame she felt as Mr. Kinner's gaze landed on her shoe. He said nothing, but she saw the surprise, then understanding flood his eyes in the two seconds that he spent looking downwards.

She couldn't bear it. Grace turned and ran. She would not wait to see the pity that surely would spring fresh on Mr. Kinner's countenance, just as it had emerged on every teacher's face for the past several years of her schooling when they began to learn where she came from, what went into the making of a girl named Grace Picoletti.

CHAPTER TWO

Glancing at the sinking sun, Grace quickened her already-fast walk to a trot. She held her schoolbooks tightly against her, as though they formed a breastplate, protecting her against the chill wind that shot through the late September maple trees. Her shoe *flop-flopped* with every step; she'd no other elastic band to hold the sole to the rest of the shoe.

Why did I even bother? she asked herself through the burning tears which she wouldn't let herself weep. *So stupid, Grace... You're always so stupid.* She could hear her brother Cliff jeering that at her, as he always did when she spilled the milk bucket or didn't get the mashed potatoes creamy enough or tripped on the stairs. He'd said it so often that Grace nearly believed it. Did believe it, sometimes.

But every now and then, a spark of rebellion rose within her, rebellion against Cliff and against her second-grade teacher who'd proclaimed her a dunce and against her mother and against everyone who said it in their minds if not in their words: *Grace Picoletti will never amount to anything. She's meant for no more than her mother was...* When the rebellious spark came into her heart, the hope that maybe, just *maybe*, everyone else was wrong, that maybe Grace Picoletti could be a great singer, maybe she would wear fine pearls and dine at fancy hotels, maybe handsome and educated men like Mr. Kinner would fall hopelessly in love with her – well, when that hope came in full force, flooding her bones, filling her spirit, it seemed to hold out the wings that would take her far-far-far from this wretched place in which she lived, from this wretched family of which she had to be a part.

6

Grace kicked the soda-pop bottle that some kid with pocket-money had left lying on the sidewalk. No matter how hard she tried, though, she couldn't seem to get the wings to fit, to give her the flight they promised.

Even as the thoughts of escape thrust themselves through her mind, Grace quickened her pace and entered the upper-middle-class part of Chetham. Usually, she liked to stroll through this neighborhood. Its nicely-designed houses smiled their welcome through freshly-updated paint jobs. Many of the plots included manicured lawns, shimmering bright green in the slant of Indian-summer light, and well-tended gardens.

Involuntarily it seemed, her steps slowed as her eyes felt the lure of a certain two-story wooden house rising up near the sidewalk. It was inconspicuous compared to some of the others in this neighborhood, with little distinction and fewer updates. But one thing compelled her eyes every day toward this particular white house, and today was no exception: Glorious red flowers bloomed from a dozen baskets hanging from the porch's eves, their rich color an exquisitely sharp contrast to the white columns.

This beauty alone brought an unwonted grin to Grace's lips each day, but today she accepted an additional pleasure: The murmured notes of a piano sounded from the open window above the porch. Grace didn't recognize the tune, but she felt certain the pianist must be the lovely dark-haired woman whom she had sometimes seen tending the red-flowered plants.

With a start, Grace came out of her reverie. She turned her feet away from the main street of the fast-growing suburb and toward the bustle of trees growing up the steep hill on her left. Tired though she was, Grace didn't slacken her pace as she ducked into the wooded area, moving along the path the Picoletti children had created over the years. The shortcut would lead right up behind the barn. With any luck and quick work on Grace's part, Mama would never realize Grace had stayed late at school. Dawdling after school would displease Mama to no end; Grace knew this from the very few times she had dared to do it.

She ducked under the low-hanging branch of a pine tree and came into the clearing behind the small weathered barn. If Papa didn't get around to painting it soon, its exterior would match the gray winter landscape just around the season's corner. Beyond the barn, Papa's large brick house stood, a testament to his hard work and cunning in the Chetham, Rhode Island, community. A pity there wasn't more food in the large cupboards within that house. But there were other things more important to Papa than whether or not his family ate.

About to pull open the door, Grace paused when she heard voices inside the barn. *Odd.* She was the only one of the Picoletti children who had barn chores before supper. Unless Mama had heard Bessie's lowing and sent out one of Grace's sisters... but it sounded like a conversation going on in there. Grace listened, ear to the door, holding her breath.

"Let go of me, you whack! What do you think you're doing?" Grace knew that voice; it was one of her two older twin sisters, Louisa. That slang talk was Lou's, too.

"Nothin'. I ain't doin' nothin'! Tryin' to give my sister a hug, is all. Guess you don't want it. You always were as affectionate as a porcupine, Lou!"

Grace frowned. It couldn't be... but she knew it was. *Ben.* Her eldest brother, hair as red as his temper, fun as an ice-cream cone in July, gone to the racetrack these past few years. *Ben... home?*

Grace couldn't stop the smile from flying to her lips, nor her hands from pulling open the splintery barn door. "Ben?" she exhaled into the cold, dim air.

He stood there, taller than she'd remembered him by a good couple of inches. Ben's face showed his surprise at Grace's sudden entrance. He turned toward her, opening his arms. She flew into them, burying her face against the warmth of his plaid shirt. She felt the solid niceness of his chest, and she knew she was secure and safe here with him. Ben smelled of horses and leather and wool. Of tobacco, too, and something stronger.

"Hey, little canary, let me see your face," he said, and Grace drew back to gaze up at him, her hair fluffing from the static of his shirt. "Well, look at you," he whistled. "My little canary, all grown up."

Grace blushed, so happy, so very happy that Ben was back. "You home for good, Ben?" she asked, biting her lip.

Her brother hesitated, then broke into a goofy grin. "We'll see, little sis, okay? Got to talk to the old man, ya know?"

Grace nodded. Last time Ben came back, Papa and he had exchanged words that almost ended with fists. But, oh, maybe this time... She couldn't even phrase the hope that rose within her heart, that organ that was ready to bust out of her chest if she didn't hug Ben tightly again.

"Better get Bessie milked, Grace." The comment came from just inside the cow's stall. Grace turned to see Lou's tight-lipped smirk. Her older sister held out the empty milking bucket toward her. "Mama won't like you being late to supper."

When Grace took the bucket from her, Lou strode out, not giving them a backward glance. Grace rolled her eyes at Ben. They both knew how Lou could be. "Mama know you're here yet?" asked Grace.

"Naw. Thought I'd surprise her at supper. Hey, look what I brought you kids." Ben reached into the sagging back pocket of his brown corduroys and drew out a small but hefty white paper sack. He unfolded the top and held it out toward Grace. She asked permission with her eyes, and he nodded, grinning again, more like a little kid than the older brother - grown man, really – that he was. Her curious eyes peered inside the bag.

"Chocolate babies!" Grace squealed, hardly believing that the bag was more than half-full of the little candy people, their faces and bodies shining darkly in the dim barn light. She glowed at him.

"Go on, have a couple," Ben urged, tumbling a good handful into her palm. They felt cool and delightfully heavy in her hand. The faint chocolate scent wafted from them and mingled with the stronger smell of hay and manure.

Bessie lowed, eager to have her udder relieved by Grace's skillful milking. Grace looked down at the chocolate babies, then up at Ben. "Sorry," she said, moving to pour the candy back into the sack. "I've got to milk Bessie, and quick, or Mama'll skin me alive. Lou'll probably tell her I was late as it is, now."

"Naw, listen, kid," Ben said, pushing her hand back from the bag. "I'll milk the cow. Fast. You sit over here." He drew her over to one of the hay bales lying on the barn floor. "Eat your candy. And then we'll go in to supper together."

Grace smiled up at him and yielded to the pressure of his large hands on her narrow shoulders. She watched as her big brother picked up the milking bucket and moved the three-legged stool over to Bessie's side, beginning the process. She picked up one of the chocolate babies and gazed at it, anticipating the sweet chewiness to come. Rarely did she have a treat like this to herself. If there were a few pennies to spare, to spend on candy or a coffee milk, Grace had to share whatever treat it was with her other siblings... which she didn't mind nearly as much as when Mama insisted that she give the whole treat – whether a milkshake or candy – to poor, dear Evelyn. *Spoiled Evelyn.*

Just thinking of it made Grace bite into the chocolate baby with even more enthusiasm. She rolled the little candy over on her tongue, felt its smooth chocolatiness between her gums and cheek, and swallowed at last with a sigh of contentment. "Thanks, Ben," she said. "These are really good."

He rested his cheek against Bessie's rounded side. "No problem, little girl." The sound of the milk pinged through the barn, rhythmically, soothing Grace's jittery emotions. First, the incident with Mr. Kinner, causing her to despair, and now the intense pleasure of having Ben home. Maybe now, with him here... maybe now their home could be a normal one at last, instead of continuing in the bizarre and embarrassing path that it had taken for as long as Grace could remember.

Sitting there sucking the next chocolate baby, Grace gazed at her brother, who seemed lost in thought. He owned the short, slightly stocky build of all the Picoletti men, deep-chested with arms made for manual labor, muscled from years of working with willful race horses. The prominent jaw that jutted out even more than was natural from its stubbornness. The sensitive aquiline nose, quivering with emotion like one of the Greek heroes Grace had read about in her textbooks. Ben's oval eyes, tapering at the edges as if God had drawn them on with a calligraphy pen; they flashed with anger sometimes and rained down compassion at others. His forehead rose, white and smooth under the thatch of auburn hair, and she could see the suntan line where his cap usually rested.

Grace popped another candy into her mouth. Yes, if anyone could help fix their family, it was one of their own: Ben. No one else would understand why every word of her father gave pleasure and pain at once. Why her mama wept late into the nights – alone – and then presented a countenance of steel at the breakfast table each morning, doling out each child's gray lump of oatmeal like she didn't care if they lived or died, but she would do her duty nonetheless. Why her papa sang like a red-breasted robin in the choir loft, burly chest puffed out, golden hair slicked back like one of the seraphim... and then sneered at Mama's soft humming over the half-broken kitchen stove. Why Ben had left in such a huff three years ago and had now returned.

All these questions, these "whys," Grace turned over in her mind as she sat there on the hay bale, tongue rolling over the chocolate babies, one-by-one. She studied Ben's broad back, the muscles pulsing beneath his worn shirt as his nimble fingers drew the milk from Bessie. "Why'd you go, Ben?" she surprised herself by asking. She heard her voice float out, a speck of sound in the air, thin as Thursday-night soup.

Her brother stopped milking for just a moment, then his hands began pulling again. He turned his head a jot and gave Grace a crooked grin – the kind you give when you're smiling through pain. "Had to go. A man's gotta make his own way, you know." He leaned his cheek against Bessie's side, tan against deep brown, and his dark blue eyes sought Grace's matching ones. "I was sixteen. Almost twenty now, you know."

"I'm nearly sixteen," stated Grace softly, "and I ain't making my own way yet."

"'Am not,' canary. Learn to speak right, and maybe you won't end up a bum like your big brother." Ben smiled, and Grace knew he was joking. "Besides, that's different. You're a girl. Mama needs you."

"Papa needs you, Ben," she answered. "More than Mama needs me. She's got Lou and Nancy."

Ben snorted. "Old Sourpuss and Fancy-Pantsy? They'll never hold a candle to you, Grace, and Mama knows it. She needs you here, so don't you go getting yourself ideas."

He stood up, pulling the stool from beneath himself and setting it against the side of the stall. Suddenly, he looked at Grace with that piercing gaze of his, usually so full of fun and laughter, now turned deadly serious. "By the way, why were you late? School got out a good hour and a half ago, didn't it?"

Grace ducked her head. "Yeah." She didn't dare refuse to answer Ben. But, oh, how to explain…

"Well, what were you doing?" Ben set the milk pail down and took a step toward her, surely meaning to intimidate her.

It worked. Grace bowed her shoulders and huddled a little deeper into the hay bale, wishing she were the size of the mice she could hear scurrying around her; then she would disappear into the crack in the wall. When Ben acted like this, he reminded Grace so much of Mama, whose quiet ways could harden into ice without much warning.

He loomed over her, and Grace jumped up, ducking by him. She fled toward the door before turning toward him, a fake smile plastered on her trembling lips. "Mama probably has supper ready," she heard herself say in a nearly-normal voice.

Ben took two steps and blocked her exit. Though short himself, he far towered over her mere five-foot stature. "Never mind about supper," he said. "Where were you, Grace?"

She stood in silence, staring at his chest, her heart pounding harder than the farrier shoeing a horse. *So stupid, Grace. How could you be so stupid? You knew you would get caught...*

They stayed still for nearly a full minute – Grace knew, for she was counting her heartbeats. Then, she felt her brother's fingers cup her chin ever so gently and urge her to lift her gaze to his. The frightened pain in his eyes startled her, and she realized that Ben seemed angry because that was the only way he knew how to express fear. *Fear of what?*

"Where were you, canary?" Ben's expression begged even as his voice remained so inflexible. "You weren't messing around with some guy, were you?"

Grace jerked her chin out of Ben's hand, flushing with embarrassment and insult. She would have to tell him. "I had to stay after and talk to Mr. Kinner," she informed him scornfully, hoping against hope that he wouldn't pry farther.

But Ben's forehead wrinkled. "Mr. Kinner? Ain't he one of the English teachers?"

She nodded.

"Why'd he make you stay, Grace? You do swell in school, don't you?" he questioned.

She nodded again; she was a straight-A student, nearly. Ben stood staring at her, confused. Finally, she mumbled, "He's got a music class after school, too."

The confusion lingered for a moment. "Yeah, so...?"

Grace looked away, toward Bessie. The small cow crunched her evening hay, her powerful jaw moving slowly in contentment. "So..." She gave Ben a flickering glance. "He's starting a choir. A special one."

"A special one?" Ben echoed. "And you. You wanna join it, is that it?"

She gave a small, stiff nod, shivering in the draft.

"He say you could?"

"Yeah." She scuffed her toe into the old hay littering the barn floor.

"Well," Ben said after a moment, "that's great, Grace. Just great. You tell Mama and Papa yet?"

She shook her head. Ben didn't realize that she and Papa barely spoke to one another. Even less than they had before Ben left... if that was possible.

"Well," he repeated, "I think it's a swell idea. You're the best singer in the family; you should be in Mr. Kinner's special choir. Good for you, kid." His hand fell on her shoulder, giving a rough squeeze. Grace couldn't stop the grin. Ben was proud of her.

"I forgot the permission slip at school," Grace remembered out loud as she and Ben made their way toward the house. Actually, she'd dropped the permission slip when running from humiliation, but she didn't tell Ben that.

"You'll get it tomorrow, kid," assured Ben, carrying the hefty pail of Bessie's milk with one hand.

Grace nodded up at him, smiling. "I'm glad you're home, Ben," she said, peaceful in the gloaming. Her eyes fell on the brick homestead, dark crimson and double-storied, the twilight settling its deep shadows over the gables, making the lights inside shine more brightly.

Ben gave her a wink. "I'm glad to be home, Grace. Whatdaya think Mama made for supper?"

Grace rolled her eyes and elbowed him. How like her brothers, always thinking of food!

CHAPTER THREE

"Where's Papa?" Ben asked, halfway through his mountain of fresh mashed potatoes. Grace looked at the chunk of coveted butter puddling in the center of the mound. Ben's filled fork shoveled another huge bite toward his mouth with an eagerness that didn't give hint of slowing down.

Grace exchanged a furtive glance with Cliff, her closest-in-age brother sitting across the table from her. His eyes widened and then slid shut, obviously not wanting to hear a response to the question.

Grace put her fork down, feeling her stomach tighten. Couldn't Ben have waited to ask until after supper, until after Mama's apple pie had been eaten with black cups of coffee and most of the children had wandered off to squander the few hours remaining before bed?

But, of course, Ben didn't bother with ceremony. No one answered him, though. Not Lou and Nancy, the twins, who sat playing with their meat loaf, afraid to eat for fear it'd go straight to their hips. Not twelve-year-old Evelyn, silently fingering her ribbon-bedecked braids. Nor Cliff, who steadily sank deeper into his chair. And Grace certainly wasn't about to volunteer any information, not when Mama stood there, a motionless statue in a graveyard. Her cheeks flushed – from the hot stove or from Ben's question?

The silence broke. "Didn't nobody hear me?" Ben demanded, swallowing the bite of buttery spuds. He looked at Grace, frowning. Biting her lip, she turned her eyes elsewhere – to the stove, to the new telephone, to the clunky washing machine crouched in the corner – seeking anything but Ben's gaze.

"Mama?"

From lowered lids, Grace saw her mother breathe deeply, sucking air into worn-out lungs. When Ben had asked his question, she'd been up refilling the bowl of corn from a big pot on the black stove. Now Mama, full of her deep breath, turned and met Ben's wondering eyes. "Your Papa is down at Uncle Jack's house. Won't be home 'til breakfast, most likely." She set the bowl down on the blue-printed tablecloth with a silent bang and turned back to the stove, busying herself with cutting up more meatloaf that nobody wanted anymore.

Ben stirred his mashed potatoes with his fork. "What do you mean, Mama?" He measured his words carefully, cut them through and hung them in the air like freshly-washed laundry on the line.

"What I said." Mama didn't turn this time, just stood with her back to them. Looking at her mama's still form, Grace felt like her insides might collapse, that the sorrow within had left such a vacuum that she might just crumple up and disappear one of these days. Perhaps everyone in their house would, as well.

Except for Papa. He was safe.

Grace risked a glance at Ben. His jaw ground, and he blinked hard and fast. Finally, he said just one word. A name. "Gertrude?" It fell into the atmosphere, a dark meteorite.

Mama didn't reply, didn't provide any indication that she had heard her eldest son. Just kept cutting meatloaf.

No matter, though. Ben pushed his chair back anyway, the scrape against the wood loud in the awkward quiet. "I'll be back," he announced. Grace threw a frightened look at Lou, who ignored her.

"Ben…" Mama's voice crawled over the heads of her half-dozen children.

Halfway to the door, Ben paused, shoving his cap on his head. His curls stuck out like tongues of fire beneath the brim. "Yeah, Mama?"

"Won't do any good, you know. Never does." Mama tucked loose strands of hair behind her flushed ears. Her blue-green eyes wore the dullness of resignation.

Ben stayed there, silent a moment. Then, jaw set, he pulled on his jacket and left. The door moaned behind him; Grace figured it was sick and tired of being opened and closed so often each day.

Mama sighed, wiped her hands on her apron, and removed it. "Nan and Lou, clean up, will you?" Mama's hand went to the back of one of the chairs, and Grace saw the knuckles whiten as she gripped it, her arm shaking.

"I got homework, Mama," protested Lou.

Grace raised her eyebrows. Lou may have had homework, but she was not known for doing any of it. Lou usually occupied her evening hours with re-reading dog-eared copies of Hollywood magazines.

"Just do it, Lou." Obviously, Mama wasn't in the mood to be argued with, which Lou must have realized. Her sister shut her mouth in a pout but said nothing more.

"Grace will help you," Mama offered, slowly making her way out of the kitchen. Her steps headed toward the living room, where Grace knew Mama would lie down on the couch and rest. And wait for Papa to come home, hopefully before morning.

Evelyn jumped up from her place, not even bringing her dirty plate and cup to the sink. Her spaghetti legs trotted after Mama into the living room as usual.

Grace saw Lou exchange an eye-rolling glance with Nancy. The twins may not have been identical in looks – though their sandy-haired, light-eyed beauty certainly had its similarities – but the two girls were carbon copies in character.

"I'm meeting Richard for a soda," Nancy stated, fluffing her finger-waves. "You wanna come? Ernie's gonna be there," she encouraged Lou.

The scowl dropped from Lou's face. Grace could see that the delight of an ice-cream soda – paid for by longsuffering Ernie – had thoroughly brightened her sister's evening. "Yeah!" she agreed. "Just let me get my sweater."

Grace looked at the piles of dirty dishes lining the table and the hills of pots soaking next to the sink. "Wait! You have to help me with the dishes first!"

Lou sneered. "Says who?"

Grace gulped. "Mama did. You know it." She sent a pleading look toward Cliff, who sat gnawing a piece of bread. But Cliff just shrugged again.

Nancy snorted. "Come on, Lou. I don't have all night."

Lou gave Grace a mocking glance and headed through the wide archway that linked the kitchen with the foyer. A grand staircase, worn by generations of feet, ascended to the house's upper level from there. Grace followed Lou toward the staircase, feeling helpless to stop her sisters. Halfway up the stair, Lou whirled and looked down at Grace, waiting at the bottom. "Don't you dare tattle to Mama on us, either, Grace!"

Satisfied with this last gesture, Lou disappeared up the stairs.

~ ~ ~

Midnight had come and gone before Grace heard the kitchen door open and shut. The elderly doorknob squeaked in weak protest as it locked.

Ben.

Grace propped herself up on her elbows, listening for his footfalls on the stair. Her bedroom — well, hers and Lou's and Nancy's and Evelyn's — lay just to the top of the curving staircase, and Grace had made sure to leave the door open just a crack before she'd turned out the light.

The heavy scuff of his boots sounded on the wood. Grace slid her legs from under the covers and felt the chill of the September night settle over her. But no matter. She needed to talk to Ben, needed to know the truth… if he'd discovered it.

A glance at Lou and Nancy's bed told her that the twins slept soundly, tired out, no doubt, from their soda-fountain dates. Lou had taken the time before bed to put her hair up in rags; tonight, she might look like a sheepdog, but in the morning, Grace knew her older sister would have an enviable head of glossy curls — her consolation for not being born a true blonde.

And Evelyn. She curled up like a flower on the other half of Grace's narrow bed, the petals of her white nightgown billowed around her. The twelve-year-old's pink mouth hung open in the sweet rest of childhood, her face a mask of peace. Fleetingly, jealousy stabbed at Grace. She couldn't remember when she'd felt so tranquil. Biting her lip, Grace turned to the door and eased it open.

No light shone in the hallway except for Ben's flashlight. He must have heard something, carefully quiet though Grace had been. The flashlight's beam turned toward her, blinding her momentarily with its brilliance. As her eyes adjusted, she saw Ben's face relax.

"Grace," he whispered. "What are you doing up? It's past midnight, don't you know." He stood, broad shoulders bowed a little, arms hanging by his sides. His voice held the weariness of an old dog, too arthritic to chase another squirrel, wanting only a soft square of bedding upon which to lay his gray muzzle.

Grace stepped out gingerly into the hallway, chillier than her bedroom. "You went to Uncle Jack's," she stated softly, shivering. Her eyes went to his, open and pleading with him to tell her, to do no more lying than had already been done, was done each day, in their home.

He met her gaze honestly, albeit reluctantly. "Yep. I did," he said and turned his face away. The harsh scent of brandy bit at Grace's senses, bringing with it a breath of fear.

There was silence for a moment. Then Grace compelled herself to speak again. "You been there all this time, Ben?"

He drew in a breath through his nostrils, tightening the corners of his mouth. "No, Grace. I went for a drink afterward. Had to cool off, ya know."

He'd gotten into a fight with Papa, then. She'd known that he would, and Mama had, too. Ben must have found what was going on with their father, what Mama and Aunt Mary Evelyn whispered about on the telephone every morning, Mama's voice a fluttering, torn-winged moth.

She laid a hand, small and quivering, on Ben's brawny forearm. "Ben," she whispered, "what is it? What's going on?"

He turned his face back toward her, and she could see the hurt ringed by bitterness in the crinkles of his eyes. "Oh, little canary-bird," he murmured, "what *is* going on?" He let out his breath in a booze-tinged puff. "God help us, I wish I knew."

Grace started back. "But… Uncle Jack's… Papa…" She couldn't finish the sentences.

Ben's lips curled up. "Oh, yeah, I know the facts. You want those?"

She nodded, desperate.

He studied her a moment, then said, "You always were ahead of the game, kid. Why not here, too?" He motioned with his grizzled jaw toward the stairway. "Grab your sweater. I'll meet you out at the barn. Can't risk Mama hearing us."

Relief flooded through Grace's limbs. "I'll be right there," she promised, almost happy to finally have some answers, terrible though they might be.

"Alright." Ben handed her the flashlight. "Here, take this. You'll need it. It's dark out tonight." He turned and disappeared down the stair without another word.

Grace clicked the flashlight off to save the battery and set it down outside the doorway while she entered the bedroom to retrieve her thickest sweater. Having done that, she picked up the flashlight again but didn't turn it on. Her bare feet picked their way down the pitch-black stair, guided by many nights' experience.

Turning on the flashlight, Grace threaded her way around the dining room table and past the looming grandfather clock, ticking the minutes of her life away on its impassive ivory face. When she was just a child, Grace had shuddered to pass the towering clock in the evening, sure that he — it, rather — would reach forward with concealed arms and grab her. He — it — would open its long front and pull her inside, consuming her in the darkness. Now, however, Grace was fifteen, nearly sixteen. Certainly no child, regardless of what Lou and Nancy said. So, she raised her chin and passed the clock without a shudder.

Almost.

The dirt path gleamed clearly beneath the full moon's gaze as Grace dashed from the back door to the barn. She caught sight of an owl swooping down in the meadow beyond the out-buildings; it caught hold of its helpless prey. A shiver ran through her body, adding more speed to her already-flying bare feet.

When she eased open the barn door, its hinge squeaked so slightly but sounded awfully loud in the silent night.

Ben sat on a hay bale, smoking a cigarette.

CHAPTER FOUR

She was still so small, this little sister of his with the hair of sunset gold. Fifteen-going-on-sixteen, just like she'd claimed, but she barely weighed eighty-five pounds, he was sure. Ben studied her standing there before him, his heart panging with the knowledge that he would break her innocent, sweet childishness, or what was left of it.

No matter what way I cut the pie, the same gross outcome...

"Canary-bird," he greeted Grace with the old pet name from their childhood... *Did we ever have a childhood?* He blew out a cloud of smoke, threw his cigarette stub down, and crushed its life out. It felt good to master something, once and for all, here at home.

"Hi," she gave a useless greeting. She was unsure of herself, he could see that from the way she kept darting her eyes from the flashlight's beam to his face, back-and-forth like a peeper frog. He moved over, making room for her. She gingerly took the seat, her slight weight causing the bale to release the aroma of sweet hay, laden with the ghosts of hot July days.

"You ain't gonna be able to get up for school, kid," he murmured, gazing at her. His sister had a nose too big for classic beauty, but the rest of her features more than made up for that, in Ben's opinion. Big blue eyes, softly curling hair, petite frame – the whole package. 'Course, she was still a kid.

"It's Saturday tomorrow," Grace replied, turning her trusting eyes to him and clicking off the flashlight. Darkness took utter possession of the barn, except for the large window behind them. That window let in enough of the pregnant moon's light for Ben to make out Grace's expression. So extremely serious, like she knew that she stood on the edge of the precipice of knowledge. *Well, you gotta grow up sometime, kid.* He consciously hardened his emotions. *Might as well be now.* Ben opened his mouth, but no words came out.

Grace did not wait for him. "Ben," she started softly, "what's going on? With... With Papa and... and..." She trailed off, not knowing how to finish.

He scrutinized her, curious. "How much do you already know?"

"Not much," she answered. "Not for sure. But more than Evelyn, I'll bet. And more than Mama thinks I do."

Ben nodded. He'd give her the basics, then. And he'd start with the least painful. "Well, the first thing you need to know is, I'm leaving tomorrow, canary-bird."

She grabbed one of his arms with both her hands, her strongest grip nothing on his horse-toughened muscles. "No!" she gasped. "No, Ben!"

He gently extricated himself from her hold on him. "Got to, sis. Papa ain't gonna want me around here after what I did to him."

Her eyes searched his face. "What do you mean, Ben? What'd you do to Papa?"

"Punched him good. Right in his kisser," Ben ground out, wallowing in the hatred he could hear in his own voice.

Grace sat silent, the dim light touching her golden strands. He had shocked her, and he knew the reason – hearing that the son of Charlie Picoletti would strike his own father. "He got me, too," he offered after a moment of silence, turning his right cheek so that Grace could examine it. It was an olive branch of sorts, to get her to listen, at least.

His kid sister sucked in her breath and reached out to touch the raised welt. Papa's backhanded whack had resulted in a wound that threatened to close off Ben's sight for a few days, if it kept swelling. "What happened, Ben?" Grace whispered, her fingers floating over the injured cheekbone before they dropped back into her nightgowned lap.

Ben couldn't face Grace when he told her the truth. He jumped up from the hay bale and stared into the blackness of Bessie's stall. He could hear the mellow crunching as the cow moved bunches of hay around with her teeth. Yet the familiar sound did not comfort him tonight. He pulled out another cigarette – the fourth this hour – and struck the match hard.

His fingers glowed orange in the small flame's light, shaking a little. Shoot, but this was hard! How did you tell your sister what everyone in town had whispered about your papa, about her papa – for years, mind you – everyone whispering but no one saying it out loud? At last, he lit the cigarette and threw away the match. He glanced over his shoulder. Grace was still there on the hay bale, like a bowed white birch waiting for the blast of a storm.

"What is it?" she asked, and he could see her pale fingers gripping the bale's edge. "What?"

"Caught him red-handed, that jerk. Caught him cheatin' on Mama with that loose sister of Uncle Jack's." Ben drew in the strength of the cigarette smoke. "So I punched his cheatin' kisser."

A half-laugh, strangled with pain, escaped him. "I threw him… threw him into a wall before he knew what hit him." He risked another look at Grace. She sat fixed, eyes wide as rain puddles on March streets.

Finally, she adjusted her position and dropped her gaze. "Is that… Gertrude?"

"Yeah. Gertrude," he spat out the name and mentally followed it with several choice curses he'd picked up at the racetrack.

He'd met Papa's brother-in-law's sister just once, right before he'd left to make his own way a few years ago. He and Papa had never seen eye-to-eye on lots of things; that much was as obvious then as now. But Ben had thought at the time that Gertrude was just a flirty woman with whom Papa liked to play. Ben didn't care to deny a man his toy, mind you, but humiliating Mama and the entire family was another thing entirely.

"Did you know? Is that why you came back?" Grace asked.

He sighed. "I didn't know for sure. One of them Polish fellows came up to work at the track. I got into a fight with him over something stupid, and, well, he brought up Gertrude. Said that Mama was the laughingstock of Chetham."

He met Grace's tear-filled eyes. "When I got back, I asked around. Seems like Papa's been open about this love affair with everyone. Except for Mama."

"Does Mama know, though?" Grace traced her toe in the dust covering the barn floor.

"Course she does!" Ben flung the words out. They slapped Grace, and he regretted his harshness.

"Sure she does," he said more gently. "Mama ain't stupid, Grace. Neither is Papa. He *knows* that she knows. And he don't care, you see? That's what gets to me. He don't care that he's killing her." Ben blinked back the weak tears that sprang up in his eyes. "And that's why I'm going. I told him what I think. With my fist." He pounded his balled-up right hand into his left palm for emphasis.

Surely, Grace would understand. Would know that he'd done all he could. How he could use another shot of brandy right now! With a sigh, he leaned against the frame of the open barn door. He stared out at the moon, sagging in the night sky.

Long silence reigned. Bessie crunched her hay. The crickets chirruped in their autumnal ecstasy. Far off, so distant that it could barely touch their hearing, a robin began his deep song. The sound gave Ben the urge to tell Grace what bit at his heart, young though she was. "We're all in the gutter, but some of us are looking at the stars," he murmured.

"What's that?" Grace asked, coming to his side.

Ben looked down into her eyes, then back out at the grassy expanse leading to the house. Would he ever return now? What was there to return for? "Nothing. Just something I read in a book once." He forced a smile. "Promise me something, canary bird."

"Yeah?" She leaned against him and gazed up into his face. "What is it, Ben?"

"Promise me that you won't settle. You'll do something with yourself." His voice had grown more earnest than he'd meant it to, and he saw fear enter her eyes.

"Whadaya mean, Ben? Do something with myself? What do you want me to do?" The words fell over each other, trembling, and, without thinking, Ben grabbed her by the shoulders and pinned her eyes with his.

"You show Papa he can't crush you with all this stuff," he insisted, willing her to understand without him spelling it out. Without the words Papa had spoken exploding through this meadow and barn.

But still Grace shook her head. "Crush us? What do you mean? What stuff? I know Mama feels bad, but…" Her voice trailed off as Ben held her gaze. "What is it, Ben? What aren't you telling me?"

He bit his chapped lip, feeling the rough skin with his tongue. "It might be nothing. Might just be something Papa said in the heat of a fight, Grace. You know, it's not every day that your son punches you out." He managed a laugh and stepped into the yard, intending to reach the house before she pulled it out of him.

But Grace caught him by the arm before he could go four feet. "What is it? What did Papa say?" she begged, eyes wide, pulling on his scrappy shirt.

Well, she might as well know what kind of man had fathered her. Ben swallowed and straightened his shoulders. "He's bringing her here," he said hoarsely, barely comprehending the statement, though he said it.

"What?" Grace frowned, obviously puzzled. "Who? Papa? Who is Papa bringing here?" With her typical nervous gesture, Grace scraped her hair behind her ears.

"Gertrude." Ben nearly vomited the name. "He said he's bringing Gertrude here. To live."

CHAPTER FIVE

Geoffrey Kinner pushed the pile of essays to the side of his desk, neatening the stack with his aching hands. Graded at last. He smiled and leaned back, glad to have finished early enough to get the lawn mowed. *One last time before winter sets in*, Emmeline had reminded him today as she'd kissed him after breakfast.

Emmeline. He could hear the old ivory keys yielding to her artistry in the room above him. Geoff's smile widened. That instrument never cooperated with him so well as it did with his wife. But then, Emmeline queened over all she touched in life, it seemed. *Even me*, he thought, fully grinning now. He rose from his chair, stretching his back, hearing the joints crack into place, feeling like a dog who had snoozed too long in a sunny patch.

The piano grew louder as he moved into the hallway, taking his time. He relished the way Emmeline embellished the old hymns, adding a little extra chord here, a long string of notes there. She played "Great is Thy Faithfulness" today; Pastor Reed probably had listed it as a hymn for Sunday's service. Emmeline always liked to practice the hymns ahead of time.

Geoff climbed the stairs softly, avoiding the creaky fourth step. He reached the threshold of the music room just as she came to the last stanza. He leaned against the doorjamb, thumbs hooked under his suspenders, gazing at his beautiful wife.

True, Emmeline had never possessed the movie-star-vixen attractiveness that seemed all the rage nowadays. When Geoff asserted that she was, quite simply, perfect in every particular, his wife usually rolled her caramel eyes and pointed out some imperfection of which she knew. But to Geoff, Emmeline's loveliness came from within, a rose opening to show its deep inner worth. He found her deep brown hair, flowing down her back like dark waves on the beach, and her olive complexion very pretty, it was true. But Geoff saw even deeper imprints of beauty in his beloved: her compassion for the poor and elderly, her zeal for the gospel, her unwavering commitment to the truth. These and so many other traits had drawn him toward Emmeline when they'd met so young – only fifteen – and kept him fixed to her now that they were an old married couple in their late twenties.

She pressed the last chord onto the upright's keyboard and paused for a moment, mouth open as if breathing in a final gasp of music. Then, whirling around on the short piano stool, she turned to face him. "Geoff." She smiled. "I'll get lunch ready in a jiffy. Are you hungry?"

He nodded. "I could eat a rhinoceros. Finished grading those papers, so I can mow the lawn after lunch."

"Super," his wife replied, rising from the stool. Gently, Emmeline pulled the hinged lid over the keys. "We're having chicken salad sandwiches," she informed him, taking her folded cardigan from the armchair near the window.

"Sounds good," he commented, and they began to descend the staircase together.

"I forgot to ask," Emmeline said suddenly. "How many children signed up for chorus? I know you were expecting a low turnout." She gave him a sympathetic smile.

"Oh, it wasn't too bad," Geoff replied as they reached the bottom of the staircase. "Maybe twenty-five." They turned into the tiny kitchen. When they'd first purchased the house three years ago, Emmeline had sewn yellow-checked curtains for the windows and cushions for the old but sturdy wooden chairs. When Geoff's mother heard about the cheerful color scheme, she'd sent some matching quilted potholders, too. Now the once-dismal room exuded a light-filled welcome.

Going to the refrigerator, Emmeline nodded. "It's tough for some students to commit to staying after school, probably. Some of the farm kids have a lot of chores." She pulled out the chicken salad she'd made from last-night's dinner remains and began spooning it onto slices of homemade bread.

"Yeah, that's true," Geoff agreed. He took down two glasses from the cupboard and poured water into them before setting them on the table.

His wife placed their lunch plates near the glasses. "For some, there's not much choice, though. It's either have the children do the chores or don't eat." Geoff pulled out her chair for her, his mouth watering as he looked at the chicken salad heaped high on the grainy bread.

"Let's pray." He reached for his wife's small hands and asked the Lord's blessing on their meal.

The chicken salad tasted as delicious as it looked, and Geoff enjoyed several bites before reviving their conversation. "Speaking of kids being poor, I did have one surprising student sign up for the chorus."

"Oh?" Emmeline raised her eyebrows, mid-bite. "Who?"

He shook his head. "I don't think you know the family. Catholic, I believe. Or, if not, they don't go to First Baptist," he said, referring to the church that he and Emmeline attended.

She nodded. The large Catholic church rose tall across the street from the high school where Geoff taught, and it received hundreds of congregants each Saturday and Sunday for Mass. "Go on," she said.

Geoff swallowed another bite before continuing. "Her name's Grace Picoletti. I had her in a literature class last year and I've got her again this year. Good student, very quiet. I had her older sisters a couple years ago… and I think I might have had her brother or maybe a cousin of hers the first year I taught." He shook his head. "Never expected her to sign up."

"Did you have her sing for you?" Emmeline took an apple and bit into it.

"Yes, and, boy, can that girl sing." Geoff reached for an apple, too, selecting a deep red one blushed with the gold of sunlight. "You wouldn't know it to look at her. She seems like just another kid from one of those poor Italian families, the ones that scrape by, selling milk from the family cow, you know?" He smiled, remembering. "Her shoe nearly fell off as she was leaving. She had attached the sole with a rubber band."

"Oh, poor thing," Emmeline exclaimed. "I hope you didn't have her sing in front of anyone, Geoff."

"No, of course not. It was after school, and I think she waited purposely until everyone else had their turn and left. Nobody but she and I was there."

"What part will you have her sing?"

"Soprano at first. That is," he paused, "if she comes back. When that incident happened with her shoe, she pretty much fled the auditorium. And forgot her permission slip." He shook his head, remembering how he'd found the paper in the aisle after the girl ran away.

Emmeline smiled. "She'll probably be back." She rose, the legs of her chair scraping the floor, and picked up Geoff's empty plate, stacking it on her own. Geoff admired his wife's easy grace as Emmeline brought the dirty dishes to the sink. She filled the basin with warm water and shook in a handful of soap flakes. "By the way," she said, plunging the plates into the soapy mixture, "I have a doctor's appointment this afternoon."

Geoff raised his eyebrows. "Why? Is something wrong?" He felt his throat tighten at the thought.

"No, I don't think anything is wrong," Emmeline answered, her back to him. He heard a happy note enter her voice.

Geoff sat for just a second, then he found himself at the sink beside Emmeline. "Emmeline!" He took her shoulders with both his hands, turning her toward him. He knew. He knew what secret Emmeline's words held just by looking at her beaming face.

Yet, his chest tightened a little. They'd been through this so often, with so many disappointments... "Are you sure?" He hated to ask it.

But his wife's eyes shone at him. "I waited until the fourth month this time, Geoff. All the other times... We lost them before then." She gave him a butterfly of a kiss. "Don't be afraid to hope, darling. I think that God has answered us at last."

At an utter loss for words, Geoff could do nothing but fold Emmeline in his arms. Joy burst in his heart like firecrackers, lit by faith.

He has answered us.

CHAPTER SIX

"Hey, Ma," Grace heard Ben say. It was his typical way of starting conversations that he didn't want to begin in the first place. Poised halfway down the staircase, Grace stopped stock-still, barely breathing. She didn't want to let Mama or Ben know that she stood just on the other side of the kitchen wall, its thin boards releasing nearly every sound into her hearing. Grace clutched her church dress in her hands; she'd been on her way to iron it.

Thwack. Thwack. Thwack. Mama's knife hit the table with a sure, unmusical rhythm as it cut through the raw carrots, surely for a soup tonight.

"Mama..." Ben dragged out her name again when she didn't reply to his first statement. A pause ensued, and Grace figured that Mama must have glanced up, urging him with raised eyebrows to continue.

"Mama, I gotta go back to the track, you know." Ben paused. "Got myself a good job there."

Mama snorted. "What, as a gambler?"

"Aw, no, Mama, I'm a groom for some big-shot politician. The guy says he's gonna be a senator."

Mama didn't speak, just kept chopping those vegetables. *Thwack. Thwack.* Ben waited through a few moments of anxious silence, then kept going out of sheer nervousness, Grace figured. "You don't need me around here, Mama. You got Cliff-"

"Cliff," Mama repeated, and Grace could imagine Mama's eyes rolling around. The knife stopped its beat, and Grace heard the

29

sound of the carrot pieces falling over each other as Mama poured them into the iron pot for boiling. "You think your brother Cliff is a help to me? A thirteen-year-old boy who can't be trusted to water the chickens? Who plays hooky every chance he gets?" She blew out a disgusted breath. "Cliff's gonna end up like his father."

"Cliff ain't like Papa," Ben ground out, a rabid tone leaping into his smooth voice. "That good-for-nothing…" His words trailed off, and Grace could only hear the water running into the pot as Mama filled it at the sink.

"You know what I found out the other night, Mama." It was just a statement, no question hidden among its folds.

Quiet, then, "Told you not to go to Uncle Jack's," Mama nearly whispered. Then, "Yeah, I know what you found."

Quiet again. "I knocked out his tooth, Mama," Ben said.

"You what?"

Grace heard Ben begin pacing, his boots thudding on the wooden floor.

"Busted out his front tooth. At least one. There was a hole there when I left Uncle Jack's and blood dripping down his blasted chin."

"Ben, why'd you do that? Now your papa's gonna have to see if he can get it fixed and-"

"Don'tcha get it, Mama? He's cheating on you!" Ben burst out. Grace heard his hands slam on the table. "How can you care about that man's teeth when…" Again, he let his words fade out, an explosion of empty shells. Ben would never use bad language in front of Mama.

Grace crept down the rest of the stairs, skipping the step that groaned. Hidden by shadows in the unlit living room, she peered through the crack between the kitchen door and the wall.

Over the bubbling pot, Mama stood slicing onions as if her life depended on it. Wiped her eyes with the back of her hand once or twice every ten seconds.

Ben moved over to her side, his steps slow and tired, sore from walking the valley of the shadow so many of his twenty years. He tenderly lifted Mama's chin with one work-hardened hand and gazed into her round eyes set in that tough little face. "Mama, why don't you just leave him?"

Deep silence reigned for seventeen heartbeats; Grace counted them. Then Mama removed Ben's hand from her chin. "Son," she said, "you don't know nothing. You think you're so smart, bringing your big-city notions here. You think the neighbors don't know what your papa does? They know, and they snicker behind my back and the children's. What do you suppose they'd make of a mother of six – seven come February – leaving her husband? And what about the priest?"

"Seven... You're gonna have another one, Mama?" Ben sounded incredulous. His eyes dropped to her midsection, then rose again to her face.

Mama nodded, staring at him with defiance for a moment. Then she turned back to slicing onions. They plunked into the pot, finding nests among the carrots.

"Since he's got that other dame, you'd think he'd leave you alone at least!" Ben growled.

Mama darted Ben an angry glance. "Don't say that about your papa, Ben!" She kept slicing the onions, wiping her eyes. "Besides, I know he loves me, no matter what he does, ya know."

Ben grunted. "Yeah, Mama, he loves you. Just like he loves us, right?" The words crawled out, so acidic that Grace cringed in her hiding place in the shadows.

"I'm leaving now," he stated more softly. "Don't know when I'll be back."

Mama barely nodded.

"Do me a favor, Mama." Ben grasped Mama's shoulders and turned her to face him. "Take care of Grace, okay?"

Mama twisted out of Ben's grip. "Take care of Grace?" she repeated. "Why? What's she done?" Her voice colored with suspicion, and Grace tensed, wondering what Ben would reveal.

"She ain't done nothing. Listen, I know you need her around the house and all, but she wants to join this choir-thing at school."

"Choir? You mean, singing? What's she gonna do with a choir?" Mama sounded skeptical, and Grace held her breath. "Sounds like a waste of time. Besides, I'll need her here to help with the new baby soon. Lou and Nancy are too busy powder-puffing their noses to do me any good."

"Yeah, but Mama, just think on it, alright? The kid's gonna bring you a permission slip to sign. I think it's only for a couple days afterschool every week, or something like that. Evelyn could help you on those days, too," Ben coaxed.

31

"Evelyn's got piano lessons to practice for," Mama replied quickly, "and she's too frail to do much in the house." Then, looking at Ben's serious face pleading with her, she added, "But I'll think on it, Ben."

He grinned and kissed Mama's cheek, flushed hot from the boiling pot. "Thanks, Mama." Without hesitation, he picked up his old leather pack, inherited from a second-cousin's Great War days, slung it over his shoulder, and moved toward the door. "I love you, Mama," he murmured, turning the knob but not his head.

Grace saw Mama nod and wipe her eyes again from those onions. Ben paused for a moment, then left. The door-latch lisped shut behind him.

~ ~ ~

Emmeline barely could keep from beaming her smile straight out at Doctor Philips. In her woman's heart, Emmeline knew. *Knew* that God had granted her prayer at last. This long list of questions, this poking and prodding was all very well... but Emmeline didn't need them. For she *knew*.

But Doctor Philips took his position as a medical practitioner very seriously, so Emmeline had humored him for the past twenty minutes or so. She'd sat atop his paper-lined examination table, not minding the cool office air or the glare from the lights shining in her eyes. *Blue or pink,* she mused, thinking of that room upstairs in their home, the one that presently housed the piano. Geoff would have no objection to her turning it into a nursery. The piano could stay; she would play hymns softly at night, soothing lullabies...

Maybe yellow...

"Mrs. Kinner, the bleeding you say that you're experiencing concerns me. Very much." The doctor kept his eyes on his clipboard as he scratched out notes. "You've had the same bleeding with each of your previous pregnancies. And none of them were viable."

Startled, Emmeline's mouth fell open. "Really? But when I used to help my mother with her midwifery, many of the women had some bleeding early in their pregnancies. It usually wasn't an issue."

The doctor didn't say anything. His grave eyes met hers, robbing the last of the hope she felt.

Her heart began a slow hammer in her chest. "I know you're a careful man, Doctor Philips, but really... I would think with something so common as..." She trailed off when she saw the doctor's already-somber face fall into grimmer lines.

"What's wrong? Is it not..." She couldn't finish the question, didn't know what she even meant to ask, as she gulped down the lump in her throat, questing for air. "I'm in my fourth month now. I've always lost the pregnancy *before* even two months passed."

Doctor Philips shook his head. "I know how much you and your husband want this baby, Emmeline. However, as your doctor, I can't assure you that this pregnancy will end happily when..." He paused, then released a heavy sigh. "When I'm certain that you will lose this one just as you did the others. In fact, I believe that you are undergoing a slow spontaneous abortion right now."

Real apprehension lurked in the doctor's expression. Seeing that, Emmeline swallowed back the tears that stung her eyes and threatened to close off her throat. She forced her lips to turn upward, her lungs to expand and deflate. "I see."

Doctor Philips tapped his pen against his lips. "Emmeline." He hesitated, evidently taking his time with phrasing what he wanted to tell her. "Some women are not capable of carrying a baby to full-term. This is the fifth pregnancy you've lost since you married four years ago. You and your husband may need to come to terms with that."

Emmeline's mind moved slowly from the shock. "Come to terms with what?" she heard herself ask. Was this conversation really happening?

"That you will never have children of your own."

Stunned to hear the doctor voice her deepest fear as a probable reality, Emmeline stared at him wordlessly.

Doctor Philips' tone softened. "And you can still have a full and productive life without children."

You will never have children of your own...

Nodding, she moved to get down from the examination table, using the little stool that stood there for that purpose. She heard her own heels click loudly on the tile. Keeping her eyes down, she carefully adjusted her clothing. She fetched her good hat from the table near the door and placed it on her carefully-styled hair before turning. She met his eyes again at last. "Thank you, Doctor."

He bobbed his head brusquely. "Because this pregnancy has

progressed so far, the loss may be more painful and difficult," Doctor Philips said, then added, "Physically, I mean. So please call the office if anything changes. Anything at all."

"Yes." She forced the words out. "Yes, I will."

If asked, Emmeline wouldn't have remembered the rest of her conversation with the town's general practitioner. There wasn't much to it; that she would have known. A good-bye, to be sure, and certainly well-wishes to be passed on to Mrs. Philips, the doctor's wife and chairwoman of the Sunday School at the Kinners' church.

Life had a way of turning out funny, Emmeline mused, as her feet found their way out the doctor's door, down the porch's two steps, and along the walkway toward home. She'd been counting on Mrs. Philips' gossipy tongue to spread the happy news which Emmeline had been sure the doctor would give her: *Emmeline Kinner is in the family way! Can you believe it? After four years of marriage and all those losses… and here she is, going to have a baby at last!*

But those words wouldn't come from Mrs. Philips' mouth now. *Though other words certainly will,* thought Emmeline as she passed a red-haired young man, roughly dressed, carrying an old army pack. His face looked as grim as she felt. *May You give him Your peace,* she prayed, barely realizing she'd done it. During all of Emmeline's growing-up years, her mother had emphasized the importance of prayer. Prayer for those closest. Prayer for enemies. Even prayer for those she met on the street, whom she might not speak to or ever see again. *"You do not know if you are the last remaining link to glory for that one. If God places you in anyone's path, it's for a reason. Pray for them, Emmeline."* Though her mother had died two years ago, her words still echoed in Emmeline's heart as she passed that cheerless young man. So Emmeline prayed, though her own grief encircled and choked her.

What will I tell Geoff? The question shouted at Emmeline as she crossed the street.

I have no idea what to tell him, she finally admitted to herself. Then, the thought-prayer burst out: *I didn't prepare for this. I didn't ask for this, Lord. I didn't expect this, and it doesn't seem fair. I even waited until the fourth month to be sure.*

The tears sprang to her eyes, and on this quiet stretch of street, lined with houses full of busy mothers, Emmeline let a drop escape to run unchecked in protest down her cheek. *I expected You to have answered me. I… I asked for bread, and I feel like You have given me a stone.*

Or that my bread has turned into a stone...

She let her feet move faster, clicking hurriedly down the remaining bit of sidewalk and up the walk to their front door. She turned the knob — always left unlocked — and let herself into the kitchen, still and sunny in the long Saturday afternoon. On the table, a note from Geoff told her that he'd run over to the school to fetch some papers and would be back by supper-time. Emmeline slipped into a chair at the table. So she had until five o'clock to figure out what to tell him.

CHAPTER SEVEN

*M*r. *Kinner looks sad today.* The thought surprised Grace as she glanced up from her literature book and peeked around Kirby McMillan's round body. In front of Grace's desk, Kirby stood stiffly, shoulders bowed over like an old potato, droning out the stanzas of *In Memoriam* with as much emotion as a four-line newspaper obituary. Mr. Kinner, normally the sort of teacher who moved constantly around the classroom, sat at his rectangular desk, dwarfed by its massive width. Throughout Kirby's reading, he'd remained motionless except for the steady blinking of his eyes.

I wonder what's wrong. As Kirby's voice whined on, Grace studied Mr. Kinner, noting the shadows circling his eyes, the tight line of his usually-mobile mouth. She'd just dropped her eyes back to her textbook when she felt a poke from behind her.

It was Ruth Ann Richards, Grace's lunchroom friend, passing a note. With a glance at the unobservant Mr. Kinner, Grace took it, unfolding the small square of lined yellow paper. She held it on her lap to read it.

What's wrong with Mr. K. today? He never lets Kirbs go on like this.

With a furtive look up, Grace licked the tip of her pencil and scribbled her reply. *I don't know. Seems kind of sad, doesn't he?*

She passed it back and waited for the reply. A moment later, she received another poke.

My mother is on the Sunday School committee with Doctor Philips' wife, and she said something is wrong with his wife.

Grace squinted down at the note and paused a minute before

scratching out her reply. *Whose wife? Doctor Philips'?*

A moment's wait. A poke. *No, silly. Something's wrong with Mr. K.'s wife.*

Grace couldn't resist the pull of curiosity. *What's wrong with her?* Her pencil asked the question breathlessly.

Ruth Ann's answer came swiftly. *Can't have a baby, I guess. She's pregnant and is going to lose the one she's carrying now.*

Grace raised her eyebrows. Not being able to have a baby might be a good thing. Letting her eyes linger on her schoolmate's scribble, she thought of Mama with her six children, seven come late winter, scraping together pennies, scrubbing floors full of mud, weeping in the night when she assumed that no one could hear her.

Whenever Mama's sister Mary Evelyn – Grace's little sister was Aunt Mary's namesake – came over to see Mama from her apartment in Boston... Well, Aunt Mary would *tsk* her tongue every time one of the Picoletti kids came in or out of the room. Grace knew what Aunt Mary thought, sitting there primly, all dressed up in her shiny patent-leather heels and her mink wrap: The children were the root of Mama's problem. *If you'd been smart like me, little sister, you'd never have had kids, marriage or no marriage. You'd never have gotten yourself stuck with a man like this.* That's what Aunt Mary thought; Grace was sure of it. And then Mama would just fetch Aunt Mary another cup of coffee, full of Bessie's cream. And the cup would pass from the work-roughened hands of one sister to the smooth tapered fingers of the other one. They would sit there sipping their coffee, both thinking, Grace was sure, of what might've been.

The note still sat on her lap, and Grace knew that Ruth Ann wanted a reply. Itching her leg with one shoe, the sole of which had been refastened with rubber bands, Grace penciled her side of the conversation.

That's all?

Ruth Ann's answer came swiftly. *What do you mean, that's all? My mother says Mr. K. probably wishes he'd married a different girl. Plenty of girls were after him, you know. And—*

"Miss Picoletti." Empty of its usual good-humor, Mr. Kinner's voice broke into her reading. Grace felt the blood drain from her face and then flood it again. She forced her eyes to look up at her teacher, but she found she could only manage to gaze steadily at his starched white shirt. "And Miss Richards," Mr. Kinner continued. "You both will be detained after class today. May I have the note, please?"

Grace's mouth turned to cotton. She heard Ruth Ann take in a quick breath. Numbly, Grace lifted the heavy note and passed it to Mr. Kinner, her ears going through various shades of pink, purple, and scarlet.

He folded it along the same lines as Grace and Ruth Ann had and slipped it into his pants pocket. For all its dangerous information, it didn't even make a bulge. Mr. Kinner turned to Kirby. "Mr. McMillan, you may continue reading."

Grace's heart sank into her soles of her shoes and onto the dusty floor. For the rest of the class, her mind drifted between what Mr. Kinner would think of her once he read the note – that she was a pitiless gossip – and whether he would send a message home to her mother. If he did, Grace certainly would receive a sound beating from Papa... if he was home. She cringed to think of his hand thudding against her ear, to look forward to bearing the bruises of his punishment to school for several days following it.

Yet that surely would not be the worst of it. The worst of it would be that Mr. Kinner would never want Grace to be in the special choir now. For Grace had taken heart when she'd heard Ben talk to Mama about her joining. She'd planned to ask Mr. Kinner for another permission slip after school today.

Grace drooped down in her desk chair. Not now, though. Not ever.

~ ~ ~

The siren of the school bell broke Grace's miserable reverie. Her eyes traveled to the clock above the classroom door. The black hands pointed out the time: 2:27 p.m. The early afternoon sun slid through the paned windows lining the far wall, but it did nothing to thaw Grace's fear.

Heart thudding from her thin chest into her fingertips, Grace rose from the desk. She was silent compared to the loud scraping of her fellow students as they gathered their books together, laughing and chattering. But then, they didn't have to think about the rebuke that surely awaited her from Mr. Kinner's mouth, the disappointment that would certainly float in his eyes. Nor did they have to dread the backhanded strike of Papa, which might meet Grace tonight.

Ruth Ann caught her eye and smirked. "Come on, Grace. Let's get this over with," she whispered, flipping her cinnamon curls over her shoulder and picking up her small stack of schoolbooks, piled up like Saturday morning pancakes. Grace knew Ruth Ann wouldn't be carrying them home; she'd only have to flutter her thick eyelashes at some boy out front of the school and he'd tote all the books she wanted home for her.

Grace tucked her own stringy hair behind one ear, fingers trembling worse than the autumn leaves still clinging to some of the trees outside the classroom windows. She forced herself to nod at Ruth Ann, pick up her own stack of books, and carve a path up to Mr. Kinner.

Beside his desk, Mr. Kinner stood in his characteristic slight slouch, intently listening to Paulie Giorgi. In his hands, Paulie held last week's essay assignment, three or four pages of paper clipped together. Mr. Kinner had returned the essays to the class today, all graded with the now-thick-now-thin navy blue ink of his fountain pen.

"So I'm just wondering, Mr. Kinner, why my grade is an A minus," Grace heard Paulie say, his peppy voice betraying no disrespect for the teacher, only confusion. "I added together the points for the components of the essay, and it seems to come to a ninety-six, sir, not a ninety-two."

Seeming to force a smile, Mr. Kinner reached his hand out for the paper. "Here, let me see, Paulie. I may have made a mistake." He flipped through the lined yellow sheets, filled to the margins with Paulie's enthusiastic cursive. His lips moved silently as he added the points marked beside each essay component while Grace resisted the urge to look at the clock again. Mr. Kinner never gave an incorrect grade; he did everything methodically as a pocket-watch. Couldn't perfect Paulie just accept the fact that this essay hadn't turned out to be his best? If Mr. Kinner didn't finish with Paulie soon, and then with her and Ruth Ann's scolding in double-quick time, Grace knew she would pay for being late from school again.

Grace sighed, and just then, Paulie turned his head a little and gave her a slight smile. *He has nice dimples,* Grace surprised herself with thinking, despite her growing anxiety. She turned red as spring beets, but it didn't matter because Mr. Kinner had drawn Paulie's attention back to the essay in question.

"You're right, Paul," he said, taking his pen from inside his suit jacket. "I didn't add that up correctly." His pen making a scratch-scratch noise, Mr. Kinner crossed out the ninety-two at the top of Paulie's essay and wrote in his new grade: ninety-six. "I'll change your grade in my log as well," he said, pocketing his pen once more.

"Thanks, Mr. Kinner," Paulie smiled. "I appreciate it." He took the paper Mr. Kinner proffered and tucked it into his leather school satchel, fastening the buckle securely. With a nod to Grace and Ruth Ann, Paulie left the otherwise-empty classroom, shutting the door behind him with a snappy click.

Mr. Kinner focused on the two girls. "Ah, Miss Picoletti and Miss Richards. The note passers," he commented, his voice void of humor but holding no anger. "Now, girls, it's the beginning of the year. I would like us all to start off on the right foot." Again, he forced a smile to his lips. "Passing notes has no place in my class. While I like to encourage friendships inside and outside the classroom, I don't care for misuse of time. Which is what note-passing is when the context is literature class. Do you understand?"

Grace nodded fervently. Ruth Ann replied, "Oh, yes, sir. We understand, don't we, Grace?" She turned wide-open blue eyes to Grace.

Grace licked her lips, desperate for moisture before croaking out, "Y-yes."

Mr. Kinner gave a single nod, letting the smile drop off his face. "Alright, you may go. There's no further punishment this time for you two."

Ruth Ann broke out into an exuberant grin, quite the alteration from her attitude of degraded penitence just moments before. "Oh, *thank you*, Mr. Kinner, sir. And I promise, we'll never do it again, will we, Grace?" She looked to Grace for her agreement, and Grace managed a weak bob of her head, her heart pounding with gratitude for getting off so easily. But her eyes traveled to Mr. Kinner's pocket, where the note must still reside. *Has he read it?*

Ruth Ann backed away, still rewarding Mr. Kinner with her smile and forgetting Grace, who stood unsure before the teacher. A moment more, and Grace's schoolmate left the room to Grace and Mr. Kinner, who tilted his head, evidently wondering why she stayed. "Grace?" he asked. "Is there something else?"

Grace swallowed. Could she... *Should* she ask? The clock ticked loudly on the wall, mocking her hesitation. But she counted five seconds and then made herself say, "Mr. Kinner…"

She could get no farther, but he must have seen how her eyes moved to his pants pocket. A ghost of his usual kind expression rested on his countenance. He drew out the folded note. "Here you go," he said, offering it to Grace. She took it, breathing a sigh of relief when it left his hands and returned to hers. "I didn't read it," Mr. Kinner added, turning toward his desk. He closed his thick teacher's edition of their literature book and shoved it into his own satchel.

Grace couldn't reply; gratitude swelled her throat. *Thank you, God,* she silently uttered a rare spontaneous prayer. If Mr. Kinner had ever read the things she and Ruth Ann had written about his wife! And about *him*! Grace felt her knees turn to jelly just thinking about it now that it was over. She squeezed the folded paper in her palm, destining it for the stove once she got home.

Home! Suddenly, her mind and feet began to work again. With a weak smile at Mr. Kinner, Grace scrambled for the door, mentally cursing the rubber-band shoe that *would* flop.

"Miss Picoletti."

At Mr. Kinner's call, Grace stopped with her hand on the heavy knob. *What now?* Dread rose again in her chest as she turned back to the teacher.

But he merely held out a sheet of mimeographed paper. "You dropped your permission slip the other day."

Grace felt so stunned she couldn't reply. He still wanted her to be in his special choir, though she passed notes in class? Though she had a shoe that flopped? Though she'd fallen flat on her face in the auditorium before him? She froze, knowing her mouth hung open like a fish out of water.

"You know," continued Mr. Kinner, "for the special choir. You do still want to be a part of it?" He raised his eyebrows questioningly.

Grace commanded her mouth to close, her tongue to moisten her lips again, and her vocal chords to work. "Yes, sir," she replied, gaining courage. "I do."

He gave a little smile. "Good. Here you go, then." He held the permission slip out to her again, and Grace moved up the aisle to grasp it. Once it reached her hands, she clasped it against her chest. She wasn't able to contain the grin that broke through all her nervousness and shame, so she let it fall on Mr. Kinner before rushing out the door.

42

CHAPTER EIGHT

Geoff gathered up the last of his papers, neatened the pile by giving it a crisp knock on the desk, and tucked it away into his satchel. The room was quiet now. He felt the heavy silence gathering around him as he finished the final tasks of the school day. He straightened the row of seven pencils on his desk, kept ready for forgetful students. He cleaned the chalkboard thoroughly, wiping every remaining tinge of white from the dust-smoked surface, breathing in that dry scent familiar to every teacher. It steadied him now. Kept his mind on the necessary, everyday things. The things that mattered. Not the things that didn't.

Because they will never be. His faith collapsed as he thought of the words Emmeline had laid before him two nights ago: *We will never have children of our own. Doctor Philips says that I'm losing this baby as we speak.*

The clock's face drew Geoff's eyes, an executioner to an unwilling victim. Two-forty-nine. Emmeline would expect him home any time. And he would leave the school soon. But first, he must prepare himself, for he would not – he could not – enter their home with this bitterness drawing new patterns across his face. He could not fail her now; Geoff would get it together before his feet crossed the threshold.

Even if my own heart breaks, Emmeline must never know it. She must believe – he must *make* her believe – that it didn't matter to him if she lost this baby. If she could never carry a baby to full-term. That his only concern was for her health.

Geoff's dazed eyes found a piece of chalk that had rolled away beneath his desk. Another excuse to delay just a moment longer. He knelt, welcoming the marble-cold feel of the tile as evidence that the present was indeed real. Once Geoff knelt on the floor, the piece of chalk no longer stood in his line of sight, but his fingers found it readily enough with a little fumbling. They closed around it, and he clambered to his feet again.

But he couldn't find the chalk box; the night janitor must have moved it. *The fool,* he thought, enjoying the unusual stinging pleasure of directing his pain toward another, more innocent man. With no chalk box to be found, Geoff stood clutching that solitary piece in one hand, staring out at the empty desks.

In one more minute, the detention bell rang. Breaking out of his trance, Geoff shook his head and breathed deeply. Without hesitation, his fingers closed firmly around the chalk-piece and bent. A snap sounded out, clear and loud. If anyone had heard – but there was no one to hear in that empty schoolroom - the crack might have reminded the hearer of a sparrow's neck suddenly broken.

Why, God? Why this?

~ ~ ~

Grace took off her shoes and socks as soon as her feet found their way off the main road and onto the tree-lined path leading to Papa's land. The September day had warmed considerably since that morning, and her toes felt hot and cramped.

Mama sat on the back steps, her worn print skirt covering some of the places where the green paint had chipped off the cement. Her auburn hair wisped around her face in sweaty tendrils, and she'd rolled the long sleeves of her dress way up above her elbows. A dead chicken drooped over her lap; Grace shuddered, glad Mama had strangled it before she'd gotten home.

"Hi, Mama," Grace offered, gripping her stack of schoolbooks in one hand, her shoes and socks in the other. Would Mama scold her fiercely for coming home late?

But Mama just nodded and glanced up, taking in everything about Grace with one blink of her emotionless eyes. Mama's fingers, thick from half a lifetime of scrubbing dishes and diapers, didn't pause in their plucking. The white feathers floated around Mama's feet, shoved into an old pair of Ben's shoes, sockless. "Careful going into the house barefoot, Grace," she said.

Grace raised her eyebrows in surprise, pausing right beside Mama, feet in the piles of feathers. "Why?" she asked, looking down at Mama's bowed head.

"Broke something earlier," Mama replied matter-of-factly. "Cleaned it up as good as I could, but there might still be some bits of glass lyin' around. Evelyn got a piece in her foot already."

"What, a canning jar broke?" Grace asked. Mama always put up lots of canned preserves and pickles at the end of summer and beginning of fall. Sometimes the newly-washed jars would slip to the floor, splintering into seemingly thousands of pieces.

"Nope."

Grace hesitated, but Mama didn't offer any further explanation, so she headed on inside the house, careful where she put her feet. The screen door screeched shut behind Grace, but otherwise, the house echoed with silence. She wondered where Evelyn had got to, and Cliff, too. Lou and Nancy were no puzzle; they worked 'til nearly six o'clock most weekday nights, Lou at a drugstore and Nancy at a fancy department store down-city.

I wish Ben had stayed. The thought crept from Grace's heart into her mind, but she pushed it away as she tucked her hair behind her ears. She wouldn't – she couldn't think about Ben. *He's gone now, so forget about him, Grace.* She saw the broom leaning lazily in the corner and decided to sweep the kitchen thoroughly so it would be ready for bare feet again. Grace took the broom with both her small, strong hands and began sweeping, scraping the corners and edges of the room to be sure to get all the glass. When she'd finished, she scooped the little debris pile into the dustpan and threw the contents into the barrel Papa had placed outside the back door.

"You want potatoes peeled for supper, Mama?" Grace offered, pausing before going back inside the kitchen. "Or you want 'em baked?"

Mama just shrugged. Grace bit her lip. If Mama was in a bad mood, she might refuse when Grace asked her to sign that permission slip. "You want me to open up a jar of beets, too, Mama?" she ventured.

Mama gave a huff. "Grace! You ask so many questions. Whatever you want, girl. It don't matter. Beets'll do. Just open the jar."

"Okay, Mama." Grace went back inside, peeled the potatoes, and opened the can of beets, red and reeking of vinegar.

When she'd finished, she went back to the screen door. Mama sat there, the chicken now plucked lying across her lap, blood staining Mama's apron. "Mama," Grace said hesitantly, "I'm going upstairs to do my homework now. The potatoes are boiling on the stove."

Mama didn't reply, so Grace turned after a moment and retrieved her books from the kitchen table. She pocketed a few soda crackers to stave off hunger pangs before trotting up the staircase. Not bothering to knock, Grace pushed open the door of the bedroom she shared with her three sisters.

Evelyn lay stretched out on the pale pink coverlet, washed by the sunlight weakly filtering in the windows. She seemed asleep, but when Grace closed the door with a click, Evelyn's eyes sprang open, bluebells in the tan field of her face. Wordlessly, the younger girl propped herself up on her elbows, staring at Grace, who sat down on the edge of the bed.

Grace touched a hand to Evelyn's face, which showed the path tears had taken earlier that afternoon. "Mama said you stepped on some glass," she said, wrinkling her nose in sympathy.

Evelyn nodded, tears rising in her eyes again. She sniffled and pointed a skinny little finger toward her feet. One foot still wore its white sock, cuffed over, but the other olive-toned foot lay bare except for a bandage.

Grace bent to look more closely at it. She could see a reddish spot oozing through the gauze, despite its double-thickness. "Mama got all the glass out?" she questioned, surprised that their mother had allowed Evelyn to hobble up to her bedroom with a still-bleeding foot. That wasn't Mama's usual way, to deal haphazardly with things. Especially when it came to her darling youngest.

Evelyn shrugged, her slight shoulders rising and falling in her floral print dress. "I think so," she mumbled, her glance turning toward the window, avoiding Grace's eyes.

For a long quiet moment, Grace looked down, studying her fingernails. *Oh, God, why can't our family be like everybody else's?* She wondered this but knew instinctively that the Almighty's ears were shut to her, a poor wretched sinner.

"What happened? Mama dropped a jar or something?" she asked at last.

Evelyn looked away. "No." She picked at her fingernails, just like Grace had been doing a few moments ago.

"What happened, then? You dropped something?" probed Grace, fresh fear entering her heart as Evelyn avoided answering her simple question. Mama had evaded answering, too.

"Mama threw a can at Papa," Evelyn blurted out, like she'd swallowed something terrible and couldn't keep it down.

Grace's spine straightened, and her breath became shallow before she could even process the thought. It was unthinkable. Often, Papa had given one of the children the back of his hand for disobeying him, or he'd even occasionally hit Mama when she gave him lip. Nothing bad. But *Mama*, throwing a can at Papa?

"It was a can of green beans," Evelyn said, as though that detail was important. She traced the spot of crimson in the center of her bandage.

"Did it hit him?" Grace heard herself ask as she stared unblinking at Evelyn, as if the action of throwing the can didn't matter, as if it only mattered if Mama's aim had been true or not.

Evelyn shook her head fiercely. "No, it didn't hit him. But she meant to." Evelyn's eyes met Grace's and the favoritism that had gone on perpetually didn't seem to matter. What mattered was, they were sisters. Sisters caught on the Picoletti train, a vehicle seemingly meant for destruction. "She hit the blue lamp," Evelyn explained. "It was right next to Papa's head, see."

"Oh." That fragile blue oil lamp was Mama's favorite, handed down from her grandmother, who came from the Old Country. The lamp had survived the sea voyage sixty years ago and two households since, but the Picoletti family had killed it. "What happened, Evelyn?" whispered Grace.

Tears brimmed again in Evelyn's eyes. "I don't know why Mama did it," she mumbled. "I came home from school, and I could hear Mama screaming from the street. I was so embarrassed in front of Natalie Quivers that I just ran to the back door. When I came in, Mama had the can in her hands. Papa stood all quiet near the telephone. Mama pitched it at him. That's... That's when the lamp broke," Evelyn finished. "I stepped on the glass coming in the door."

Hearing the story, Grace's chest hurt. Thinking of Mama in that way, screaming at Papa like a wild animal... What could have possessed her to do it? And throwing the can at him? Grace closed her eyes. That was even worse. "And what'd Papa do?" she breathed.

Evelyn wiped her nose on the back of her hand and pushed her tousled stray hair out of her eyes. "He just stood there for a second. Then he walked out the back door past me, got in the car, and drove off. I don't know where he went." She shrugged and flopped back down on the bed, eyes on the ceiling. "That was, I don't know, maybe an hour ago."

Grace opened her mouth, unsure of what to say next, but before she could speak, she heard a car grinding its way into the hard-packed dirt-and-pebble driveway out front. She listened as the car moved around the house – to park, she guessed. Evelyn's eyes met hers. Grace rose from the bed, quick as a cat, and walked to the bedroom window overlooking the backyard and barn area. Ever so gently, she lifted the curtain to the side, veiling herself in the shadow and dingy lace. If whoever was below looked up, he would not catch sight of her.

Grace's peering eyes found Papa just stepping out of the car, his short stature masked by the vertical distance between them. He wore his good hat, a clean-looking shirt, and dress pants. All this, Grace took in at a glance. When Papa closed the car door with a bang, her focus switched to the person in the car's passenger seat. Grace couldn't make out the face from her position above them, but she could see tightly-permed blond hair under a smart little hat that seemed to match the woman's brown tweed suit. Papa strode to the woman's side of the car and opened her door. He gave her one of his heavy tanned hands, and she stepped out, one hand clasping a small carpetbag. Another bang closed her door, and Papa went around to the trunk. The woman waited for him, hands smoothing her skirt, head turning to look this way and that. Another moment, and Papa pulled out two large suitcases, their obvious heft having no effect on him as he toted one in each hand.

"Who is it?" Evelyn's question broke into Grace's inspection of the scene below their bedroom.

Briefly, Grace turned her head to answer her younger sister. "Papa's back." Something stopped her from telling Evelyn about the woman he'd brought with him, something gnawing that made her hands shake a little as she turned back to the window. She gripped the ledge this time for strength before allowing her eyes to fall on the scene below.

But she needn't have concerned herself. Papa and the strange woman had already gone inside. Grace heard the screen door whack shut. Suddenly, she thought of Mama, plucking that chicken on the stoop. Of the broken glass. Of Ben's words to her the night before he'd left. The night he'd given Papa a solid blow in the kisser, as he put it.

He's bringing her here. To live.

Grace choked. *Oh, please, no.* It was one thing for Papa to run around a bit. Mama was sick all the time, pregnant often, with so many kids to care for... Really, Papa couldn't be blamed for needing some reprieve from responsibility. So what if the good kids from school snickered at her family behind their hands? They didn't have to wear rubber bands around their shoes; their Papa didn't sell junk for extra money. They couldn't understand.

But this... She'd thought Ben had too much booze running through his brain that night. To bring another woman into Mama's house, a woman with permed, bleached hair while Mama plucked a chicken for Papa's supper... "I'll be right back," she stammered to Evelyn. Her feet took the stairs two at a time, never stopping their forward motion until Grace reached the archway that opened into the kitchen.

It was like seeing a waxwork museum scene. Mama stood motionless, a frazzled, frumpy china doll. She leaned against the kitchen counter, while the dead chicken's feet hung out of a pot of scalding water on the stove next to her.

Mama looks like she's been gutted. Mama's eyes stared from her white, white face. Her hands still wore traces of blood from the fowl; they hung useless before her soiled apron. Her gaze – that unblinking gaze – fixed on Papa, who had taken his stand at the head of the kitchen table, suitcases still in his hands.

His face, though – His face wore such an expression! Grace had never beheld that look embedded so deeply upon Papa's countenance. It... It held hatred; it held disdain; it held *triumph*, all mingled together there, a bitter cup for the witness to drink. His arm curved around that woman, who stood next to him, her twitching eyes and willowy hands the only movements in the room.

All at once, it seemed, the threesome became aware of Grace's presence. She trembled as Papa kept his narrowed eyes intent on Mama and yet addressed Grace. "Grace, this is your Uncle Jack's sister, Gertrude. She ain't got work right now, so she's staying with us for the time being." He let his eyes drop to the blond woman for a second. "One of my daughters. Grace."

The woman seemed to gain courage from Papa's introduction. She threw a little contemptuous glance at Mama and moved a couple of steps from under Papa's protection. The thought flitted through Grace's mind that the strange woman might have been pretty, in a coarse sort of way, if it had not been for the arrogant politeness that haunted her eyes and her painted mouth.

The woman extended one of her slim, polished hands toward Grace. "So pleased to meet you, Grace," she purred, low and throaty. The scent of cheap tobacco stained her breath. Grace's own hands remained clasped, trembling, behind her back, as her eyes darted from Mama's eviscerated face to the woman's smile-pasted one.

Grace would not shake hands with this snake.

The kitchen rang silent. The woman glanced at Papa from under thick-lined eyelids, then back at Grace. She opened and closed her pouty lips twice before any sounds emerged. "You... You're how old, Grace? Chuckie told me, but I'm sorry to say, I can't remember," she tittered with an expression of exaggerated apology plumping out her cheeks into a lopsided smile.

Chuckie? With a start, Grace realized that the woman meant Papa. *Chuckie!* Nobody called him that. Mama always called him Charlie, just as Papa's family and the men at the lunch counter did. For the first time in her life, Grace raised eyes of contempt to her father. To let this woman nickname him something different, and to stand there smugly as if he approved it!

Papa hadn't answered the woman, though, because his eyes still pinned Mama against the countertop. The scalding water nearly boiled over the pot, the chicken legs bobbing up and down. Mama had forgotten it; usually the chicken only hung scalding for a couple of minutes at most. *It'll be ruined.*

As if it mattered. As if anything at all mattered except the terrible scene taking place now. And she, Grace, was one of the actors.

"You're what, seventeen?" the voice asked in determination, obviously anxious for Grace to answer, for this awkwardness to somehow dissipate. As if it ever could with *her* here.

"Fifteen. Grace's goin' on fifteen," Papa said, snapping out of his rigor mortis.

Grace just stared at him. *Going on fifteen... I'm fifteen now!* Did he really not know her age? The thin blade of her Papa's self-interest bit a little deeper into her chest. She couldn't bear to watch Mama expire before her eyes.

"I have to go check on Evelyn," Grace gasped. Her feet found the stairs – she didn't know how – and she fled to the attic, where the spiders could listen unsympathetically to her sobs.

CHAPTER NINE

One more, and she'd be done. Emmeline closed the hymnbook before settling her fingers upon the ivory keys again. She didn't need the music to guide her on this one. Pressing her fingers gently down, sweeping them along the keyboard, the chords sang out:

Be still, my soul, the Lord is on thy side;
Bear patiently the cross of grief or pain.
Leave to thy God to order and provide;
In every change, He faithful will remain.
Be still, my soul, thy best, thy heavenly Friend;
Through thorny ways leads to a joyful end.

As the final notes lingered in the still room, Emmeline let her hands rest on the piano, tears dropping from her eyes, running between the keys. The late afternoon sunlight trickled through the white curtains, fell across the old wood floor, and puddled at her feet, gilding all it touched, turning the fallen teardrops to prisms. A great sigh tore from her chest.

For many moments, Emmeline sat bowed at the instrument, not putting off what she knew she *would* do but waiting until the Lord Christ ripened the desire in her heart. At last, she heard Geoff's footfalls on the porch. He hadn't whistled a cheerful hymn as he usually did on his way home from school, she noted briefly.

But Geoff's approaching presence gave her the impetus to drive forward. *This will eat away at me, at him, at us, if I continue to carry it.* Slowly, ever so slowly, Emmeline turned her hands over, palms open. She had no strength to raise them but kept them resting on the ivory-and-black expanse. "Lord," she whispered – and a witness would have testified to the iron in her tone, "I am Yours. All of mine is Yours. You give what You deem is best, and I will pour it back at Your feet as an offering."

As she continued there in silence, she felt the burden of the weekend – no, of the years she and Geoff had waited for a child – lift from her shoulders. The relief felt so palpable that Emmeline nearly gave into the desire to look in the mirror on the far wall to see if anything had changed in her appearance. A sorrowful peace had replaced the anxious weight. She felt she could breathe again without the anchors of unmet expectations holding down her lungs.

Emmeline heard Geoff making his way upstairs and turned on the bench to greet him. Knocking once, her husband pushed open the door. He stood there, a burnt-out match, expression full of care. Emmeline rose and kissed the worn cheek. Geoff's tense arms gathered her against him. They were strong arms, yes, but not nearly strong enough to carry their trouble alone.

She nestled her head against the five o'clock shadow of his cheek. "Don't fear, beloved one," she whispered. A tear – one of his – dropped into the dark ocean of her hair. "He will not give us a stone for bread. He will not." Her eyes closed, sharing his weeping. "He'll give us what is good, beloved."

~ ~ ~

The moon had shone for hours by the time Grace finished her homework. She leaned back as much as possible in the upright desk chair, stretching out her overworked arm. Her gaze fell on the two double-beds, occupied by her three sisters. Evelyn appeared as a round lump under the covers, curled up like a cat. Only her two braids showed, spread out on her pillow. Evelyn nestled right in the center of the bed, and Grace knew that she would have a difficult time of getting her little sister to move onto her own side.

In their own bed, Lou and Nancy lay, the latter's mouth open in a light snore. Both had come home too tired to hear much about the new situation with Mama, Papa, and the woman he'd brought into their house. When Grace had explained what had happened, Lou had just shrugged and Nancy snorted, "Oh, Grace, you always think of the craziest things."

When Grace had persisted in talking about it, whispering furtively in the privacy of their bedroom, her older sisters became angry. "Look," Nancy had finally said, "just keep your trap shut about it. Our family is embarrassing enough as it is. If you keep talking like that, how d'you think Lou and I'll ever get dates?"

So Grace had shut her mouth and given the smallest possible account to Evelyn, who didn't understand all that adult stuff yet anyway. Cliff lived in his own world, so Grace didn't waste her breath on explanations to him. While Nancy and Lou did their hair up in rags and Evelyn played with her homemade paper dolls on their bed, Grace sat and did her homework. But now that all of her sisters slept, she closed her textbooks and tiptoed to the open window. She thought of her Mama's face – unfair, partial Mama; hardworking, dogged Mama – and of what Papa had decided to do to her, and the tears rose to Grace's eyes. They bubbled over, streaming down her cheeks so steadily she didn't think they'd ever stop. *Why? Why would he do this? To Mama? To us? Have we done something so awful, so bad that he needs something else, that it's right for him to bring this woman here?*

And no answer came. The tears continued to flow, Grace as helpless to stop them as she was to dam the breakage in her home, to mend Mama's surely-bleeding heart, to make Papa into a real father. *No hope,* she thought numbly, digging her fingernails into the white-painted windowsill, watching as her tears splattered there. *There is no hope.*

After many long minutes, Grace ceased weeping, having nothing left to cry, and what was worse, knowing no one cared whether she shed tears or not. No catharsis awaited her, but rather a raw, empty ache. She drew the curtains shut, still allowing the warm September breeze to make its way into the room.

She turned off the dim lamp on the desk all three sisters shared. In their bureau's bottom drawer, Grace fished around in the dark until she found her old-fashioned white cotton nightgown, so unlike Lou and Nancy's silky and skimpy nightwear. She removed today's clothing and laid it over the desk chair, so that it would be ready for tomorrow, relatively unwrinkled. As she arranged her cardigan, she saw a sheet of white paper sticking out of one of her books.

Frowning, Grace pulled it out, holding it in the moonlight to see what it was.

The permission slip. She'd meant to ask Mama to sign it, but with everything that had happened, Grace had forgotten completely. She bit her lip, thinking. Mr. Kinner had wanted that permission slip back as soon as possible. The special choir would start to rehearse later this week. *I can't ask Mama about it now that Papa has gone and done this.* Her mother had too much to worry about without Grace complicating their family life even more. With a sigh, Grace tossed the permission slip into the waste paper basket, letting it fall next to the pencil shavings.

But, wait. Mama had pretty much said yes when Ben had asked her if Grace could join Mr. Kinner's special choir. She'd never really denied Ben anything he'd wanted in earnest. Grace's eyes lighted on the pencil near her schoolbooks. Not daring to let herself think, she flattened the slip of paper on the desk and picked up the pencil, sharpened just enough for the job. With a quick, flowing hand, Grace scratched out her mother's signature. And – relief of reliefs – she felt a guilty courage course through her heart.

CHAPTER TEN

The soft knock came just after school the next day. Geoff didn't turn from erasing the stray marks on the blackboard. "Come in," he called, trying to keep up the effort he'd made all day: to give his voice its usual upbeat sound. "Be right with you," he continued as he heard the classroom door open and click shut quietly. With a few brisk strokes, he finished up and turned, ready with a brave smile.

The Picoletti girl stood there, silent and grave as always. Her guarded eyes turned to the clock, then back to him. Geoff smiled again to put her at her ease. "Did you need something, Miss Picoletti?" he asked.

The student nodded. Wordlessly, she opened one of the textbooks she carried and drew out a sheet of paper. Geoff recognized it as the permission slip for the choir. "Wonderful!" he exclaimed with a cheerfulness he didn't feel. "You've got it signed?"

The girl hesitated for a brief moment and then nodded. She held the paper out to him. He saw calluses marking the bird-like hand, signs of repetitive hard labor, and he looked into her face for just a moment. There, he found other marks of difficulty, yet of a different kind.

"Thank you, Miss Picoletti," Geoff said, more gently, as he took the paper, running his eyes over the signature briefly. "We start practice this Friday after school. Attendance is mandatory at all rehearsals." He waited for her agreement and received a short, unsmiling nod. "Alright, that's it," he finished, seeing that she seemed anxious to go.

The girl turned toward the door. Geoff looked after her for just a moment, wondering what her little story was – the literature teacher in him made him curious, he supposed. Then the clock above the door arrested his attention. Nearly three o'clock. Emmeline would be returning from her ladies' Bible study, where he knew she would share her need – their need – for prayer. Geoff wanted to be home when she returned. To comfort her.

If she needed to be comforted. Last evening, her strength had amazed him. Here he had expected to find her curled up on their bed, weeping in the certainty that she would never hold their child in her arms.

But Emmeline had risen like a robin from its nest when Geoff entered the piano room. Yes, Emmeline had cried; that much evidenced itself on her weary pale face, her washed-out eyes, her hoarse voice. But a new intensity undergirded all of that, made the sorrow a set of notes rather than the entire opus. She'd lain her head gladly on Geoff's chest, but he rather suspected she'd taken that action to console *him*.

~ ~ ~

Aunt Mary had never thought well of Papa, and when Grace walked into the kitchen after school, her mother's sister sat there at the table, reminding Mama of just that. "I warned you, Sarah," she jittered out in her high-heeled voice. Aunt Mary pursed her lips together into a tight sandwich around the teacup's rim.

She paused mid-sip and lifted narrowed eyes to Mama. "This teacup's chipped," she proclaimed, as if everybody in the Picoletti household needed to know.

Mama's weary face didn't show its usual shame when Aunt Mary made that kind of announcement; she just stared down, blank as fresh notebook paper. Without turning, she asked, "Grace, get your aunt another cup of coffee, will you?"

Grace nodded, her chest caving at the sight of Mama leaning her chin on her plump hands, too tired to support her head without a prop. "Yes'm," Grace answered quickly, dropping her stack of schoolbooks on the table and moving toward the cupboard.

"Leave it! Leave it," Aunt Mary's command interrupted her

actions. Grace turned to look back at her and Mama, ur ,ure.

"I do not want another cup of coffee, Sarah," Aunt Mary explained to Mama. "I am just stating that this cup is chipped. It was part of our grandmother's china set, you know, Grace." Her blue eyes glared at Grace, as if she was to be blamed.

Grace nodded. In Aunt Mary's economy, offspring were to blame for mostly everything that went wrong in life.

"Disgraceful. That's what this household is, Sarah. Just a disgrace." Aunt Mary paused and switched her weight from one crossed leg to the other. Grace noticed how perfectly straight her aunt's stocking seams were.

Mama sat there, slumped silently over her full cup of cooling coffee, waiting for her childless sister's next pronouncement of doom. Grace stood motionless, listening.

"And now this: Your husband has a woman. Living in the cottage. Behind your house." She punctuated the phrases precisely, like the priest did during Confession when he especially wanted someone to feel sorry for their sins.

She talks like Mama and us kids should be the ones repenting. Aunt Mary raised her thinly-penciled eyebrows. Grace thought they could compete with the arches in their church for height. She bit her tongue to keep from saying anything. After all, Aunt Mary was Mama's sister and Evelyn's godmother.

"Mary…" Mama murmured, her gaze darting toward Grace, who had stayed right near the cupboard, ears fully open, mouth shut.

Aunt Mary gave a mirthless smirk. "Oh, really, Sarah, you think the girl doesn't know what her daddy's doing out late at night? She knows what's what, don't you, Grace?" Aunt Mary directed the last part to her.

Grace pressed her lips together and said nothing.

"I thought so. Well," continued Aunt Mary Evelyn brusquely and, Grace thought, mercilessly, "it *is* true, isn't it, Sarah?"

Mama nodded and looked down into the dark liquid of her cup. "Where did you hear it?" she asked, softly.

Aunt Mary Evelyn snorted. "Where did I hear it?" she asked in mock wonder. "My Johnny's second cousin heard it at the club last night. He told Johnny on the telephone this morning, so I rushed on over here. Your husband evidently has no problem tossing the news around. It's only in this house – and maybe the church, I suppose -

that he keeps it hush-hush. As if a wife didn't suspect something when her husband keeps a mistress. Behind her house, to boot! Who does he think he is, the king of Greece?"

Grace looked over at Mama, but Mama didn't say anything. She just kept her eyes lowered, looking into her coffee as if it would give her some answers that might halt her sister's tirade.

"Well," Aunt Mary continued, "there's nothing to be done for it. Of course, you can't leave him, what with *six* children. Going on *seven*. And the Church would never approve. So that's out of the question. Though I have no idea why you thought that so many children were necessary with that bum of a husband of yours."

"Charlie's a hard worker," Mama inserted in that tone of hers that disallowed argument. At last, having found the right words, she picked up her cup and took a deliberate sip, her pale lips clinging to the china edge.

"Yes, in more ways than one," Aunt Mary retorted, setting her teacup down with such a force that Grace feared it might break altogether.

Rebuked, Mama sat silent.

"I'll come for her on Friday, then," Aunt Mary said, rising to her feet. She layered her words with an official air. "I've been telling you I'd take her for years. I'm glad to see that you've come to your senses."

Grace glanced at Mama. What did Aunt Mary intend? For whom would she come? And why?

But Mama didn't say anything to enlighten Grace. "Yes," Mama said in the same voice with which she would give an order at the grocer's. "Come for her on Friday." When Grace looked into Mama's eyes, they seemed like holes in the night sky, places where the stars had died.

Without a good-bye to Grace, Aunt Mary swept out of the kitchen, her shiny black heels tattooing her path with efficiency. Grace heard the door of Aunt Mary's car slam shut, the engine start, and the wheels grind their way out of the drive. In the ensuing quiet, Grace listened as the grandfather clock ticked the seconds of their lives away.

"Mama," she asked finally, "what did Aunt Mary mean?"

Mama turned toward her, eyes floundering, unfocused. "What? What?" The words tumbled out, unsure if they could find their footing. "What do you want, Grace?"

"Nothing, Mama. Just," Grace began tentatively, "Aunt Mary said she would be back on Saturday to pick up someone. What did she mean?"

"She's going to take Evelyn, Grace." Mama's voice remained vacant. To Grace, the sentence made no sense.

"What do you mean, Mama? 'She's going to take Evelyn?' What do you mean? Take her where?" Grace dared to place a trembling hand on her mother's shoulder, rounded under her faded print dress.

"Home." With the suddenness of a Rhode Island thunderstorm, Mama's face crumpled. Grace watched in dismay as the sobs gained control over her mother's petite frame. "To live… with her and Uncle J-Johnny."

Mama gasped for breath, choking and weeping, but Grace couldn't comfort her. She'd heard the words that her mother had spoken, but they seemed to have no meaning. "Why?" she finally managed, feeling nothing. "Why?"

Mama didn't respond, but as soon as Grace had asked, she'd known the answer, spoken or not. *Evelyn is Mama's favorite, outside Ben. Mama wants Evelyn at least to have a chance. A chance to live without the stain of… this.* Grace swallowed hard, desperate to accept the truth of the kind of life her papa was creating for them. She sat there as Mama wept, shoulders shaking hard, nose running. She waited until Mama had no more tears to cry, and then she asked, "Does Evelyn know yet?"

Mama shook her head. Wiping her eyes and nose on her dirty apron, she muttered, "No, not yet." She hiccupped from the sobbing. "But she'll be glad. Your aunt and uncle have the money to give your sister the right kind of life. The kind of life she deserves."

With one harsh motion, Mama stood and pushed her chair into place at the table. Her small, quick feet brought her over to the cupboards and countertop, where she began to prepare supper for the family.

CHAPTER ELEVEN

Emmeline woke with a jolt. Dread rose in her chest, numbing her, as she realized what had broken her sleep: Her legs felt sticky and moist. Her abdomen panged with cramping.

Geoff slept solidly beside her, his breathing calm and deep, such a contrast to the ragged gasps making their way up her throat. Resolvedly, Emmeline pushed back her side of the bedcoverings and forced herself to look at the sheets, illuminated by the moonlight.

Blood soaked the linens where she'd lain. *The life is in the blood...*

The loss had begun in earnest, then. *Doctor Philips was right. I will never carry a baby to full-term.*

Emmeline's nails dug into her palms as she struggled to contain her sobs. When she realized she couldn't, she dropped to the floor beside the bed, pulling her pillow with her. Face buried to muffle the weeping, she spent a long, dark night.

~ ~ ~

The smoke coming from behind the barn alerted Grace. *Papa's burning.* In the quiet after-supper darkness of her bedroom, she leaned against the windowsill, arms crossed, breathing in the earthy scent of orange flames consuming orange leaves. She hadn't seen Gertrude since yesterday when Papa'd brought the woman home. Sometimes, Grace tried to push the whole idea of it out of her head, tried to conceal it as a corpse in the clods of her heart. But, like a vampire not buried at a crossroads, the knowledge that *this* really was happening continued to resurrect in her mind and heart.

Maybe if I talked to Papa... True, Evelyn always held first-place in Papa's heart, just as she did in Mama's. But occasionally, Grace had seemed to see a regard for herself in Papa's eyes. Perhaps if she talked to him, let him explain, she could understand... Maybe he could show her that the situation really wasn't as bad as it seemed, that he wasn't the gross monster whom Ben had understood him to be.

I'll talk to him, Grace decided and rose from her kneeling position.

~ ~ ~

Charlie threw another chunk of yard debris and garbage into the barrel. The container's sides rose up four feet, rusted tangerine from years of use. His father – an Italian straight from the Old Country – had always burned his garbage along with leaves and wood waste, and Charlie Picoletti saw no reason why he, his father's son and proud of it, should do differently, town garbage ordinance in place or not.

His eyes fell on the large brick homestead towering over the nearer barn. His father had built that too, and now Charlie's own family dwelt there, made safe and secure by the sweat of his brow and the work of his large, rough hands. This Depression had turned out to be a tough time for the state – no, for the country - and Charlie had done a little of everything to get by: junk-collecting, other folks' butchering, gambling, and, yes, even politics. He was a smart man, Charlie was, and he knew it. He would get by in life. He always did.

Now if only stupid Sarah could get it through her thick skull: that this thing with Gertrude had nothing to do with her. Charlie shook his head. Sarah'd moaned and whined a bit in the past when he'd had flings – truth was, he'd rarely *not* had a girlfriend in the years since they'd been married; he was, after all, a very attractive and fascinating man – but his wife'd never carried on like this – as if it was the end of the world!

"You brought that woman into my own house!" Sarah had screamed at him, tears running down her cheeks like a lovesick teenager. 'Cept she weren't a teenager no more, with rosy cheeks and honeyed glances that could melt his heart.

He'd stared at her. Was she serious? "Into *your* house?" He'd stated the question. "Into *my* house, you mean. I'll bring whoever I want into my home. You got that?"

And he'd not even kept Gertrude in the house! He'd gone to all the expense and trouble of fixing up that old ramshackle cottage for her, when they all could've saved a good deal of money by her staying in the guest bedroom. And yet he'd done all this to please *Sarah*; she was so finicky!

Charlie gave a kick to the barrel. *Women.* You couldn't live with them... and he, for one, certainly couldn't live without them.

Speaking of women – well, girls, at any rate – his middle daughter had come out of the house just now. Grace paused on the back stoop, hesitating like she was waiting for something, someone, or maybe she was just catching her breath. Grace was turning out to be pretty good-looking, if Charlie did say so himself. Small of stature like all the Picolettis, her thin frame caused her to take on the appearance of a tiny bird, golden-feathered, soft-featured, except for her slightly-bigger-than-average nose. *That nose comes from her mother's side.*

Grace's face stayed turned away from him, looking toward the sky, and Charlie stood studying her, wondering if she was waiting for a boyfriend to swing by, or whatnot. She was fourteen; she must have one, he figured. Not that it mattered to him at all. Grace would talk to her mama, or to Lou and Nancy about all of that. Let the women handle themselves.

Back when he and Ben had been on speaking terms – before his son had bashed in his tooth for no good reason – Ben had said something about Grace having a nice voice, too. It was why his eldest son called her, "canary-bird" or some such silliness. Charlie sniffed in the smoky air, appreciating the melded scents of burning rubber and wood. Now, if you wanted hear a good voice, all you had to do was listen to Grace's mama, Charlie's Sarah. He smiled in the gray light cast by the fiery barrel. There was a time, past now – long past – when he and Sarah'd sit at that old piano for hours, singing one popular tune after another. Charlie remembered that season in their life together the way a little boy remembers his birthday cake from the year before: sweet and rich, and he didn't care if it didn't have no nourishment. He liked the taste of it; that was for sure.

He poked at the flames rising up over the side of the rusted barrel, eyes smarting from the smoke. *That time's past, Charlie,* he reminded himself, even as the picture of Sarah, bright-eyed and lighthearted, pushed itself into his mind. Her fingers had flown over the ivory keys like a swallow catching bugs at the dusky lake nearby. Her voice had combined with his, challenging Charlie with the ease with which Sarah switched keys and changed harmonies. *Sometimes, she overreached herself,* he thought with a brisk poke at the pile of smoldering debris. *As if she wanted to outdo me.*

And such could not be borne. It wasn't a woman's place to tell the man what to do or how to live. Which was why Charlie had every right to bring Gertrude into *his* home. What did it matter to Sarah, as long as she and the kids ate good? Why did she care whose bed he slept in on the nights he wasn't in hers?

Sometimes a man just got sick and tired of coming home to the same barefoot porridge of a woman. Couldn't Sarah understand that? When Charlie walked in the door, night after night, he saw Sarah standing there at the stove, making his dinner with her once-smooth hands roughed up by housework. The sight certainly didn't lift the cares of the world from Charlie's shoulders. And she'd invariably have one kid or another bothering her about something – school, chores, whatever.

And then there were the potatoes. How many potatoes could a man eat, no matter how your woman tried disguising them, mashing them, buttering them, boiling them? Of course, she blamed him for that, too – said there weren't no money for anything else.

And her hair... Charlie could remember when Sarah's hair ran lush and heavy down her back, a burnished, enticing path. She'd not cut it when all the running-around women had bobbed theirs. But she *had* sacrificed it on the altar of motherhood, snipping it right around her shoulders. Charlie spit in disgust at the memory of Sarah sitting in the rocking chair, the first day she'd had her hair cut. She'd not even asked him, as if his permission wouldn't have mattered. That'd been right around the time Sarah'd disappointed him in another way too; she'd lost three babies, one right after another. And when he'd done all in his power to make sure she'd get pregnant each time, knowing she'd felt bad about it all! Women! You just couldn't please them.

Whereas, Gertrude...

Charlie tossed more rubbish into the barrel, feeling the heat on his fingertips. Well, last night was a good example of the difference in the way Gertrude and Sarah treated him. Right after supper, Charlie had run down to that snug little cottage he'd fixed up for her. Gertrude had met him at the door – thrown the door open actually and pulled him inside. She'd smelled like fresh-cut roses; the scent lingered in her hair, washed over her petal-soft skin, wafted through her ready-made clothes. Her lips had met his, and he'd tasted mint on her mouth, covering up her cigarette habit. Now *that* was how a woman ought to prepare herself for her man!

In that husky - some mistakenly called it hoarse - voice, she'd murmured right into his ear, "Here's my handsome, hard-working man. I've been waiting for you, Chuckie."

Handsome. As if he was a young man of twenty again, vigorous with the spirit and good looks of youth. She'd captured him in an embrace, and he had no desire to resist her. "I can't stay tonight," he'd protested, weak as a toddler in her soft arms. She'd changed into a silky robe and had taken her hair down from its pinned-up style. "Sarah ain't happy with me..."

She'd laughed the way she might laugh at a silly, roly-poly puppy, and he'd stiffened, insulted. A man had his dignity, after all. But then she'd drawn herself against him again. She'd whispered, "Now, you just tell me, why Chuckie Picoletti minds what that old-woman-in-a-shoe thinks? Let her stew her life away in misery; it's none of *our* concern." She'd kissed his cheek, gentle as a spring breeze through the lilac bushes. "Come..."

The very memory of Gertrude's fingers – smooth and light as butter made from Bessie's fresh milk – tracking through his hair made shivers run down Charlie's arms now. He poked at the fire, anxious for it to burn down so that he could let his feet run over the field beyond the barn, out to the cottage at the back of his property.

~ ~ ~

Grace swallowed hard, staring up at the night sky. She'd not glanced over the expanse from the house to the barn, but she knew Papa stood out there, tending to his barrel-fire. All during Grace's growing-up years, Papa had burned a fire nearly every evening. When she'd been young, no more than five or six, she clasped Papa's finger, big and meaty, in her whole hand, and he'd led her out into the yard to help him tend the burning trash and wood stuff.

Standing here now on the back steps, Grace remembered what it had been like when she was a little girl, tiny and innocent, knowing hardly anything at all about Mama and Papa's problems. Mama had cried from time-to-time, had peered out the curtains when the hour was late and Papa had not returned for supper, had whispered quietly in a worried voice with Aunt Mary at the kitchen table over coffee. But nothing that much disturbed the simple sweetness of a five-year-old's natural trust in her papa or love for her mama. How Grace longed for those times back again now, nearly a decade later!

In the darkness of nights like this, standing here on the back step, Grace recognized the real reason that nobody but Ben and Aunt Mary dared bring up the festering wounds so blatant to the rest of the world: Grace – and Mama and Nancy and Lou, even Evelyn – they were all afraid that voicing the terrible possibilities might award them breath and life. That acknowledging the ghosts might give them leave to walk the earth.

But Grace found she could be silent no longer. Not with Mama beginning to swell with her seventh baby; not with a strange, permed woman living in the cottage beyond the barn; not with Ben running off after knocking Papa's tooth out – so he said; Grace hadn't seen the hole yet, and Ben sometimes exaggerated.

Papa's tooth aside, the questions burned in Grace's heart, and she feared they'd consume her without her consent. Thus, here she stood on the back step, willing courage into her chest as she thought about approaching Papa, burning at his trash barrel.

"Mary, Mother of Jesus, help me," she begged aloud, barely moving her lips, afraid her papa would see and think her crazy for talking to herself. "Mary, Mother of sweet Jesus, answer my prayer." Grace knew she would have better luck trying Mary than directing her prayer straight to God, like the Protestants did. Mary was, after all, a woman like Grace and hopefully would sympathize with her human weaknesses.

"Bring my prayer before your Son, Mother of God," she whispered. While Grace herself had no claim on the Son of God, surely Jesus would listen to His mother. "May it... may it *all* be alright," she stammered, her tongue lame, then stopped, silent, trying to find the right words. Her heart and mind swarmed with so many thoughts that she couldn't get a single one clear. "Help me," she implored and hoped it would be enough. She was taking a chance, she knew, since she hadn't gone to Confession since last week. But her prayer would have to do.

Grace breathed deeply one more time and forced her feet down the steps. She kept her eyes on the dirt path through the prickly fall grass, not daring to raise them to see if her father saw her coming. The night air clamped coolly on her shoulders; she wished she'd worn a cardigan at least.

But it was too late to turn back and retrieve one from inside the house now. Grace's steps brought her right up to the burning barrel before she'd thought it possible.

Papa glanced up, his dark eyes glowing amber from the firelight. He grunted, his way of greeting someone familiar, then gave his eyes back to the barrel's contents.

"Hi, Papa," Grace swallowed. She found an ancient rotting log near the barrel and sat down, knowing her legs were ready to give way.

Papa's gaze shot up again, obviously surprised to see Grace sitting down, like she planned to stay awhile. He shifted his position, as if uncomfortable. "Milk the cow?" he finally said, probably as a way of finding something to talk about.

"Yes, Papa," Grace replied. She'd milked Bessie that afternoon, just before supper.

"Fed her?" was the next question.

"Yes, Papa," Grace answered. "Bessie's all set."

Papa grunted his approval, and silence fell again. But it was an uneasy silence, full of unexplained matters, brimming with questions that neither wanted to ask or answer. Grace perched there, feeling the cold wood underneath her goose-pimpled legs and the fire's warmth brushing the front of her body. Heart so much afraid, she studied Papa beneath lowered eyelids.

"Look," Papa suddenly burst out, giving a vicious poke at the flames. Grace jumped. "I know Ben talked to you afore he left. Don't know what he said, but it weren't true. None of it."

Something lifted in Grace. Funny thing was, she recognized the falseness of Papa's words, but, oh, they were so good to hear! They would be so nice to believe! She let herself play-act for a moment, buoyed up by what she knew was a phony hope. "Really, Papa?" she murmured. "None of it?" She raised her eyes to meet his, but he kept his own gaze on the fire.

"Of course not," Papa replied. "You're fourteen, Grace, big

enough to recognize a slur when you hear it."

Fourteen...

And just like that, the breath pulsed out of her little cherished self-deceit. "I'm fifteen, Papa," she stated quietly. "Turning sixteen in November."

"Of course you are. I know that..." Papa blushed red and blathered on, but Grace had stopped listening. She stared into the bright flames, waiting for the train of his words to chug to a halt.

"Why did you bring that woman here, Papa?" The question came out baldly, ugly and harsh, even filtered through the soft autumn night.

In the loud silence that ensued, Grace dared to glance up. Papa's eyes fastened on her, expressionless. His long, blackened stick had frozen mid-poke; it, too, had been shocked by Grace's audacity, by speaking out loud what no one else in the Picoletti household had dared.

No. That wasn't true. Ben had spoken it. Had hissed out his revulsion at his papa's promiscuity and encouraged Mama to split the joint, dragging her kids with her. He'd spoken it, alright. And where was Ben now?

Gone.

Grace shuddered, then rubbed her arms, pretending that the cold had made her shiver like that. She licked her lips, suddenly dry as a mitten left too long on the radiator, and dropped her eyes to the dirt.

Silence. Grace counted out ten beats of her heart before letting her gaze flicker up again, timed to match the crack of moist wood in the barrel. Still Papa's eyes lay on her, dark and burning cold. She opened her mouth, forcing out the lie. "I... I mean, why didn't, uh, Gertrude-" Her tongue soured at the poisonous name. "Why didn't she stay with Uncle Jack?" Hopefully, the question would tamp down Papa's anger with Grace for meddling where she had no business. Her heart thudded painfully against her carved-out lungs.

Papa stayed grim for just an instant longer, then relaxed. He turned his eyes away from Grace, and the stick began to thrash at the fire again. "Told you. She didn't have no work. They've got too many mouths to feed over at Uncle Jack's to keep her there with no pay."

Too many throats to pour beer down, more's like. Grace's thought surprised her. *I'm thinking like Ben talks,* she realized, with a little shame coloring her cheeks.

Glad that the darkness shaded her face, Grace nodded her understanding. "She looking for work now?" Grace heard the question leap out of her mouth before she could stop it. She bit her bottom lip hard, wincing at the pain of the necessary action. That should stop her wayward tongue.

Papa's jaw pumped angrily, and his eyes flashed over to where Grace sat. She tried to look as innocent as possible while braving the aftermath of her query: slouched over her shoulders, hugged her knees with white-clenched hands. From experience, she knew that Papa's mercy extended farther when his subject appeared submissive. "Mind your own business, Grace," he finally barked, the ends of his words growling through the smoke. A moment more, then, "Dontcha have homework to do?"

"Yeah, Papa. I got homework to do," Grace replied, rising with shaking knees. Despite her fear, she let her gaze fall for a long moment on her papa, taking in his heavy but handsome jaw, the sweep of his golden hair, the deep-toned complexion that spoke of old Italian beaches and of long hours under a blistering Rhode Island sun.

Drawing her eyes away, Grace started back to the house, feeling the fire's heat fall from her body. She felt the moisture of sharp, unbidden tears but blinked hard to drive them back to where they belonged. *Pity... and longing... and hurt... How can they all mix so in my heart?* She shook her head, trying to make everything fall into place. *I don't know what to feel!* Her feet quickened their pace, and Grace dashed into the house, past a surprised Mama, and clattered up the stairs, as if the devil himself nipped at her heels.

Entering the dim bedroom, Grace shut the door, pressing her whole body against its old wood, comforted by the solidity. She remained there at the doorway for a good long while, waiting for her breathing to calm.

Finally, Grace regained control. She moved away from the door and sat on the edge of her bed, tucking one leg underneath her. *Nothing has happened that will change anything. Papa has... has had women before.*

Admitting what everyone knew brought an internal cringe but Grace forced herself to continue her quieting self-talk. *The only difference is that this woman lives here with us now.* Grace sighed. If the woman – Gertrude – kept to the cottage that Papa had prepared for her, well, then, Grace decided that she and the rest of the Picoletti kids – Mama, too – could cope. She couldn't understand Papa, but maybe it wasn't her business to do that.

Clenching her jaw, Grace picked up her notebook and began her science homework. She had a quiz tomorrow; she was determined to get a perfect score.

CHAPTER TWELVE

There were only two left. Emmeline lifted first one and then the other from their hooks, feeling the packed weight of the baskets transfer to her hands. The brilliant scarlet flowers hadn't faded at all in the crisp early autumn nights. Yet, Emmeline knew that their season in the sun had finished for the year. She didn't want to risk losing the geraniums to a bad frost.

In that September morning, she looked at the empty porch eves above her and at the red-petaled plants cradled in her arms. Despite the cheerful wren's call from the nearby pine tree, Emmeline felt a heavy wistfulness draw its shroud around her heart. She forced a small smile onto her lips to combat it. Geoff would leave for school soon, and she didn't want him to find her out here, despondent. She hadn't told him about last night's heavy bleeding. Or the continued cramping. Before Geoff had woken, Emmeline had drawn the bedcoverings over the stains, hiding them from him.

Hoping against hope…

She bent her head over the red flowers, looking into their clustered faces. "Come now," she admonished the geraniums, "time for you to come inside for the winter."

"Bringing the plants upstairs?" asked a deep voice. Sure enough, here was Geoff now, full satchel in one hand, lunch pail in the other. Dressed in the white button-down she'd ironed for him earlier that week, he looked to her as handsome as the day she'd met him as a young girl.

Emmeline sighed despite her resolution to remain optimistic.

"Yes, it's time for them to come inside. I'm afraid of a frost." She smiled at her husband and placed the hanging baskets down on the porch. "Here, wait a minute," she said, moving toward him. "You forgot one." She pulled off the tiny swatch of toilet paper he'd used to staunch the nick he must have gotten shaving this morning.

Geoff dropped a kiss to her forehead and returned her smile. "What would I do without you?" he asked, his eyes twinkling from behind dark lashes.

"You would have children." The words slipped out without Emmeline thinking about them. She let her gaze fall back to the geraniums, embarrassed.

"What?" He sounded incredulous.

She forced herself to say it again. It was true, wasn't it? "If you'd married someone else, you'd have had children of your own." She fingered the red blossoms, smelling the plant's spicy fragrance.

Then Geoff's hands gripped her shoulders. "Don't say that, Emmeline. I would rather have you as my wife than have half-a-dozen children." He kissed her forehead gently. "You are the Lord's most precious gift to me."

A tear escaped the crack in her heart. "You'd better go to school," she said softly, picking up the plants, clutching them for security.

He kissed her cheek. "Have a good day, beloved. I'll see you tonight," he murmured.

She watched as he trotted down the three steps to the sidewalk. More tears rose to her eyes, but as quickly as they came, Emmeline shook them away. She picked up the hanging baskets at her feet, checking for any stray spiders, and brought them inside the house. The screen door squeaked and banged shut behind her.

~ ~ ~

"Mama." Grace stood in the doorway of her parents' bedroom, picking at her cuticles so hard it hurt.

Her mother kept making the narrow double bed, as if she didn't hear her middle child calling her name.

"Mama," Grace tried again, taking a step into the room.

Mama glanced up this time, her grown-out hair falling all over her cheeks. "Oh, Grace. Didn't see you there," she said, tucking the bottom sheet underneath the mattress with those rough, capable hands. "Don't you have to get to school?"

"I got a couple of minutes," she answered, shrugging her thin shoulders. Grace knew that she'd have to run all the way because she took the time for this brief conversation.

She placed her lunch pail, battered from years of use, down on her mama's antique dressing table and went to the bedside opposite her mother. She began tucking the sheet underneath the mattress, folding the top over it. All the while, her eyes kept going to Mama's worn-out face, wondering how to ask the question she had to put forward.

But Mama broached the subject first. "What is it, Grace?" she asked, her hands picking up the pillows to fluff them. None of the soft caring resided in Mama's tones that Grace had heard in other mothers' voices – Ruth Ann's mother, for instance. Mama's voice always wore a practical, severe dress, uncompromising and somber enough for any occasion.

Grace swallowed down the anxiety that kept creeping up her throat. "Mama," she began, "there's a special choir at school now. Mr. Kinner – you know, the English teacher – started it."

Mama didn't say anything, just kept fluffing those full-of-goose-down rectangles.

Grace picked up one of the other pillows to keep herself from picking at her nails again, but she felt too nervous to fluff it. She just clutched it and heard herself say, "Practices are only on Fridays." Grace held her breath, hoping Mama would understand what she was asking. "Today is the first one."

"And?" Mama stepped into a patch of sunlight, let in by one of the windows. She picked up the bedspread from where it draped over Great-Grandma's rocking chair and shook it, letting it unfurl over the bed.

"I thought…" Grace hesitated, unsure of how to continue in a way that would guarantee a positive response. "I thought maybe I could join it?" She bit her lip after the last word, waiting for her mama's answer.

But Mama just sighed, quick and full, and kept smoothing out the bedspread, drawing it up and folding down the top edge.

Grace unclenched her teeth from their hold on her lip. "Ben said-" she tried again, appealing to her mother's love for her firstborn.

Mama turned sharp eyes on her, straightening up her short, hen-like body and folding her arms tightly across her middle. "Don't go telling me what Ben said," she informed Grace. "Ben talked to me 'bout this singing choir, and I told him what I thought 'bout it then." She shook her head. "Well, I ain't changed my mind, Grace. I think it's a waste of time. Yours and mine."

Desperation overtook Grace. "But, Mama," she stammered. In her heart, she'd been sure that Mama's love for Ben would win out. "I - I thought…"

"I know what you think, girl," said Mama, staring at Grace with those weary, drained eyes. "You think you're gonna join this special choir, and everybody's gonna make a big fuss 'bout how pretty your voice is."

Grace flushed. How did Mama know what had been in her thoughts since the day she'd heard about Mr. Kinner's choir? Her forefinger found its way to her mouth, and she began to gnaw the cuticle, sweetly distracted by the sting. She wished she'd never asked Mama.

"And then, somehow, you'll get a solo part. Some big whig'll notice you and put you in a Hollywood movie or on some fancy stage in New York City. You'll be famous and rich and beautiful. That's what you think, ain't it, Grace?"

Embarrassed at the truth of Mama's words, Grace twisted her toe into the floorboard. She finally uttered, low and soft, "I just… I just want to do *something*, Mama. It's only one day a week, Fridays." She ran her tongue over her dry lips and glanced at the cuckoo-clock hanging on the wall over her parents' bed. She was impossibly late for school.

Mama unfolded her arms and picked up the patchwork quilt that she always placed at the foot of the bed. Her hands busied themselves with folding it neatly. "Yeah, well, I was young once, too, and not so long ago," she replied, her tone softening just a little. "It'll do you no good indulging in those silly daydreams, Grace. 'Sides," Mama's voice returned to its usual brusqueness, "I need you here after school, what with Evelyn going to live with Aunt Mary and Ben gone for good." She laid the quilt at the foot of the bed.

Mama had made up her mind, then. Grace knew better than to argue; doing so would only irritate Mama and put her into a silent, foul mood for days. She pushed down the protest that wanted to spring from her mouth. "See you after school, Mama," Grace choked out, picking up her lunch pail from the dressing table.

She was almost out the bedroom door when Mama replied, "Mind you shut the screen door tight. I don't want any flies coming in."

Grace nodded and escaped.

CHAPTER THIRTEEN

Sarah finished straightening up the bedroom, accompanied by the tick-tick-tick of the cuckoo-clock. She glanced over at the glossy wooden timekeeper. Nearly nine o'clock. Time to get the bread dough mixed and set out to rise. She'd bake this afternoon when the noon heat of the September day had died away. No ready-sliced, store-bought bread for Sarah; she baked hers from a sourdough starter. Fact was, the bread that Sarah baked descended from her mama's bread starter. When Sarah'd married Charlie Picoletti – What? Twenty years ago now? Only fools and young lovers kept track of such dates – her mama had given her a cupful of bubbly yellow flour and water, ripe with the scent of yeast. Since then, twice a week, Sarah had made all her bread from that starter.

Glad to be left alone on her baking days, Sarah often used the silent hours to remember her own mama, gone now for more than a decade. Her mama had birthed many children, even more than Sarah had: Four sisters and five brothers made their homes throughout the Northeast and the Midwest. One brother had even moved out to Canada. Quebec, Sarah thought, but she hadn't heard from that brother since 1924, a year after their mama's death.

Passing the dusty dressing table with barely a glance, Sarah moved with heavy steps into the kitchen. *Good thing is, my bedroom's downstairs.* No long steps to climb. Though only in her fourth month, Sarah didn't feel like trudging up a steep flight of wooden stairs.

Funny. When had she begun to refer to the bedroom which she and Charlie shared as "hers?" *Used to be "ours."* She shook her head as her hands reached for the flour canister that sat ready on the kitchen counter. And when had her hands become so wrinkled? So full of brown spots from hours spent plucking chickens on the back step and hanging out wet laundry on the line?

Nothing turned out the way it was supposed to. Retrieving her mixing bowl from the cupboard, Sarah added a splash of starter, then shook a good heaping of flour into it. She'd always scorned the use of a measuring cup. And she'd always mocked – once upon a time, long, long ago – the idea that her Charlie – laughing and sparkling-eyed – would cheat on her like this.

Blinking back the tears threatening to march to the front of her vision, Sarah rummaged around for her long wooden spoon to stir up the mixture into smooth, sticky dough. She found it and plunged it into the bowl, remembering how her own mama used to remind her to scrape the sides.

Mama had liked Charlie when Sarah had brought him home with her a few years before the Great War. From that first evening he'd sat in their kitchen, complimenting Sarah's mama on her chewy cookies and drinking two full glasses of milk, Charlie had seemed like he just… belonged in their family. And Sarah… Well, seventeen-year-old Sarah had felt like she'd belonged to Charlie. That he'd protect her. Stick by her. Especially since her first love – actually, her first fiancé - hadn't. But, well, that was best left forgotten, stashed away like her wedding dress deep in an attic trunk.

And the early years with Charlie hadn't been bad. They had their arguments, but all couples did. And the babies came one after another. Sarah remembered the pride etched in Charlie's face when the midwife had presented him with their firstborn son, a fiery boy they'd named after Charlie's own grandfather Benjamin. And Lou and Nancy soon followed, twins whose appearance heralded a strain on the family finances. Sarah made reductions in her food budget to help scrape by and had exclusively breastfed the twins until they passed their first birthday, despite the stress to her own body.

Lucky I did, too, thought Sarah, sprinkling more flour across the wooden table surface. *Otherwise, I would have had another one even sooner.* As it was, she'd become pregnant again before she could catch her breath. Charlie'd seemed a bit uneasy about it, though he said he was glad. Work at the lumber mill that employed him had increased, but the owners kept hiring more immigrant workers who would accept lower wages. That cut into Charlie's hours some. So Sarah tightened the financial belt even further to make up for the lost pay.

Despite his decreased hours, Charlie wasn't home much. "Looking for work," he always told her as he pushed his cap over his golden curls each morning and headed out the door. But his steps were unsteady when he arrived home at night and his pockets even emptier than when he'd left that morning. Sarah would sigh and cut the bread a little thinner for hungry-eyed Ben and the two toddling twins. At least they had their own cow for milk and cream. Secretly, Sarah had begun to sell some of the butter and soft cheese which she made, thanking the Sweet Mother of Jesus that she had customers for it.

Remembering it, Sarah couldn't bring a blush to her cheeks when she thought of her own relief at losing that third pregnancy. True, the doctor had put her on bed-rest for two weeks because she'd lost so much blood. She couldn't keep down more than a mouthful of chicken soup sent over by a kindly neighbor. But Sarah had paid Doctor Philips no mind in the end. So weak that she could feel her legs shaking together, she'd gotten out of bed in four-days' time. Even today, more than fifteen years later, Sarah couldn't suppress a mirthless laugh from escaping her lips. Stay in bed for half of a month? With a three-year-old boy running around the house and two one-and-a-half-year-olds? Sure, her mama had come to help out. Sarah'd only been in her early twenties, after all. But Sarah told Mama that she could handle everything herself, that she'd be fine on her own. Really, though, she hadn't wanted her mama to see what kind of a man her sweet Charlie had shaped out to be.

She'd thought it wouldn't get any worse. But then Sarah had peered out the front window one day, pulling the bleached curtains to the side to let in a little sunlight during that tired winter. She'd been waddling around with Cliff in her belly then; Grace was just a very little girl, barely wobbling around on her unsteady legs. Sarah had put lemon squares in the oven, Charlie's favorite dessert, and the sharp citrusy-scent brightened up the day considerably.

Through the rain slamming against the old panes, she'd seen Charlie's car chug up the road. It'd been a black Ford, she remembered now as her hands massaged the dough. Sarah had wondered at her Charlie arriving home so early in the afternoon. *Must've been cut... again!*

Funny, when they were first married, his early arrival home would have brought a leap of joy into her young heart. But now Sarah felt nothing but anxiety at the sight of Charlie's familiar form behind the steering wheel: Would his measly paycheck cover their bills? How would she ever save enough money for shoes for Ben? He needed them for school! Never mind Sarah's hair, which hadn't been styled for months and grew around her neck like an untended brambly bush.

She'd been about to let the curtain fall back into place when she realized that Charlie hadn't slowed down so that he could take an easy turn into their curving driveway. Curiously, she looked at his moving car closely as it approached the house, traveling along the lazy side road. She could make out a figure in the passenger side. A woman.

They had driven on by the house, surely never thinking that child-saddled Sarah would be peeking out at the rain-sodden world. But she had been. And that was the first in a long series of similarly-rooted events that choked what was left of Sarah and Charlie's marriage.

But that was 1921. This was 1934, and Sarah had bread dough to put on the windowsill, allowing the sunshiny lumps to rise in the warmth.

Wish Grace was at the age to quit school, she thought. Having someone with whom to share the household chores would certainly help, especially when the new baby came. *Come to think of it, Grace'll have to stay out of school once February comes so that she can help me with the baby.*

A little pang of guilt struck Sarah, but she pushed aside the feeling. *It's not my fault Grace can't finish school. I need her here. Lou and Nancy are no help with the house, too hoity-toity for it. And Evelyn's going to live with Mary.* Sarah tied on a fresh apron with unnecessary firmness. Grace's pleading face appeared in her memory: her middle daughter's wide eyes begging to join that foolish singing group. *"Practices are only on Fridays,"* Grace had said, the hope practically spilling out of her mouth along with the words. *"Ben said..."*

In the empty house, Sarah let out a snort. "Ben said!" As if that should make a difference! Sarah's eldest son, who lived from day-to-day on the odd mix of gambling earnings and fairly-earned wages at a horseracing track, of all places! And he thought he could get his mama to change her mind...

Yet, he almost had done it. Grace would never know that Sarah hadn't made her final decision until her daughter actually had asked for her permission. Well. Good thing Sarah had thrown out all cotton-candy feelings, all warm remembrances of her own youthful yearnings in the face of Grace's supplication. Only an unloving mother would allow such nonsense to fill up her children's heads. Better that Grace learn early that the world was a hard, cruel place which would ruthlessly crush any dreams she might possess.

~ ~ ~

"Hi, Grace."

The cheerful male voice broke into Grace's near-stupor. She'd been sitting at her desk in Mr. Kinner's class, just moments after the last bell rang. Startled by the interruption of her thoughts, she raised her eyes to see who addressed her.

It was Paulie Giorgi, Mr. Perfect-Score. He stood, inclining his head a little bit so that his warm maple-syrup eyes could look into Grace's face. "You look like you're deep in thought," he smiled, bringing out those beautiful dimples again.

"Uh, yeah," she stammered. "I was just... thinking." Truth was, she'd been sitting there trying to figure out a way to tell Mr. Kinner that she wouldn't join his special choir after all. A way, that is, in which she wouldn't have to admit she'd fudged Mama's signature.

"Well, don't sit there thinking too long," he grinned, all-out friendly. Grace felt like the sun had just spread its warm beams on her, despite the drizzle that pattered outside the classroom windows. "I heard you're joining Mr. K.'s after-school chorus," he continued.

Now where did he hear that? Grace wondered. "I... I..." she trailed off, not knowing whether to nod or shake her head. After all, she wasn't joining now. Mama had refused to let her. But she didn't want to get into that with Paulie Giorgi. She didn't even *know* him!

"Teddy Bulger told me," Paulie went on, not seeming to notice Grace's sudden-onset speech impediment.

Well, that made sense. Teddy chummed around with Ruth Ann's brother, and Grace had let the news slip to her school friend. *Boy, Ruth Ann can't keep her mouth shut to save her life, can she? Not that I asked her to keep it a secret, but for Pete's sake!* Grace nodded to show that she understood.

"What part do you sing?" Paulie asked, and Grace wished he would just go away. Her stomach hurt with him standing there, smiling down at her.

She swallowed and managed to mumble out, "Soprano, I think." Her hands twisted themselves into knots beneath her desk.

"Mr. K. tested your voice?" Paulie questioned, not looking like he planned on moving until she did.

"Uh, yeah." The sound of shuffling books caught Grace's attention. Mr. Kinner stacked and placed his books in his satchel up front. She had to tell him now that she would not be able to join the chorus, but Paulie's solid body hemmed her in. She'd have to ask him to move, but the words wouldn't come to her lips. *Couldn't he just go away? Why is he talking to me, anyway?*

Mr. Kinner finished latching his satchel. Paulie said something about a song he hoped the choir would sing, but Grace was too preoccupied with Mr. Kinner's actions and her fast-disappearing chance to explain the situation to the teacher privately. She heard none of Paulie's words.

Realizing that, satchel in hand, Mr. Kinner approached the classroom exit, Grace began to glare at Paulie. He apparently didn't notice her angry look, however, and kept on chattering. *Mama would say he talks the hind leg off a mule! Never heard a boy blabber so much!*

Grace's frustration overcame her timidity at last. She rose to her feet, slipping from the seat worn smooth by hundreds of schoolchildren's bottoms. Doing so forced Paulie to step back so that Grace didn't bump right into him. Surprised, he finally stopped talking for just a moment, his eyes following her gaze, directed toward the classroom door.

But it was too late. Mr. Kinner disappeared into the corridor, and Grace had lost her chance to explain, to make everything right. Sort of.

"You needed to talk to Mr. K.?" came Paulie's friendly query.

"Yeah." Fleetingly, Grace noticed that even though Paulie abbreviated their teacher's name, he attached a respectful title to it. She glanced at him. "Guess it will have to wait," she ended, filling with hopeless panic. Today was the first rehearsal. Mr. Kinner needed to know she wasn't participating. Today.

"Hey, well, just talk to him at rehearsal," suggested Paulie with an encouraging smile.

This time, Grace couldn't refrain from letting her own lips respond by turning up tentatively.

"Here, can I carry your books for you?" Paulie offered, reaching out for the four-book stack piled on Grace's desk. "The choir meets in the auditorium."

Grace paused in the act of pulling her thin cardigan from the back of her chair. No boy had ever asked to carry her books before now! She tucked a stray strand of hair behind her ears with a trembling hand, her throat as dry as chalk. Should she let him carry them? But she wasn't going to rehearsal!

She didn't need to worry about giving Paulie a reply. When Grace didn't give him an immediate, "no," he picked the stack right up. "Is this all you have?" he asked.

Grace shook her head and opened the top of the desk, where she stored her pencil case, tablets, and a few other textbooks. She gathered them together in a neat little pile with the pencil case topping it all. Paulie added that accumulation to the stack in his arm. Then Grace reached beneath the desk chair and retrieved two more books. Paulie reached for these as well, but Grace hesitated. "These are my library books," she explained, feeling a little more shy. She hid the emotion by tucking the two books under her arm quickly and looking Paulie straight in the face like she didn't care what some boy thought about her being a bookworm.

No matter how charming his cheek indentations were.

But Paulie's smile didn't fade. In fact, it just grew wider. "Okay," he said. He gestured toward the classroom door. "Shall we?"

~ ~ ~

She wasn't scary at all. Paulie wondered why he'd never had the courage to talk to Ruth Ann's friend Grace before today. Well, that wasn't true. He and Grace had gone to the same school together for two years, so they must have said *something* to one another at some point. But, of course, Paulie meant really *talk*. Like he was doing now, walking down the school corridor at Grace's side, letting his lips flap about who-knew-what.

She was certainly quiet; that much was obvious. Hurrying so they wouldn't be late for rehearsal, he noticed how Grace kept her head bowed a little, not really looking where she was going. More staring at her feet than anything else. He wondered what went on inside her head, beneath that sweep of golden hair, every last strand combed into place. Except for that one lock that she continued to twist and tuck behind her small pink ear.

"So, what books are you reading?" he asked, smiling down at her from a full ten-inch advantage. He expected it would be some female-in-distress romance or a Nancy Drew – which would be worse. *She is, after all, Ruth Ann's friend.*

She shot a glance up at him. "Tennyson," she answered, almost defiantly. "*Idylls of the King.*"

Paulie's grin widened. "Hey, you're a girl who knows how to pick out a book," he complimented sincerely and was glad to see her wary countenance relax a little – a very little – bit. "I love Tennyson," he offered as they reached the auditorium's double-doors. *Maybe it'll bring another smile to her face.* "I thought I was the only one who liked it when we read *In Memoriam* in Mr. K.'s class."

Grace's eyes grew large in surprise, and they paused before the doors, Paulie's fingers closing around the door handle. "Oh, no. How could you *not* love Tennyson? His poems are so… so wonderful," she finished, red blushing over her face like a McIntosh apple in the autumn.

"Agreed." Paulie pulled open the door, letting out the sound of chatter from the students already gathered in the auditorium. Wow, a lot of kids had showed up. They filled the front two rows of the large room, stretching across from left to right. Mr. Kinner sat at the piano up front, apparently looking through some music before they began to rehearse.

Paulie began to stride down the center aisle. Suddenly, he realized Grace hadn't continued at his side. He turned to see where she'd gone and found that she lingered near the entrance. Her pale face with its large unblinking eyes stood out in the dim entryway lighting.

"Hey, you coming?" asked Paulie, backtracking a few steps.

Grace's gaze flickered from Mr. K. at the piano to Paulie. "Uh… I think… I have to use the lavatory." The words stumbled out of her mouth.

"Oh, sure." Paulie smiled and placed her stack of books on one of the auditorium's back row seats. "I'll set your books here for you."

"Thanks." But she didn't sound grateful at all. Just preoccupied. With what, though? This was the first rehearsal of the new choir!

Girls. You couldn't figure them out.

"No problem," Paulie replied. "Hey, don't be too long. Mr. K.'ll probably be starting soon." Sure enough, just then, Mr. K. rose from the piano bench, climbed the short stair to the stage, and walked to the center of it. His footsteps echoed on the wooden flooring, shiny with wax. Paulie watched the teacher for a moment before the sound of the auditorium door clicking shut caught his attention. Grace had slipped back out to the corridor to use the lav.

"Paulie! Paulie, over here!" His chum Elliot Krieger stood up in the second row, beckoning to him. "Got an empty seat for you, buddy!"

Paulie glanced one more time at the closed auditorium door before shrugging off Grace's odd behavior and moving with quick steps to join his friends.

~ ~ ~

Grace scurried through the corridor, looking over her shoulder to see if Paulie had followed her. *Why should he follow you, Grace? You're paranoid! He just thinks that you're using the lavatory.* And she would visit the lavatory, too, because she didn't want to commit the mortal sin of lying, after all.

As she came up to the creamy-tiled girls' restroom, Grace caught her breath as she realized, *I already did lie. I forged Mama's name and told Mr. Kinner that she had given me permission to join the chorus.* The guilt rose as bile from her stomach. Now she would have to receive the sacrament of Confession as soon as possible. Mama always told Grace and the other kids about her great-uncle who had lied about something and hadn't gone to Confession before he died. Mama still prayed for her great-uncle's soul, but she said she had doubts regarding whether it would do any good, seeing that he had committed a mortal sin.

Grace entered the lavatory with slow steps. She could see two high-heeled feet below the stall dividers, but she couldn't say for sure to which teacher the feet belonged. Before the occupant could emerge, Grace ducked into the other stall and latched the door, leaning against the green-painted metal. The girls' bathroom smelled heavily of bleach and ever-so-lightly of smoke. *Some of the bad girls must have been lighting up cigarettes in here today.* She was glad that the teacher in the next stall – whoever she was – had come into the lavatory first and so couldn't suspect Grace of smoking.

The toilet flushed in the stall beside her, and Grace felt the tremor through the metal as the door unlocked and opened. The high-heels tapped their way over to the sink. Grace listened as the woman washed her hands and dried them. Then more taps came, and Grace could be sure the woman had left the lavatory.

Slowly, Grace unlatched her own stall door and came into the silent bathroom, like a scared rabbit hopping oh-so-gingerly into the twilight surrounding his burrow. She walked over to the smeary mirror, reflecting the bathroom's glaring light, and stared at her own face.

I wish Mama had said yes.

That would have prevented all these problems, after all. The priest surely would excuse her forgery because she had not willfully misled Mr. Kinner. Now, Mama had denied Grace's request, and so Grace's falsification of Mama's signature appeared an outright falsehood, something she'd meant to do.

Why did I sign Mama's name, anyway? she wondered, looking at her own large eyes in the mirror. *I could have just asked her if I'd thought she would say yes.*

And the answer came to her: In her heart, she'd known that Mama would say no.

And I didn't want to face that. I… I want to be in this choir so bad. The tears bubbled up and over the rims of Grace's eyes. Trying hard to stop them, she crossed her arms over her chest and bit her lips.

But it was no use. The tears wouldn't stop but merely increased at her attempts to stem the flow. *Stop! Stop!* Her mind screamed it but for once, Grace knew herself unable to force her emotions to bow the knee to her will.

I want this, she realized, thinking of the auditorium with its brightly-lit stage; the popular, nervy kids practically bouncing excitedly out of their front-row seats; Mr. Kinner standing there, exquisite as one of the heroes in Grace's books; and even Paulie shining his welcoming smile at her. "Don't be long," he'd grinned before she fled to the lavatory to try to figure a way out of this mess she'd gotten herself into.

Mama has no right to take this away from me. The thought popped into her brain suddenly and with a force that knocked the breath out of her heart. She saw her mother scrubbing, scrubbing, scrubbing the kitchen floor on calloused knees; operating that clunky antique washing machine twice a week; baking and cooking constantly for her thoughtless kids and her unappreciative husband. *That's how I'm gonna end up,* thought Grace. *That's how Mama wants me to end up.* Her fists clenched into balls at her sides. She remembered her mama's mocking words that morning before Grace had left for school, and she knew she was right. *I won't – I won't – I won't!* Grace stared hard into the mirror, watching as her eyes turned to ice.

I will be in Mr. Kinner's choir. I'm nearly sixteen years old. Mama can't stop me, Grace asserted, lifting her chin boldly and dashing away the rest of her tears. A weight seemed to lift from her chest. She breathed in deeply and turned on the sink faucet. The cool water refreshed her flushed cheeks. Grace wiped her face on a paper towel and raked her fingers through her hair to neaten it. Hopefully, no one would see the red rimming her eyes. Other than that, no visible signs remained of her sobbing attack.

With a feverish heart, Grace rushed from the lavatory. Her skipping steps brought her back to Mr. Kinner and the chorus. She could hear the throb of voices in the auditorium, warming up.

CHAPTER FOURTEEN

I t was tough to please two women at once.

Charlie put his back into raking, scraping the ground with vigor, shoveling thoughts of Gertrude and Sarah from his mind. The pile of dead leaves grew into quite a mound. The front lawn looked pretty good; he'd go around to the back after poking his head into the priest's house to see if he couldn't snag a drink. A lemonade, at least. Though he *was* a priest; maybe he had some good red wine available.

The church building rose high and gray behind Charlie, giving him the shadow of its blessing. As it should. The Picolettis had always paid their dues to God. Charlie had seen the arrival and departure – some through death, others through reassignment – of four priests during his lifetime in Chetham. The first priest had baptized him and his two siblings. The second had administered Charlie's First Communion and confirmed him. The third had performed the Sacrament of Marriage for him. Father Fredrick was number four. He hadn't done anything for Charlie yet, but maybe he'd bury him one of these days.

Setting his rake to the side, Charlie had just determined he'd go inside and ask to use the restroom or something when the Father himself appeared, smiling out the church door at Charlie. Father Fredrick wasn't a bad chap as far as church men went. He kept to himself and let folks keep their business to themselves. Charlie appreciated that kind of thoughtfulness in a priest.

"Looks like you've got quite the pile here," remarked Father

Fredrick. He hadn't quite reached his fifties, yet he had a full crop of hair as white as confectioner's sugar. His eyes bulged pleasantly as he talked, joining with the priest's stocky build to remind Charlie and the other parishioners of a polite, pious bulldog. "Do you think you'll finish by dinner?"

It was already three o'clock in the afternoon. Charlie started to give the priest an odd look, but then he remembered that the priest had come from a snooty background. The religious man called "supper," "dinner," and "dinner" to him was "luncheon." So Charlie nodded. "Oh, I think so," he said. "At the latest, by five o'clock."

The priest smiled benignly. "Good. You wouldn't want your wife's dinner to get cold." Suddenly, the cheerful expression fell from Father Fredrick's fleshy, mobile face. In its place, the priest attached a different mien: a concerned and somewhat stern one. Startled, Charlie put up his guard, ready for whatever the priest might say.

"You know, Charlie, I've always seen you as a family man," Father Fredrick began, his well-fed jowls flapping a bit in the wind that whipped around the corner of the church.

Warily, Charlie nodded his agreement. "That I am, Father." He wrapped both meaty hands around the rake's handle and waited.

Father Fredrick held Charlie's gaze, his bright blue eyes scalding. *You can't intimidate him, that's for sure!* "Well, I've heard reports…"

The priest seemed to be searching for just the right words to explain. His lips tightened together, then released. He must've figured out how to say it. "A reliable source tells me that you are not entirely faithful, Charlie." The priest glanced left and right, as if afraid someone might have overheard.

Faithful? What'd the priest mean? Of course Charlie was faithful! He provided for his family, didn't he? Wasn't he doing yard work right now, earning a pittance from the parish to add to his weekly wages? His eyes narrowed in disbelief. "Faithful?" he echoed aloud, cocking his head to the side.

"Yes, faithful to your wife," the priest clarified.

"To Sarah?" Charlie would have snorted at the humor of it, if he hadn't been so insulted by what the man insinuated. "'Course I'm faithful to my wife, Father. No man's more so. And if he tells you otherwise, he's a lying Kaiser." Charlie ground those words out, turning them up and out of his mouth like fresh sod in a flowerbed.

Faithful? Didn't he provide for Sarah? And all them kids? Hadn't he given her six – no, seven children? What further faithfulness did the priest require? Charlie knew that he was loyal to Sarah in every way that could be expected – realistically, at least.

Trying to keep his anger down, he clamped his jaws shut so that the muscles pumped with blood. He should not – he would not become angry with a priest, may his mother rest quietly in her grave! To show his honesty, Charlie lifted his square chin up and stared Father Fredrick straight in the eyeballs. *I'd love to see him flinch.*

But Father Fredrick retained his calm demeanor, merely returning the gaze with his own cool eyes. After a moment, he let the corners of his neat mouth turn upward ever so slightly in what Charlie had come to see as the sign of the priest's benevolence. "Well," the father said, "that's good to hear from your own lips, Charlie."

Charlie nodded, brows contracting into a cloud against his will. His hands throttled the rake handle. *I'd like to find whoever's been having a good time telling the priest about me and thrash them good!*

"Would you care for some fresh lemonade? That's very thirsty work you're doing," the priest remarked, the same slight smile touching his mouth.

Suddenly, Charlie's desire for lemonade fled. "Uh, no, Father. I'm not thirsty at all." Without waiting for the priest to go back inside the church, Charlie turned back to raking, lashing the ground with gusto.

~ ~ ~

Grace flew all the way home. The tops of her shoes shook free from the soles; the rubber bands had broken on the first block. *I'll have to ask Cliff for some more,* she thought, knowing that Cliff had lots of the cheap "ammunition" for his rubber-band gun. Sweat began to run down her back, but she didn't want to take the time to stop, remove her cardigan, and tie it around her waist. She could feel her blouse untucking from her skirt's waistband.

I have to hurry! Mama's gonna be so mad! Grace pumped her legs faster, not caring as much about the people who saw her running as about her fuming mama, waiting for her at home.

Oh, but the chorus rehearsal had been glorious while it lasted! Grace couldn't remember the last time she'd enjoyed anything so much. Except for the occasional pang of guilt she'd felt when she glanced at the clock or at the stack of permission slips resting on Mr.

Kinner's piano, the hour glowed. Mr. Kinner had placed her with the other sopranos, to the bottom right of the choir. They'd warmed up their voices with challenging exercises, and Grace felt a thrill run up her spine at the sound of all the other students singing up and down the scale together, all around her. *If only it hadn't ended!*

There wasn't enough time to stop at the red-flowered house today, to just stand there gazing at the hanging baskets' flaming beauty. She dashed by it, not slowing down for an instant. Yet Grace couldn't resist peering out the corner of her eye at the porch just to see that flash of scarlet that had glanced back at her for the past month. After all, she hadn't paused this morning, either, on her way to school; she'd been too distraught over Mama's refusal to grant Grace permission to join the choir. So, now, at the end of the event-filled day, Grace stole a glance at the porch with one straining eyeball.

But the red flowers were gone.

Grace's steps slowed to a jog, and her head fully turned toward the white house. Her eyes widened in disbelief. The baskets, too, were stripped from the porch without warning. Grace came to a complete and dazed halt. To say the least, she'd not expected it, and she felt now as empty as that porch, swept clean but lacking anything to fill it.

That is your punishment. The thought startled Grace with its sudden clarity. Of course! She had disobeyed Mama, had *lied* and kept that lie alive knowingly. So God had taken the red flowers away from her, that bright spot of joy in her rather dreary existence. *Even the piano doesn't play,* she realized, noting how the floral curtains blew at the partially-opened second floor window. Grace swallowed, feeling the lump of guilt grow in her throat. With one more stare at the pretty house with its hollow porch, she bolted toward home.

~ ~ ~

"You did what?"

Grace heard her papa's incredulous tone as she entered the kitchen. The guilt that steadily wrapped itself around her brain caused her to think that Papa addressed her. Holding the screen door as it shut so that it wouldn't slam – something that irked Papa to no end – Grace opened her mouth to explain her lie with trembling words.

But Papa's face turned toward Mama. He didn't even peep to see which one of his children had entered the house. His jaw pumped heavily, like a boxer's fist, and his eyes barely blinked as they trained on Mama.

Mama. Her defensiveness coated her vulnerability as she sat crouched at the kitchen table. Her hands wrapped around her cup of black coffee like it threatened to jump out of her grasp.

Trembling with fear, Grace turned her eyes toward Papa. The china-thin silence gave her thoughts time to ramble. What was this all about? Gertrude, again? But then, why would Papa say that *Mama* had done something? She waited just inside the doorway, frozen as one of the blocks that the ice-man brought.

"You. Had. No. Right." Papa spit out each word separately, bullets to pierce Mama's head. Grace could see his teeth bared like one of the feral mutts that roamed around the neighborhood. "No right at all." He stared down at Mama, eyes ablaze, nostrils flaring with wrath.

Mama responded by jutting her chin out, pressing her thin white lips together. "I had to do it! And I have every right. I'm her mother."

"And I'm her father!" Papa roared, neck muscles bulging. Grace cringed as his hands cracked down on the table. Mama's coffee bounced and spilled out of the cup, running over her hands.

"What do you think you're doing, woman?" His face lunged into Mama's, but Mama barely flinched.

The sunlight filtered through the screen door, streaming by Grace, touching on Mama's pale face. "I did what I had to do, Charlie. And I don't want to hear another word about it." Browned and wet from the spilled coffee, Mama's hands kept their grip on the cup. Her eyes stayed fastened on Papa, ignoring Grace's presence.

Grace watched as Papa's lips curled into a smile of mockery. "Oh, *now* you don't want to hear another word about it? After you give away my daughter to your sister? Is that how it is? Jezebel!" Without warning – though Mama should've known she had it coming to her – Papa's open-palmed hand struck hard, right across the side of Mama's head.

Mama hadn't been prepared for the blow. Her head reeled to the side, the graying brown hair falling over her face. She wobbled on the chair but managed to regain her balance. Then Mama surprised Grace by sweeping her hair back away from her eyes and standing up, holding onto the table's edge for support. "How dare you? How *dare* you call me that?" Mama hissed at Papa, using a voice Grace had never heard. "I've given you six children. I keep up this house for *you!* I cook three meals a day with that skimpy thing you call a paycheck for *you!* I wash your clothes. I do your ironing. I garden. I churn butter. *For you, Charlie!*"

Grace watched in silent wonder as Mama finished her outburst, bosom heaving. Papa stood wordlessly as well, his jaw evidently taking a break from pumping, his eyes staring hard at Mama.

Mama paused, then stepped toward Papa. "I've put up with your runaround ways for twenty years. I would've let you keep going with them, too, in spite of the humiliation you've caused this family-"

"That *I've* caused!" Papa interrupted, folding his heavy arms across his square chest, a smirk growing on his face again. "What about you? Look at you! You think I'm proud of a wife like you?"

The arrow went straight to Mama's heart; Grace would have seen that no more clearly if the well-aimed dart had been visible. A red flush crept up Mama's neck and face, hiding in part the welt that grew near her hairline. Grace squirmed inside, her heart throbbing in pity, tensing with the agony of seeing Mama appear so pathetic.

Papa's words had silenced her. Red-faced, Mama bowed over, arms loose at her sides, the picture of a beseeching captive whose plea for freedom the ruling monarch had denied.

"You make me so angry sometimes, Sarah," Papa's tone softened just a bit. "And now you – or your fool man-hating sister – is spreading lies about me to Father Fredrick. How am I supposed to keep up our family's reputation with you doing that? Huh?"

"Father Fredrick?" Mama asked, regaining her shell of steely non-emotion. She picked up the half-full coffee cup and carried it over to the deep sink with only slightly trembling hands.

"Said he'd *heard* that I wasn't so faithful to my family. Now where'd he get that from, I'd like to know?" Papa stuck out his chin like a teenage boy looking for a fight. For an instant, he looked just like Ben.

Mama shrugged, turning on the tap to run a dishrag under it. She brought the wrung-out cloth back to the table and began mopping up the spilled coffee. Her hands moved with small, efficient strokes.

"Where'd he hear it?"

Grace whirled her head at the echoed question. Nancy poised

herself in the large archway between the living room and the kitchen. Grace's older sister wore her clothes for working down city: a smart navy-blue skirt suit handed down from Aunt Mary, accessorized with a tiny perky hat. In her manicured hand, she clutched her matching pocketbook. Without glancing at Grace or Mama, her eyes flung steak-knives straight at Papa. "How does Father Fredrick know that you're a cheater?"

Grace's eyes opened wide as Nancy took two long steps into the kitchen. Her tall sister ended up standing nearly nose-to-nose with Papa. Nancy laid a mocking finger aside her smiling lips. "I don't know, Papa. Could it be the fact that you've got a kitten living in the cottage behind our house?"

What is Nancy doing? Grace couldn't believe what she saw. Of all her siblings, only Ben had ever taken a stand against Papa. *And he left once he had done it.*

But Nancy... Why would Nancy, of all people, burst out like this? Nancy had always been content to escape the house when things got bad; to fling off responsibilities onto Grace's thin shoulders; to hole up in their shared bedroom, door locked, reading the latest edition of *Film Weekly*. She nor Lou had ever seemed to share Grace's concern for Mama or anyone else in the family.

But here Nancy braced herself, angry-eyed, a derisive smile turning up the corners of her lacquered lips, raising her plucked eyebrows. Grace chanced a look over at Papa, wondering what he would make of this phenomenon... and what he would do about it.

He showed her soon enough. For an infinite moment, Nancy and Papa stared into each other's eyes, seeming to dare the other to back down. But neither did.

"Get out." Papa gnashed out the words, fists shaking. "Get out before I do something I don't want to do."

Nancy's sneer grew. "What are you going to do, Papa? Kill me? Oh, wait," she mock-gasped. "That would ruin the family reputation, wouldn't it?"

His hand shot out then, that Italian palm, meaty as a sausage, and smacked Nancy's mouth. Head thrown back for a moment, Grace's older sister didn't even wince. A thin stream of blood threaded down her split lip, but she grinned through pink-tinged teeth. It looked like she'd eaten deviled ham from a can and forgotten to swallow.

"Made you feel manly, didn't it?" Nancy scoffed, letting out a little snort of a laugh. Papa seethed, jaw popping.

Frightened, Grace watched as Nancy turned her back on Papa and sauntered from the kitchen, moving toward the stairway. Nancy's eyes didn't flicker once toward either Grace or Mama. She wiped the rivulet of blood with the back of her hand as she walked, probably trying to avoid getting stains on her blouse.

Papa gave Mama a glare of disgust and stalked out the screen door. Grace shrank back as he passed, but he shoved her aside anyway. Mama had stood motionless during Nancy and Papa's exchange, coffee-soaked dishrag in hand, but when the door slammed shut, Mama regained mobility. She took wooden steps over to the kitchen sink and rinsed out the dishrag with slow handwringing.

Nerves tingling, Grace glanced out the screen door. Sure enough, Papa marched across the back pasture. *Toward Gertrude's cottage,* ached Grace. Her father would take his comfort from the arms of a permed blonde to whom he'd made no sacred vows and who had never sacrificed her body to bear him children. Grace left the kitchen, taking the stairs to her shared bedroom.

She could hear shuffling inside the bedroom. Nancy had shut the door, but the lock had never worked for as far back as Grace could remember. She gave a slight knock, then squeaked open the door and entered the dimly-lit room.

Nancy stood before the four sisters' common closet, pulling her few skirts and dresses off the hangers. She looped each over her arm and deposited them on the bed before moving to the room's sole bureau, a beat-up hand-me-down from Mama's family. Yanking open a drawer, Nancy's nimble fingers pulled out camisoles, underwear, stockings, garter belts. She gathered them all in a messy ball and stuffed them into the open carpet bag sitting on her bed.

Grace watched silently for a moment. *It's like when Ben left for the first time, years ago.* "Whatcha doing?" she asked, though she already knew the answer.

Nancy didn't hesitate or look at Grace. "Leavin'." She gave the heap of clothes a final shove and buckled shut the carpet bag. "Shut the door, kid."

Grace nodded and obeyed, closing the door with a gentle click, feeling the cool brass knob yield to her pressure. "Where'll you go, Nan?" she said softly.

Her sister glanced at her, jaw set like cement. "Richard's got a place now. Above Barry's auto garage." A smile hardened on Nancy's lips. "He's been pushing me to marry him for who-knows-how-long. I've been putting him off, telling him I need more time." Nancy snorted. "Well, I guess now's the time, huh, kid?"

Grace's eyes widened. "What about the priest? Father Frederick wouldn't marry you just like that, without Papa and Mama-"

"I didn't say anything about Father Frederick, Grace," Nancy interrupted. "There's a Justice of the Peace, you know."

No priest blessing the Sacrament of marriage? Grace couldn't believe her sister would do such a thing. "But Mama-"

"I don't really care what Mama thinks, Grace," Nancy huffed, glaring at her for daring to object. "Mama and Papa were married by the Church, and I don't see that it did them any good."

Grace hung her head, studying her fingernails. *The whole family... everything... is just fallin' apart.* She felt Nancy's hand squeeze her shoulder then and looked up to see her big sister's toffee eyes fastened on her face. "I gotta do what's best for me, kid," Nancy explained, her voice a little softer. Her hand dropped off Grace's shoulder. "Hey, at least you'll have more space now, huh?"

Grace managed to nod, blinking back the stinging tears. There would only be her and Lou sleeping in the bedroom now. But instead of relief at the thought of no longer being squashed together with three sisters, Grace felt only an ache. "Good luck," she offered.

"Thanks, Grace." Nancy picked up her bulging floral bag, and Grace stepped away from the door. She opened her mouth to say good-bye, but the words wouldn't creep out her throat. "See you, kid," Nancy said and was gone.

The room was so silent that Grace could hear the tick-tick-tick of the old mantle clock counting the seconds on the desk. She moved with noiseless feet to her bed and perched there. *I don't feel anything,* she thought wonderingly. *I know I'm sad and hurt and all that, but I just can't feel it anymore.*

Though Grace had been on the verge of crying only moments before, she now sat tearless and dry-spirited. No sound came from the kitchen below the thin floorboards; Grace vaguely wondered whether Mama had seen Nancy leave or if her older sister had just slipped outside without saying a word to the woman who birthed her, who raised her.

95

She didn't raise us. We raised ourselves! The truant thought sneaked through Grace's mind. Acutely conscious, she felt the bitterness rise up as she remembered Mama all during her growing-up years: colder than the blocks that the ice-man brought on Tuesdays, less caring than a cowbird was for its young.

The room felt so empty. Evelyn had left, too. Aunt Mary had taken her namesake to live with her and Uncle Johnny today. Grace looked at the two double beds, one of which she sat on, made so neatly that a quarter could bounce on them. Then her eyes went to the big closet, where the four sisters' clothing had fought for legroom. It was more than half empty now; Evelyn and Nancy had taken all their things.

Evelyn's saddle shoes were gone from their place beneath the bedside table. Somehow, that made the emptiness unbearable. Bending over, Grace pulled off her own shoes and placed them in that spot.

CHAPTER FIFTEEN

On Monday morning, Emmeline had just finished crimping the crust of an apple pie when the phone rang. She wiped her hands down her bibbed apron, brushed back the wisps of hair from her face, and picked up the black receiver.

"Mrs. Kinner? This is Doctor Philips' office."

Emmeline's fingers gripped the phone, knuckles bleaching as she anticipated what words might come next. "Yes," she swallowed, "this is Emmeline Kinner."

"Doctor Philips would like you to come in for another consultation." The starched voice paused. "He'd like to be sure that everything is going as it should."

Going as it should? But nothing was going as it should.

Emmeline's mouth parched. She forced herself to swallow, nearly choking, then asked in what she meant to be a calm tone, "When would the doctor like me to come in?"

"When it's convenient for you," the nurse replied.

Emmeline barely heard the times and dates offered next. Her mind had turned to wood, it seemed. When she didn't reply to a question, the speaker on the other end said, "Mrs. Kinner? Are you alright?"

Lord, help me. "Yes," she managed. "Yes, I'm alright. What... What are the possible appointment times again, please?"

The nurse rambled off a list of available days in the next week. Then she added, "Or you could come in today. Doctor Philips has an opening this afternoon at one o'clock."

"Yes," Emmeline answered. "I'll come today."

~ ~ ~

Behind his massive oak desk, Doctor Philips tapped his fountain pen against his lips. In the silent moment, Emmeline remembered the medical man once telling her that he didn't like to write in pencil, ever; it seemed too changeable. "When I write something," he'd said, "whether prescription or diagnosis or symptoms, I don't intend to alter it."

Clutching her small black purse in her lap, Emmeline crossed her ankles and tried to appear as serene as possible. *Oh, God of my fathers, You alone are in control.*

Doctor Philips gave a final tap, and leaned back in his padded chair. "Mrs. Kinner," he began, "this is a most difficult conversation for me to have with a patient whom I've known for as long as you."

Emmeline could not reply, could not even nod. *I know what you're going to say…*

The doctor cleared his throat. "As I informed you at your last visit, your pregnancy seems at an end."

Emmeline felt the word *seems* like a jolt. "Seems?" Her gaze sought the doctor's. "Do you mean… Do you mean that I *am*, in fact, still pregnant, then?" Hope stretched its wounded wings in her heart, despite the doctor's grim expression. Her hands shook; she gripped her purse tighter to quiet them. "I thought… the bleeding… I thought that I'd already lost the baby?"

The doctor's shoulders lifted and fell with a sigh. "Losing. Lost. At this point, we can't be certain which it is." He looked straight into her eyes, compassionate but unflinching. "Mrs. Kinner, please prepare yourself. I am certain that your body is aborting this fetus. What you've related to me – the experience you had the other night – only confirms my belief."

"Is there no chance at all, then?" Emmeline heard herself ask.

Doctor Philips bushed his eyebrows together, his mouth relaxing a little. "Not much of one, Mrs. Kinner." He shook his head. "I would be a cruel man to let you think that there is. I would rather prepare you for the inevitable." He leaned forward in his chair, searching her eyes with his.

Her breath came slow and shallow. "So I will never have children,

Doctor?" She stared down at her white knuckles, firmly clinging to the purse for safety.

Doctor Philips paused. "Only God knows that, Mrs. Kinner. But, speaking as your doctor, no, I don't think so."

"I see." She stared down at her lap, feeling his kindly gaze on her.

~ ~ ~

"Hey, Mr. K. is really booking it today," Paulie observed, looking down the hallway. He carried Grace's books in his hands once again, grinning.

Grace tried to find a polite way to tell him to give her back her books and get lost. *I don't want Paulie finding out where I live,* she thought, her eyes following Mr. Kinner as well. He really was in a hurry. He practically ran down the corridor, not seeming to pay any attention to the stares of other teachers or the surprised looks of students.

"Must be in a hurry to get home." Paulie grinned, showing off those dimples.

"Where are ya going, old boy?" Teddy Bulger's chipper voice sounded right behind Grace. She felt her face growing warmer as the number of boys around her increased. *How can I escape?* But Paulie blocked her way — not meaning to, of course — from the front and now Teddy came alongside her, freckles shining on his oily face.

"Walking Grace home," answered Paulie, keeping her books tucked securely under his arm. He didn't look ready to give them up anytime soon.

Grace stood miserably, ignoring the boys' conversation until she heard her name again. "Well, I'm walking Grace home right now," Paulie said to his friend. "I can come over to help you with your essay right after that."

Teddy turned curious eyes toward Grace, and she could just hear his thoughts: *Why would he want to walk her home?* But Teddy didn't say anything out loud. He shrugged and said, "Okey-doke. See you, Paulie." Hefting his own load of books under his arm, he trotted toward the main entrance.

This is it, Grace. This is when you make Paulie give you back your books and flee. But even as the thoughts ran through her mind, Grace found that she didn't want to say them, not in her heart.

Especially when Paulie turned his broad smile back to her. "Ready?" he asked.

Grace nodded, the faintest smile touching her own lips.

~ ~ ~

Sarah pressed a hand to her back, feeling every surge of the pain shooting up her spine. Biting her chapped lips, she bent once more to the task before her: scrubbing the kitchen floor on her hands and knees. "Blast that girl," she muttered. If Nancy hadn't been so fresh with Charlie the other night, Charlie wouldn't have told her to high-tail it out of the house.

And Sarah would've had just a little more help around here. "Not much, though," she grumbled out loud. Nancy had always been the independent sort. Not lazy, exactly; just bent on doing what she wanted, when she wanted. Lou acted similarly. And, in some ways, Sarah had always admired her twin daughters for that streak of selfishness. *Least they grab what they want outta life. Unlike me. Unlike Grace.*

Just at that moment, the screen door banged. Sarah picked up her head to see Grace entering, flushed and hot in the Indian-summer weather. "Don't slam the door," Sarah huffed. *How many times do I have to tell the girl?*

"I'm sorry, Mama." Grace stood just looking down at Sarah, lunch pail dangling from one hand, books cradled in the other arm's crook.

Pathetic. Just like me. "Well, don't stand there like a pelican. Get changed. I need your help with supper," Sarah snapped, not feeling the least bit bad about it. Fact was, lashing out at someone felt kinda good, especially when you knew that they weren't the type to bite back.

Grace opened her mouth, then closed it. "What?" questioned Sarah. She shifted back on her heels, feeling the ache rip down her spine.

Her daughter seemed hesitant. With a slight clink, Grace set her lunch pail down on the kitchen counter. "I... I got a lot of homework, Mama."

Did Grace think of nothing else but school and homework and singing? Didn't she understand that Sarah needed her help? Didn't Grace realize that Sarah had no one else upon whom she could depend? "You can do that later if you want," Sarah answered, lacing the words with sarcasm. Grace might as well know now. "This'll be your last few months of school anyway, so I don't see why you're all worked up about your homework."

She shot a glance straight into her daughter's eyes, willing the innocence out of them, before turning back to her scrub bucket. Sarah dunked her bristle brush and tore away at the floor. She let a couple of minutes pass before looking up to see the effect her words had.

Grace turned pale, her eyes two blue holes in a white-clouded sky. "Whatcha mean, Mama?" she nearly whispered.

A painful pleasure throbbed through Sarah as she knew that she'd hurt Grace. Sarah thrust the brush deep into the bucket, splashing soapy water over the edge. "Just what I said. I guess you know about the baby coming in February."

Grace stared, but Sarah thought she saw her head bob a tad in acknowledgment.

"Well," Sarah continued, scrubbing the wood as if her life depended on it, "I'll be needing you here once February rolls around."

"But..." Grace looked like a sunfish some cruel boys had left to flop on a summer riverbank. "But I have to finish school, Mama."

A fifteen-year-old daughter telling her mama what she had to do! Sarah sat back on her haunches, looking at Grace, scrawny and threadbare, and her heart softened just a bit. Then she heard Charlie's car pulling up the long drive, grinding through the stones in the dirt. A bang of one car door, then another. Laughter followed, high and nervous and quickly hushed. Sarah's mouth hardened into a thin line. "I need you here, Grace. There'll be no arguing about it, is that clear?"

Grace began nodding, tears pooling in her eyes. Sarah didn't feel the kind of satisfaction that she had thought she'd feel, but she went back to scrubbing. Without looking at Grace again, she said, "Go on now and change your clothes. I need your help with supper."

"No."

Sarah whipped her head up, sure she'd heard wrong, though the word had been said in such a strong, unmistakable voice.

Grace stepped forward, coloring rising in her cheeks, dashing away tears with the back of her hand. "No, Mama. I'm not gonna quit school, no matter what you say, and I've got homework tonight!" With a glare that seared her mama, Grace dashed from the kitchen.

Sarah heard her daughter's feet thud up the stairs and then the bedroom door shut with a loud bang. The kitchen stayed silent for a long while, the only sound being the weeping that shook Sarah's shoulders.

CHAPTER SIXTEEN

None too patiently, Geoff waited for the nurse to bring Doctor Philips to the telephone. When he finally heard the older man's calm voice, Geoff's words poured out in a deluge of panic – *vomit, blood, pain. My wife. My wife!*

"Yes, so she is experiencing spontaneous abortion, just as I thought," Doctor Philips replied. "Usually, there's only mild bleeding, but with Mrs. Kinner's pregnancy having reached four months, some vomiting and cramping should be expected."

Geoff heard Emmeline retching in the bathroom. His blood pressure rose rapidly. "So what do you recommend we do, Doctor?"

"Do? There's nothing to do, Mr. Kinner." Doctor Philips sighed. "I *am* sorry for the loss. But, as I told your wife last week, I expected this unhappy conclusion."

"There's *a lot* of blood, Doctor!" Geoff couldn't stop himself. "I don't think this is normal. Emmeline is very ill!" Didn't the man understand? Geoff wasn't just worried about the loss of the baby; he was concerned about his wife!

"Sometimes the body retains some of the tissue if the pregnancy is of a two-month duration or longer. Then, she may need a minor surgical procedure to stop the bleeding and prevent infection."

"A surgical procedure?" Just when Geoff had thought it couldn't get any worse.

"Yes. Actually, I'm going to refer you to a specialist, just to be on the safe side. Doctor Samuel Giorgi. You may know him already."

Sam? Of course, Geoff knew him; Sam and his son had attended

First Baptist for a few years now. The Kinners had hosted them for dinner several times. "Yes, of course," replied Geoff. "We know him from church."

"Good. You'll be comfortable with him, then. As you may know, Doctor Giorgi is the foremost gynecological surgeon in this region. You'll be in good hands with him. Let me give you his office telephone number. See if he can get you in today."

Leaden-fingered, Geoff penciled down Sam's office phone number. He would call the specialist as soon as he let the school know that he wouldn't be in today.

And I'm cancelling that choir. I can't concentrate on something so inconsequential when Emmeline needs me so much.

~ ~ ~

"Say, Grace, did you hear?"

Paulie's grinning face appeared just to the right of her locker. Somehow, he seemed to materialize wherever Grace was. And Grace found herself blushing worse than an apple-blossom tree whenever the dimple-cheeked boy did materialize. *I wish he would go away!*

Maybe he wouldn't see how red her cheeks got if she kept her face hidden in the depths of the metal cubby. Conveniently, Grace found that her pencil case required immediate attention. She set it on the narrow shelf inside the locker and began to straighten its contents, not even glancing at Paulie. *If I don't answer him, maybe he'll leave.* She lined up her pencils so that the erasers lay snugly together.

But Paulie wasn't in any hurry to leave, heedless of Grace's silence and total absorption in her pencil case. After a few moments, Grace looked in Paulie's direction from the corner of her eye. There he still stood, tanned forearm leaning up against the locker next to hers, eyes sparkling like hot caramel, his usual wide grin toned down to a serious smile. He would've looked like a young Hollywood heart-throb in one of Nancy's magazines if it weren't for the slight meaty scent on his breath. *He must've had bologna for lunch,* thought Grace, a little envy spreading shoots inside her.

He's not gonna leave unless I talk to him. Hoping her face had cooled, Grace turned toward Paulie, keeping her hands in the pencil case for safety. "Hear what?" she asked, her heart gaveling against her chest. Her eyes dropped down for just a fraction of a second to make sure the pounding wasn't shaking her blouse visibly.

"Mr. K. dropped the choir." Paulie grimaced. "It's a real letdown, huh?"

Grace's tongue lay paralyzed. For several seconds, she stared at Paulie, mouth open as a trout's. Then she realized how she must look and clapped her lips together. A moment later, she managed, "W-W-Why?"

Paulie shrugged, his thick shoulders rising and falling with easy confidence. "Don't know yet. Mr. Jeffries told me on my way inside this morning."

Grace's heart fell into her ankles. It must be true, then, if Paulie had gotten the news straight from Mr. Jeffries. Proud of being born on the day the Civil War ended, bow-legged Mr. Jeffries was the principal of Chetham High School. "Why'd Mr. Jeffries tell you?" she couldn't help asking. Why did Paulie get first dibs on info from the principal?

He shrugged again. "I asked him if he knew why Mr. K. was in such a hurry yesterday. He got all tight-lipped but then he let that leak out about the choir." Paulie folded his arms across his chest – but Grace noticed how the gesture didn't make him seem like a tough guy. *Just... Just... manly,* she decided, then bit her lip, glad that he couldn't read her thoughts.

"I sure was looking forward to it," he added.

Grace nodded and turned back to her pencil box. "Yeah, so was I," she said.

Really, Grace? Were you planning on going back after what happened last night with Mama? Her fingers felt the smooth wood of the pencils as they rolled about the box.

Yeah, I was. I really was. The clarity of the thought scared her, froze her fingers in mid-caress. *I was going back.* Her index finger and thumb pinched one of the pencils until the skin under her fingernails turned bloodless white. *No matter what Mama said, I was going back to the choir.*

She knew why, too: Her brother Ben's words kept vigil in her mind, haunting her in the early hours of the morning when her bedroom was so cold and empty. They whispered comfort when she brought the buckets out to milk Bessie in the gloaming; they sang to her as she worked on homework late into the night. *We're all in the gutter, but some of us are looking at the stars,* he'd said. His eyes, so serious and sad in that darkened barn, pleading with her: *Promise me, canary bird. Promise me that you won't settle...*

The tears brimmed before Grace knew what had happened. Panicked to think that Paulie might glimpse her outbreak of emotion, she stuffed her head further into the locker, not taking into account her now-violently trembling hands. The pencil box clattered off the locker shelf, its contents scattering in a five-foot radius all around Grace. Humiliating as it was, she half-welcomed the diversion. She dropped to her knees to pick up the pencils, feeling the solid tile chilling her skin where her stockings had drooped.

Paulie was beside her in an instant. "Here, lemme help," he said, and his hands pooled the pencils with a few quick swipes. Grace's icicle fingers brushed against his warm ones; she knew he didn't notice it, but she sure did. Of course, she was forced to acknowledge it with a face full of fresh floridity.

With a grin turning up his mouth, Paulie poured his handful of pencils into her box and stood to his feet. He grabbed Grace's elbow as he rose, helping her up as well. She jerked away from him as soon as she regained her footing, the unaccustomed courtesy making her feel awkward.

Paulie looked surprised at her repulsion. Surprised, and Grace thought, just a smidgen hurt. She tucked a piece of hair behind her ear to cover her embarrassment. A brief expression of confusion seemed to hover on his face for just an instant, but then he replaced it with his usual cheery smile. The bell shrilled above their heads. "Well, I'm off to World History," Paulie said, hefting his books under the crook of his arm. "See you later, Grace."

She nodded, so many feelings – some familiar and most completely new - roiling inside her, and watched the springy figure retreat down the hall.

~ ~ ~

"Mr. Kinner has taken a leave of absence." The rookie substitute shifted from one leg to another. Paulie noticed that the young man – he couldn't be more than twenty-one – had a very twitchy mouth. Maybe he wasn't sure whether he should smile to show he was good-natured or if he should frown to show how stern he would be if anyone dared to disobey him.

"Who is this guy?" Toby Simmons whispered in Paulie's ear from the desk behind him, spraying Paulie with a light mist of saliva.

Paulie grimaced and wiped his neck. Why did Toby have to have a space between his front teeth *and* an overbite to rival a beaver's?

"Oops, sorry, Paulie," Toby muttered.

Paulie wished he hadn't wiped his neck so conspicuously. He turned his head a bit to offer Toby a grin. "Forget it, Tobes. And I don't know who the sub is," he whispered.

"Wish Mr. K. was here," Toby murmured.

Paulie nodded, his eyes turned back toward the front. "So do I."

The substitute wobbled over to the blackboard lining the classroom wall, picked up a thin piece of chalk with shaky fingers, and began to scrawl something on the black expanse. Only, the chalk broke halfway through, falling on the floor in several unusable pieces. The classroom broke out into laughter as the man turned a red-and-white face back toward them. "Class! Class!" he emitted in a strained voice, and Paulie felt pity for the poor man as he grasped for authority that he hadn't earned.

Without bothering to raise his hand (It wouldn't have done much good since the whole class rollicked with laughter.), Paulie jumped up from his desk and headed for the front of the room. He'd taken out the box of spare chalk from Mr. Kinner's desk before the substitute could protest. "Here you are," he smiled, offering the box.

The young man took it from Paulie with a stiff little nod. "Thank you," he answered. "You can take a seat now."

Paulie grinned again and headed back to his desk. On his way, he noticed Ruth Ann passing a note to Grace again. He glanced back over his shoulder at the substitute. *Hope he doesn't catch them.*

The substitute had busied himself with writing his name on the blackboard, however. He seemed oblivious to all else but his own quest to obliterate the students' memories of his mishaps by means of impressing them with his elaborate cursive.

"I am Mr. Crookshank," the substitute announced, turning back to the class. His cheeks glowed with the triumph of having written his name. "I will be your teacher until Mr. Kinner returns."

Two rows over from Paulie, freckle-faced Gerry Turnbull raised his hand. "When's Kinner coming back?" he asked, chomping hard on a wad of bubblegum.

Mr. Crookshank's lips tightened. "He has taken a leave of absence for the time being. That is all you need to know, Mr...?"

"Oh, Turnbull, sir. Gerry Turnbull," replied Gerry, happily smacking away at that gum.

"Mr. Turnbull. You will refer to your absent teacher as *Mr. Kinner.* And you will please dispose of that disgraceful chewing gum *immediately.*" The substitute seemed to be gaining his academic sea-legs by force.

He must've known he made a bad first-impression and is trying to fix it now, figured Paulie, sitting back. The substitute surveyed the classroom coolly, his eyes raking each student. Suddenly, his gaze stopped near the back of the room to Paulie's right.

Oh, no. He caught them.

Sure enough, Mr. Crookshank strode toward Grace and Ruth Ann. Ruth Ann saw him coming before Grace did. She shrank back and pretended to be flipping through her literature book. When Mr. Crookshank came to a halt in front of Grace's desk, she still was reading the note Ruth Ann had passed her.

Whack!

The ruler fell across Grace's hands with a force that made Paulie wince. She hadn't expected it; the note bounced out of her hands onto the floor, and her head jolted up to stare at Mr. Crookshank. From his seat, Paulie could see the deep red marks the ruler had left on Grace's white fingers. Crimson rose in his own face as he bent his eyes to stare at his desk.

"Well," Mr. Crookshank stated, a glimmer in his eye, "I can see we have our work cut out for us in the next few weeks. Bubble-gum chewing, disrespect, passing notes," he listed, giving extra emphasis to the last action as if it was truly diabolical. "I thought I was here to teach English literature, but I see that I truly have been hired to instruct this class in manners."

"Oh boy," muttered Toby in Paulie's ear. Paulie didn't dare answer.

Mr. Crookshank still hovered over Grace, who had drawn her shaking hands into her lap. "For how can we expect to appreciate the heights of taste and culture, to mine the depths of Cowper, Shakespeare, Dickens, and..." His voice trailed off. Amidst the creak of desk chairs, Paulie shifted to see what had caught Mr. Crookshank's attention.

The substitute's eyes fixed on Grace's golden hair, shining like a buttercup under the school's lighting. *For heaven's sake, what in the world?* Paulie waited, barely breathing, to see what would come next.

"Is that a..." Again, Mr. Crookshank's voice faded away as he squinted at Grace's bowed head. "It is!" he announced at last, as if he had discovered a new continent peopled with cannibals. "It is! It's a *louse!*"

The classroom erupted into laughter again, and Paulie watched, horrified, as Grace turned redder than a robin's breast. If she shrank any deeper into her desk chair, she'd become part of it. Paulie glared at the substitute.

Mr. Crookshank, however, had no interest in Paulie's anger. He gripped Grace's elbow, forcing her to her feet and moving toward the classroom door. Her face was a frozen mask of horror. "Young lady, you march straight down to the office, and you tell them that they are to check you thoroughly for lice."

With that, he pushed Grace briskly out the door.

~ ~ ~

I can't believe that just happened. Grace shook in the empty corridor. She could hear the laughter quieting down within the classroom from which she'd just been ejected. *They were all laughing at me.* Her cheeks burned so badly that she touched them with her icy hands to see if they were really on fire.

The slap with the ruler hadn't bothered her. It wasn't fair; after all, Ruth Ann had also been passing notes, and she'd gotten away with it. But Grace would've just taken that patiently and gotten on with her day.

But *lice!* She wandered aimlessly down the hall a few steps before coming to a numb halt. She laid her head against the cool tiled walls. *Why'd he have to announce it like that?* Her fingers found her scalp and scraped through the hair, glad to feel the physical pain.

I can't. I'm not going back. She sniffed away the tears pushing at the back of her eyes and gritted her teeth. *Mama was right. I don't belong in school anymore. Ben was wrong. I don't have any other choices. Sometimes... Sometimes, you have to settle, Ben.*

It felt like a day of death as she went over to her locker, touching the metal door for the last time. She made sure that she had all her books and pencils before closing the locker with a clink that echoed in the empty hall. *Like closing a coffin,* she thought. *Except there's nobody in it. Like me. Nobody.*

Grace paid no mind this time to the flop of her shoes as she made her way to the office. *I'll return my books. Say that Mama needs me at home right now 'cause of the baby coming.*

After wiping away those first tears, Grace couldn't say what she felt. Happy? Certainly not. Fated? Perhaps… And there was a morbid comfort in knowing you were fated to be miserable, that it wasn't just chance, after all.

She was reaching out her still-stinging hand toward the worn brass knob of the office's varnished oak door when she heard a familiar voice call out softly, "Grace! Grace, wait up."

As she turned reluctantly, Paulie dashed down the hallway toward her, dark hair bouncing as he ran. He slid to a stop right in front of her, breathing deep. Grace dropped her eyes, staring down at her saggy stockings. Her hands went to her hair, tucking it behind her ears. *He probably laughed at me, too.*

He stood there silently for just a moment, then said in that straightforward way of his, "I'm sorry that guy did that to you, Grace."

She looked up to see real sincerity shining out of his face. His mouth bore a sympathetic smile, which Grace found her own lips returning, albeit with timidity.

"Thanks," she said softly. "You better get back to class." Without waiting for his answer, Grace turned back to the office door. *I'll probably never see Paulie again.* Grace couldn't help the little sigh her heart gave.

"I can't," Paulie said, reaching around her to get the door knob.

She turned curious eyes toward him. "Can't what?" she asked.

"Can't go back to class yet," he answered, grinning this time. "Gotta go to the office myself."

She tilted her head at him, puzzled. What'd he do in such a short time to get sent to the office?

"Lice," he smiled. "I got dozens of them. Crawling all over my head."

Grace's mouth fell open.

"Fact is," said Paulie, pulling open the door, "you probably caught them from me. I told the sub that I felt them creeping. In fact, I think the whole class will have to be checked."

"But…" Grace couldn't find a response. Paulie told the substitute he'd found something in his own hair? *Dozens of them,* according to him. She felt gratitude for this strange act of mercy, for she knew Paulie didn't have bugs and she knew that she most likely did.

"Come on," he said before Grace could say anything more. "We gotta get our heads checked before we go back to class." And he gave her a wink as she passed in front of him.

CHAPTER SEVENTEEN

His coffee had long since cooled off, gathering a white film of cream across the liquid's top. But holding the paper cup gave Geoff something to do with his hands, a necessity. The anxiety he felt now surpassed the feeling he'd had on the morning of his wedding. But that nervousness had grown from joyful expectation, whereas this found its root in raw fear. Fear to which Geoff Kinner did not want to admit.

The waiting room held half a dozen other anxious relatives of those in surgery. Some, like Geoff, nursed a cup of coffee or tea; others pretended to read the newspaper, drowning out their terror with trivialities.

He traced his finger along the top of the cup once more, then got to his feet and walked over to the receptionist's desk. The seated older woman barely glanced up.

"Mr. Kinner," she said, "I've told you three times now. When your wife's procedure is over, we will let you know."

Geoff nodded numbly. He'd just found his way back to his seat when the door swung open. He sprang to his feet, but the man in scrubs wasn't Doctor Giorgi after all. This surgeon pulled down his mask and sat next to a young woman who clutched her gloves too tightly in her lap.

Geoff watched them openly, the stress of the waiting room liberating his normally polite nature. Though he couldn't hear what the doctor said to her, he saw tears fill the young woman's eyes. She fumbled about for a handkerchief in her black purse, finding it at last.

She wiped her wet eyes and stood with the doctor. Geoff observed them as they went through the swinging door.

Something went wrong with that surgery. Was it for her husband? Her mother?

His thoughts returned to Emmeline, even now undergoing the procedure. *Her eyes must be closed as in death. O Lord, do not let her die.*

Yet the prayer felt somewhat hollow, and he wondered if Anyone listened at all. Emmeline had said to him that God would not give them a stone for bread. *But didn't He? We prayed for a child, and the Lord gave us a child, but He planted it without much thought.*

Either God wasn't listening very well or He didn't care very much. *In either case, prayer will do no good.* Geoff sank his head into his hands. But he prayed anyway because he had promised Emmeline he would. And because he was afraid of what God might do next if he didn't.

~ ~ ~

The sun had long since sunken low in the autumn sky, heavy as an overripe orange on its branch, when Doctor Samuel Giorgi pushed open the door and entered the waiting room. Geoff had never seen his friend right after a surgery, and he felt some surprise at how tired he appeared. Sam's eyes sank deeply into their red-rimmed sockets, and his olive-toned cheeks looked bleached; his creased forehead had deepened its lines.

He spotted Geoff right away, at the same moment that Geoff picked up his head from its cradle in his hands. Geoff jumped to his feet with the arthritic quickness of one who has sat for too long a time. He met his friend halfway across the room. "How is she, Sam?"

Sam didn't smile, but Geoff knew that wasn't unusual for him. The doctor took his job with acute seriousness, which trait Geoff figured had made Sam the best regional surgeon in his field. "She's in the recovery room," he replied, his square chin bumping against the surgical mask he'd already pulled down.

"Why did the procedure take so long?" Geoff couldn't help but ask.

Sam paused, hands burrowing deep into his surgical coat pockets. "We couldn't stop the bleeding with curettage alone. I had to perform a hysterectomy to prevent the hemorrhaging from becoming fatal."

A hysterectomy… Emmeline would be devastated when she awoke. *This is the end of the road for us to have children. There's no chance anymore.* He kept his eyes on the floor, memorizing the pattern of miniature pink-and-gray tiles at his feet as tears blurred his vision.

Geoff felt the doctor's hand fall on his shoulder and squeeze it with firm gentleness. The gesture of compassion released the floodgates in Geoff; his eyes welled with tears before he could make any attempt to control himself. Blinded, he stood, shoulders shaking, hands covering his face as he wept. And he knew then something of the Heavenly Father's grief when He, too, lost His only Son.

"May I see her?" Geoff asked at last. "I… should be the one to tell her."

~ ~ ~

"Walk you home, Grace?"

The gladness outweighed the dread for the first time as Grace heard Paulie's voice behind her. She picked up the rest of her books from the locker shelf and turned toward him. "Sure, that'd be alright, I guess," she answered, a little smile creeping up on her face.

"I figure we've got time to amble since Mr. K. cancelled the choir." Paulie grinned at her. "Guess that wasn't all bad, was it? I get to walk you home now."

Grace couldn't prevent her heart from picking up speed. But she would be careful. Paulie most likely didn't know from what kind of family she came; he'd only moved to town a couple of years ago. She took in his brand-spanking-new sweater and neatly-ironed trousers, his shined-up shoes. *Paulie comes from a whole different planet.*

He fell in step with her as she shut her locker, and then he grabbed her books, bestowing plenty of his wide grins. *He smiles at everyone,* Grace told herself.

Not like he does at you, her inner voice replied. She promptly ignored that voice and straightened her cardigan, hoping Paulie wouldn't notice the growing holes in both of the elbows.

"So," Paulie began as they stepped into the fresh autumn air, "are you going to let me really walk you home this time, or are you going take your books back halfway there and hightail it?"

Grace felt the blood leave her face. It was true; each of the half-dozen times Paulie had insisted on walking her home, she'd stopped a good half-mile before the turn-off path. She'd always made the excuse that she had to hurry; she had chores, and Mama wouldn't want to be kept waiting.

"Where do you live, anyway?" Paulie asked now, and Grace sure was glad that he couldn't hear the pounding of her heart.

"Uh... just through Main Street, over the hill." She hoped – no, she prayed – he wouldn't press for a more exact location. *I shouldn't have let him walk me home.* But she couldn't very well say no to a boy who'd let the school nurse treat him for lice just for her sake.

Paulie nodded. "You live on Main Street, then?" They stepped up onto the sidewalk that began right after the school's tiny parking lot.

"Uh, yeah, sort-of," she half-lied, swallowing down her guilt like castor oil. Let Paulie think she lived in one of those grand, newly-built homes near the center of town. Better for him to believe that fib than for him to know the truth: that the Picolettis resided in a ramshackle brick farmhouse that her father could care less to repair because his mind was on his mistress.

"The church Dad and I go to is on Main Street. First Baptist," Paulie commented as one of their teachers pedaled by them, astride her shiny black bicycle. Her textbooks sat primly in the basket attached to the handlebars.

"That looks like fun." Grace remarked, watching the teacher fly down the sidewalk, the feather on her small hat bobbing to-and-fro.

Paulie stopped short. "Haven't you ever ridden a bicycle?" he asked, squinting in the bright mid-afternoon sunlight.

"Yeah, of course," Grace responded, not liking the surprise she detected in his voice. "Well, once, when my cousins from Massachusetts came." That had been when she was five years old and she'd only gotten to sit on the handlebars while Ben pedaled, but Grace figured it still counted.

"Don't have one yourself?" Paulie asked, shifting the books from one arm to the other.

"No," Grace answered, pulling her cardigan more tightly closed and wishing the bottom button hadn't fallen off. What'd he think, everybody was rich? Was he trying to make fun of her or something?

But he wasn't. "Wanna come over and ride mine sometime?" he offered, and Grace let her defenses lower just a little.

"What'll you ride if I'm riding your bike?" she asked cautiously as they turned onto Main Street and Grace caught sight of her brother

Cliff popping into the Old Man Turner's candy store with a gang of his buddies. *Probably leaching off them,* she figured. *That one's got no pride.* But she couldn't really blame Cliff; the last time she'd had a sweet was when Ben had brought the chocolate babies weeks back.

Paulie shrugged. "Dad's got a bike. I can always borrow his. Wanna come over tomorrow after school?"

"Why?" The question popped out of Grace's mouth before she thought about it. Followed, of course, by a blush to beat the band. Good thing that Paulie had several inches on her; it made it that much harder for him to glimpse her scarlet cheeks.

"Whaddaya mean, why?" Paulie laughed and shook his head like she made no sense at all.

A very nice laugh, Grace thought even as she scrambled for an explanation.

But she needn't have worried. Paulie kept talking; that was surely the Italian in him. "Cause I think you're swell, Grace Picoletti. And I want to spend some time with you, but you're always rushing off to get something or other done after school. So if luring you with a bicycle is the only way to get you to stop a minute, I'll happily offer you a bicycle ride!"

He means that. He really means it. The smile spread slowly over Grace's lips even as Paulie's words sank into her soul. They'd come to a stop on the sidewalk without meaning to, and an old man carrying a crate full of apples nearly crashed into them. "Watch it, kids!" the man barked, giving them a glare.

"Sorry, sir." Paulie pulled Grace to the side of the walk, and the old man hobbled on his way. Paulie waited until they could no longer hear his grumbling before turning back to Grace. "So how about it? Tomorrow after school?" He raised his eyebrows expectantly.

But no. Grace wouldn't let him persuade her. Beneath that dimply grin, deep inside those warm eyes, Paulie was a man – well, he would be one soon. *Like Papa.* Mama had always said Papa had been the perfect gentleman when she met him. Had promised her the world. Mama had accepted Papa's offers, first of a soda downtown, later of dates in the moonlight, and finally his proposal of marriage.

I ain't gonna become like Mama. Grace forced the smile off her face and shook her head. "I can't." The words hurt her, but she would buck up and bear it. *Look at the stars, canary...*

"Why not? Just for a little while?" Paulie appealed, frowning slightly.

See, he's just like other men. Now he'll get mad at me 'cause he didn't get his way. But Grace would stand her ground, unlike Mama. "No," she stated. *I don't owe him an explanation.* She saw her books tucked under Paulie's arm. "Here, gimme my books. I gotta get home." She raised her chin, waiting for his anger to shoot out at her.

Yet it didn't. Paulie nodded and slowly handed her the books. "You sure? That's a lot of books; they're heavy. I'd like to carry them for you." Instead of irritation, friendly concern spread over his countenance.

"I've carried them before," Grace replied, marveling at how firm she could be when she tried. She ignored the pain in her heart. Taking the stack from him, she cradled the books in her arms.

"Oke-dokey," Paulie said, serious-faced. *But not mad.* "I'll see you in school tomorrow."

Grace couldn't help but feel a bit of pity for him. But she wouldn't let it show. "See you," she answered, short and sour as a baby dill pickle. Turning on the dusty sidewalk, she dashed toward home.

She didn't let herself look back until her feet had carried her a good block away.

Paulie was gone.

CHAPTER EIGHTEEN

Mr. Kinner returned to school three weeks later. Paulie thought he looked a bit drawn, and while never a giddy teacher, Mr. K. now wore a faint expression of preoccupied sorrow as he taught his lessons.

On his first day back, he stood before the class and apologized for cancelling the choir. "I know that several of you hoped to continue in it all this year," he said. "Unfortunately, it will not be possible for me to direct it. Perhaps next year. We'll see."

In his careful, private way, Dad had let Paulie know that he'd performed some kind of serious surgery on Mr. K.'s wife. Paulie felt bad for Mr. K. and his wife, that was for sure, but he also wished that the special choir could have continued. Stealing a glance at Grace's bowed head near him, Paulie knew the true root of his desire: He'd been looking forward to getting much better acquainted with Grace Picoletti. So pathetic she looked, yet... something about her thoroughly intrigued Paulie. She had strength of mind and spirit that the other girls lacked.

She'd not allowed him to walk her home again, rushing out of the school building like a frightened mouse running from a cat. *I scared her off with the invitation to ride bicycles, I guess.* Paulie passed the mimeographed worksheets back to Toby. *You shouldn't have been so forward,* he scolded himself. *You know that she's shy.*

Paulie sighed and turned his attention to the first instruction on the worksheet: *List three adjectives describing a person whom you admire.* Barely thinking, Paulie's pencil scratched out, "Delicate, mysterious,

118

enchanting." His eyes sought out Grace again; yes, he'd described her perfectly.

He turned to the second instruction: *Use those three adjectives in a sentence.* Smiling now, Paulie wrote, "Bejeweled with enchanting blue eyes, her delicate white face held a mysterious charm for him."

She deserved better, but it would have to do, for Paulie was the son of a doctor, not a poet.

~ ~ ~

A cool late October breeze caused the remaining leaves on the steady oaks to rustle and woke Emmeline from her doze on the front porch. She winced as her consciousness rose, reminding her of her still-healing incision. It stretched several inches long across her abdomen and looked rather grisly, but its appearance – however horrible – could not compare with the excruciating pain Emmeline had experienced after the surgery. Just in the last two days or so, the agony abated enough to allow her to sleep without the aid of drugs.

Her left arm tingled a little. She must have slept on it the wrong way. Carefully, flinching a little, Emmeline adjusted her body position on the long wicker lounge chaise and pulled up the light quilt until it tucked under her arms. The day nurse could not have known it when Emmeline had asked her to find a quilt before she left an hour or so ago; but Emmeline's own grandmother had stitched this delicate covering almost forty years ago when she was a young woman in her thirties. Emmeline knew that her grandmother had been a devout woman and that she often used her quilting time as extra prayer time. Warmth swelled in Emmeline's heart as she pondered the idea that she was covered – literally and figuratively – in the prayers of a faithful grandmother.

She lost all three of her sons. Emmeline traced the delicate hand-stitching with one finger, brooding. Two had died in the Great War and a third had committed suicide unexpectedly some years ago. *Yet Grandma never walked away from her faith.* Emmeline squinted down at the pin-straight patchwork pattern. Actually, her grandmother was fond of saying, "God only gives good gifts, though the wrapping on them seems ugly at times."

He only gives good gifts...

Emmeline's hands floated over her abdomen, covered by both her nightgown and the lovely quilt. *Empty.* There was no gift there. And never would be. The place where she had expected the blessing – the only logical place from which it could come – that place was barren and scarred. It seemed that God had cruelly snatched away the half-formed answer to her and Geoff's prayers.

"Barren," she said aloud. Even the word sounded terrible.

Hopeless.

A deep breath.

And then...

Thy best, thy heavenly Friend, through thorny ways, leads to a joyful end...

The tears rose up, welling at her lower lids. Emmeline brushed them away with a patient hand. The tears would come, and she would not be frightened of them. She would not be ashamed to admit her sorrowful heart's cry. But now Emmeline knew a hunger for hearing God's voice, desiring it to drown out her own pitying whimpers. Her heavy hands picked up her small personal Bible, tucked away between the side of the chaise and her wounded body.

Before the surgery, Emmeline had been reading in the minor prophets; since then, she'd not stuck with a particular reading plan, as the initial physical pain seemed to make it difficult for her to even think. But now that the pain had diminished somewhat, the steadying routine of having a reading plan again appealed to her. Emmeline smoothed her hands over the worn Bible – Geoff had purchased it as his wedding gift for her – and asked the Holy Spirit to open His Word to her heart. "And open my heart to Your word, Lord," Emmeline finished, her fingers finding the place in Haggai which she had last bookmarked:

And now, I pray you, consider from this day and upward, from before a stone was laid upon a stone in the temple of the Lord: Since those days were, when one came to an heap of twenty measures, there were but ten: when one came to the pressfat for to draw out fifty vessels out of the press, there were but twenty.

The tears nearly blinded her, but she dashed them with her hand and kept reading.

I smote you with blasting and with mildew and with hail in all the labours of your hands; yet ye turned not to me, saith the Lord. Consider now from this day and upward, from the four and twentieth day of the ninth month, even from the day that the foundation of the Lord's temple was laid, consider it. Is the seed yet in the barn? yea, as yet the vine, and the fig tree, and the pomegranate, and the olive tree, hath not brought forth: from this day will I bless you.

Hope, tender and as yet trembling, gleamed ever so faintly within her. Hers was truly a great God. He was a God of mercy, a good God who would bless her and Geoff, though the notion itself seemed utterly false. True, the Lord addressed Israel in those verses, yet wasn't Emmeline part of the remnant? And didn't the Lord still speak to His people?

"Though He slay me, yet will I trust in Him," she recalled aloud. *Not because I want a bloodthirsty God, but because I believe He is as good as He says... that He will bring life where I see only death.*

Emmeline picked up her journal, eager to remember the things God had spoken to her that day. Before she could begin writing, however, her gaze caught on a slight figure hurrying along the street. Staring for a moment, Emmeline recognized her as the young woman – a girl, really - who often hesitated in front of the Kinners' house every weekday. Strange, though Emmeline had seen the girl often enough as she watered her geraniums or swept the porch, she'd never thought to talk with her or even say hello. A rueful smile grew on Emmeline's face. Funny how being laid-up caused you to consider small things like that!

Perhaps the girl doesn't want you to say hello. Emmeline brushed the thought aside. *If she doesn't, she can keep walking and ignore me,* she answered herself, watching the skinny girl take short, quick steps. Sure enough, the girl slowed down and cast a long look at the Kinners' home. Her eyes caught sight of Emmeline reclining there. Emmeline could tell that the girl was about to quicken her pace and hurry away.

"Hello, there!" Emmeline called, anxious to greet her before she escaped.

Obviously startled, the girl stopped in her tracks. She glanced over her shoulder, as if wondering whether Emmeline addressed her or someone else. Seeing no one, she turned her surprised eyes back to porch.

Now that the girl stood still, Emmeline could get a better picture of her. The girl appeared to have skipped lunch for a month: her ratty cardigan hung like a curtain around her scrawny frame, and her baggy skirt slouched off her hips. Emmeline couldn't be certain from this distance, but she thought she saw the glint of a safety pin holding the skirt up. "Hello, there," she said again, sitting up as much as she could manage. Oh, that she wasn't crippled by these stitches and this pain!

The girl seemed like she might not answer at first. Then, unsmiling, she replied, "Hello."

"Won't you come up to the porch for a moment?" Emmeline asked. Something about the young woman drew her; she felt urged to not let this opportunity pass by.

The girl looked in the direction she'd been headed and appeared hesitant. Emmeline's heart sank faster than a stone in the mill pond. She wouldn't come. But then the girl answered slowly, "Alright."

~ ~ ~

Why am I doing this? Grace asked herself as her feet seemed to move of their own accord up the path to the beautiful white home. But another question overtook that one quickly: *Is this woman the one who played the piano?*

I need to hurry. Grace knew that Mama would want her assistance with supper. But the woman on the porch appeared so inviting, so different from that to which Grace was accustomed. *I'll only stay a minute,* she promised herself. *Just long enough to find out why she threw out those red flowers.* Her feet took the porch steps quickly, her heart thudding along.

At the top, Grace couldn't bring herself to raise her eyes from her rubber-banded shoes. Intense embarrassment crept up her neck and froze her arms tightly against her sides. *Perhaps it was a mistake to come...*

"I'm Emmeline Kinner, dear."

The woman's words jolted Grace's head up. Was *this* Mr. Kinner's wife? The one who couldn't have children? Grace stood gaping for a moment, then realized that the woman waited for her answer without a hint of impatience.

"I'm Grace Picoletti," Grace managed. The woman appeared so likable that she felt bold enough to ask, "Does your husband teach at the high school, ma'am?"

Mrs. Kinner's smile spread. "Yes, he does, in fact. Do you have

Mr. Kinner as a teacher?"

Grace nodded. Mr. Kinner certainly had a swell wife, as Ben would say. *I wish I could ask her about the flowers.*

"I see you come by nearly every day, Grace," Mrs. Kinner went on, "and I wondered about you." Suddenly, gently, she grasped Grace's hand. "I'm so glad that we could meet one another today."

The woman's smile infected Grace, and she found herself returning it, though she felt so uncomfortable with her hand in Mrs. Kinner's. "I'm glad to meet you, too, ma'am," she replied. And she realized that she meant it.

"Now, Grace," Mrs. Kinner said, releasing her hand, "every time you pass our home, I see that you slow down a bit. Are you looking at anything in particular?"

Had it been so obvious? Hopefully, Mrs. Kinner wouldn't mind that Grace had been staring. "Your flowers, ma'am. The red ones," she added when Mrs. Kinner looked puzzled.

Mrs. Kinner's face lit up, and her eyes sparkled. "Oh, the geraniums! My geraniums. You like geraniums?" she asked. "I like them, too! They're beautiful, aren't they?"

Grace nodded and stayed silent for a moment. But the question wouldn't stay put. "Then why did you get rid of them? They were so pretty."

Mrs. Kinner laughed. "Get rid of them? Get rid of my geraniums? Never!"

Now it was Grace's turn to be puzzled. "But... they're gone. They've been gone for a while now."

"No, no. They're not gone, Grace. I just take them inside for the colder months, you see," Mrs. Kinner explained. "You'll see them again on the porch, hanging in those baskets, when spring comes."

A smile burst out; Grace couldn't help it. The disappearance of the flowers had felt like a little death to her. Knowing that they would be resurrected, well... Something inside her rejoiced at the thought.

"I would bring you inside the house to show you them – I keep them upstairs in my piano room – but I recently had an operation and find myself rather immobile for the time," Mrs. Kinner continued.

Grace realized that Mrs. Kinner had changed her position on the chaise very little during the time in which they'd been talking. *She must be in some pain.* "I have to be getting home anyway, but thank you, ma'am," Grace said reluctantly. "I'm so glad about the flowers." It was silly, she knew, but Mrs. Kinner could little know how happy she had made Grace today!

"You must come by again, dear, when I'm up on my feet," Mrs. Kinner encouraged. And she looked as if she truly wished it!

"Alright," Grace heard herself saying.

"Good!" Mrs. Kinner smiled, her hands smoothing the quilt.

Standing there on that porch, without warning, Grace believed that she had found a real friend, though it seemed brazen to even think that of this kind, lovely woman – that she would want to be Grace's friend! "Goodbye," she said, backing away a few steps.

"Good-bye, dear. Come again soon!" The voice echoed in Grace's head as she ran the entire remaining half-mile home. She didn't even realize until she'd arrived that the rubber bands had broken off both her shoes.

CHAPTER NINETEEN

A week after Grace refused to let him walk her home anymore, Paulie decided it was high time to discuss the situation with his father. *He always gives good advice,* he assured his anxious mind as he joined Dad at the dinner table.

After the usual surface bits and pieces of chatter, Paulie brought up Grace, a little nervously. Taking a bite of broccoli, Dad listened as Paulie carefully described his interactions with her.

"I know I've had crushes in the past, Dad," he finished, "but I've never... *liked* someone so much as I like Grace. I'm just not sure what to do about it because it seems like she's suspicious of all of my approaches toward her. She even took her books back the other day. I was walking her home – though she never lets me bring her all the way to her house – and she suddenly got all funny and grabbed them."

Paulie shook his head, so confused. "I'm just not sure what to do. Is it wrong for me to like Grace so much? When she obviously wants nothing to do with me?" He raised his eyes to look at Dad. He hoped there would be no censure in Dad's gaze.

And there wasn't. Dad ran his index finger over the rim of his water glass, apparently searching for the right words. "If it's meant to be, it'll be, son, without you forcing it," Dad stated finally, taking a sip of his water. "But I'd like your promise in this matter on two accounts."

Something in Dad's tone demanded Paulie's full attention... which Dad had anyway. He looked his father straight in the eyes.

"What's that?" Paulie asked.

"First, that you don't get serious about any girl who doesn't love Jesus Christ. He must be the foundation of the deep, lifelong relationship of marriage." Dad hesitated, waiting for Paulie's agreement.

Paulie reddened. "I wasn't thinking of marriage, Dad. I'm only just seventeen." He looked down into his mug of hot cocoa, swirling with freshly-whipped cream.

Dad nodded. "I know that. But for us as Christian men, that's where serious relationships with women should be headed. And, like you say, you and Grace are both a bit young for that." Dad smiled. "At least in our culture. And then there's a second thing."

"What's that, Dad?"

"That you stay open with me about how things are going with Grace so that I can keep praying for you about it."

Paulie sighed. "Well, updating you sure won't be a problem. There's not going to be much to update you on. Grace hasn't spoken to me since that incident with her books. Other than saying, 'hi,' you know," he said, adding to himself, *When I say it first, that is!*

He glanced up to see Dad giving him a sympathetic look. "Well, pray about it, Son. Like I said, if it's meant to be, you can trust your Heavenly Father to bring it to pass. Right?"

"Right, Dad," Paulie agreed aloud and hoped that he really believed it.

"So I have your word on those two things?" Dad interrupted Paulie's thoughts.

Paulie nodded. Dad always had Paulie's best interest at heart; of this Paulie had no doubt. "Yes, Dad," he affirmed.

"Now, why don't you ask Grace to come around some time afterschool? You could play checkers or ride bikes while the weather's still good," Dad suggested. "Mrs. McCusker will be here, you know."

Paulie blew out a breath. "I already tried that. When I asked her to come out here to ride bikes, she grabbed her books back and wouldn't let me bring her the rest of the way home."

"Ask her to do something else," Dad advised.

Surprised, Paulie raised his eyebrows. "I thought you said that I shouldn't force it, Dad?"

Dad grinned. "Force it? No. But every real man should exhibit some perseverance, son. Nothing wrong with putting feet to your faith." Dad winked. "Right?"

Paulie felt a slow smile growing on his lips. "Right."

~ ~ ~

A few days later, Paulie felt that unusual pounding in his chest as the end-of-school bell rang. His eyes found their way over to Grace Picoletti's seat. She bent over, pulling books from the metal shelf underneath her chair. *Come on, Giorgi,* he sternly rebuked himself. *Get your act together. She's just a girl, after all.*

Just the loveliest, most interesting girl he'd ever laid eyes on, ever talked to. Looking at Grace, Paulie felt relieved that he had spoken to Dad about her, even though the Lord knew he'd felt a bit awkward about it.

She's the bee's knees, alright!

He took a deliberate breath to steady himself. Though his body might not cooperate, Paulie felt peaceful in his heart, knowing that God would do His good will in this... this *liking* he had for Grace. *Is it from You?* He'd asked the question often this week in his morning prayer-time. And God didn't seem to be giving him a direct answer, but Paulie at least knew that he would trust in the Lord in this little thing ... and that he would, by God's grace, keep the promises he's made to Dad.

His eyes fastened on that golden head, Paulie rose to his feet, book gripped tightly in his hands.

~ ~ ~

"So I told Henry that there was no *way* I'd go with him to the movie-house, talkie or no talkie," Ruth Ann buzzed, picking up the conversation with Grace right where she'd left off before class. Ruth Ann's big eyes glowed with insinuation as she leaned close to Grace.

Ruth Ann talks so loud half the class could listen in if they wanted to. Grace plucked up her pencils and returned them to their case.

"You know what I mean, Grace?" Ruth Ann asked. "Why would *I* go to the movie-house with *Henry*?"

The way she said it, you'd think Henry had never washed a day in his life. Grace shrugged, hesitant to voice an opinion. Henry had always seemed like a nice boy to her. Of course, she didn't know him too well, but she didn't know any boy really well. Though she wished she could have known one boy – Paulie - a little bit better...

"Hey, what's so bad about Henry?"

Grace nearly jumped. The familiar voice that Grace had missed hearing every day as she walked home now came up right beside her. She hardly dared to look at him, sure that he'd see the delight he'd caused just by appearing there by her side. *Grace, have some self-control,* she admonished, schooling her features into nonchalance before turning her eyes toward the speaker.

Wearing an unguarded smile, Paulie stood waiting for a response from Ruth Ann, whose dark eyes flashed at him for the interference.

"Pardon me," Ruth Ann said with a lofty tone, "but I don't remember you being part of this discussion, Paulie Giorgi."

Paulie grinned. "Nope, I guess not. But I couldn't help but overhear what you said."

"And what's it matter to you?" Ruth Ann asked, eyes narrowed. Grace held her breath; Ruth Ann did *not* like being crossed.

Paulie raised his chin, and when he spoke, his voice held not only firmness but kindness, too. "Henry's a good chum of mine, and I don't like hearing him talked about behind his back. If you're going to say something bad about him, at least do it outright, Ruth Ann. With some proof. So that's why I asked you: What's so bad about Henry?"

Ruth Ann's pretty pink lips tightened. "Well, maybe you aren't aware of this, but *I* certainly am." She leaned closer to Paulie and dropped her voice a fraction. "Last week, Lisa-Marie saw Henry's brother Michael *smooching* Marsha Thomasina in the back of the movie-house!" She folded her arms across her chest. "Now do you think I'm that kind of a girl? The kind who *smooches* at the picture show?"

Grace glanced at Paulie. *Surely, now he'll see that he was wrong to butt in.* Though she had enjoyed every moment of his defense of Henry thus far.

Paulie tilted his head to the side. "Thought you said Henry asked you to go, not his brother?"

Ruth Ann sniffed, fingers playing with her pearly sweater clip. "That's right."

"Well, why are you judging Henry by hearsay of what his brother did?" Paulie asked. "I'm not saying you should go to the picture show with him, Ruth Ann. I'm just saying that you shouldn't judge Henry by what his brother's like. That's all."

I wonder if he really means that? Would he mean it if he knew... knew what my family was like? Would he judge me by them? Hugging her small stack of textbooks, Grace waited for Ruth Ann's answer.

"And I'll bet you're going to tell me that not judging Henry is *biblical*, aren't you?" Ruth Ann spat the word out. Grace thought that her friend's glare could have roasted a chicken.

Paulie grinned. "Sure it is, Ruth Ann. Where would Abel or Seth be if God had judged them by Cain's actions?"

"Ugh!" Ruth Ann groaned. "Here comes a Sunday School lesson." She gave a final "humph" and stalked out of the classroom, letting the door slam behind her.

With only a little shyness, Grace met Paulie's eyes. He had won a new respect from her. Boys didn't usually stand up to Ruth Ann. First off, they often wanted to get on her good side because she was awfully pretty; and secondly, she had a terrible temper and could hold a grudge longer than anyone else Grace knew. But Paulie had believed what he'd said, that much shone clearly, and he wasn't afraid to take a little heat for it. Yet he had said what needed saying kindly, without a hint of malice. Even Ben would have lashed Ruth Ann with his tongue. *What makes Paulie different?*

"Got chores to do today?" he asked as the classroom emptied. He moved to pick up Grace's books. "May I?"

Despite the fear that curled her toes, Grace nodded, albeit hesitantly. What harm really could come from her letting him carry her books? She wouldn't let him walk her any farther than Mrs. Kinner's house. Then, she would take her books back from him and scurry home, quick as a lightening bug, through the wooded shortcut. After all, she so much *wanted* to talk with Paulie. *You want his attention,* she rebuked herself. And she realized that she couldn't deny it. Grace was glad that she preceded Paulie out of the classroom so that he couldn't observe the prominent grin displayed on her face.

It seemed like seconds had passed when Grace saw that they were already approaching Mrs. Kinner's house. *I'll wait a little longer, and then I'll visit her again.* Grace bit her lip at the sudden thought: *Maybe Mrs. Kinner was just trying to be kind; maybe she doesn't really want you to come again, Grace.* If that was true, Grace surely didn't want to humiliate herself by dropping by again. *Maybe I'll wait until she calls out to me again one day...*

"Hey, I've gotta stop off here," Paulie interrupted her thoughts. They'd been walking in slightly uncomfortable but pleasant silence for a couple of minutes. Only their feet broke the quiet as they scuffled through the autumn leaves littering the sidewalk.

They were at the Kinners' house. Surprised beyond words, Grace knew that her astonishment must beam right off her face.

"It's Mr. K.'s house," Paulie explained, obviously unaware that Grace already knew that. "Dad said that Mrs. K. might want some company afterschool until Mr. K. got home."

Paulie knows the Kinners personally? Grace stared at him wordlessly, then turned her gaze to the porch to see if Mrs. Kinner reclined there on the chaise. But Grace didn't see her.

"They go to our church," Paulie said, as if he had heard her silent question. "Mrs. K. had an operation a few weeks ago – Dad did the surgery – and she's still recovering. The Kinners don't have the money to hire a full-time nurse, so, from the time the day-nurse leaves after lunch until when Mr. K. gets back from school, Mrs. K. stays by herself."

Grace nodded, not sure how she felt about this connection between Paulie and the woman whom Grace was beginning to think of as a friend, though she'd met her only once.

She was just about to reach for her books when Paulie's eyes lit up. "Hey, you want to come inside and meet her? She'd like you a lot; I'm sure of it."

Grace felt a smile creep onto her face. "I already met Mrs. Kinner the other day."

"You did?" Paulie appeared astonished, but in a good way.

"Uh-huh. She was layin' out on the porch couch, and she called out for me to come get acquainted," Grace explained, enjoying the warmth of Paulie's gaze on her.

He broke out into his wide grin. "Well, then! You've gotta come inside to say hello! Please say you will, Grace. It'll mean a lot to her," Paulie cajoled.

Thoughts of the chores – the milking, starting supper, sweeping out the kitchen – and her homework rushed through Grace's mind, but with one decided motion, she pushed them away. *What will five minutes matter?* One more look at Paulie determined her choice, though she feared that, if she once gave into the kindhearted appeals of his eyes, she would not be able to say no ever again.

~ ~ ~

Ten minutes later, Grace flew down the sidewalk toward home. Her heart felt light as whipped cream. Mrs. Kinner had still been too weak to climb the staircase and show Grace her "geranium room." But she'd said that, if Grace returned a few days later, she surely would have the strength to do it then.

CHAPTER TWENTY

"A perfect paper again." The now-familiar voice sounded very near. Almost halfway home, Grace swiveled her head to look behind her. Sure enough, Paulie was there, just two steps behind her.

"Thought you were gonna join the chess team," Grace commented. "Weren't sign-ups today?"

Paulie quickened his pace to catch up with her. "Yes, but I found out that they practice three times a week after school."

"So?" Grace asked, then wished that she hadn't been quite so blunt.

"So, you think I'm going to miss walking you home three times a week just so I can move a few pieces of ivory around on a gameboard?" Paulie questioned, raising his eyebrows.

I'm more important to him than joining the chess club! Grace reddened at his words and her thoughts. Why did she have to have such light skin? If her skin was a nice olive tone like Papa's, these infuriating blushes wouldn't show up so strikingly!

"Oh, good job on your perfect paper, by the way," she said, desperate to change the subject.

"Perfect paper?" He sounded surprised.

She was sure she hadn't misheard him. "Didn't you say that you had another perfect paper? Right when you came up behind me?"

The confusion on his face cleared, and he grinned. "Yes, I have another perfect paper, but it doesn't have my name on it." He held out a sheet of paper in his right hand.

Grace glanced over at it and saw her own name swirling in neat cursive at the top. "That's the math test we got back today. How come you have mine?"

"You dropped it a little ways back," Paulie explained, offering it to her. "So I guess the onus is on me: Good job, Grace. I think you were the only one in the class who got a perfect score. That test was hard!" He shook his head wonderingly.

Grace shrugged, embarrassed at receiving his unabashed praise. She looked off to the side of the road, watching the postman make his final deliveries for the day.

"What, does your daddy crack the academic whip?"

Startled, Grace stopped in her tracks, her lungs out of air. Was he serious? Did Paulie have *any* idea how things at her home really stood? She figured not – hoped desperately not – and squirmed inside, trying to make up a somewhat-truthful answer without giving anything dreadful away. Anything about cottages and burning trash and scraping the bottom of the barrel so hard that your fingernails hurt from the splinters under them.

But Paulie winked. "I'm only kidding you, Grace. I bet your parents are swell. It's *you* who's the perfectionist, right?"

What did you say to that? Sucking in the crisp autumn air, Grace merely gave another shrug instead of trying to figure out how to verbally respond. Why *did* she strive so hard to get perfect scores when no one at home cared if she failed or passed?

Because then I am worth something.

The thought sprang into her mind without warning, vivid and scalding. Its very unsought suddenness declared its veracity. And then, just as quickly, its light faded and Grace focused on her conversation with Paulie.

"I'm stopping to see Mrs. Kinner," Grace told Paulie as they came to the white gate.

Just then, the screen door on the front of the house opened. Grace saw Mrs. Kinner, dressed in a pale-pink housecoat, standing at the threshold. "Grace!" she called, waving. "I've been watching for you. Do you have time to come in and see my geraniums today?"

So Mrs. Kinner hadn't forgotten! Chest tight with excitement, Grace nodded. "Yes! I'm coming."

"You want to come, too, Paulie?" Mrs. Kinner asked, smiling at him.

Grace looked at Paulie, half-hoping that he'd say no. She kind of wanted to meet the special geraniums without him distracting her.

To her relief, Paulie shook his head. "Naw, but thanks, Mrs. K. I promised Dad that I'd give the lawn one last haircut this year." Grinning, he handed Grace back her books. "Thanks for letting me walk you home, Grace. See you tomorrow."

"See you," Grace echoed. Their eyes locked for just a moment before Grace swung away, feeling the red creep up her neck. Her feet carried her up the path to the Kinners' porch steps, where Mrs. Kinner greeted her by extending both of her hands and clasping Grace's.

"Grace, Grace, it is good to see you," Mrs. Kinner exclaimed. She gave Grace a smile as honest as lemonade is sweet. "Now," she said, and the hint of anticipation that entered her voice thrilled Grace, "are you ready to see my geraniums?"

~ ~ ~

Mrs. Kinner still felt very weak. Grace could tell by the way her hostess' hand gripped the doorframe as she held the screen door open for Grace to pass by her. Was it too much to ask of the woman? She'd told Grace that she kept the geraniums upstairs, and as much as Grace longed to glimpse the scarlet blooms again – and up close, for the first time – she didn't know if it was right to ask Mrs. Kinner to brave what might be a long flight of stairs.

"Are you sure that you're not too sick, ma'am?" she said before stepping into the house. She didn't want to ask the personal question but felt conscience-stricken if she refrained. She glanced up into Mrs. Kinner's face, expecting to see her own hesitancy reflected there.

But though a shadow of pain flitted across Mrs. Kinner's countenance, a smile of joy more authentic than Grace had ever seen came with it. "I've been waiting to show you my geraniums all week, Grace; ever since you stopped by my porch. The Lord God has been very good to me with this operation, and I'm healing, slowly but surely. Now come inside, dear," she urged, and Grace obeyed, her heart lifting as if she really was a canary like Ben often called her.

The first thing Grace noticed was the bowl of apples sitting in the middle of the table. Not that apples were an uncommon sight in autumnal New England, but Mrs. Kinner had arranged the fruit carefully in such a way that pleased the love of beauty that Grace hadn't known she'd possessed. The Golden Delicious apples nestled near the chubby Macs, picking up the color of each other. Then, Grace's eyes turned to the embroidered placemats, neatly lined up at each of the four chairs. The stitched flowers and vines complemented the crocheting both on the placemats and, Grace noticed, on the window curtains. The kitchen itself shone with cleanliness but in a way that made Grace feel happy and peaceful there, rather than rigid and uncomfortable.

"Come along this way," Mrs. Kinner invited her, moving toward the opening that seemed to lead into the parlor. Grace followed her, glancing this way and that, first at the long bookshelves lining the parlor, then at the glass-faced cabinet filled with a collection of teacups.

The stairway jutted out into the parlor, and Grace trailed behind Mrs. Kinner as they climbed to the second floor very slowly. Mrs. Kinner wore ballet-style house slippers, nearly soundless, but Grace's flappy saddle shoes threatened to make a slapping noise with each narrow, tall step. Hoping against hope that Mrs. Kinner wouldn't notice if they did, she curled her toes to decrease that likelihood and moved up the staircase like a wooden soldier.

At the landing, Mrs. Kinner stopped for a long moment, eyes closed, just breathing. Unsure if she should offer help (but what kind of help could she give?), Grace stood silently. A step up from the landing, the short hallway provided the mooring for several dark-wooded closed doors. If Mrs. Kinner hadn't accompanied her, Grace would have found the upstairs a little spooky.

Finally, Mrs. Kinner opened her eyes and gave Grace a quiet smile. "This way," she said and stepped across the worn carpeting to one of the closed doors.

The knob turned easily, though the hinges squeaked as Mrs. Kinner pushed it open. Grace felt her nostrils awaken as an unfamiliar spicy scent met them at the threshold.

Mrs. Kinner smiled. "That's the scent of geraniums, Grace. I don't think a person can forget it once she smells it."

They stepped into the light-filled room, and Grace let her eyes rove from the large windows facing the west to the piano perched in the room's center and, finally, to the long table near the windows. There the baskets of geraniums sat.

Where were their scarlet flowers? Suddenly, Grace felt ill. She stepped closer and saw that someone – Mrs. Kinner? – had cut the stalks to a savage stubbiness; not a bloom remained. Gone was the beauty she had so hoped to see.

She couldn't help it. Speechless, she threw a look of deep betrayal at Mrs. Kinner.

"Why, what is it, Grace?" Mrs. Kinner asked, obviously confused. "Is something the matter?"

Somehow, Grace forced herself to find her tongue. "The geraniums... They're dead..." She could say no more. Silly though she knew it must seem, the loss of the flowers – no, their ruin – struck her deeply. Her chest grew tight; she feared that she might cry. Unwilling to permit her tears to fall in front of Mrs. Kinner, Grace turned toward the door, desperate to leave and find a place to weep by herself.

But Mrs. Kinner caught her by the arm with a gentle hand. "Grace, no. You don't understand."

Grace hesitated, her thoughts so tangled with distress. She'd been unable to keep the tears at bay, so she impatiently brushed her fingers across her eyes before turning to face Mrs. Kinner. The woman's voice was so kind, so quiet. Despite her grief, her feelings of betrayal, Grace couldn't just rush out on Mr. Kinner's wife.

Mrs. Kinner's beautiful hazel eyes looked right into Grace's light ones. She seemed to be hiding nothing. "Grace, I always cut the geraniums down after I bring them inside for the winter. That's how you make geraniums grow well. They need a time of cutting back, of pruning, so that they become stronger for the next year."

Dazed by this revelation, Grace stared past Mrs. Kinner, her gaze on the plants. "The red flowers... will come back?" she dared to ask, lips trembling.

"Yes," Mrs. Kinner smiled. "Next spring, they'll be new again. They will stay in this cool room all winter, and then I'll bring them out in the springtime. They'll be hanging in my baskets by May, Grace. And you are very welcome to come and check on them any time you'd like to, all winter."

Suddenly feeling rather foolish, Grace nodded and blinked away the remaining tears. *She must think I'm a real dolt!*

But Mrs. Kinner's face showed no sign of that. With the same warmhearted expression, she asked, "Now that you've seen my geranium room, would you like a snack before you go home? I have fresh oatmeal cookies just out of the oven."

Almost before she realized it, Grace nodded again. In less than five-minutes time, she and Mrs. Kinner sat at the kitchen table, sharing cookies and milk.

CHAPTER TWENTY-ONE

The cold water felt good on his skin. Paulie gave one more splash to his face and then wiped it with the bleached hand towel. He'd already mowed the lawn; now he had an hour to go before supper. Might as well crack open his math book. His class had a huge test coming up in two weeks, and Paulie knew that he was nowhere near ready for it.

Pulling his button-up shirt back on, he sighed. Funny, as the son of a doctor, you'd think he'd be good at math. *Well, you don't stink at it, Paulie. You just don't get perfect scores.*

Like Grace Picoletti did.

As his fingers nimbly fastened the white buttons, Paulie's face broke into a grin. He had an idea.

Quite a swell idea, actually.

~ ~ ~

"Grace, you milked that cow yet?"

Mama's voice, full of its usual irritation and weariness, called out the door as Grace hurried up the back walkway. Hearing it, Grace's stomach twisted into a knot. *I stayed too long at Mrs. Kinner's house.* She broke into a run and reached the screen door in two seconds flat. Taking a deep breath, she pulled open the rusty door and entered the kitchen. She hoped that she could grab the milking bucket without Mama noticing.

But no such luck could be Grace's today. Broom in hand, Mama stood facing the back door, eyebrows furrowed like she'd heard that a storm was coming. "Hi, Mama," Grace gulped. She avoided Mama's eyes as she set her schoolbooks down on the table and picked up the milk bucket.

"So you didn't milk her yet?" Mama stated rather than asked. "Where under heaven have you been since school let out?"

"Nowhere, Mama," Grace replied, fear freezing her thoughts. Then, realizing that she'd have to confess another lie to the priest if she didn't elaborate, she forced out, "A lady asked me if I wanted to come inside and see her flowers. That's all." Tense, she waited for Mama's response.

But Mama just harrumphed. "Flowers," she muttered. "She goes to see flowers while I'm here working my tailbone off so that she can keep going to school."

"Mama, it only took a little while. I'm sorry that I'm late…" The words stumbled out as Grace felt the guilt rise. Mama *did* look so worn-out, standing there with her hair in bedraggled strands around her saggy cheeks.

"As if I don't have enough stress what with your father… Oh, never mind. Just milk the cow, Grace, and stop giving me your silly excuses," Mama muttered, her ragged broom scraping the floor again. "I can't wait until you're old enough to quit that school, anyway. Least then you can earn a little money with a job or something."

Quit…

At that moment, surrounded by the hollow, dark cheerlessness, Grace longed for the bright peace of the Kinner home – more than she had wished for anything else in her whole life.

~ ~ ~

Geoff Kinner arrived home from school to find his wife on her hands and knees. Her garden tools at her side, Emmeline's hands moved skillfully as she pulled out errant tufts of grass and shook the soil from them. She hadn't noticed his presence, and so he stood watching her for several moments, listening to the hymn she softly sang:

"Neither life nor death shall ever, from the Lord His children sever; unto them His grace He showeth, and their sorrows all He knoweth."

The tears rose to Geoff's eyes as his listened. The recent sorrow they'd experienced together still burned so fresh in his heart. Sometimes he wondered how Emmeline could move forward seemingly unhampered by the hopelessness he often felt.

The memory of their child's loss caused Geoff to think about how fragile his wife's health still was. "Should you be out here gardening, Emmeline?" he asked, concerned.

She started, falling back on her heels, but then smiled when she saw him. "Oh, Geoff," she said, "I didn't see you there. Yes, I'm feeling much better lately, and this couldn't wait any longer. It's November. I had to get these in before the first hard frost." She pointed to a small pile of bulbs at her right.

Once Emmeline made up her mind to do something, nothing outside of a direct command would have any bearing on her actions. And it was her determination that he loved so much. "Here, let me help you," Geoff offered, rolling up his shirt-sleeves.

Emmeline nodded her agreement, and he felt the ground's autumnal moisture seep through his pant-legs as he knelt down beside her. "Show me where you'd like the holes dug," he requested, and she pointed out the spots.

Geoff asked her about the happenings of her day, and Emmeline inquired about his, and they accomplished the planting quickly. Enjoying the gratification of seeing the job well-done, Geoff helped his wife to her feet. They stood there for a moment, looking at the neat circle of plantings around the base of the old weeping willow.

"I didn't know you planned to put bulbs out here," Geoff remarked. "I would have helped you get them in the ground earlier in the season."

Emmeline shook her head. "I thought of this recently." She met his eyes. "It's a remembrance garden, Geoff."

He could almost hear the ticking of his pocket-watch. Compelling his throat to swallow the hard lump that caught there, Geoff managed, "What do you mean, Emmeline?"

Her expression asked him to understand. "It's in remembrance of the baby," she said, her voice low, her eyes on the fresh plantings.

Sorrow, crisp as the leaves littering the ground at their feet, rose in Geoff's heart. The mere mention of his little dead child – of the death of their hopes - had done it. Though Geoff ground his teeth, hardened his jaw, stiffened his shoulders, the tears came anyway.

Oh, Lord, I wanted to be strong for Emmeline, his mind cried out as his chest began to shake with silent weeping. Since the day of Emmeline's surgery, he had not cried, determined to resign himself to God's will, hard though it was, resolved to display not a chink in his armor... at least, until he could repair it.

But he had failed. Through the cloak of grief, Geoff felt Emmeline's arms encircling him, quiet and soothing. *She would have made such a good mother. Why? Why? Why?* The cries no longer merely revolved in his heart and brain but ricocheted toward the heavens.

But there was no answer. If rending his garments could have forced a response, lashing his body, begging, he would have done it. Yet he knew in his heart that none of those actions would compel an answer from God's lips. Only the song of the wren, sharp and clear and high, rang out through the rustling trees.

"It is a garden of hope as well," Emmeline whispered, her hands still on his ribs. "In the spring, these bulbs – so dead as they seem – will rise to life."

He wiped the back of his hand roughly over his eyes. "Hope... Hope of what, Emmy? Certainly not that God will answer our prayers for a child. Surely even you can see that His answer is no." He paused, then numbly continued, "And so we must simply submit."

She didn't answer for a long time. Geoff was about to turn from the tree and go inside the house when Emmeline finally murmured, "We hope in Him. Don't you think, Geoff, that perhaps – just perhaps – He answers all sincere prayers with a yes, but we might not see His answer in this life? Or that His yes might appear different than the way that we expected it to look?"

Perhaps... Perhaps, she was right. Confusion – and the desire to believe - and even anger fought hard for control in Geoff's heart. He didn't speak or move for long moments.

At last, he shrugged. "I don't know, Emmeline. I just... just don't know." He kissed her hair, right where it met the skin at her temple. That she would know his despondency had nothing to do with her!

She leaned against him, returning the kiss to his jawbone. "I love you, Geoff, darling."

CHAPTER TWENTY-TWO

The following Monday, Paulie decided to bring his idea out into the open. As usual, he walked by Grace's side as they made their way from the high school toward Main Street, where Grace would undoubtedly inform him that she would make her own way from there.

What's she hiding? He'd asked himself that a million times. Her family's poverty? A lot of families had dug themselves into a hole, what with buying on credit and the Market Crash a few years back. And businesses weren't hiring people anymore; it was hard, really tough, to make ends meet. Paulie's family hadn't experienced much of that; his dad's work as a leading obstetrical and gynecological surgeon secured plenty of business, yet Paulie knew that many of their friends had gone – were going – through a difficult time. Naw, it couldn't be that. It was too common a problem to hide it.

So what is it? One day, he promised himself, he'd find out.

But right now, he had a question that needed asking. "Grace," he started as they turned a corner, heading away from the school. Several students trailed behind them and walked ahead of them, but nobody with whom either of them was friends.

Grace looked up at him, her gaze shy but full of life. "Yeah?"

He shifted the stack of schoolbooks from one arm to the other. "I have a favor to ask." Paulie watched her face carefully and saw that he'd definitely surprised her. "I'm wondering if you would mind giving me some tips in math." He held his breath, wondering whether she'd see right through his ploy.

But she just looked quizzical and a little guarded. "Tips?" she questioned, slowing her pace.

"Yeah," Paulie said, hoping to explain it right. "You know, we have that big math test coming up in a week-and-a-half. I haven't been doing great in math lately – not terrible, just not great – and I'd really like to get my average up again. You do swell at math," he added and then held his breath.

Grace had come to a complete halt. Her expression blank, she stared at him. *Great, what'd I say now? She's probably gonna grab her books and run home!* Paulie groaned inwardly. But he kept his smile on his face, trying to appear as winsome as possible.

"You mean help you cheat?" she finally said.

What? "No, not at all. I don't cheat," he stated, a bit offended. "I'm wondering if you could, I don't know, maybe help me understand the concepts better."

He was unprepared for what came next.

"I'd have to charge you," she said, glancing to the side, as if she didn't want to meet his eyes.

"What?" He almost laughed. Was she joking?

But no, she was not. That much was apparent from the way in which she responded to his exclamation by raising her chin with a defiance Paulie had not known she possessed.

"How much?" he managed at last, choking down his disbelief.

At this, she seemed unsure. "Uh…" Her eyes went to the stack of books in Paulie's hands, and he knew that she was about to take them and leave him. And he didn't want to lose her company for a second.

"Hey, how about you think on it and let me know?" he suggested.

Slowly, Grace nodded. He offered her a smile, and she gave him one – a very tiny one – in return before they resumed their trek toward Main Street.

~ ~ ~

Walking along at Paulie's side, Grace couldn't believe her good fortune. Here Mama had just been saying that she couldn't wait until Grace quit school so that she could earn some money for the house, and Paulie popped up with this question. True, he hadn't known Grace was going to *charge* him for help with his schoolwork, but then, Grace hadn't known it either until the words dashed out of her mouth. But it certainly did seem like the perfect solution. *How can Mama complain if my schoolwork pays hard cash?*

And though Grace felt a slight twinge at charging her friend – she could call Paulie no less than that – she brushed the spasm of conscience aside. Hugging her thin cardigan tight to her body, Grace shivered in the chilly late autumn air. Not everyone could live a cushy life.

CHAPTER TWENTY-THREE

December 1934

"The order of operations, Paulie. Remember the order of operations," Grace sternly reminded him, forcing herself to keep a straight face when he winked.

"Okay, Grace. Order of operations," Paulie repeated, grinning silly.

Her finger tapped the book sprawled out on the table. "Do the next ten problems, and then I'll look them over," she said. She still couldn't believe that she was doing this: tutoring Paulie Giorgi in math at Mrs. Kinner's kitchen table. The Blessed Mother must have heard her prayers after all.

"Yes, ma'am," Paulie answered, winking up at her again.

Flustered, Grace turned to her own work, an easy history assignment. "You joke it off, Paulie Giorgi," she said, keeping her voice even so that he wouldn't know that her heart skipped beats when she was so near him. "But you're the one losing the ten cents every day 'cause you don't try hard enough."

He went silent then, and Grace felt sorry that she'd been so harsh, just to hide her own discomfiture. She was about to soften it up, but Mrs. Kinner entered the room. Wearing her apron as usual, the woman smiled at the two of them; Grace returned the friendly expression shyly.

How strange that Paulie hadn't minded what Grace had assumed was a high price for her tutelage! And that, when they'd stopped together at the Kinners' house last month and mentioned Paulie's proposition, Mrs. Kinner had offered her kitchen as the perfect spot to conduct the tutoring. *Insisted was more like it,* thought Grace now as she put her pencil down to watch Mrs. Kinner move elegantly toward the cookie jar.

"Anyone hungry for a snack?" Mrs. Kinner turned suddenly, and Grace dropped her gaze, not wanting to be caught staring.

Paulie perked up. "I am!" he announced. "What kind of cookies, Mrs. K.?"

Mrs. Kinner brought the jar over to the table. "Let's see," she said, pulling the lid off. "I see sugar cookies and sugar cookies and more sugar cookies."

"I should've guessed," Paulie laughed. "It *is* Christmas-time."

"Two weeks left," Mrs. Kinner added. Apparently excited, she smiled at Grace, but Grace felt hard-pressed to return the gesture this time. Christmas at the Picoletti house would be awful this year; Grace was sure of it. They hadn't heard from Ben since he'd gone back to the track in early fall.

And Aunt Mary barely brought Evelyn to visit. *Thanksgiving was a joke,* remembered Grace miserably. She'd seen Papa swing out of the driveway early that morning, Gertrude at his side, surely on their way to Uncle Jack's house. Nancy spent the holiday with her new husband's family, and Lou... Who knew where Lou was any day of the week now? Mama hadn't even bothered to fix a turkey since it had just been the three of them: Grace, Cliff, and Mama. Grace had cracked open a few cans of tomato soup; they'd crumbled Saltines into their bowls and called it Thanksgiving dinner.

Would Christmas be any different? Grace guessed not. She blinked back the tears that sprang so unwanted into her eyes and pretended to focus on her history assignment while Mrs. Kinner and Paulie chattered about their upcoming happy holiday.

"We're going back to New York to visit Mother's family," Paulie said. "It'll be nice to see them again, but I kind of wish we could spend Christmas in our home."

"Will you leave before the twenty-third?" asked Mrs. Kinner. "That's the special Christmas Sunday service at First Baptist."

Grace peered through the lace of her eyelashes at Paulie. He bit his lip thoughtfully. "I don't know. I've gotta ask Dad." Then he turned to Grace. "Hey, Grace, you should go to that service. I bet that you would like it. We sing all sorts of Christmas hymns, and we light the next-to-last Advent candle..." He trailed off, then added, "And the pastor usually gives a good sermon, too."

"It *is* a beautiful service," Mrs. Kinner agreed.

Grace stiffened. "I'm a Catholic," she reminded them. She hoped that her cold reply would dissuade them from trying to coax her further. What would Father Frederick say?! Her family already had enough gossip making the rounds without Grace attending a Protestant Christmas service!

But Paulie paid no mind to her coolness. "Well, that's perfect," he enthused. "Go to... what do you call it? Mass?"

She nodded.

"Right. Couldn't you go to Mass on Saturday night, and then come to First Baptist on Sunday morning?"

Never! Grace licked her lips, unsure of how she should phrase her definite refusal without losing Paulie and Mrs. Kinner's favor.

"Won'tcha think about it, Grace?" Paulie persisted, biting into a large snowman-shaped sugar cookie.

"You could sit with us, dear," Mrs. Kinner offered.

Grace thought of Mama fingering her rosary each night as she sat in her rocking chair. Mama would skin her alive for even *considering* this; Grace was sure of it!

"I... I'll think about it," she finally replied and bent her head feverishly over her homework.

~ ~ ~

Sarah looked at the clock and then at the back door. Nearly eight, and Grace wasn't home yet. There were probably still chores to be done; didn't Grace know...?

She shook her head. *No.* If she was honest, Sarah would admit it: She was lonely, and knowing Grace was in the house alleviated that.

It's my own fault, Sarah chastened herself. When Grace had come to her last month, pleading to be allowed to tutor some boy in math, Sarah had agreed solely for the sake of the extra fifty cents it would bring in every week. "As long as you come home first and do your chores," Sarah had cautioned her middle daughter.

And Grace had kept her part of the bargain. Every day after

school, since November, she arrived home to complete her chores, wolf down an early supper, and leave for some woman's house where the tutoring took place. Who the woman was, or why the tutoring took place at her house, who could say; Sarah certainly didn't pay attention to such non-important details.

'Specially since Charlie had taken to spending nearly every night either at Gertrude's cottage or at his brother Jack's. Glancing out the window, Sarah saw that a light snow was beginning to fall – the first one of the year. If Charlie was planning to come home tonight – Sarah didn't count the cottage at the back of their property as his "home" – he'd have been inside by now.

"Where is that girl?" Sarah mumbled again, banging the teakettle down on the Plymouth gas stove. She waited over the burners, craving the heat the stove threw into the cold house. At last, the water boiled hot, and Sarah poured herself a generous cup of tea. Normally, she preferred coffee, but tea was cheaper since she could reuse the bag three or four times. And cheaper equaled better, especially with Christmas coming…

She'd buy nothing for Lou and Nancy, of course; they wouldn't expect it and, for all Sarah knew, they probably wouldn't even stop at home for Christmas. And Grace shouldn't hope to receive anything, either, at her age. Cliff, certainly, would have a little something; he was a boy, and boys were by nature and habit greedy things. For Evelyn…

Jealousy stabbed into Sarah's heart, making her grit her teeth as she calmly stirred a quarter-teaspoon of sugar into the tea. *The last time Mary brought her here, Evelyn acted like she barely knew me. Me, the one who gave birth to her!* Dressed in a raccoon fur coat and bright patent-leather shoes, Sarah's youngest child had half-hidden behind Mary, not attempting to leave her guardian's side during the entire visit. In an odd way, Sarah had felt relieved when the two left; it had caused too much pain to know that her physical separation from her favorite child had turned into an emotional estrangement as well. *Who knows what Mary has been telling her…*

But Evelyn would fare better where she was, Sarah reminded herself. Already, Mary spoke of sending Evelyn to a fine all-girls boarding school, perhaps next year; and after that, maybe college. *Yes, Evelyn will make something of herself,* Sarah assured her heart as she picked up the chipped, steaming teacup and took her customary seat on the kitchen's rocking chair. A radio – bought with the little money Sarah's mama had left her when she died – balanced on the small table beside the chair.

With a deep sigh, Sarah sank into the chair cushions and flicked on the dial. She settled her head against the chair's back and held the warm teacup steady on her plump belly. *Seven months already. The baby will be here in February.* At least, she hoped so. The women in her family had a habit of carrying babies well past their due-date; she'd carried Ben almost a month over his expected arrival. And who knew exactly when this baby had been conceived, anyway? Sarah had too much on her plate to keep definite track of anything so inconsequential.

Somehow, the banter of the two radio comedians sounded banal and foolish tonight. Maybe it was because Grace wasn't home yet, and so Sarah couldn't quite concentrate on the jokes the man and woman exchanged between them. Impatiently, she leaned toward the dial, clicking through the stations, trying to find something that didn't grate on her nerves. At last, she found what sounded like old-fashioned singing; something through which she could just rock numbly. Satisfied, Sarah leaned back and sipped the steaming amber liquid.

A few minutes passed. Sarah felt the tension of the day rocking away, soothed by the sweet singing. Then suddenly, her half-closed eyes shot open: This was a Protestant radio program! Perking up her ears, Sarah listened more closely to the lyrics:

What a Friend we have in Jesus, all our sins and griefs to bear!
What a privilege to carry everything to God in prayer!
Oh, what peace we often forfeit, oh, what needless pain we bear,
All because we do not carry everything to God in prayer!

Yes; it was Protestant. Sarah was sure of it! She pushed her weary body forward to click over to the comedy show again, but before she changed the station, the thought that she actually *liked* what she was hearing went through her mind.

She glanced uneasily around her and then chuckled. *As if someone was watching me! If I like listening to it, there's no reason I shouldn't,* she reasoned. But her own mother's warning about Protestants fought against her own logic: "The Protestants – all of them – would like nothing better than to eat us Catholics alive!" Her mother had meant spiritually, of course, but her words still sent a shiver of fear down Sarah's back.

Yet the words of the song drew her. The choir sang another verse:

Are we weak and heavy laden? Cumbered with a load of care?
Precious Savior, still our refuge, take it to the Lord in prayer.
Do your friends despise, forsake you? Take it to the Lord in prayer!
In His arms He'll take and shield you; you will find a solace there.

Well, in her younger years, Sarah might have been taken in by those words, but now she was older and wiser. Prayer had never unburdened her, really. Had it ever made her hopeful for a time, that things would change, maybe get a little better with Charlie?

Yeah.

But it never helped in the end. It never answered the cry that burned in Sarah's bosom, no matter how tight-lipped she kept her face: *Why, God? Why did you place me in such misery? And why, oh, why am I so alone?*

CHAPTER TWENTY-FOUR

"So... I thought you'd like to know."

Grace met Paulie's grin the next evening with a smile. He'd arrived at the Kinners' house before her, but he'd waited outside, despite the freezing temperatures.

Well, he is dressed for the weather, unlike me, thought Grace as she quickened her steps. No thick woolen coat for her; instead, she'd donned a jacket that Ben had left behind, thin as frost and not much cozier. But she was glad about one thing: She'd discovered a way to make her floppy shoes a lot warmer. When Mama had taken home their box of groceries that week, Grace thought of an idea. She'd taken her shoes, traced the outline on the triple-thick cardboard, and cut out the shoe-shapes with Mama's sewing shears. My, but it had been difficult to cut through that cardboard! Grace's fingers had ached when she was three-quarters of the way through the job, but she pressed on, certain that her reward would be great.

And the result proved Grace correct. After cutting out the shapes, she'd fitted them into her shoes and snapped the rubber bands on as usual. Her feet fairly sighed in relief at the cushioning and warmth that cardboard provided.

True, she'd have to replace the inserts as the cardboard flattened and became wet from the snow. But Grace figured that she would have a fresh supply of cardboard each week from Mama's grocery shopping. She only wondered that she'd not thought of this before now!

"What would I want to know?" Grace asked, stopping at the

Kinners' gate. She looked up at Paulie, dimly lit by the few streetlights.

Paulie's breath came out in frosty puffs. "Cold tonight, isn't it?" He shoved his hands deeper into the pockets of his wool coat. *Bet that isn't second-hand,* Grace marveled. She always marveled at Paulie's attire.

"Hey, you must be freezing!" he exclaimed, jolting Grace from her state of icy admiration. "Here," he said, starting to unbutton his coat.

Grace knew what he would do next, and she rushed through the gate, calling behind her, "What did you say I would want to know?"

She'd made it halfway up the snow-dusted porch steps by the time Paulie caught up with her. He brushed past her to get the door. *He's mad that I didn't let him give me his coat.*

But the face that showed under the porch light held no malice. "I was going to say," Paulie replied, opening the door and holding it for her, "that you would like to see this." He stepped into the toasty house behind her and withdrew a folded paper from his coat pocket. He offered it to her, and she took it, slowly banging the snow from her shoes on the doormat.

Opening it, she saw a red "A+" circled at the top of the paper. "You got a perfect score on this week's math test," she smiled, glancing up at him. "Good work."

"Thanks, but I know I wouldn't have gotten it without your help, Grace. You know, you should become a teacher," Paulie encouraged.

Embarrassed but happy at the praise, Grace shrugged and turned her attention to unbuttoning her coat.

"I've got some cocoa on the stove, kids," Grace heard Mr. Kinner announce from the room beyond the kitchen. Her heart lifted to hear that friendly, masculine voice hold a frank welcome for her.

"Okay, thanks, Mr. K.," Paulie called back, wiping his feet on the mat. "Where's Mrs. K. tonight?"

Mr. Kinner appeared in the doorway that joined the kitchen and parlor, spectacles on the end of his nose, book in hand. "Went to a women's prayer meeting at church," he explained, "but she should be home before you two leave. She said that you should help yourself to the cookie jar," he added with a smile.

"Thanks, Mr. K.," grinned Paulie. "That's awfully kind of her. We sure will, won't we, Grace?"

Blushing, Grace shook her head. Would Paulie ever stop teasing her?

"Well," said Mr. Kinner, "I'll let you two get to work. I have some lesson plans to do, but I'll be right in the parlor if you need me."

Grace shook her head once again as Paulie dashed for the cookie jar, pulled off the lid, and bit right into a thick oatmeal cookie. "Didn't you eat dinner?" she asked.

"Sure, but that was an hour ago, Grace," he replied, munching happily away on his third bite.

"Come on," she urged, putting her little stack of schoolbooks down on the freshly-scrubbed table. "We have work to do, you know." She frowned at him to prevent herself from giving him a liberal grin instead. "Just because you got one A+ doesn't mean you should slack."

"Yes, ma'am," Paulie obediently answered, placing the cookie jar in the center of the table, "but couldn't we have some cocoa first?"

CHAPTER TWENTY-FIVE

She still had some supper dishes to wash up, but Sarah remembered that the radio program to which she'd been listening – that Protestant one – came on around eight o'clock. So she turned on the radio to that station while she washed up the rest of the forks and plates.

The program seemed to mix in some preaching – a lot of it full of fire and brimstone – with the singing some nights. When the preaching came on, Sarah felt tingles up her spine when the minister talked about the fate of the wicked. Funny, he never mentioned Purgatory. Sarah figured that he must not be as well-educated as Father Frederick was. But that radio preacher sure could pack a powerful punch with his words when he wanted to!

Tonight, however, he'd quieted his tone down. Sarah let the water fill the sink, added some soap, and plunged her rag into the warm bubbly mixture, listening all the while.

"I want to talk to you tonight, dear people, about the birthday we are about to celebrate. Whose birthday, you ask? The birthday of the Christ Child, whose advent into this world heralded the peace on earth and good will toward men of which the Scripture speaks," the crackly voice spoke, filling the dim kitchen. Only the soft splash of the dishwater accompanied it.

"And what peace do we see? Certainly not peace in the world. Wars and rumors of wars we hear of almost daily, almost hourly, friends. Hourly! Then, perhaps it is peace in our homes, in our families?"

No, thought Sarah, her mind drifting to the busted-up family which she and Charlie had tried to create. She shook her head as she picked up another chipped plate and wiped it clean of grease.

"No, my friends. Almost daily, I receive letters from listeners to this little radio program, detailing the heartbreak wreaked upon your homes by wild youth, by adulterous hearts, by reckless behavior. No, this peace cannot be found in our families. Where, then, is this peace?"

Where? Sarah perked up her ears. She hoped he'd give the answer and not just segue into the musical portion, like he sometimes seemed to do.

"It is found in the manger in Bethlehem, where the little Child lies asleep. It is found in the carpenter's shop, where the Lad learns at the hand of Joseph. It is found in the temple, where the Youth answers the questions of the religious leaders of His day. It is found at the well in Samaria, where the Teacher asks a woman for a drink. It is found in Gethsemane where the Supplicant begs His Father to let the cup of suffering pass by Him and yet resigns His will to His Father's. It is found at Golgotha, where the King refuses to call on His army of angels to rescue Him. It is found in the empty tomb, where the Prince of Life shook off the bonds of death... forever!"

The preacher's words drew Sarah like no words of any religious man had ever done. She felt hungry and thirsty, but she didn't know for what. It wasn't a physical hunger, but a spiritual and emotional one. As he'd spoken on and on, her mind pictured that Jesus. Not Jesus as He hung week after week on the wall at church, but as a Man who really lived and died and... rose again!

"This is where peace is found, this peace of which the angels sang," the preacher continued. "Every man, every woman, every child can only find true peace *in Him!*"

Finished with the dishes, Sarah blotted her wet hands on her skirt and went to the stove to set the kettle on to brew her tea. *Peace in Him, peace in Him, peace in Him* swirled around in her mind. She shook her head, feeling muddled. How could she have peace in the Lord Christ? The minister seemed to be saying that peace from God was the result of an *individual* choice, a decision.

But that didn't make sense, did it? After all, Sarah knew the rules of the Church. She'd been baptized into it as an infant, celebrated her First Communion, and received the Holy Spirit during her

Confirmation. She and Charlie had married in the Church, of course, and while Sarah had a lot of catching up to do – she'd been terribly careless of late with prayer and Confession – she knew that she remained a good Catholic.

Yet this radio religious man seemed to believe that everyone – Sarah included – could have a *relationship* with God's Son…

"Receive Him, then, dear friends," the radio man continued. "Receive Him not as the innkeepers of Bethlehem, too busy making money to give Him room. Receive Him not as Herod, too greedy for power to welcome the kingly Babe. Receive Him not as the teachers of the Law, too fond of their own ideas to let Him overturn them. Receive Him not as Pontius Pilate, too concerned with his own safety to stand with the Savior. How, then, how shall we receive this King of Peace, you ask?"

How? Sarah's own heart wondered as she poured her tea.

"Repent, my friends. Turn from your sins and turn your face to Christ. 'Come unto Me, all ye that labor and are heavy-laden, and I will give you rest,' the Lord Jesus tells us. Believe that He suffered, that He died for you… for you, my friends. Believe that He lives, yes, lives in Heaven for you, pleading on your behalf before the Father."

The voice continued, but Sarah stood, not listening. What did he mean? The radio minister couldn't be preaching for Catholics, too; after all, Sarah already knew all of that and had no peace. *Peace for Catholics must come in a different way,* she finally settled as she took her seat in the rocking chair. Tonight, the radio choir sang a lovely Christmas hymn. Feet on the floor, Sarah rocked back-and-forth, back-and-forth, letting her mind rest in the crackling music coming from the radio.

~ ~ ~

Grace tiptoed up the back steps. *Oh, Mama, please don't get mad,* she begged silently as she eased the screen door open and slowly turned the wooden door's brass knob. Maybe it wouldn't squeak this time, and Grace could creep up the stairs unnoticed, especially if Mama had already gone to bed.

She'd seen the twinkle of lights in the cottage down at the property line. *Papa's probably with Gertrude,* she concluded. If he was home, Papa was almost always down at Gertrude's cottage; which made Mama more irritable than ever.

The door squeaked, of course.

"That you, Grace?" Mama's question came from the dim kitchen.

Cringing, Grace stepped inside, much as she wished she could stay out in the barn tonight and avoid a big blowout with Mama. "Yeah, Mama," she answered, pulling the door closed behind her. She saw Mama sitting in her old rocking chair, moving back-and-forth, back-and-forth as she usually did after she'd done the evening chores.

"Make sure that door's shut tight. It's cold tonight," Mama advised without opening her eyes.

"Yes, Mama," Grace replied, shuffling her shoes a little to remove some of the snow. *Mama's not upset,* she realized, in her surprise stealing more than one glance over at her mother. "Sorry I'm late," she offered hesitantly. "I had to take it slow through the woods because of the snow and ice."

But Mama still didn't rebuke her. Keeping her eyes shut, leaning against the rocking chair's back, she only shook her head slightly, evidently dismissing Grace's tardiness. "You got homework?" she asked.

"No," Grace answered, shocked that Mama wasn't boiling over. Maybe the advancing pregnancy just tired her out too much? "Today's the start of Christmas vacation."

"Oh, that's right," Mama murmured. "I forgot."

Grace stared at her for a good long moment, but she couldn't figure out the reason for Mama's forbearance. Finally, she just turned toward the stairway. It *was* late, and she was tired. It'd be nice to get a few hours of good sleep before waking up with the chickens.

As she passed Mama, Grace's ear caught the strains of a song. It was peaceful, clear, and sweet. Odd, because Mama usually turned on a loud comedic show when she wanted to relax. Turned her mind off, she said. Grace paused and listened:

Come, Thou long-expected Jesus,
Born to set Thy people free,
From our fears and sins release us,
Let us find our rest in Thee...

The sound of the choir filled Grace with longing – the wish that Mr. Kinner's choir could have continued; that her own voice, and not that soprano's, could sing a high note and receive applause; that she could use music to drown out the drab bitterness of her life…

And yet, hidden beneath all of that, behind all those open doors of desire, Grace sensed a pull, a drawing toward the words of the song itself. She had the uncanny feeling that something – Someone? – looked into her soul… or perhaps that she peered into the windows of Someone Else's heart.

A mist rose in her eyes, unbidden and incomprehensible. Shifting the schoolbooks tucked into the crook of her arms, Grace tried to shake off this strange, new emotion. It was a more intimate drawing than the affectionate attraction she felt toward Paulie. But a pull toward what? Or toward Whom?

She did not know. "Goodnight, Mama," she said softly. She turned to the staircase and made her way up the long, dark flight.

~ ~ ~

The pencil twirled, spun, and fell for the twelfth time in less than five minutes.

Come on, Grace. Concentrate!

She'd spoken the truth to Mama; she had no real homework, except for this literature essay, not due for a few weeks. But Grace had already read the required book, and since she had tossed and turned sleeplessly for well over an hour, she figured that she might as well sit up and accomplish something.

But, despite her best efforts, she found her mind pitching back and forth between two different trains of thought, neither of which had anything to do with her literature essay.

Can I really be considering this? Grace wondered as she pondered afresh Paulie's – oh, and Mrs. Kinner's – suggestion that she join them for the Christmas service at First Baptist Church.

She almost laughed out loud in her nervousness. What would Mama say if she knew? What would Father Fredrick say if he ever found out that one of his flock had strayed so far as to be caught sitting in a Protestant church? And only two days before Christmas, too!

Yet, I want to go…

Stiffening at her own boldness, Grace turned to the other thought that seemed to have instigated her sleeplessness: that song – hymn? –

that the radio had played. Mama had long since turned off the music and gone to bed; sitting at her desk, all alone in the bedroom she'd once shared with three sisters, Grace had heard the cessation of the crackling sound and Mama's slow shuffle toward her bedroom.

But the memory of the song remained with Grace. And with it, the desire, the longing toward... *what?*

Certainly not for the "long-expected Jesus," sung by the choir. Grace knew this Jesus; He dangled, cold and lifeless at the end of Mama's rosary. He hung, eternally grief-stricken, behind the altar at church. His aloof stone countenance had peered down at her from Grace's grandmother's elaborate gravemarker. Grace worshipped that Jesus, yes, just as Mama and Papa worshipped Him: with fear and gratitude. She knew that He'd carried the sins of the world, and she was part of that world. Grace understood that, somehow, God forgave her and that Jesus' death on the Cross had something to do with it – some kind of holy swap. But to long for this Jesus?

No, I don't long for Him.

She half-shuddered, thinking of the morose statue on her grandmother's grave. Actually, a thrill of relief coursed through her heart, a terrible gladness that she could recognize that *that* Jesus had no place in her desires. No connection to her hunger.

What, then? Why did I have that feeling of such yearning with the song? A feeling of intense craving that had come and fled and left her coveting more. Again, Grace shook her head to break the cobwebby thoughts. She pursed her lips and forced herself by sheer willpower to concentrate on her essay.

CHAPTER TWENTY-SIX

A s usual, that Saturday morning, Grace dropped her week's pay on the kitchen counter. The five shiny dimes jangled lightly as they settled there on the nicked surface. She knew Mama would add the money to whatever funds Papa felt disposed to provide that week.

Lou or Nancy would've made a fuss, she realized for the hundredth time. When they lived at home, the twins usually had kept any money they'd earned. They would have squawked fiercely if Mama had asked for their paycheck. But Grace knew the price of her freedom: Ten cents a day – fifty cents a week – bought her every evening at Mr. and Mrs. Kinner's kitchen table, studying with Paulie.

Every cent is worth it, thought Grace as she opened the bread box and cut herself a narrow slice of Mama's bread. Opening the cupboard quietly so that Cliff wouldn't hear, she took down the jar of homemade blackberry jam and spread a thin layer on the slightly-stale slice.

Crossing herself quickly, Grace sank her teeth into the sweet breakfast. Just then, she heard the mattress groan in Mama's bedroom. *I thought Mama was up already.* Ever since Grace could remember, Mama had been first to rise, often in the kitchen before the sun had fully risen.

This baby is really hard on her, Grace realized, pity dawning in her heart. Setting her own breakfast down on the counter, she cut another slice of bread and slathered it with a generous glob of jam. Pouring a small cup of coffee for herself and one for Mama as well, she set Mama's cup and slice at the table just as her mother trundled into the kitchen.

"Morning, Mama," Grace greeted her, making sure her voice wasn't too cheerful. Mama disliked any hint of fakeness.

Mama nodded, blinking red eyes.

"I cut you some bread," Grace offered and saw Mama's face relax when she saw the mug of black coffee waiting beside the darkly-spread slice. With a sigh, Mama drew out a chair for herself and plopped down. Ignoring the slice of bread, she picked up the coffee with trembling hands and took several tentative sips.

Grace leaned against the counter, nibbling her breakfast. *Should I ask Mama about going to First Baptist?* Her internal debate on the previous night had lasted beyond her late waking hours; she tossed through her dreams with a hint of Paulie's invitation always flavoring them.

"Cold today," Mama commented, breaking the silence.

"Yeah," Grace agreed. She glanced out the window. "But at least it's not snowing." Her eyes narrowed as she saw a bulky figure making its way up the back walkway. *Papa.* She swallowed hard through the last bite of her bread. "Mama," she said, turning from the window, "Papa's coming in."

Mama's hand went to her hair, mussed and tangled from sleep. The pity that Grace had felt earlier grew and gathered strength as she realized the pathetic situation in which Mama found herself: aging fast, pregnant, competing with a younger woman with whom Papa seemed smitten, though Mama was the one who wore a wedding band. Anger, bright and steely, filled Grace as she saw the old door swing open. Papa entered, harrumphing at the cold that bit through his heavy coat and turned his ears crimson.

Raising his eyes, Papa saw her and Mama but made no acknowledgment of them. Banging the crunchy snow off his boots, he clomped his way over to the coffee pot. The hot liquid sounded loud as it poured into Papa's large mug. He lifted it with strong hands, accustomed to manual labor, and took a deep draught of the brew.

Quietly, making no more noise than necessary, Mama rose from her chair, leaving her bread uneaten. With slow, somewhat unsteady steps, she moved toward her bedroom.

But Papa spoke, surprising Grace. "Make sure I've got a good clean shirt pressed for Mass tonight," he addressed Mama's retreating back.

Mama paused but didn't turn. "You singing?" Grace heard Mama's emotionless voice inquire.

Papa swigged his coffee again. "Father Frederick asked me to. Can't say no to a priest."

And Papa wouldn't want to, besides. Grace knew how much Papa delighted to raise his tenor voice above the church choir in a solo part. Everyone said that he had the voice of an angel. And it was true.

When Mama didn't reply again, just stood, back to the kitchen, Papa set his mug down. "You'll have my clothes ready, yeah?"

Grace winced at the hint of irritation in his voice. *Answer him, Mama. Say, "Yes," like you always do.*

But Mama shuffled off into her bedroom before replying, "Why don't you have your fancy woman iron your clothes for you?"

The words jolted Grace. Outside of a few loud arguments, Mama *never* confronted Papa. His iron fists and bull-like countenance forbade it. Barely breathing, Grace glanced over at Papa.

He was livid. His swarthy face turned from red to dark purple, and he stared unblinking after Mama.

Then, in five long strides, he lurched across the room and into the bedroom behind her. Grace's stomach turned upside-down when he slammed the door, locking Mama into the room with him.

Sinking down to the floor, head dropped to her arms, Grace listened to the storm raging in the bedroom.

"Do you hear yourself, woman?" Papa bellowed. A string of curses followed, each directed at Mama's audacity in answering him back.

"You're my *wife!* You do what I say! You listen to me, Sarah!" he bellowed. "You hear? If I want my clothes ironed, you iron them!"

"You think you can keep that woman-" Mama's words snapped suddenly, and Grace cringed as she heard a vase crash to the bedroom floor, followed by the thud of a body hitting the dresser. *He hit her.*

"I can keep whoever I please! You hear?" Papa growled. "Who gives you food? Huh? Who gives you money for clothes? Whose daughter is standing there in the kitchen? Whose car is in the driveway?" He paused. "Whose baby you got in your belly? Huh?"

Another silent moment. *I wish he were dead,* Grace thought numbly.

"Huh? Whose? Whose? *Whose?*" He ended with a near shriek. "Answer me, woman!"

At last, she heard Mama's voice, a murmur blanketed with soft sobs. "Yours, Charlie. They're all... yours."

"That's right." Papa sounded triumphant. "And you remember that, Sarah. You remember that."

The bedroom door opened, and Grace nearly swallowed her tongue in nervousness. But Papa could care less about her, it seemed. He turned one last time toward the weeping that emerged from the bedroom and ordered, "Make sure you got my clothes ready for four o'clock. I'm getting together with some of the boys before Mass."

Grace followed him with her gaze to the door. He slammed it vehemently. *To show her that he meant what he said.* Rising to her feet, Grace thought about going to the bedroom to comfort Mama, awkward as she felt about that.

But Mama simplified the matter; the bedroom door shut with a click before Grace could move one step.

CHAPTER TWENTY-SEVEN

"What do you think of asking Grace to come for Christmas dinner?" Her fingers busily tying the bows on presents, Emmeline finally broached the question that had lingered in her mind for several days.

Geoff looked up from his book. "Don't you think she'll be spending it with her family, Emmy?"

He was probably right, but still... "I know. I just thought that..." Emmeline let her voice trail off, unsure of what *exactly* she thought.

"Thought what?" Geoff prodded.

Choosing a gold ribbon for the next package, Emmeline squinted in thought, trying to figure out how to explain herself. "Well, when Paulie mentioned that he and Grace couldn't do the tutoring at her house last fall, I assumed – and perhaps it's a wrong assumption – but I assumed that there must be something that Grace wishes to hide about her home. Something she doesn't want Paulie – or us, for that matter – to know."

Geoff looked at her. "Her family's very poor," he commented. "That's certain."

Emmeline nodded. "You can tell that from Grace's clothes alone. But nobody's rich anymore." Slowly, she looped the ribbon into a bow. "I think it's something more than poverty, Geoff. I know that there's no hard evidence; it's just intuition, I suppose."

"A woman's intuition is usually right," Geoff smiled. "Why don't you invite her? She can always say no."

Glad for her husband's generous spirit, Emmeline returned his smile. "Alright," she replied. "I'll ask her." Happy anticipation filled her as she turned her full attention to wrapping the presents.

But Grace wouldn't be coming back until after Christmas recess! Emmeline groaned. "I can't believe it!" she said aloud, putting her scissors down with a clatter.

Again, Geoff looked up from his book. "What is it?"

"I can't ask her. I forgot: She won't be coming back until after school recess. And we don't know where she lives." Emmeline shook her head. "If I did, I would send her a note. I didn't even give Grace her Christmas present!"

"You can give it to her after Christmas," Geoff suggested, grimacing a little. "I forgot, too. I'm sorry."

"It's not the same, giving a gift after Christmas," Emmeline replied, her heart sinking. Receiving a *late* Christmas present was the last thing a girl like Grace needed!

Geoff shrugged. "I'm not sure what else you can do, Emmy."

Sighing, Emmeline turned back to her work.

Paulie. Surely, he knew where Grace lived! She rose from her seat, eager to get to the telephone before Paulie left for New York with his father.

~ ~ ~

A pail of milk in her right hand, Grace shut the barn door tightly behind her. Bessie's milk supply had dropped off significantly, which Grace had expected, seeing that Papa had bred the cow last summer again. Bessie would dry up soon and bear a calf sometime in early spring. Grace's heart twisted at the thought. Papa would surely sell the calf for meat, leaving Bessie disconsolate for days. But there was nothing that Grace could do about that, other than give the poor mama cow extra scratches around her thick, soft ears.

The sound of a car pulling into the driveway distracted Grace from her gloomy thoughts. *Maybe it's Evelyn.* Hope rose within her. *Mama will be glad if it is. Aunt Mary should bring Evelyn to visit more often.*

Grace hurried her steps around the curving path that led to the driveway from the barn, eager to greet her sophisticated aunt as well as to hug her little sister.

But the older beige car stalling in the driveway didn't belong to Aunt Mary. Startled, Grace's blood froze as she watched Mrs. Kinner emerge from the driver's side and then walk up to the back door.

This isn't happening! Grace tried to swallow, but her throat stuck. Her body felt numb. Remembering just in time that she carried a bucket of milk, her fingers tightened around the handle. *How does she know where I live?*

Suddenly, Grace realized that if she didn't hurry, Mrs. Kinner surely would knock on the back door. And who knew whether Mama would answer, eyes red with weeping, bruise freshly apparent on her cheekbone? Or if Papa would swing wide the door, his hairy chest popping out of his undershirt for the whole world to see? Grace was certain that Mr. Kinner *never* bared his chest.

She found her tongue at last and called out. "Mrs. Kinner!" Not waiting to see whether the woman heard her, Grace rushed down the path toward her, the milk sloshing in the bucket.

But Mrs. Kinner turned right away, a ripe smile blooming on her lovely face. She wore a thick black winter coat that made her skin glow even whiter than it usually did. Paired with the crimson lipstick shining on her lips and her vivacious dark eyes, Mrs. Kinner appeared a snow queen to Grace.

A snow queen about to discover that Grace came from the abyss.

"Grace," Mrs. Kinner greeted her, reaching out a hand to grasp Grace's. "I'm so glad you're home. I just came by to give you your Christmas present."

"My... Christmas present?" *Should I have gotten Mrs. Kinner a gift? Does she expect one?*

Mrs. Kinner smiled. "Yes, I'd forgotten that you wouldn't be back to our house until after Christmas, and I dislike giving Christmas presents *after* Christmas."

I hope she doesn't think I'm going to invite her inside the house. "Oh, yeah. That's right," Grace answered aloud. "I won't be coming over again until we go back to school."

Mrs. Kinner nodded. "I didn't know where you lived, but I thought Paulie might know. And he did!"

She sounded triumphantly happy, but Grace just wondered how in the world Paulie knew her address. *He must have followed me home one day,* she mused. The blood rose in her face.

"So," Mrs. Kinner interrupted Grace's thoughts, "let me give you your gift! It's in the car."

Grace followed Mrs. Kinner over to the car and waited while the woman bent into the interior. Despite Grace's embarrassment, she wondered what the gift could be. A book, perhaps? A pretty hairclip? It might be the only gift Grace would receive this Christmas, and so she couldn't help the way her anticipation bubbled up.

But Mrs. Kinner's gift took Grace by surprise. With a happy smile, Mrs. Kinner held out a beautifully-sculpted pot of deep brown clay. A rich crimson ribbon clasped the pot just below its rim, contrasting with the dark greenish-brown stems sprouting from the nearly black soil.

Speechless, Grace looked from the pot to Mrs. Kinner, and then back to the pot.

"It's a geranium," Mrs. Kinner explained. "Seeing how much you appreciate mine, I thought that you might like to have one of your own. It won't bloom for months, but you can certainly look forward to the flowers that will come in the warmer weather."

Oddly, the gift frightened Grace. She felt as if Mrs. Kinner had opened a door from a dark room into… Grace didn't quite know where the door led. And that frightened her.

Yet the fright was not enough to overcome her joy at the geranium plant. *Stop shaking,* Grace commanded her trembling hands as she reached out to receive the gift.

~ ~ ~

She placed it on the windowsill of her bedroom, where she could see it as soon as she woke up in the morning and last thing before sleep claimed her eyes.

Glancing at it as she dressed for six o'clock Mass, Grace remembered Mrs. Kinner's recent invitation to Christmas dinner at the Kinner house, as well as Paulie's urging that Grace attend services at First Baptist tomorrow morning.

Will Paulie be there? Grace buttoned her white blouse with nimble fingers and weighed the reasons for and against going to the Christmas Sunday service at First Baptist.

The Kinners will be there. Certainly, that weighed heavily in its favor.

Mama probably won't like me going. I know Father Frederick won't like it. The thought of the priest's somber eyes caused a shiver to run down Grace's spine.

Paulie might go, if he hasn't left for New York yet. She bit her lip to keep from smiling, even in the privacy of her empty bedroom, as she imagined her friend's sparkling brown eyes and delighted grin.

I don't have anything nice to wear. True, she could don the same worn-out clothing that she wore to Mass tonight, but... no one at First Baptist knew about her family's poverty. And the God of First Baptist seemed to be a rich Fellow, if one judged Him by His followers. She'd seen the people entering that place of worship: fancy hats with feathers, shiny high heels, silky white blouses on all the ladies. And the men? They all wore smooth dark suits with polished shoes and snowy shirts. Looking at her reflection, Grace knew that she'd stick out like a sore thumb. And just at a time when she wished to be invisible.

Sinking down on her bed, Grace knew that she couldn't go. She wouldn't expose herself and her family to the pointing fingers and tittering lips of a bunch of rebellious Protestants. Much as she wished to, she would not attend First Baptist's Christmas service.

~ ~ ~

Papa sang beautifully that night. His throat quivering with the golden notes, he closed his eyes, the picture of reverent worship and manly strength. An angel in God's throne room could not appear to better advantage. Stealing another glance to the balcony behind the congregation, where Papa and the rest of the choir stood, Grace could not recall the hateful words that Papa had poured from that same throat this very afternoon.

Sitting beside Grace, Mama, too, shut her eyes, seeming to forget as well.

CHAPTER TWENTY-EIGHT

Grace woke early the next morning. The house sat silent, draped under a newly-fallen blanket of snow. *First Baptist's Christmas service is today.* The thought popped immediately into her brain as soon as Grace's gaze landed on the pot of geraniums.

Shivering in the winter dawn's chill, she pushed back her blankets, getting her fingernail stuck on the top one's ragged edge. Her toes curled on the ice-cold floorboards, despite the double layer of socks she wore. She pulled one of the blankets around her shoulders as a makeshift robe.

The quiet of the room still unnerved her a bit; her sisters had long since taken leave, but they had shared the bedroom with Grace for so long that it was difficult to become accustomed to life without their presence. *Nancy hardly comes around anymore.* And Lou had moved into a Providence apartment with two other girls just a week ago.

Turning the knob slowly, Grace avoided making the hinges squeak. Her quiet steps took her down the stair and into the dimly-lit kitchen. She could hear Mama's soft snoring escaping through her half-open bedroom door. As usual, Cliff hadn't woken up yet. He'd probably sleep in for as long as Mama let him.

Grace filled the coffee pot with water and coffee grinds, anticipating the rich scent of the brewed beverage filling the stale house. Cozying up the blanket around her shoulders so that she'd be warm as she waited, Grace peered out the kitchen window just in time to see Papa and Gertrude dash toward his already-running car. *Probably going to Uncle Jack's.* On weekends, Uncle Jack often had a house full of rowdy guests, sweet Italian cookies, singing, and homemade wine. Likely, Papa would stay there all day, having done his duty by God last night.

Through the panes of glass, Grace heard the happy gurgle of a robin issue from the pine trees. The bird chirruped once more and then flew from the trees down to the frozen ground just in front of the window. His bright black eyes peeped up at Grace, and she couldn't help but smile at the little creature in his crimson vest. His chest feathers could compete with geraniums for ruddiness…

Why shouldn't I go to First Baptist today if I want to? Grace glanced toward Mama's bedroom. The sound of sleep hadn't abated at all. And First Baptist's service started early. *If I come back before I'm missed, what harm could it do?*

~ ~ ~

Determination lifted Grace's chin, though her heart skittered, playing dodgeball with her lungs. She straightened her dress one last time and hoped that it would be warm enough in the church to remove her ratty jacket quickly.

How fortunate that Lou had left a couple of grown-out dresses in the very back of their closet! Grace hadn't thought of looking for anything salvageable belonging to her departed sisters before this morning, but she'd thanked the Sweet Mother several times in the last hour for this boon: a slightly-worn dress of dark green cotton with a white lace collar. Its lowered waist attested to its age, and Grace knew that the material didn't really match the cold weather. *But it's green for Christmas, at least,* Grace tried to reassure herself, *and it fits.*

She'd hurried to get ready, pushing all doubts from her mind. Now, however, standing before First Baptist, Grace wondered if she'd been too hasty.

The light gray stone church rose before her, intimidating her with its soaring arches and steeple. The other churchgoers milling around her didn't seem to notice First Baptist's imposing demeanor; they hustled into the building, calling out greetings and tossing smiles here and there. Looking at them, Grace knew that she'd been correct last night in her thoughts: even in this green hand-me-down, she would stick out like a sore thumb. Many of the ladies and girls Grace's age wore fur-trimmed coats and sophisticated hats. *A rich church, just like I thought. I don't fit in here.*

She hovered just before the stone steps, trying to decide whether or not she should plunge through the dark doorway.

Perhaps I should go home.

"Grace?" Paulie's voice sounded as welcome in her ear as the rattle of the feed bucket did for old Bessie. "Grace!"

She turned around, eager to see Paulie's familiar face. But hesitancy rose when she saw that a tall older man accompanied him. *Must be his papa.* Acutely aware of the pilling fabric of her jacket as well as the ugliness of her hat, Grace avoided the man's eyes. She hoped that Paulie would quickly move by her and go inside the church with his father.

But apparently, Paulie would have none of that. "Grace," he said, eagerness dancing across his face, "I'm so glad that you came!" His smile attested to the sincerity of his statement. "Oh, let me introduce you to my dad. Dad, this is Grace."

Well, Paulie's smile certainly came from his papa. The older man – Grace guessed that he was no more than forty-five – gave her a kind nod. "My son has told me about you, Grace. I hear that you're very talented in mathematics."

Unable to make her tongue work, Grace just shook her head. Oh, how foolish she must appear to Paulie's papa! Her fingers played with the edge of her coat buttons, and she wished hard that Paulie and his father would go inside the church.

The bells pealed just then, signifying that the service would begin soon. Grace found her voice and croaked, "I have to find the Kinners."

Without waiting for a response, she bounded up the steps as quickly as her dignity would permit and escaped into the church.

~ ~ ~

The Mass – er, worship service – was nice. Grace had to admit that. She enjoyed the music very much, but she'd expected to. Seeing the choir singing those beautiful Christmas hymns made her envious. Grace could picture herself standing up there on that platform, performing the soprano solo to the awe of the listeners. Though she didn't know all of the hymns, she tried her best to sing along with the congregation.

Mrs. Kinner had saved a seat for her, and Grace proudly sat beside her friend on the curved wooden pew. Bible open on his knees, Mr. Kinner sat on Mrs. Kinner's other side, focused on the men who led the service. A smile crept onto Grace's face. *It's almost as if they're my family…* The thought lightened her heart.

During the sermon and prayers, Grace let her attention wander. She knew that Father Frederick would not be pleased if she participated in the rituals of the Protestants. So Grace spent the hour or so watching the congregants, guessing at their personalities and names. Paulie and his father must have found a place in the back of the church because Grace's roving eyes didn't spot them.

Suddenly, during the hymn sung after the sermon, a notion popped into Grace's mind. *Is attending this church a very serious sin? Will I have to confess it and do penance?*

She felt the blood drain from her face at the idea of confessing this to Father Frederick. Hastily, Grace reviewed the Ten Commandments in her mind. No, she didn't think merely *attending* this service could be considered a sin.

~ ~ ~

She came! Paulie could hardly keep still in his seat. *Grace came!*

He'd been praying – praying hard – all weekend that Grace would come to First Baptist today. He'd even asked Dad if they could delay travelling to New York until Sunday afternoon. And this, this was God's answer to his prayer!

I wonder if the sermon meant anything to her. Or did she just come to see the Kinners? Paulie's mind whirred even as his voice joined in the singing of those around him. *Did… Did she come to see me, too?*

Paulie glanced up at Dad, standing there beside him as they sang the final hymn. His father's mouth curved into a smile. Dad had prayed, too.

And now Dad had met Grace. *What does he think of her? She acts so shy, but that doesn't usually put Dad off.*

Well, his father and he would have a lot to discuss on the way up to New York this afternoon. That much was certain!

~ ~ ~

"You know," Emmeline tried to keep the excitement from her voice while at the same time remaining friendly, "we would love to have you come over for Christmas dinner." The service had finished, and she, Geoff, and Grace lingered in the foyer.

Was she urging too much? Should she just let Grace make her own decision without any prodding? Emmeline bit the inside of her cheek as she waited for a response.

The petite girl hesitated, thin arms hugging her jacket closed. "I'm not sure what my family has planned."

Emmeline forbade disappointment to show on her face. "Well," she encouraged, "if you find you have time, feel free to come over. Bring your family, if you wish. We always have plenty of food."

Beside her, Geoff patted his stomach, winking at Grace. "Yes, indeed. I usually gain several pounds on Christmas Day alone."

"Speaking of which," Emmeline added, "I have a roast in the oven that I have to take out. But if you do decide to come," she said to Grace, hoping she wasn't trying too hard, "we'll have dinner around three or so. And we'd love to have you."

Grace nodded in a noncommittal way and wouldn't meet Emmeline's eyes. Emmeline's heart sank. *She's not coming. Why, Lord? Why, when I so long to reach out to her?*

Geoff spoke up, turning his friendly smile to Grace. "Do you have a ride home, Grace? We could bring you if-"

"No," Grace interrupted him, then explained, "I walked here. It's only a short way to my house. But thanks. I should get going."

Emmeline noticed that Grace's serious eyes turned here and there, as if looking for someone. *Paulie,* Emmeline knew.

And who should come trotting down the church steps, nudging the crowds aside, but the young man himself? Emmeline held back a grin as Paulie bounded up to them. "Grace!" he exclaimed. "Am I glad that I caught you!"

Grace looked quizzically at him.

"I have a Christmas gift for you," Paulie stated. "Hang on a second. It's in Dad's car. I'll be right back." He jogged away a few steps, then turned. "Stay right there, huh?"

Grace nodded, and Emmeline watched the red creep up her neck and the anticipation build in her eyes.

Less than a minute passed before Paulie ran up again, his scarf flying in the light wind. He clutched a small square package, only a couple of inches high and wide. A jewelry box; Emmeline was almost certain of that. Good.

"Merry Christmas, Grace," Paulie declared, his breath puffing out like steam rising off hot cocoa. "This is for you." He offered her the present wrapped in silver paper; a neat red bow crowned the top.

Grace seemed unsure about whether to take it or not. Several seconds passed before she opened her hands to receive the package, and even then, she didn't unwrap it. "Thanks," she said at last. "I... I didn't get you anything," she added.

Paulie laughed outright. "I don't care about that, Grace. I hope you have a really nice Christmas."

In one of his flashes of impetuosity, Paulie pulled Grace into a quick hug. Emmeline *thought* that she heard him say softly in Grace's ear, "You look swell in that green dress, too, Grace."

She was *certain* that she'd heard it when she saw the girl's embarrassed, happy face after Paulie dashed away.

CHAPTER TWENTY-NINE

I'll wait *until Christmas morning to open it.* Grace bit her lip in anticipation. She gave one more stroke of her finger to the silver wrapping paper and whisked out of her bedroom.

A hymn she'd heard at First Baptist's service hummed in her throat as Grace tripped gaily down the stairs. *I haven't felt so happy in years.* It wasn't just receiving the Christmas present from Paulie – though, of course, that was grand – but also the feeling of acceptance the Kinners offered her… as if they really believed that she was worth something, as if they really wanted her company. *As if they really care.*

She'd decided to make sugar cookies, like Mrs. Kinner did. Surely, on Christmas Eve, they could spare a little butter and sugar for cookies! Especially if Aunt Mary brought Evelyn to visit Mama.

Maybe I could make icing, too!

Grace had just begun measuring out her ingredients – sugar, flour, butter, eggs, baking soda, vanilla – when she heard the back door open behind her. A cringe spread up her spine.

Papa.

She stiffened but kept measuring her ingredients out. Most likely, he would simply ignore her; he usually operated like that now. *Who knows where he'll go for Christmas? Or if he'll suddenly expect Mama to throw a big Christmas dinner and act like we're a happy family?*

She jumped when a rough hand clapped over her eyes. "Guess who?" asked a familiar deep voice.

It couldn't be… "Ben!" Grace gasped, wrenching away from the hand and swirling around to meet her brother's teasing gaze. "You came home for Christmas!"

She fell into his fierce bear-hug, breathing in the well-loved scent of horses, sweat, and cheap cologne. "I can't believe it!" The tears rose to her eyes, bubbling over and obscuring her vision. She wiped them away with hasty fingers; she wanted to see as much of Ben as she could while he was home.

"Hey, canary, why're you crying?" Ben held Grace back to look into her eyes. "Things that bad here?" He hugged her to himself again without waiting for her answer. "Where's Evelyn?"

Grace gripped Ben in one final embrace, gathering strength from his solid muscular frame. Then she pushed back. "A lot has happened since you've been gone, Ben," she started. "Here, sit down. Mama's napping. I'm baking cookies."

Ben whistled softly. "Cookies? My little canary-bird's baking cookies?" He gave her a wink. "Guess I *will* sit down then."

~ ~ ~

Sarah could hardly believe it. *Benny... My darling, sweet Benny!*

Wiping the blur of sleep from her eyes, Sarah rushed across the floor toward her firstborn. Ben met her halfway, taking her into his strong, grown-man arms. *So like Charlie when he was young...*

She felt Ben's tough, thick fingers run over her graying hair as she rested her head again her son's hard chest. He stank of that rotten racing-stable, but what did Sarah care? Her son was home for Christmas!

"You can't stay here," Sarah said after a long moment of silent joy. "Your papa, he hasn't forgotten."

She glanced up to see Ben clench his jaw but give her a smile, too. "Yeah, I know, Mama. I'm sleeping at Red's house. They got a spare bed. Don't worry about it. Okay?"

"Okay," Sarah agreed. "How'd you get here?"

"Hitched a ride with a guy going to Providence," Ben replied, shrugging. "I'll get back the same way."

"Still working at the track?" she asked, already knowing the answer.

"Yeah, Mama."

Watching Grace as she cut out the sugar cookies with a clean empty can, Sarah bit her lip. "We ain't got no tree this year, Benny," she said apologetically. "I... I just didn't feel up to it."

The slight sadness that crossed Ben's face brought a pang to Sarah's heart. "Don't worry about it, Mama," he assured her. "Who needs a tree when we got sugar cookies?"

"And hot cocoa," Grace added, her face beaming as she placed the dough rounds on the rectangular cookie sheet.

"And," said Ben, getting up from where he'd sat down at the table, "we've got the best little mama in all of Chetham, right, Grace?"

Sarah rolled her eyes, and before she knew what was happening, Ben had swept her into his arms and began jigging around the kitchen with her, loudly humming a jazzy tune. Their shoes clomped on the wooden floor as Ben swung her around.

For the first time in months, Sarah felt laughter pulse from her heart and out of her throat. Feebly, she pulled away, but Ben would have none of it. They passed the radio, where he paused, keeping a firm grip on her, lest she escape from his arms.

"Let's have a little *real* music," Ben proposed, switching on the knob.

The radio crackled and poured out a rendition of "Jingle Bells." No wonder; it was Christmas Eve. Ben swiveled round and round the kitchen in time to the music, dragging Sarah along with him.

At last, the song finished, Ben allowed Sarah to drop breathlessly into a seat at the table. She looked up and saw Grace's delighted yet shocked eyes on her. *We haven't danced in this house for years,* Sarah realized as the next song streamed through the radio and filled the room:

O Little Town of Bethlehem, how still we see thee lie!
Above thy deep and dreamless sleep, the silent stars go by.

Something about the Christmas hymn's simple melody struck a deep place in Sarah's heart. The radio minister's words from a few days ago reverberated through her mind: *This peace is found in the manger of Bethlehem where the little child lies asleep...*

Resting her hand on her own growing belly, Sarah looked at Grace and Ben, curious to see if the song had affected them in a similar fashion. But no, it seemed not; Ben sat teasing Grace and sipping a mug of cocoa, while flushed Grace pushed pans of cookies into the hot oven.

Suddenly, an idea nudged its way into Sarah's thinking. Without a word, she went to her bedroom and gathered her coat and pocketbook, checking to make sure that she had a little change.

"Where you going, Mama?" Ben asked when she returned to the kitchen.

Feeling a bit shy – whoever knew why – Sarah just shook her head. "I'll be back in a jiffy."

She would let it be a surprise.

~ ~ ~

Harold Quincy was ready to close up the shop. Sarah could tell from his loud sigh when she stepped into his tiny five-and-dime store on the corner of Main Street and Trellis Avenue. The doorbell rang above her head, announcing her entrance, though Harold had already seen her.

"Evening, Mrs. Picoletti," Harold greeted her in his crisp baritone. He didn't smile.

He knows a cheap customer when he sees one.

"Evening, Harold," Sarah answered. She could remember Harold from back when, as a kid, he went frogging with her brothers. "You don't close 'til five o'clock, right?" She glanced up at the prominently-displayed clock ticking above the cash register. The hands read quarter-to-four.

"Usually, no. But it's Christmas Eve. Gotta get home early tonight, you know," Harold replied, scratching with a pencil on some receipts.

"I'll just be a minute. I already know what I want." Hoping that no one had bought her intended purchase, Sarah traveled down the tightly-stocked aisles full of trinkets, necessities, and little gifts of every kind, from miniature china dolls to pocketknives.

There it was. Just where she had seen it on her shopping trip last week. Carefully, she picked it up and brought it to the front of the store. She laid it down on the heavily-nicked wooden counter.

Harold looked up from his receipts. "Done already?" he said, raising his bushy black eyebrows in surprise.

Sarah couldn't keep the small smile from her lips. "Yes."

Removing the ticket, Harold held out his hand. "That will be one dollar and five cents, please."

The extravagance of such a purchase nearly stopped her, but Sarah refused to give way to prudence this once. She placed the five dimes, seven nickels, and twenty pennies into Harold's hand and snapped her purse shut. "Wrap it up good for me, please. Don't want it to break or nothing."

A few minutes later, Sarah stepped onto the curb just as the street lights began to glow. Her chest lifted in a happy sigh, and she clutched her small package close to her plump body, trudging through the snow toward home with a lightened heart.

CHAPTER THIRTY

"I don't think she's coming, Geoff." Emmeline let the lace curtain drift back into place. She turned from the window with a sigh. The extra stuffing, pies, and ham would stock the refrigerator for the rest of the week.

Geoff offered a sympathetic smile from his seat next to the Christmas tree. "I'm sorry, Emmy. I know that you look at Grace almost... well, almost as a daughter, short time though you've known her."

Emmeline shook her head and walked over to the tree, staring up at its star with a rueful expression. "It's silly, isn't it? Of course Grace has her own family. Of course she wants to spend Christmas Day with them."

She fingered one of the glittery red balls hanging from a needled branch. With a wisp of laughter, she went on, "I suppose I've been picturing myself as Grace's salvation of sorts. Thinking that she needs *me* when perhaps..." Emmeline let her words trail off as she met Geoff's eyes.

He rose from his cozy armchair, putting his mug of hot cider aside, and wrapped his arms around her. She could smell nutmeg and cinnamon on his breath. "When perhaps Jesus is who she really needs?" he questioned softly, finishing her thought.

Emmeline nodded, fingers still tracing the shimmery lines of the ornament. "What do you think?" she ventured, half-hoping he'd disagree with her.

Geoff paused before answering. "Yes and no, I think, dearest one," he replied at last. "Ultimately, yes, Grace does need only Jesus. I've told you that my own heart has ached for her more than once during this school year. Not merely for her obvious poverty, but also for her evident desire for approval, for praise. Grace wants worth, but only Jesus can give that to her."

Again, he hesitated, then said, "And no, too. Because in a way, *you* are Jesus to Grace. I don't mean literally, of course, but you are making Him real to her. She sees Him in you, Emmy, and I pray, in me, by His grace. And when she comes face-to-face with Him someday, I hope that He will seem to her like coming home." He smiled; Emmeline felt it in the curve of her neck.

Glad in expectation, Emmeline lingered for several minutes with Geoff near the tree, twinkling with dozens of lights. And later, when they'd consumed far too much dessert, she and her beloved husband knelt down and, together, brought Grace and her family before the Lord of Hosts.

~ ~ ~

The moonlight climbed steadily across her bedroom wall, but Grace's eyes continued to drift open. Usually, she felt too worn out from the day's work to have a problem sleeping. Yet this Christmas night differed.

Flipping onto her back, she pulled the blankets up higher and snuggled down into her bed. She would have to wake up early tomorrow to milk Bessie and start breakfast. Determined, Grace closed her eyes and tried to inhale the deep, steady breaths of sleep.

A minute later, she gave up. Gathering a blanket around her shoulders, she padded over to the geranium plant perched on her windowsill. Beneath its stems, in the shadow of the sculpted pot, she'd placed the gift from Paulie, opened alone early this morning.

For the twentieth time that day, Grace picked up the small box labeled *Timothy Simmons, Jeweler.* Fingers tingling with pleasure, she opened the lid, basking in the sight of the two creamy pearl clip earrings nestled comfortably on their soft cushion.

Paulie bought them for me. For me! Biting her lip to keep from smiling too widely, Grace plucked one earring from its velvety socket. Of course, she'd never wear them. They were too beautiful, too obviously costly. Wrapped in her old blanket, she gazed at the gift for a long time, a smile touching her lips, her mind recollecting the past twenty-four hours…

Last night, Mama had returned with a package. Unwrapping it, she'd pulled out painted figurines: the Holy Mother, Saint Joseph, a shepherd boy with his sheep, the Three Wisemen, an angel, and, of course, the Lord Jesus in a manger bed. A glued-together stable, in which all the figures fit, completed the scene.

Mama didn't say much about it; just that she'd seen it the other day in Harold Quincy's five-and-dime store and thought it would be nice to have a manger scene. Ben hadn't seemed to think much of it; he only appeared happy that Mama had gotten what she wanted.

But staring at those figures, particularly the one of the Baby Jesus, so small and helpless… Well, Grace felt something echo inside of her that she couldn't put her finger on. His arms outstretched in the manger bed… outstretched just as they were on the cross in church. *Why?* It made her uncomfortable, fearful. She wished she could dismiss these nagging thoughts.

Cliff came home in time for supper, after which they all – except for Ben – attended Mass. There at church, Grace tried hard to reconcile the Man hanging on the cross behind the altar with the tiny painted figurine in Mama's manger.

What difference does it all make? What does it all mean? The thoughts were new ones for Grace, spurred by the music Mama had played on the radio several nights ago. Grace dared not share them with anyone.

Not even Ben, who'd met them when they were halfway home so that he could walk by her side. Their feet crunched through the hardened snow drifts. She'd breathed in the ice-cold air, feeling the hairs in her nose freeze, trying to forget everything but the fact that Ben had come home for Christmas…

Now, alone in the dark, Grace lightly ran her fingers over the round earrings, delighting in the glow of the creamy color. Just beneath her window, an automobile chugged quickly up the driveway, startling her.

Papa's home. Grace's heart sank into her socks. He'd been gone all day, leaving before dawn with Gertrude; why did he have to return now? Why did he *ever* have to return?

The crunch of his boots on the snowy driveway followed by the titter of Gertrude's annoying, muffled laughter reached Grace's ears.

Clenching her teeth, she refused to torment herself by looking out the window at their dark silhouettes, drunkenly staggering under the moon.

And there Mama lies in the bedroom below, pregnant with his child.

Grace thought again of that manger scene on the side table, of how Mama had placed each figurine inside the stable just-so, making certain that Joseph and Mary stood at the right angles to the adored Child. *If I'd been Mary, I would've chucked Joseph,* she decided, listening to Papa and Gertrude's steps fade away.

The tears rose to her eyes, though her chest tightened to suppress them. *Joseph, he was probably just like Papa.* Grace's fingers tightened around Paulie's gift, and she held herself erect, desperate to squash the hollow weeping that she sensed approaching.

Or was he like Mr. Kinner?

The thought pushed in, and Grace considered it. Not many men were like Mr. Kinner – kind, generous with his time, loving toward his wife.

The pearl felt smooth beneath Grace's fingertip. *Paulie.* Though not yet a man, Paulie had all the markings of Mr. Kinner.

What made them different from most men, even from good-natured but unreliable Ben? What caused Mr. Kinner to open his home to her and Paulie's lessons every weeknight? What made him continue to cherish Mrs. Kinner, a wife who couldn't give him what every man in their right mind should want – a son?

And Paulie… Why would he care about *her?* Grace touched her cheek in thought. Perhaps she had a little beauty – Ben said so – but was that enough for Paulie to humiliate himself with that lice incident? She had no money, no popularity, no pretty clothes. Why, then, did Paulie take such pains to show his regard for her? And why was his regard so… so sincere?

"I've never met a man – a boy – so nice," she murmured aloud, staring down at the earrings for a long moment before snapping the box shut. Carefully, Grace set the gift beside the geranium plant.

She had just lain down when she remembered. *The Kinners.* They'd invited her for Christmas dinner. Smiling, Grace snuggled down into her bed. Funny, when Mrs. Kinner asked her, Grace had thought that the Picoletti's Christmas Day would turn out bleak and that she'd wish that she'd gone to the Kinners.

Yet it hadn't. Aunt Mary had brought Evelyn for a few hours, which delighted Mama to no end. And Ben and Cliff had shared jokes. Mama had cooked a canned ham and boiled potatoes and baked a pie. And, in the privacy of her bedroom, Grace had opened Paulie's gift.

Still, Grace wondered what joy she had missed at the Kinners' house. It was a place of such warmth and love that even having Ben home couldn't prevent her pining to be there... a bit.

~ ~ ~

Ben came around the house the next morning to say goodbye. He'd spend the day hitchhiking his way back to the racetrack or wherever his winter quarters were. He never said outright.

"You're still in school, right?" he said to Grace for the ninth time, it seemed. She'd decided to walk through the woods toward Main Street with him. "No choir, but you're still in school, kid?" he repeated.

"Yeah, Ben, I'm still in school," Grace assured him. *But for how long will Mama let me stay there?*

Ben took a long drag of his cigarette, giving her a satisfied nod. "That's good, kid. Sorry about the choir, but you'll figure out another way."

"Another way?" Did he think she should pursue music, then? Another way to what?

"Remember what I told you? We're all in the gutter, but some of us are looking at the stars?" Ben kept taking his long steps as he talked, and Grace had to walk double-time to keep up with him.

"Yeah, I remember," she said, but her heart wasn't in it.

"Hey, don't say it like that. You were born to look at the stars," stated Ben.

His affirmation lifted her spirits a little. If not the choir, perhaps something else. Grace felt the square box bang against her leg. She'd put Paulie's jewelry box there to show Ben, and now she remembered it. "Wait," she said, her breath a cloud in the frigid air.

They stopped in the middle of the icy path. Grace pulled the jewelry box out of her pocket, glancing up to find Ben's eyes narrowed in curiosity. Gently, she opened the embossed lid, revealing the pearls, shimmering in their square sea of blue velvet.

Ben whistled low. "Somebody give you those, canary?"

Self-consciously, Grace nodded. She held her breath, waiting to see what else Ben would say.

Without asking her permission, her older brother reached for the box. His eyebrows shot up as he inspected the quality of the earrings. "Well," he said at last, "somebody with lots of dough is sweet on you, that's for sure, kid. It was a boy gave 'em to you, right?"

"Yeah," she answered, glad that Ben agreed with her assessment of Paulie's gift.

Then he frowned, looking down at the earrings. "See here. I ain't home to look after you, like a brother should."

She cocked her head. What did he mean? What was he getting at? Ben licked his lips.

"Just say it, Ben," she urged, her heart starting to thump. A squirrel chattered in the branches above their heads, the only sound in the still patch of woods beside their own breathing.

He stared down at the earrings. "Well, it's just this, kid. Guys don't give expensive stuff like this unless... they want something in return. Got it?"

Suddenly, the earrings didn't hold the same pure delight. Grace shivered, feeling the cold bite through her thin jacket. *He's right...*

Clearing his throat, Ben snapped the box shut and offered it back to her. She reached out a mittenless hand and took it, feeling the velvet exterior against her numb flesh. Visions of Gertrude intruded into her mind, unwanted... Gertrude wearing the latest hat or a new pair of high heels as she minced down the driveway to Papa's car. Where did she get all that new stuff?

From Papa.

"Just be careful, alright?" Ben's voice broke into her thoughts.

She looked up at him. "Yeah, I'll be careful, Ben."

CHAPTER THIRTY-ONE

January turned out so cold that year, even fire would freeze.

When Grace returned to the Kinners' after Christmas break, she expected Mrs. Kinner to evidence some sort of disappointment that Grace hadn't shown up for Christmas Day. But the woman didn't do anything of the kind. Instead, Mrs. Kinner asked small questions about Grace's family holiday.

"So your brother came home for Christmas? That must have been a treat for you all," Mrs. Kinner smiled, her hands busy breaking up ground hamburger in a sizzling frying pan.

Grace nodded, standing to the side of the stove. Usually, she didn't arrive until after six o'clock, but she'd rushed through her chores today, hoping to spend a little extra time with Mrs. Kinner before she and Paulie settled down to do their homework.

"Will your brother – Ben, right? - be able to come home again soon?" asked Mrs. Kinner, eyes on the hamburger.

Dread crept up Grace's throat. How far would Mrs. Kinner's questions go? "Uh... no. I don't think so. He works pretty far away," Grace managed. She ran her fingernail along the countertop to alleviate her nervousness.

"Oh? What line of work is he in?" came the horrible question. In her family's own circle of friends, Grace would've had no trouble saying that Ben was a groom. She'd brag about how he brushed the horses for some big-city fellow. But somehow, Grace knew that being a horse-groom at a racetrack wasn't a suitable profession for people like the Kinners... for people who attended church at First

Baptist and ate hamburger – real hamburger! - for supper on a weeknight.

How could she tell Mrs. Kinner the truth *without* telling her the truth? Suddenly, Grace remembered something she'd overheard Ben say back in the fall: that he groomed horses for a local politician. "He works for a politician," she answered Mrs. Kinner. Relief lifted the dread from her chest.

"Oh, so your brother is in politics?"

What? "Uh, I guess," Grace stumbled, hoping that she wasn't *really* lying.

A bright rap sounded on the kitchen door then, announcing Paulie's entrance and allaying one of Grace's anxieties while introducing a fresh one.

Paulie. Grace stole a glance as he let himself in. Snow covered his head, and he laughingly dusted it off his dark curls.

"It's freezing out there!" he exclaimed, unwrapping his scarf.

Grace had seen him only once since the day he'd given her his Christmas gift, and it had been during class, so they'd just had the chance to exchange pleasantries. No time to talk; no time for Paulie to say what he'd meant with his gift.

For he had to have meant *something*. Oh, she hoped against hope that Paulie differed somehow from what Ben had said: that he'd only given it 'cause he wanted something in return.

And Grace wasn't her mama's daughter for nothing. She knew precisely what Ben meant.

~ ~ ~

Mrs. Kinner had offered them a plate of macaroni and hamburger, but since Grace declined it, Paulie felt a little awkward digging into a mound by himself. Besides, he'd eaten a nice big plate of steak, potatoes, and cooked carrots before coming here. The Kinners weren't badly off or anything, but Paulie knew that Dad and he lived on a higher scale than they did. It didn't seem right to take food from them when he was sure that they could use the leftovers.

He and Grace settled to work at a small table in the parlor while Mr. and Mrs. K. ate in the kitchen. Paulie couldn't help glancing more than once at Grace as they opened up their textbooks and organized their pencils. What was she thinking? She seemed quieter than usual tonight...

Was it the earrings? Did she not like them? She's not wearing them. But then, Grace never wore earrings. Maybe it was the wrong gift! But Mrs. K. said that girls liked jewelry, and Dad had approved it as well.

Then why didn't she say anything about the gift? And why did he feel so thick-tongued? Paulie licked the tip of his pencil, preparing to dive into his math homework.

"Paulie," Grace surprised him by starting a conversation. He set down his pencil, but she kept her eyes glued to the literature book splayed on the table in front of her.

He waited.

"I don't think you should pay me for the mathematics help anymore," she said in her feather-soft voice.

Well, this came out of nowhere. "Why not?" he asked, frankly curious as to her reason. The fifty cents didn't matter one way or the other to Paulie. "You think I'm a hopeless case," he added, joking to lighten up the mood.

One side of Grace's thin lips pulled up in a smile, but she seemed to strangle it. *Why?* "I don't mind helping you, Paulie," she said. "I'll do it without pay, whenever you need help. As a friend, you know."

"And here I thought you were doing it as an enemy," he joked again. Grace didn't return his grin, and then the meaning of her pointed phrase took hold of him.

She means only *as a friend.* His heart plummeted into his shoes. Grace had ascertained why he'd given her the earrings, alright. And she was saying no to his affections outright. Without a second thought.

"Well, sure, Grace," he managed to gulp out, trying to keep his voice from cracking like a thirteen-year-old. "If that's how you want it."

He saw her quick nod. Her golden hair spilled across her face, and her huge blue eyes remained fastened to the page. Stunned, Paulie picked up his pencil but didn't begin the first problem yet.

How could I have so misjudged things? I thought there was something between us for certain. I even told her that I liked her back in the fall! Paulie shook his head, dazed at Grace's rejection.

And he'd prayed about this, too. Asked the Lord to prevent Grace from coming to First Baptist that Christmas Sunday if God didn't want him to give her the gift. And she'd come. Paulie had thought

God had answered his prayer.
    Evidently not.

CHAPTER THIRTY-TWO

Mama's belly kept rounding more and more. *Soon, she's gonna tell me she needs me at home.* Nervously, Grace finished her chores every day and took her homework over to the Kinners' house. *I can't give Mama the chance to speak her mind about me quitting school.*

True to her word, Grace hadn't taken one dime from Paulie since that day in January. She'd come up with the idea as a way to even things up between them with the pearl earrings. *If I keep helping Paulie with his math, he can't expect "payment" for the earrings.* Not that Grace felt opposed to affectionate feelings toward her from Paulie; but what Ben spoke of was different. It cheapened the whole thing. And Grace wouldn't have this precious friendship with Paulie cheapened any more than she would her friendship with Mrs. Kinner. She didn't *want* to find out if Paulie was like Papa.

At first, she'd feared that Mama would stop her from going to the Kinners once the dimes stopped flowing into the Picoletti home each week. But, surprisingly, Mama didn't seem to mind; she asked once or twice, "You sure those people want you to keep bothering them?" Otherwise, Mama didn't say anything against Grace bundling up her books each night after supper and trudging through the woods and then down the road.

Often, Grace returned home from the Kinners' to find Mama sleepily listening to a preacher or some hymns on the radio. Grace still felt a little startled every time she entered the house to the soothing sound of "Tis So Sweet to Trust in Jesus," rather than to

190

the tinny blare of an evening comedy hour.

One evening, as usual, Grace tapped a couple times on the Kinners' door, hugging her jacket tightly around her body to keep warm. She'd layered two cardigans beneath it. The snow poured down, bright white under the street lights; Grace hoped it would let up before she had to leave for home.

"Come on in, Grace!" Mrs. Kinner called, and her voice filled Grace with joy right down to her darned stockings.

Grace turned the knob and stepped into the house. The warmth shocked her, as it did every evening. The aroma of cookies filled the kitchen, and Mrs. Kinner stood at the sink, washing up the last of the supper dishes. "Hello, Mrs. Kinner," Grace greeted her, not feeling too shy around the older woman anymore. She picked up a dish towel to help dry.

"Oh, thanks, dear," Mrs. Kinner smiled. "I wondered if you'd come tonight, what with the snow. Mr. Kinner's headed off to a meeting at church, and I thought I might have to be all by my lonesome self."

Sure enough, Mr. Kinner popped into the kitchen just then, Bible in hand. Grace noticed it was worn. *Like he reads it,* she thought without surprise. Grace had never known anyone who read the Bible outside of church except for the Kinners. Perhaps Father Frederick did, but that was part of his job. *Maybe Paulie does, too...*

Mr. Kinner swiped a handful of snickerdoodles off the plate that sat on the kitchen table. "Geoff, are you stealing my cookies?" Mrs. Kinner asked without even turning around.

He winked at Grace and sidled up to his wife, holding out his handful of cookies. "Guilty as charged, darling."

Grace watched Mrs. Kinner struggle to keep her lips from turning up as she gave her husband a mock-stern look.

"But I'll pay for them," Mr. Kinner went on, a serious expression on his face.

Mrs. Kinner placed the last clean dish in the strainer to drip and wiped her hands on her apron. "Oh? And how do you plan on doing that, Geoff?" she asked, turning to face him.

Quick as a wink, he grabbed his wife by her elbows and his mouth pecked hers. "With a kiss," he grinned, releasing her.

Mrs. Kinner shook her head and gave him a playful shove toward the door. "Go on with you, Geoffrey Kinner!"

Chuckling, Mr. Kinner ambled toward the door, still clutching his cookies and Bible. "Well, I'm off. Good-bye, Grace, if you're not here when I get home." He pulled on his thick coat, gloves, and hat before popping out the door.

Grace smiled her good-bye, her mind turning over the affectionate scene she'd witnessed. Even years ago, when Mama and Papa had gotten along better, she couldn't remember them having such a simple delight in one another. This… This was *love*, pure and simple, that she saw and heard and felt in the Kinner household. And it was this that kept Grace coming back every night that she could. She wanted to have a piece of that love, or at least feel the wind of it ruffle the sails of her soul. Even though it scared her to get too close to it, sometimes.

"Men," Mrs. Kinner commented, giving Grace a smile. But she didn't say it in the disgusted voice Mama or Aunt Mary might use. She just said it in a way that made Grace feel like she and Mrs. Kinner had a special kinship as well.

"Speaking of which," Mrs. Kinner continued, untying her apron, "I wonder if Paulie will come tonight." She hung the apron on its hook near the sink.

Grace froze in the middle of hanging up the dish towel to dry. She felt heat rushing from her neck into her face. Ever since Paulie had given her those beautiful earrings and she'd rejected his fifty cents, she'd felt a little tongue-tied around him, though he still walked her home from school most days. *He probably doesn't notice your foolishness, Grace, so don't worry about it.*

"He's a nice boy – Paulie. How old is he?" Mrs. Kinner asked as she began to neaten a stack of papers on the countertop.

Grace swallowed. "A year older than me," she managed, "Seventeen."

"That's the age I was when…" Mrs. Kinner broke off as a firm rap sounded on the door. "That must be him now," she smiled. "Come on in, Paulie."

The door swung open. Paulie walked in, and so did another visitor. Grace's mouth dropped open.

A petite dark-haired girl stepped – no, bounced, Grace decided – into the kitchen. Her heart-shaped face wore a perky pink smile, her round cheeks glowed rosily in the warm lighting, and her perfect black eyebrows arched over large mossy green eyes. The young woman was, quite simply, flawless, from the tiny hat perched atop her fresh bob, to the colorful scarf knotted at her white throat, to the furry snow boots covering her delicate feet. Laughing, she dusted snow from her own shoulders and then… from Paulie's, as well!

Mrs. Kinner looked surprised. "Well, hello." She glanced at Grace, then at the girl. Grace squirmed inside but wouldn't let on. *What in the world?*

Paulie gave his usual hearty grin. "Mrs. K., Grace, this is Angelique. She's from Montreal. Her daddy just started working at the hospital, and they're staying with us until they can find the right house to buy."

Angelique fluttered her very long, dark lashes. "My father is an orthopedic surgeon, Mrs. Kinner," she explained in a softly-accented voice. "I hope Paul didn't overstep by bringing me here. Both of our fathers are on duty tonight, and…"

"No, no, not at all," Mrs. Kinner assured her, smiling, and Grace felt her hackles rise in jealousy. Who was this Angelique, to shove in on their study-time?

"Great!" Paulie exclaimed. "I didn't think you'd mind if I brought her, Mrs. K."

Grace suddenly noticed that Paulie carried a larger-than-usual stack of books. *He must be carrying Angelique's books! Well, why shouldn't he, Grace? You have no claim on Paulie's undivided attention,* she reminded herself.

Grace busied herself with laying out her own textbooks, notebook, and pencils on the kitchen table. She made sure that she left enough room for Paulie and Angelique's things. She knew Mrs. Kinner would knit or sew in the rocking chair that sat in the corner.

"Angelique, this is Grace," Paulie said as he set down his load of books with a thump.

"It's so nice to meet you, Grace," Angelique said. Even her voice sounded like a poem. "Paul has told me quite a lot about you."

Grace glanced up from her math problem. She saw Angelique's bright eyes examining her with a quizzical expression and then darting to Paulie. Flushing, conscious of her unstylish haircut and threadbare sweater, Grace fastened her eyes back on her paper. "Nice to meet you, too," she mumbled.

Paulie and Angelique took seats at the table, and he immediately reached for a couple of cookies from the plate. "Help yourself," he told Angelique. "Mrs. K. makes the best cookies ever. Want one, Grace?"

"I'm not hungry," Grace replied, though her stomach protested. She refused to glance up again and tried to lose herself in the order of operations.

"Nervous about the math test on Friday?" Paulie commented. "Boy, Angelique, are you fortunate! Sixteen and already finished with school."

Grace paused and sneaked a look at Angelique. The girl sat erect with a thick novel clasped in her long white fingers. She smiled at Paulie. "Well, finished for now, Paul," she corrected. "I plan to attend university, you know." Excitement spread over her pretty features, adding even more color to her cheeks and brightening her wide eyes.

"Of course," agreed Paulie, "but it sure must be swell to have finished high school. I've still got another year to go after this." He groaned and flipped open his own math book. "And then college. Dad keeps telling me to pray about which school to head off to. I know that, in his heart, he really wants me to go to Brown, like he did, but Harvard... Harvard's just so *enticing*. You know what I mean?" Paulie cocked his head to the side like a robin red breast and grinned. He popped an entire snickerdoodle into his mouth and chewed it before continuing. "Then again, there's always the possibility of going overseas, you know, to Oxford or Edinburgh..."

Angelique nodded, smiling that she understood exactly what he meant. But Grace didn't. Couldn't fathom it. *Harvard? Brown?* She straightened her skirt hem over her knees. *Can he ever know how differently I live?* Grace knew she'd count her blessings if she managed to finish this school year, never mind attempt higher education. Mama's baby was due soon. *And, if Mama gets her way, I'll be staying out for good.* The thought burrowed into her mind as she turned the pencil around in her fingers.

"Where do you want to go, Grace?" The question came from Angelique's perfectly-formed lips.

Grace's tongue turned numb. She felt the blush branding her face again. *What am I supposed to say? The truth? The truth is, I probably won't even finish high school.* "I... I don't know," she finally mumbled.

I can't take this anymore.

Grace rose suddenly, knocking over her chair. Paulie jumped up to right it, but she didn't stop. "I've gotta go home. I can't concentrate," she stated, shutting her books and stacking them in a wobbly pile.

"Hey, are we talking too much?" Paulie asked. "I'm sorry, Grace. Stay. We'll be quieter; I promise." His big brown eyes implored her.

She refused to be persuaded by his dimples. "No, I've gotta go." Calling out a good-bye to Mrs. Kinner, who'd gone to retrieve her knitting from her bedroom, Grace darted out the door, grabbing her jacket from its hook.

The snow had nearly stopped. Grace breathed a shaking sigh of relief as the silent night closed around her. She stuffed her hands into her pockets. Somehow, the loneliness of the evening hours comforted her; she understood what it was to be alone, to be the one on the outside looking in.

It was nice while it lasted. Her eyes gazed up at the light glowing inside the Kinners' kitchen – warm, welcoming, completely "other."

I won't be going back. Finally, she admitted what she'd always known in her heart: She didn't really belong; she never had, and she never would. She didn't fit in with loving people like the Kinners or smart, kind boys like Paulie Giorgi. They corresponded with the Angeliques of the world, with their neat picket fences, their red geraniums, their brick walkways, their diplomas from universities, the other well-dressed members of First Baptist, and their perfectly-round snickerdoodles.

They just don't get it. They don't get that life for me is fated to be one long thread of despair. Gritting her teeth, Grace refused to look back at the house again, afraid that her resolve might soften, though she knew that her conviction was right.

Her heart felt too heavy to do any more thinking, any more feeling. She put one foot in front of another. *I need to change out the cardboard,* she realized, feeling the slush soak through her shoes.

Mama would be glad to see her walk in early, though she wouldn't say it. She could see Mama in her mind, sitting there all swollen with the baby coming, rocking away by the window. Papa never came inside at night anymore; he spent all of his nights with Gertrude in that dumpy cottage.

I wonder if I'll end up just like Mama? The thought brought a dull shiver of horror. *Who knows what's in the cards for me, I guess,* she reflected. *Mama sure couldn't have thought this would be her life.*

Grace had just turned the first corner when she heard footsteps pounding up behind her. Ever alert, she whirled around on the deserted sidewalk. She prepared to run if necessary and peered through the soft veil of falling snow.

Paulie. His dark curls flew back from his forehead as he jogged toward her, face full of heavy concern. "Grace, wait up!" he called out. He'd only pulled on his coat; he must have been in a hurry to catch her.

Half wanting to relent, she hesitated for only a second, then turned and kept walking. He came up alongside her, panting. "What's the matter, Grace? You always do your homework at the Kinners. That's why I brought Angelique over there tonight, to meet you."

"Well, I met her." Grace clutched her books tightly in the crook of her arm, keeping her ice-cold hands jammed down in her pockets. She looked straight ahead, not trusting herself to meet Paulie's eyes.

In two quick strides, he moved in front of her, compelling Grace to stop. "What's wrong, Grace?" he asked, and when she looked up, she saw genuine confusion thick in his eyes. "Did I do something?"

"No, you didn't do nothing... anything," Grace answered, ducking her head. How could she meet the gaze of this young man who was so far above her in every way that mattered?

"Did Angelique...?"

She forced herself to raise her eyes, determined to maintain a modicum of dignity. "Angelique is fine. I mean, she didn't do anything wrong. She's a swell girl, Paulie. She's great for you." Grace kept her voice even, emotionless.

Paulie raised his eyebrows. "Great for me? What are you talking about, Grace?" Realization and then surprise replaced the confusion in his eyes. "You don't think..." He gave out a shout of laughter, and then Grace found herself seized in a fierce brief hug.

Dazed by the unexpected expression, Grace just stood blinking in the quiet glow of the streetlamp when Paulie released her. "Grace, are you kidding me? I care about *you*," he said earnestly. "Don't you understand?"

From deep inside Grace's heart, anger bloomed and spread suddenly, surprising even her with its ferocity. "Well, you shouldn't care about me!" She moved around him and burned the pathway beneath her feet, desperate to get away, to get back home where it was safe. Bleak, perhaps, but always safe. Always safe.

But Paulie grasped her elbow, stopping her again and turning her toward him. "Why not, Grace?" he asked. "Why won't you let me?"

Because I'm afraid. Afraid to hope. "I just don't fit, Paulie. That's why. You... You come from this gilded, happy-go-lucky life. I... I..." Her voice limped to a halt, broken-toned.

"You...?" he urged, and she glanced up to find his quiet eyes set on her face.

"I was born on a dead-end road," she said, her words cracking with tears she wouldn't shed. Not here. Not in front of him. *Better for him to know the truth now.* Grace turned away from the light shed by the streetlamp, turned her face into the shadows so that Paulie could only see her back.

"A dead-end road?" Paulie repeated. "What do you mean, Grace?"

The smile had fallen out of his voice. Was he confused? Or was he truly disturbed by what she said? "I know where you live. I know that you're poor. You don't have to hide that from me," he murmured.

Would he never understand?

"Look." Grace breathed deeply. "Your papa's a doctor. Well, mine never finished grade school. And he's never held a steady job for as far back as I can remember. He keeps a mistress in a cottage out behind our house. She's my uncle's - his brother-in-law's - sister."

She dared to look straight at Paulie, wanting to see his reaction. He flinched. Good. Better for them both to understand the real deal.

Grace continued, knowing that once she stopped talking, it'd be nearly impossible to start again. "My family's broken in pieces, Paulie. Mama's nearly cried herself to death this year, and I know that she wants me to drop out of school to help her with the baby that's due any day now. Your life... Well, it's fun for me to visit it, doing homework at the Kinners and all, but I have to admit it to myself, Paulie. I have to admit: I don't live in your world. I live in my world, bad as it is."

Her quiet words had stunned him. Grace could see it in Paulie's eyes. Good. Now he knew. And she could quit hiding and she could stop dreaming and she could just settle for the way things had to be.

They stood there a few feet apart for several moments. Finally, Grace murmured, "I don't mean to hurt you. It's just the way it is, you know?"

But he shook his head, eyebrows furrowed. "No. No, Grace. It doesn't have to be that way. *You* don't have to be that way. You're

197

thinking you have to live your life the way your family does? You don't. You really don't."

Her anger flared again. "And how am I supposed to get out of it, huh? I don't have a daddy with loads of money so that I can coast my way to Harvard. 'Or maybe I'll go to Oxford,'" she mimicked bitterly. "And what am I supposed to do, desert my pregnant mama? Nobody else is gonna help her. My older sisters left the house. There's only me!" She jabbed at her chest to underline her point. "I'm in the gutter. There's no way out for me. I can look up at the stars, but I'm still in the gutter, Paulie! Alone."

He hesitated just a moment – Could those be tears in his eyes? "You aren't alone," he said softly.

"What?" Great, was this going to be some dramatic love-speech? Grace really wasn't in the mood. Even for Paulie.

He looked directly at her, his eyes glittering in the streetlamp's light. "You're not alone, Grace. Jesus is with you, in the gutter."

She couldn't believe that he would bring something so off-topic into this. "Jesus? What does He have to do with this?"

He breathed deeply. "A great deal. I should have talked to you like this before. Honestly, I feared coming across like I was preaching to you, or was against you being Catholic or whatever."

Grace stiffened.

"But I know that you struggle with your lot in life and-"

"Struggle with my lot in life?" Grace cut him off. "You have no idea what you're talking about, Paulie Giorgi. No idea at all!" She let her words out blood-red and clawed, hoping to wound him. Perhaps that would rid her of some of the pain that twisted its way up her throat, nearly choking her with grief.

Paulie swallowed hard, obviously bitten by her tone. "I'm sorry," his voice came low, his breath frosty. "I'll pray for you, Grace."

She laughed. She couldn't help it. "Thanks a lot. My mother prayed to the saints for years, and look where it's gotten her." She felt the tears coming, hot and bitter, and knew she wouldn't be able to stop them for much longer. "Bye, Paulie," she said.

This time, he didn't stop her.

CHAPTER THIRTY-THREE

I t was over between them. Grace knew that now. Their friendship couldn't stand the gust of reality which her harsh words blew. *It's better this way,* Grace reflected sometimes over the next few days. That thought soothed the pain of their encounter.

The day after their argument, she removed the little velvet jewelry box from its place of honor beside the geranium plant. In the privacy of her bedroom, Grace didn't bother to stop the tears from scalding their way down her cheeks and staining the box's material. She muffled her sobs so that Mama wouldn't hear, and she placed the jewelry box deep inside her desk.

She begged her heart to forget its existence. If only the box could just disappear forever. If only her memories could disappear forever – They only made her present reality even more wretched.

Grace quit school immediately. She was sixteen now, and she knew that the school would never question it. Lots of kids dropped out at that age.

Why wait any longer? I'll be forced to do it in the end, anyway, she reasoned as she placed her borrowed textbooks on the school secretary's desk. Mama looked ready to pop with this baby. Grace couldn't screw her face up and look away every morning when Mama turned pleading eyes on her, begging her to help. *There's no way out.*

Did I do wrong? Grace pondered the question as she scrubbed the kitchen floor, swept out the bedrooms, and fluffed the pillows. She remembered Mr. Kinner's lively voice talking about metaphors and similes as she fed the chickens, milked Bessie, and boiled spaghetti for supper. She pulled the ticks off the family dog, squashing them with her thumb on the rocks and thinking about Paulie Giorgi sticking up for her with the lice incident last fall. Grace mended clothes and baked bread and rounded up junk to sell to the peddler who came on Wednesdays while the memory of Mrs. Kinner's kindnesses replayed in her mind. The geranium plant stood on her window sill yet, the last thing Grace saw before her weary eyes closed for the night.

Finally, two weeks after her argument with Paulie, Grace found that she had an hour or so of spare time on her hands. She'd emptied the mending pile, and supper waited on the back of the stove for whenever Cliff and Papa decided to tramp inside the house, bringing more mud for Grace to sweep up. For Papa still took his meals at home regularly. *I guess, for all her charms, Gertrude doesn't know how to cook, and diners get expensive.*

One hand on the doorframe, Mama rubbed at her lower back. Her belly stuck out like a July watermelon, ripe and hard and tight against her faded print housecoat. Several sizes too large, the garment slouched off one of Mama's shoulders, revealing her worn doughy flesh. Her hair stuck in damp, snarly tendrils that wormed their way down her neck, despite the chilly March weather. "Think I'll go lay down for a while, Grace," she murmured.

"Alright, Mama," Grace answered. "Want some water?"

Mama shook her head. "No, I'm just tired. Wish this baby would come." She rested a hand over her enormous belly and winced.

Grace frowned. Mama wasn't one to show pain unless it really mattered. "You alright, Mama? Is... Is the baby coming?" Grace remembered when Mama had delivered Evelyn; she'd been just four years old and scared nearly witless by Mama's screams. Papa had shuffled her off to a neighbor's house to wait out the delivery.

Now Grace was sixteen. *I'm old enough to handle it, I bet.* She raised her chin, wanting Mama to see how strong and capable she was. Of course, Mama would need a midwife, too. "You want me to get Mrs. Bailey?" she asked. The old Irishwoman played midwife whenever called upon by her impoverished neighbors, enjoying the extra gin she could purchase with the small payment for her services.

But Mama wasn't paying any attention to how tough her middle daughter was. She just shook her head. "No. Not yet, Grace. The baby hasn't dropped. I'll be alright. I just have to lie down." She hobbled off into the bedroom, leaving the door cracked open. Grace heard the mattress groan heavily as Mama settled on it.

Grace had read only a page of her book when she heard a soft rap on the kitchen door. Surprised, she waited a moment to make sure that she'd heard right. The knock came again, a little louder this time.

Dog-earing her page, Grace glanced at the driveway through the kitchen window. She hadn't heard anyone drive up, and sure enough, no car loitered in the driveway. *Aunt Mary Evelyn would bring her car.* A sliver of hope leaped into her heart. *Maybe it's Ben!* What she wouldn't give to see her big brother now.

Her hand was already on the knob when she realized, *Ben wouldn't knock.* The hope vanished, but her curiosity grew. "Who is it?" she asked through the closed door, unwilling to open it to an unknown person when she and Mama were alone in the house.

"Grace? It's Mrs. Kinner," the familiar voice answered, a little muffled by the wooden barrier.

Grace's heart jolted with sudden happiness. Mrs. Kinner stood just on the other side of the portal. Then it plummeted to her knees. *What will she think of me dropping out of school?* Her hand remained paralyzed on the knob.

She realized she'd waited too long to open the door when Mrs. Kinner called hesitantly, "Grace, couldn't I come in? For just a moment?"

Grace swallowed hard and turned the knob. She opened the door enough to reveal herself. Mrs. Kinner stood on the top step, giving Grace her lovely, cidery smile. Grace could see concern in her friend's eyes.

"Hello, Grace," Mrs. Kinner said. "May I come in?"

Grace nodded and stepped back to let Mrs. Kinner enter. She smelled the familiar powdery perfume Mrs. Kinner wore as she stepped past Grace and moved into the kitchen.

"I brought this for your family," Mrs. Kinner explained, holding out a rectangular loaf wrapped in waxed paper and tied with a little red ribbon. "I always bake too much for just me and Mr. Kinner. It's cranberry nut bread."

"Th-Thank you," Grace stumbled over her words as she reached for the bread. It was so awkward, this meeting between her and the woman whom she loved best in the world. She busied herself with placing the loaf just so on the table.

201

"Grace," Mrs. Kinner began, once Grace had arranged the bread thoroughly.

Grace felt her entire body tense. She knew what was coming. She tucked a stray piece of hair behind her ear and swallowed. *I should offer her some coffee,* she thought desperately and moved over to the kitchen counter, avoiding Mrs. Kinner's gaze. "Can I get you some coffee?" she asked, the grown-up phrase feeling too big on her voice.

"Coffee would be nice," came the soft reply. Grace took her time setting up the coffee pot and measuring out the coffee.

As the inviting smell drifted through the room, she realized that Mrs. Kinner still stood with her purse in hand, hat pinned to her head, and coat in place. "Oh, I forgot. Please, sit down. Let me take your coat," Grace flustered.

As Grace hung the coat on the peg near the door, Mrs. Kinner sat down. She paused just a moment before speaking again. "Grace, I came to ask why you haven't been to see us lately. I miss having your help with my geraniums, you know. And I know Paulie misses your company while he does his homework in the evenings."

Grace stayed silent out of necessity. Her throat filled with tears she wouldn't – *couldn't* – liberate. She'd finished hanging up the coat but stayed right where she was, in front of the pegs, her back to Mrs. Kinner.

"And Mr. Kinner says you've not been to school," Mrs. Kinner continued, her voice undemanding. Just gentle and a little sad. Her words and voice broke Grace's heart to hear.

Finally, she turned and faced Mrs. Kinner. "I dropped out." There. She'd said it.

Mrs. Kinner scrunched her eyebrows, obviously perplexed. "Why, Grace? I thought you liked – I thought you loved school."

"I do. I did." She forced herself to meet Mrs. Kinner's gaze. She would tell her the plain truth without the situation between her and Paulie clouding things. "My mama, she's near having her baby. She needs my help around the house now."

Grace couldn't encounter those kind eyes any more. She moved toward the coffee pot. Surely, it had finished brewing by now! "Seeing I didn't have homework, there was no point in going to your house anymore, I guess." She selected the least-chipped mug from the cupboard and poured out the dark brew. "Did you want cream, ma'am?" Grace knew there was no sugar in the house. Thanks to

Bessie, there was cream, though.

Mrs. Kinner shook her head. "No, black is fine. Thank you." She accepted the steaming mug carefully. "But I thought you came over to my house for more than homework, Grace. You've become quite a friend to me over the past few months."

Despite the tenseness, Grace felt a blush of pleasure rise to her cheeks. Mrs. Kinner counted her, Grace Picoletti, as a friend?

"Certainly, I understand that you must help your parents and do as they bid you. And I *am* sorry that you must drop out of school. But couldn't you come over to our house from time-to-time even without needing to work on homework?" Mrs. Kinner coaxed, her hands clasping the mug. "It's nearly springtime, and I'll be starting my garden and hanging the geraniums again soon. I would love your help with that, if your mother could spare you for just a while, every so often."

Grace couldn't help but smile just a little. After all, what harm could there be in helping Mrs. Kinner with her garden? Just once in a while? She slowly nodded. "Well, I..."

"And Mr. Kinner would be more than glad to lend you books from our library so that you could continue your studies at home, if you'd like," Mrs. Kinner added, taking a little sip of coffee.

The notion tempted Grace sorely. Just because she didn't belong to the same sort of people as Paulie didn't mean she couldn't educate herself, did it? She wouldn't pretend to be like them, headed off for high things, but she could learn for her own pleasure, couldn't she?

"And Paulie would love to see you again," Mrs. Kinner continued. "He keeps mentioning that he misses your help with his mathematics."

No.

Grace shook her head. "No," she murmured softly but firmly. "I can't." Her hands trembled in her lap, and she began to pick at the cuticles.

Now Mrs. Kinner was really puzzled; Grace could see that. "But..." she trailed off, shaking her head.

"I'm awfully busy," Grace said. "Mama needs my help. I don't really have the time to go over to your house anymore. I'm sorry."

CHAPTER THIRTY-FOUR

Half of Papa's face seemed on fire as he burst through the door. Staring at him, Grace dropped the plate that she was drying and gaped, not even hearing the china shatter. The top part of Papa's countenance wore a mask of shining, blistering crimson. His eyes shut against the horror. *Are his eyes even there anymore?*

The smell of burning flesh – she knew she'd never forget the nauseating scent – preceded him. Papa stumbled forward, falling, hands feeling for the way into the kitchen.

Grace felt frozen to the spot where she stood near the sink, unable to move her hands from the dish towel or her feet toward Papa. He rolled on the floor in agony, hands clasping his head.

But Mama…! Barely had Papa fallen when Mama let the broom drop right where she'd been sweeping up the crumbs from the sandwiches they'd eaten for lunch. The broom fell with a crash, and Mama ran to Papa's side, her huge stomach bouncing beneath her housecoat.

Mama's reaction shocked Grace after the frigid separation between the two of them for so long, but there wasn't much time for pondering it. Kneeling down, Mama grabbed Papa's hands away from their scraping at his face and gripped them tightly in her own fists. All while struggling to tame Papa's agonized flailing, Mama shouted out to Grace, "Get me a bowl of cold water!"

Mama's sharp voice snapped through Grace's immobile state. She grabbed a bowl from the cupboard above her head, letting the doors bang shut while she dashed to the sink. The cool water poured from the faucet, taking so long to fill the mixing bowl. Her eyes fastened on the stream of water, Grace's ears took in the wild-animal groans coming from Papa. A glance over her shoulder showed that he still thrashed like a rabbit caught in a boy's snare.

There! The water filled the bowl. Without bothering to turn off the faucet, Grace pulled the bowl out of the sink and hastened to Mama's side, recoiling at the sight of Papa.

"Set it down there!" Mama commanded, not taking her eyes off Papa for a second. Grace's hands trembled as she obeyed. "Get me a rag!" Mama directed, but then she saw the dish towel hanging from where Grace had tucked it into her skirt's waistband.

"Never mind!" Mama let go of Papa's hands and plucked the towel from Grace. She plunged it straight into the cold water and pulled it out, laying it sopping wet across the top of Papa's head and face, leaving just his mouth uncovered so that he could breathe, Grace guessed.

Papa had stopped pawing at his face. He lay stiffly with his head in Mama's lap, gasping and moaning. Tremors began to shake his body, so slowly at first that Grace could hardly discern them, then stronger and more pronounced. "Grace," Mama breathed out the words quickly, "get the doctor. Run!"

Grace scrambled to her feet, tripping over the hem of her skirt, hearing it rip a gaping hole at the waistband seam. She glanced back just once before plunging out the screen door into the harsh evening air. Crouched there on the wooden floor, Mama held the soaking towel on Papa's face, rocking back and forth from hip to hip. She stayed silent amid Papa's moans.

Not daring to waste another moment, Grace clattered down the back steps. The dog rushed from the side yard, barking at her and wagging his tail, but Grace didn't pause for a second. Toward the wooded path she ran like a young child, mindless of appearances, catching her hem on low branches. Unable to see clearly in the dusk, she fell in the mud-filled path twice, scraping open her knee on a tree root the first time and nearly twisting her ankle the second time. *Get the doctor, Grace! Get the doctor!* Mama's words played in her mind to the pounding rhythm of Grace's flying feet. The memory of Papa – *her* Papa – groaning and floundering across the floor boards joined the phrase and spurred her on to an even faster speed.

By the time she reached the almost-vacant Main Street, the March twilight had become night. From Main Street, it was just a short sprint to Doctor Philips' tidy house-and-office. A lamp shone in the bay window, pink roses stenciled around its globe. Panting, Grace cut across the lawn. Her cold fingers fumbled to open the white-washed gate, fairly glowing in the darkness.

The latch seemed stuck, and she jerked it toward and away from her, desperate to open it. *Mother of Jesus, help me!* With a final yank the latch gave way. Grace let the gate rattle shut behind her and dashed up the brick pathway to the doctor's neat front porch. *Doctor Philips won't be in his office now; he'll be in his house, finishing supper.*

Her fist slammed into the ornate door, not paying mind to the brass door-knocker hanging just above her eye-level. She pictured the doctor pausing over his supper, raising his eyebrows at his syrupy-as-candied-sweet-potatoes wife, and rising to get the door. "I'll answer it, Dolores, dear," he'd say, dabbing at his mouth. He'd put aside his napkin and...

Grace's eyes swung from their roving back to the door as the knob turned. She opened her mouth, ready to ask the doctor to come with her. To beg, if necessary.

But the doctor's wife, not the doctor himself, waited on the other side. "Yes?" she inquired, her silvery head tilted to one side. A look of slight irritation spread across her face when she glanced down to see Grace's muddy shoes dirtying her pristine porch. Known to be a fastidious housekeeper, Mrs. Philips always reminded Grace of one of those fancy house finches.

"Please, ma'am, I need Doctor Philips to come with me right away," Grace pleaded, her breath emerging in faint white puffs.

The doctor's wife smiled, but the expression didn't reach her eyes. "I'm sorry, but that's impossible. Doctor Philips is away this weekend at a medical conference in Boston." She emphasized the last phrase, as if to impress and intimidate Grace with Doctor Philips' importance.

Get the doctor! "But..." Grace trailed off, panic setting in.

The woman began to shut the door until there was just a crack left open. "If you need medical assistance, you can visit Doctor Kelver in Smithfield. He'll be happy to help, I'm sure." She smiled again to close the conversation and inched the door shut.

But Grace stopped her from closing it with a desperate hand.

"Please! It's an emergency, ma'am! My father burned himself — I don't know how — and we don't have a way to get him over to Smithfield — and-"

"Well, then, you'll have to call the ambulance if it's a real emergency, dear. I'm sorry that I can't be of more help. Goodnight." The door clicked shut decisively, and Grace let her hand fall to her side.

There was no money to pay a hospital bill; Grace knew that. *We can't call the ambulance.* Doctor Philips would have accepted milk and butter, maybe some eggs, in exchange for his services, whether his wife liked it or not. The hospital, on the other hand, didn't accept that last relic of the barter system. Its cold white halls demanded cash money, which the Picolettis did not have. And neither Mama nor Papa would beg for charity, even for an emergency such as this.

Who can help us? Who? From the corner of her eye, Grace saw the curtain move; the doctor's wife waited for her to leave the clean-swept porch. Her heart thudded in her chest as Grace made her way down the steps. *Where can I go? Who will help us?*

The bells of First Baptist rang out sharp and clear in the night, announcing the hour. The notes touched Grace's ears even as the chill wind brushed her hot cheeks. And she knew to whom she would go.

Paulie.

Paulie Giorgi's father was a doctor. She would go to him. Paulie had mentioned once that he lived on River Avenue, and Grace knew that she could find him.

CHAPTER THIRTY-FIVE

Ten minutes later, Grace gasped up the even tidier path to the Giorgi house on the east side of town. She hadn't even needed to knock on someone's door to ask which house belonged to the Giorgi's; Doctor Giorgi had engraved his last name on a stone pillar at the beginning of their long driveway. Pruned-back rose bushes lined the walkway, and they bowed to her like commoners to a princess.

Some princess, Grace thought, slowing down as she reached the four marble steps ascending to the front entrance. A porch light illuminated the front area fairly well. Enough so that Grace could see how very dirty she'd gotten, falling through the muddy, slushy wooded pathway from her home to town. *It can't be helped... If something happens to Papa...*

Gritting her teeth, Grace clambered up the four steps and pressed the doorbell hard. She heard it ring through the large rooms within the house, and she drew her dirt-smeared hands behind her back. Then, she caught sight of the hole yawning at her waistband and remembered how she'd stepped on her skirt in her hurry to get a doctor. Undecidedly, she pulled one hand from behind her back to cover the tear, then put it behind her back again...

The door opened.

"May I help you?" a puckered voice inquired.

Grace gathered all of her courage and met the middle-aged woman's vigilant eyes. "Please, ma'am," she panted, "I need to see Doctor Giorgi!"

"I am Doctor Giorgi's housekeeper. I regret to say that the doctor is in his study and cannot be disturbed."

The door threatened to close, but Grace, desperate, stepped forward, gripping the doorpost so that the woman would have to shut the door on her hand. "Please, ma'am! It's my papa who's hurt. If you'll just tell Doctor Giorgi that Grace Picoletti is here…"

The housekeeper shook her head. "I don't care who you are, young lady. Doctor Giorgi gave explicit orders-"

"Grace, is that you?" The familiar boyish tone brought a blush to her cheeks, and she found herself glad for the dark night and the shadows in which she stood.

Sure enough, Paulie peered over the housekeeper's shoulder. Mrs. McCusker pursed her lips but made way for her master's son. "Grace! Thought I heard your voice." He grinned in his old way, dimples showing. "Boy, am I glad to see you!" He seemed to really mean it, too.

"Hello, Paulie," Grace managed. She let him catch her eyes at first but found herself unable to maintain the connection. What must he think of her, despite that smile, when their last words had been so sharp on her part?

"So… why did you come here? I mean, so late at night?" Paulie asked. Mrs. McCusker lingered in the background, pretending to inspect the hall mirror for dust.

"I need your papa – I mean, your dad," Grace blurted out, realizing the minutes were ticking away. How long had it been since she'd left Mama with Papa lying in her lap? Twenty minutes? Even longer? "He's a doctor, right?"

She saw that her words took him aback for a second. "Why?" he questioned.

It was a strange request, she knew. "My papa. He got burned. Bad, I think. Doctor Philips isn't home. I tried…" The words tumbled over each other, but somehow Paulie seemed to make some sense of it.

"Well, hey, come in, Grace. I'll get Dad. No problem there." He swung the door open wide for her to enter and rushed off, down a long brightly lit hallway. As Paulie called for his father, his voice fairly echoed in the vast house.

Mrs. McCusker stood to the side, chin raised, allowing Grace to step into the house. Clutching the hole in her waistband, Grace hurried inside, head ducked. The door shut decisively behind her.

She glanced up. Mrs. McCusker stood guard parallel to her, the housekeeper's droopy eyes pinning Grace to the square of tile upon which she stood.

The woman needn't have worried. Grace had no plans to move farther into the rooms filled with domed antiques. The silent yellow lights above her head glinted off the crystal vases and, in the room just off the entryway, gleamed on chandeliers. *Like a palace.* Grace dropped her widened eyes to her smeared shoes again. *My socks are filthy,* she mused, glumly staring at her besmirched, formerly-white stockings.

In just a few moments, hurrying feet sounded on a staircase somewhere nearby, and then came nearer. Finally, Doctor Giorgi strode into the entryway, followed by Paulie tagging along right at his elbow. Dressed in casual but well-tailored trousers, the doctor rolled his sleeves down as he walked.

"Grace, what brings you here?"

She glanced up to see a warm smile stretching across Doctor Giorgi's face, lighting up his tanned olive countenance and crinkling the corners of his eyes. That smile emboldened her to ask what she must. "Will you come? My papa's hurt bad – got burned – Doctor Philips ain't home," she explained, realizing too late that she'd slipped back into low-class speech in her nervousness.

Doctor Giorgi's eyebrows knit together. "If he's hurt badly, why not call the ambulance?" He cocked his head.

Shame colored Grace's face, and the richness of her surroundings pummeled her. "Ain't no money for that," she forced herself to mumble, scrunching her toes inside her shoes and feeling the place where the soggy cardboard edge met the sole.

The housekeeper sniffed. "Well, if that isn't nice, Doctor!" She folded her arms across her shriveled bosom and stared at Grace with smirking eyes. "She expects you to work for nothing, I guess. Those n'er-do-wells—"

"Mrs. McCusker, have the goodness to be silent, please," Doctor Giorgi interrupted, and Grace wondered at the soft authority his voice held. He kept his gaze on Grace, and she knew he took his housekeeper's words into small account. "I'll be right back with my bag," he stated. "Son, wait here with Grace, please."

"Sure, Dad," Paulie agreed, a study in seriousness.

Doctor Giorgi could not return soon enough for Grace's comfort. As the loud hall clock ticked the slow seconds, Paulie sought to catch Grace's eyes while she kept them locked on the freshly-vacuumed carpet. Whenever she lifted them, she found Mrs. McCusker staring at the hole in her skirt, chin tucked deep into the fold of flesh at the housekeeper's throat.

"All set," Doctor Giorgi announced as he reentered the hallway at last. One hand grasped his black leather medical bag, and the other held his coat. "We'll drive," he said.

"Can I come, too, Dad?" Paulie spoke up.

Grace's heart skipped a beat before she heard his father's answer. "Yes, son. I may need you. Let's go; we've wasted enough time."

Conflicting emotions swirled in her chest as Grace followed Doctor Giorgi out to his intimidating car. Silver-gray with shining mirrors, it waited in the driveway; a man – Grace guessed that he must be an employee – had driven it from its place in the garage. He stood holding the driver's side door open for the doctor.

"Thank you, Taylor," Doctor Giorgi said to the stocky man before hurrying over to the passenger side. With the courtesy due to royalty, Paulie's father opened that door and gestured. "Grace," he invited.

Awed and pleased in an uncomfortable-sort-of-way, Grace slid past Doctor Giorgi and into the front seat. Seeing the smooth leather interior, feeling its soft give beneath her light weight, Grace regretted that her filthy dress would surely dirty it. Well, she would try to keep her muddy shoes from soiling the floor too much, at least, by holding them slightly above the mat. It might be difficult to keep her balance thus, but Grace had her pride, too.

Paulie jumped into the backseat, and Doctor Giorgi placed his black bag beside his son before going over to the driver's side and entering the car himself. "Alright," he said, "and where do you live, Grace?"

CHAPTER THIRTY-SIX

The short ride across town passed in a blur. Doctor Giorgi attempted no conversation. He seemed to understand how tense Grace felt. Paulie sat silent, too, fidgeting a little in the backseat and clearing his throat a few times. The car moved smoothly through the inky darkness; there was no moon tonight.

"Turn here," Grace directed the doctor. Her voice sounded loud in her own ears. She squeezed her lips shut, anticipating the meeting of her parents and Paulie's papa.

Nodding, Doctor Giorgi maneuvered the massive car around the back road's bend and down the stony driveway that led to the house's back door. Grace saw that Mama had turned on the kitchen light, but the rest of the house loomed dark above them. *I wonder where Cliff has got to?* The thought moved fleetly through her mind, but Grace shrugged it away. Far more important matters than Cliff's absence occupied her.

Doctor Giorgi switched off the engine and hopped from the car with one fluid movement, slamming the door. He immediately strode toward the house. "Paulie, bring my bag, please," he called out behind him.

"Yes, Dad," Paulie replied, grabbing the soft leather satchel and bounding into the yard.

Grace scrambled out. Her hand clutched her waistband together as her numb legs carried her up the pathway behind Paulie and his father. Humiliation crashed over her in waves as she saw Doctor Giorgi mount the broken-down steps. *I'm so embarrassed for them to know where I come from!*

Grace knew that she should be worrying about Papa, not caring about what a virtual stranger thought of the Picolettis' lifestyle. But she couldn't help it; he was Paulie's daddy, and she had never wished harder that they lived in a nicer neighborhood... that her parents were better people ... that her daddy didn't burn garbage in a barrel in his backyard and keep a mistress in a cottage way out back. The tears pressed against her eyes, but she fought them back

Upon reaching the back door, Doctor Giorgi gave only a short rap with his knuckles, and without waiting for an answer, he turned the knob. The scent of bacon grease and soap wafted out as he pushed open the door. The doctor stepped inside the dimly-lit house, ducking his head a bit because of the low doorway.

Grace scuttled in right behind the doctor, her eyes slowly adjusting to the light of the single lamp. Mama must have helped Papa to get up onto the long, ratty horsehair couch that leaned against one of the kitchen walls; the couch had occupied that spot for as long as Grace could remember, perfect for any ill family members. Moaning low, Papa lay there, one leg lolling off the couch. His pants had rumpled up, displaying his mismatched, much-darned socks and a healthy swath of dark Italian leg hair. Grace ground her teeth in embarrassment. She couldn't imagine Mr. Kinner or Doctor Giorgi lying there like that. Anxiously, she risked a glance at Doctor Giorgi, but he seemed unfazed by his patient's uncouth display.

Mama looked up then from her place sitting beside Papa. "Who's this?" she barked, squinting into the shadowy entryway. Her unkempt, graying hair snarled around her worried spherical face, accenting the thin, tight line of her mouth.

Grace sucked in a deep breath. "I brought Doctor Giorgi, Mama. He says he'll look at Papa."

"Doctor who? Where's Doctor Philips?" Mama halted in her nearly-continual administration of wet cloths to Papa's face and head. As soon as she paused, Papa's groaning grew louder, though, so she quickly dunked the cloth down deeply into the cold water and applied it.

Grace hadn't counted on Mama disliking that she'd gone elsewhere for a doctor. But what choice was there, other than bringing Papa to the hospital? "Doctor Philips ain't home, Mama," she said.

Doctor Giorgi stepped out of the entryway toward Mama. His feet took him from the shadows and into the circle of soft lamplight. "I'm Doctor Samuel Giorgi, ma'am. I'd be glad to see to your husband, if you would like." In his quiet, kind way, Paulie's papa crouched down so that he could be at the same level with Mama, sitting there on that stool. Mama turned from sponging Papa's face to look the doctor square in the eyes, her usual tough manner displayed.

And then Grace saw it – the shock suffusing across Mama's countenance. The line of Mama's lips broke as her mouth fell open a tad, and she stared at Doctor Giorgi with unblinking eyes.

Mama knows him.

Curious, Grace flashed a glance, lightning-quick, at Doctor Giorgi. For a split second, he appeared confused at the surprise dawning plain-as-day on Mama's face. Then, recognition emerged. *He knows her, too,* Grace realized, looking from one to the other.

"Sarah?" The name stumbled out of Doctor Giorgi's mouth, sounding as if he found himself using a second language he'd not known he could speak. "Sarah… Antonelli?"

Grace saw a red flush rise to Mama's cheeks. Her mother swallowed hard, the sinews in her neck straining. "Sam Giorgi," she acknowledged in a voice as quiet as a dying cricket. "Didn't know you'd come back."

Doctor Giorgi nodded. "Yes," he said, low and controlled. An expression rose in his eyes that Grace could not read as he peered at Mama. Certainly, it could not be any tenderness, for Mama sat, a crumpled mess, shiny with sweat and big with the baby that should be coming any day now. But for several seconds, Grace watched as Doctor Giorgi held Mama's gaze gentle as he might cup a butterfly. Mama broke the silent grip first, turning her face to look at Papa.

"I understand your husband burned himself badly," Doctor Giorgi straightened up and turned his attention to Papa, too.

"Yeah, he did," Mama replied, swabbing at Papa's face with her wrung-out dish rag. "Burning trash out back, I think. Don't know what happened. Came in like this, face nearly on fire."

Doctor Giorgi leaned forward, and Grace crept forward a little, too, hardly aware of Paulie's presence behind her at all. Mama lifted her dish rag off Papa's face so that the doctor could see the extent of the injury.

A chill prickled through Grace's limbs as she gaped at Papa's burns. The crimson skin, extending from Papa's singed hairline to his lips, appeared glossy and bubbly like soda-water. His mouth open in a guttural groan, Papa seemed hardly aware that anyone but Mama was in the room. His eyes remained closed against what Grace knew must be searing pain. Papa was a strong man; it took significant agony to debilitate him.

"What's your husband's name, Sarah?" Doctor Giorgi asked.

"Charlie," Mama managed to reply, fluttering away from the couch now that professional hands had come to do their job. She rose from her seat and went to stand behind Grace. *Almost as if I was a shielding wall.*

Doctor Giorgi sat down next to the couch. His hand grasped Papa's shoulder with great gentleness. "Charlie, I'm Doctor Giorgi," he spoke near Papa's ear. "Your wife has asked me to look at your burns. I'll be as gentle as I can, alright?"

Grace watched as Papa gave a slight nod, and Doctor Giorgi began his examination.

CHAPTER THIRTY-SEVEN

Sarah's nails bit into her palms as her eyes followed the brilliant headlights of the doctor's car. The beams cut through the dark night as the man and his son pulled out of the driveway and onto the dirt back road.

Her shoulders relaxed into their usual rounded posture, and she released the breath which she felt like she'd been holding since meeting Sam Giorgi's gaze earlier this evening.

Sam Giorgi. Sarah could hardly get over it. No, she really couldn't. In a dull, detached way, her heart thudded like she was sixteen again and he'd pulled up in front of her papa's front stoop. Many years had passed since then, and they'd sure been kinder to Sam than to her. With a glance over her shoulder at Charlie lying prone on the couch, eyes bandaged shut, Sarah tiptoed to her and Charlie's bedroom – well, hers, really, 'cause Charlie hadn't slept there in months – and waddled her pregnant self over to the little mirror drooping against the yellowed wallpaper.

Half-fearful, half-bold as brass, Sarah forced herself to look into that mirror. And as she gazed, the red rose to her cheeks as if she'd spent all day ironing clean laundry.

I'm an old woman. The thought made her mouth sag deeper into its already-grooved wrinkles. *An old, fat woman with bare feet, too many kids, and a good-for-nothing husband.*

And she couldn't even pay Sam. Perhaps that was the most humiliating part of this night. As he finished cleaning and bandaging the burns, Sarah had fished around in her old butter crock, hopelessly wishing she could draw out enough money from the makeshift piggy bank to compensate the doctor for his services. But her chubby fingers had managed to scrape out only a dime and a few pennies. Sarah felt her own face burning as she remembered how she'd turned to Sam – that is, Doctor Giorgi – and sucked in her breath before mumbling, "Doctor Philips usually takes a down payment... Don't know if you'd be willing to do the same?" She'd held out the grimy coins, putting steel in her eyes to show him she wasn't ashamed.

He'd given her that reserved, sweet-as-red-licorice smile and pressed the money back into her palm. "No payment is necessary, Sarah. My reward came from seeing you again tonight." He shook his head, as if he couldn't believe it. "I never expected this. Not in a hundred years, Sarah."

Surprised at the tenderness – there was no other word for it than that – in his voice, Sarah hadn't said a word. Just stared at him and then back at the boy standing behind him. A handsome boy, just like Sam had been two decades ago.

A few more moments passed, just the two of them looking at each other, Sarah growing more and more awkward and Sam seeming as if he wanted to say something. Then Charlie had groaned, and Sam shook himself. "Paulie," he'd turned to his son, "are you ready?"

Paulie – whose attraction to Grace was unmistakable, though the girl didn't seem to realize it – finished packing up his papa's satchel. "Yes, Dad," he replied, fastening the buckle. Sarah heard the boy murmur something to Grace, who stood nearby with that embarrassed stance she *would* adopt, no matter how many times Sarah told her to pick up her head!

"I'm leaving some ointment for the burns," Sam explained, more guarded now. "Change the bandaging every day and clean the wounds. Let me know if there's any sign of infection. I'll return to check on him, but those burns should heal nicely within a few weeks. Not much scarring, either, I should think. As I said, it's a second-degree burn. Extensive, but not disfiguring or life-threatening."

Suddenly, desperation to keep Sam there had overtaken Sarah. "You want some coffee?" she asked, wishing she could offer him some cake to go with it but knowing that her cupboard was empty.

Sam shook his head. "No, we must be getting home," he'd answered.

Heart sinking, Sarah kept her expression emotionless. "Your

wife'll be waiting up for you, I guess," she'd managed.

But a sad smile found its way to Sam's lips. "No, only a housekeeper. My wife – Paulie's mother – died six years ago this April."

"I'm sorry," Sarah automatically answered, but wasn't she glad that a beautiful wife didn't lie awake for him?

"Thank you," Sam replied, "but the memory doesn't come with such a painful twinge now as with the reminder of the mercies of God to me."

The mercies of God...

Even now, looking into the bedroom mirror after Sam and Paulie left, Sarah narrowed her eyes in disbelief. The mercies of God? What were they? The mercies of the Mother of God she could understand. At times, Sarah herself begged the Mother of the Lord to plead for her before her Son. But the mercies of God himself? She shook her head. All of her life had become one long marathon to escape a cold God's sickle-blade, it seemed, no matter what that radio preacher said. What mercy had God shown to her? What mercy did she even deserve?

"None," Sarah whispered aloud. Though she'd always tried to live decently. And she couldn't be blamed for being born. Didn't God owe her something for that, at least?

And how could Sam find the mercies of God in the *death* of his wife? The question puzzled Sarah. Perhaps his wife had been a nasty old hag. But if she'd had anything to do with the raising of their son – a polite, good boy by all appearances – Sam's wife couldn't have been *too* bad. Not bad enough for Sam to consider her death a mercy in and of itself.

A groan from the kitchen couch roused Sarah from her reflections. No sense in pondering such useless things as this, at any rate. She had a sick, grouchy husband to tend. With his eyes bandaged shut, Charlie wasn't likely to be in good humor. *Second-degree burns,* Sam had said, probably from a flash flame in that stupid barrel where Charlie always stood tossing in the trash and leaves.

I really oughta get a haircut, Sarah sighed as she turned from the mirror and waddled back to the kitchen.

CHAPTER THIRTY-EIGHT

E mmeline had just finished watering her geraniums when she heard the front door open and shut. *Geoff's home from school.* She couldn't keep her lips from smiling. Setting down her small watering can, she wiped her hands on her apron and headed for the staircase.

On her way down, Emmeline discerned more than her husband's voice below. *He must have brought a visitor.* She glanced in the hallway mirror to make sure that she looked presentable and then moved into the entryway to greet Geoff and his guest.

Sure enough, Sam Giorgi stood with her husband, hanging up his thick coat. Geoff dropped a quick peck on Emmeline's cheek. "Hello, darling. I found Sam sitting out on our front porch, so I decided to let him in." He gave a wink to Sam.

Surprised, Emmeline looked at Sam. "I didn't hear you knock. I'm sorry if you were sitting out there long."

Sam shook his head. "No, I was waiting for Geoff. He promised to lend me a particular book when I saw him in church on Sunday."

"Will you stay for dinner?" Emmeline asked, hoping that she had bought enough cubed steak.

But Sam declined. "No, I have to get home, but thank you. Paulie's waiting for me. I promised him that we would go fishing. The stream's fully thawed behind the house."

"I won't keep you, then. Excuse me while I go fetch that book," said Geoff, and he scurried off toward the parlor.

"I miss Paulie coming to see us," Emmeline commented as a way to pass the moments until Geoff returned. And she truly did miss Paulie... but she missed Grace more. "It seems our little homework circle has broken up."

Sam nodded and seemed like he was about to say something. "What is it?" Emmeline urged, hoping that he'd not had any objections to his son's participation at the unofficial Kinner Homework Parties.

"Nothing, really," Sam smiled. "My guess is that Paulie doesn't come any longer because Grace doesn't come. He means no slight to your household, Emmeline, I'm sure."

So she wasn't the only one who had noticed Paulie's fascination with Grace. "I didn't think your boy did, Sam. I just wish..." She couldn't go on. Didn't know how to phrase the desire of her heart: to see Grace happy and whole, no longer hobbling under the pain of a difficult life.

Again, Sam paused. Then he said, "You know, I visited Grace's house recently. Her father received a nasty burn on his face, and the family sent for Doctor Philips to come. Philips was attending yet another one of his conferences, so Grace ran for me, instead."

"I've never met her father. What is he like?" wondered Emmeline aloud. Perhaps that would give her more clues into how to help Grace find her way.

Sam shrugged. "I'm not really sure. He was in a lot of pain when I was there. Not entirely conscious. But her mother was the surprise for me." A curious smile grew on Sam's lips.

"Oh?" Emmeline's interest deepened.

"Yes. You see, almost as soon as I saw her, I recognized her." Emmeline saw faint pain tinge Sam's countenance even as he maintained a collected expression. He continued, "Her name is Sarah. She *was* Sarah Antonelli; now she's Sarah Picoletti, is that right?"

"Yes, that's Grace's last name," replied Emmeline, hoping he would continue. Gingerly, she prodded, "So you knew her before she married Grace's father?"

A chuckle escaped Sam's mouth. "I knew her when she wore her hair in pigtails. Sarah and I went to school together. Well," he corrected himself, "I was a few years ahead of her, so we were in different classrooms."

Emmeline smiled, wanting to encourage him to keep telling the story. But she wasn't prepared for what he said next.

"We were engaged," he murmured, his voice lower now.

Emmeline's eyes grew wide as she took in his words. "What happened?" she asked, hoping Sam wouldn't feel that she'd pried too much.

The slight smile dropped off Sam's face. He looked down, his usually commanding demeanor bowed low. "I broke the engagement," he replied. "My family didn't approve of Sarah – too plebeian, too common a girl, they said – and so I dropped her. Truth be told, I thought I could come back for her after I'd used my father's money to get through medical school." He shook his head slowly. "But by then, I'd heard that Sarah was married. You know, I left this town for almost twenty years? And I suppose, when I accepted the position at the hospital a couple of years ago, a little part of me wondered what had become of Sarah Antonelli."

Geoff returned with the book just then, but Emmeline tucked away Sam's story in the back of her mind. She brought it out later, in her evening prayer-time with Geoff.

~ ~ ~

Scrub-scrub, back-and-forth. Grace's hand molded around the chunky bristle-brush as she moved it in short motions across the kitchen floor. The hard, old boards cut into her knees, but the job would only feel more difficult to finish if she stood up for a minute or two. Getting back down on your knees always hurt more than just staying down in the first place.

And wasn't that the truth? Even now, tears smarted at the back of her eyes as she remembered the high joy of the Kinner household. Going in through the kitchen door, schoolbooks in hand... munching cookies or biting into a slice of pie... hearing Mrs. Kinner play hymns on that piano upstairs... enjoying school all the more because it meant that Grace would have homework to bring to the Kinners'... working on essays and math problems with Paulie...

Dunking her brush into the soapy water, she shook her head, trying to clear away those memories that clung like cobwebs to the rafters of her mind. *It's all over,* she told herself. *No point in thinking about any of it – even Paulie – especially Paulie – anymore, Grace!*

Even though he had spoken low in her ear that night that Papa got hurt: "Grace, I miss you. Couldn't I come by and see you

221

sometime?"

And she'd shook her head fiercely: *No.*

A light knock sounded on the back door, startling her. Grace glanced toward her parents' bedroom. Mama had gone to lie down after breakfast; she'd said that her head ached. No wonder with Papa so peevish lately; his burns were healing nicely, but, like the man he was, he still griped about them. Grace just tried to stay out of his way.

The knock sounded again, and Grace set aside the brush. Wiping her hands on her already-wet skirt, she went to the door, curious to see who would visit at this hour of the morning. Most women she knew did their housekeeping chores around this time.

"Hello, Grace." Once again, Mrs. Kinner stood on the other side of the door. And once again, she carried a loaf of bread in her hands.

She's back. Even after I nearly ran her off last time. Grace had never felt so glad to see anyone, had never been so hungry to talk. A bit shyly, she pulled the door open even further. "Won't you come in, Mrs. Kinner?"

~ ~ ~

An hour later, Grace waved her good-bye to Mrs. Kinner. Her heart fairly bubbled with delight. The one subject Grace had been afraid Mrs. Kinner would broach – Grace's return to school – had never been mentioned. *She must realize how impossible it is,* Grace assumed, her momentary joy sinking a little at the thought. *Impossible.*

We're all in the gutter, but some of us are looking at the stars.

Ben's words returned to Grace, but she smirked at them now. *For some of us, there are no stars, Ben,* she replied inwardly, closing the door.

"Who was that, Grace?" Mama leaned against the bedroom doorway, weariness etched into every line of her body. The baby had grown so large. *Surely, Mama'll have her baby soon. It's so late this time.*

"Just Mrs. Kinner, Mama. The lady whose house I used to go to, remember? She came once before," Grace replied, kneeling down by her bucket again. She still had a little of the floor to finish, and noon loomed near. "She brought apple bread, if you want some."

"Not connected with the government, is she?" Mama asked, tucking her gray-streaked hair behind her ears.

"No, Mama," Grace answered. She picked up the brush and felt the muscles in her arms protest as she began to scrub once more.

Mama heaved her way into the kitchen, hand pressed against her lower back. "Good. 'Cause I don't want no government interfering in this family. What happens in our house is our business. Nobody else's."

"Yes, Mama," Grace agreed, going at the floor with fatigued vigor. She certainly didn't want anyone knowing everything that went on in their house, either!

"You almost done with that?" Mama asked.

"Nearly," she managed to reply between scrubbing.

"When you're finished, want to make up some jelly sandwiches for lunch?"

"Sure, Mama. Is Cliff coming home?" Grace asked. Her brother sometimes brought a paper-bag lunch to eat in the schoolyard; other times, he trotted home to eat leftovers or a jelly sandwich or two.

Mama shrugged. "Not sure. I think he took something with him today." She eased her bulk into a chair at the kitchen table.

Grace heard her groan. "You alright, Mama?" she said, anxiety wrapping around her throat.

Wincing, Mama sighed. "Yeah. Wish this baby would come. Must be jumbo size by now."

Grace stood, feeling her knees pop into joint again. She carried the bucket to the back door and tossed the soapy water into the yard, then set the empty bucket and bristle brush beside the door. Returning to the kitchen, she set about slicing bread, thickly spreading strawberry jam across it. Two sandwiches for Mama; one for Grace. She brought them over to the kitchen table as they were – no sense in dirtying napkins. Setting the sandwiches down, Grace plopped into a chair, grateful for the break in her work.

"Bless us, O Lord, and these Thy gifts, which we are about to receive from Thy bounty. Amen," Mama mumbled, crossing herself.

"Amen." Grace echoed Mama's crossing and brought the sandwich to her lips. How wonderful the jam felt as it squished between her teeth. It seemed so long since her small bowl of oatmeal at breakfast.

"Doctor Giorgi... How'd you find him, Grace?" Mama asked suddenly. She chewed bites of her sandwich carefully; Grace knew Mama was missing a few of her back teeth.

"He's Paulie's daddy. I know Paulie from school," Grace answered, fingers picking apart her sandwich. Why did Paulie's name alone conjure up such awkwardness within her?

Mama nodded silently.

"You knew Doctor Giorgi from somewhere, Mama?" Grace ventured to ask. The question had burned a hole in her since the night of Papa's accident. She kept her eyes on her sandwich, waiting for Mama to answer.

A few seconds passed before Mama opened her mouth. "I knew Sam Giorgi when I was a young girl. Hadn't seen him in a long time. A real long time. He left Chetham when I was seventeen. Didn't know he'd moved back here, that's all."

Grace glanced up and found that Mama's eyes contained a distant expression that forbade any more questioning. Sweeping the crumbs from their sandwiches into her palm, Grace rose from the table to continue with her household tasks.

CHAPTER THIRTY-NINE

Two days later, at nine o'clock in the morning, Grace heard that same determined knock on the kitchen door. She wasn't surprised this time when Mrs. Kinner stood there. The woman didn't carry any baked goods, but a workbasket hung on her arm.

"Hello, Grace," she smiled, showing her pretty white teeth. "I wondered if your mother might be up to seeing me today?"

"Mama?" Grace echoed, surprised. Mrs. Kinner had never expressed any interest in meeting Mama before now. What did she want to talk to Mama about?

Mrs. Kinner nodded. "Yes." She gestured to her basket. "I brought my knitting. I'm having trouble with the pattern I'm using, and I remember that you mentioned once that your mother is an excellent knitter."

Vaguely, the memory of telling Mrs. Kinner that Mama had knitted her cardigan came to Grace's mind. Hesitantly, unsure of how Mama would receive her, Grace let Mrs. Kinner into the house.

"Let me just see if Mama's feeling alright. She was sick earlier." Grace headed off to the bedroom, where Mama rested in a wooden rocking chair.

"She wants to meet me?" Mama furrowed her eyebrows when Grace told her Mrs. Kinner's intention.

Biting her lip, Grace nodded. "She... She has some knitting project that she wants your help with." When Mama didn't answer her right away, Grace hurried on, "I can tell her that you don't feel too good today."

But Mama shook her head. "No, I'll come." With a groan, she rose to her feet, stumbling toward the bureau. "Let me just get dressed. Show her into the sitting room, Grace."

Surprise making her heart beat double-time, Grace backed out of the bedroom to settle Mrs. Kinner in the rarely-used sitting room.

~ ~ ~

After that, Emmeline returned to the Picoletti house every few days. She couldn't explain it exactly – couldn't point to chapter and verse in her Bible – but she knew that God wanted her to get to know Grace's mother. And Sarah seemed to welcome her visits, whether Emmeline asked for help with her knitting or merely sat and chatted about mundane things.

Emmeline hadn't given much thought to the woman before Sam Giorgi explained his link to Sarah. And it was an odd connection, certainly! Yet, Emmeline sensed that God had not woven the threads of all their lives together without purpose. Had Grace come into her life, perhaps, so that she could minister to Sarah?

Minister – such a professional word. Emmeline really meant another: *Love*.

~ ~ ~

The moon rose high above Paulie as his feet took along the familiar path to Grace's home. How many times had he walked this way over the past weeks? Ten? No, more like twenty. Each time, he'd stayed just out of sight, gazing up at the room which he guessed belonged to Grace.

What happened? Over the winter, he'd thought Grace had softened toward their friendship. Then, while he blinked, she'd slammed the door on him. Abandoned their afterschool sessions at the Kinners' house. Dropped out of school. Dazed by her words and actions, Paulie had lain low, hoping for Grace to return to them. To him.

But she hadn't. Oh, Paulie had hoped that the night she'd come to beg for Dad's assistance, she would acknowledge his friendship again. But she'd not done that. Not even when he'd told her that he missed her and wanted to visit her. No pressure to go back to school or to the Kinners.

But she'd dropped her eyes and shook her head so fiercely that Paulie was afraid to raise the question again. Instead, almost every night now, he slipped from his sleepless bed and wandered to the Picoletti house, his heart aching. Though she'd refused to accept his visits, Paulie figured that he didn't need Grace's permission to wait.

Or to pray.

CHAPTER FORTY

The baby hung on until the first week of April. Five weeks late. Grace found Mama gripping the corner of the stove with a white-knuckled hand one morning, so early that the frost still clung to the window panes.

"Want me get Mrs. Bailey, Mama?" Grace asked for the tenth time since Christmas. Her heart sped up in anticipation. *The baby's coming! I'm sure it is.*

Mama turned a grimaced face toward her. "No, not yet, Grace."

Grace heard a dripping noise and realized that Mama stood in a puddle of fluid.

Mama glanced at her uneasily, almost apologetically, like a dog who'd vomited and felt bad.

"Don't worry, Mama," Grace hurried. "I'll clean it up."

Weariness already gnawing her face, Mama nodded. "Thanks." She held her hands against her back and shuffled toward the bedroom.

"Tell me when you want me to get Mrs. Bailey," Grace called after the retreating figure. She grabbed an old towel and began mopping up the puddle, nervousness making her fingers shake.

~ ~ ~

Grace gritted her teeth at the guttural moan issuing from Mama's bedroom. She'd long since fetched the old midwife, who relaxed in the rocking chair beside Mama's bed, her knitting held in sun-spotted hands.

Chop the carrots. By the time you finish, her labor will be over. Grace coached herself through each task. She was preparing chicken soup at Mrs. Bailey's instruction. "Your Mama," Mrs. Bailey had said earlier, "will feel weak and want something nourishing to eat after the baby's born." So Grace filled the afternoon hours with making the soup, glad to have something with which to occupy her hands.

"Ouch!" A line of liquid red sparkled on her finger. The knife had slipped. Grace inspected the offending digit. Not too deep. She sucked away the tangy blood and wrapped a scrap of rag around the cut as a makeshift bandage.

Finishing with chopping the vegetables, she poured them into the pot – celery, carrots, potatoes. They plopped into the chicken stock, and she covered the pot with its lid. They'd take a while to soften up.

The sun set. Its rays filtered through the window above the sink, turning the kitchen orange and yellow. Grace pulled the curtains closed a bit and turned impatiently toward Mama's bedroom door.

Silence. Was the baby born, then? No, babies screamed when a woman birthed them, when they came face-to-face with this new reality called life. *I don't blame them.* Licking her lips, Grace edged toward the bedroom door, wondering if Mrs. Bailey would get upset if she knocked.

But Grace didn't have long to wonder. The door opened just wide enough for her to see Mama stretched out on the bed, stifled by her pain. Mrs. Bailey squeezed her short round figure through the doorway, shutting the door behind her.

Unable to speak, Grace beseeched Mrs. Bailey with her eyes.

The Irishwoman's mouth set in a firm line. "Now, listen, child. Your mama's time has come to give birth, but the baby refuses to enter this world. It's come to the end of my ability, I hate to say. Where's your papa? He should get your mama to the hospital."

Numb, Grace shook her head. "I don't know where he is," she managed. Papa had headed out early that morning. "But Mama will never go to the hospital. It's where people go to die, she says." *And it costs far more than we could ever afford to pay.*

The midwife's jaw tightened visibly. *She's afraid.* The sturdy woman usually took everything in easy stride; if Mrs. Bailey sensed something was getting out of control...

"Let me ask Mama," Grace heard herself say, swallowing the lump in her throat.

The midwife hesitated, then nodded. Her crepe-paper hand popped open the door behind her, and she allowed Grace to enter the darkened bedroom.

Mama moved restlessly beneath a thin sheet, her complexion matching it. "Mama?"

Mama's eyes fluttered open, struggling to focus. "Grace," she swallowed. "You shouldn't be in here."

"Mrs. Bailey let me in." Seeing Mama so helpless tore at Grace's chest. "Mama, she wants you to go to the hospital. She says—"

But Mama interrupted before Grace could finish the explanation. "No," she gasped out just before Grace saw a contraction wrestling her body into paralysis. Finally, the pain apparently releasing her, Mama murmured, "Is Mrs. Bailey sure... sure she can't deliver me?"

Grace turned to glance back at the midwife, who immediately gave a nod. "Yeah, Mama. She's sure."

Mama stayed silent for another long moment. "Then get Doctor Philips. I ain't going to no hospital."

Grace nodded and moved to the door.

"Sweet Jesus give wings to your feet, child," Mrs. Bailey intoned, making Grace's heart pound even harder.

"Grace," Mama called just before Grace passed through the door. "Yeah?"

"Do you... Do you think Emmeline would mind coming round?"

"Mrs. Kinner?" Grace blinked in surprise.

"Yeah." Mama grimaced, trying to roll over but not managing it.

"She'd come," Grace said, knowing it for certain.

"Then... Then get her, too."

~ ~ ~

A scream pierced the still black night, waking Charlie from a thick slumber.

"What's that?" He felt Gertrude tense beside him as she asked the question.

"She must've had the baby," Charlie mumbled. Gertrude didn't like it when he referred to Sarah outright, so he always used a pronoun. They both knew of whom he spoke.

His girlfriend shivered, clutching the coverlet to her chin. "Does it always sound so... so awful? Like someone got themselves murdered?"

In that moment, Charlie felt more than his usual serving of disdain for Gertrude. "Yeah," he said. "She has big babies. Hurts coming out, ya know."

Gertrude stayed silent for a moment, maybe contemplating his words. Then she offered, "Or she's just a crybaby."

"Yeah," said Charlie carelessly, knowing it was far from the truth.

"I mean, she had the baby, didn't she? She didn't die or nothin'." Gertrude persisted. "Couldn't have been that bad."

"Naw," he agreed, to shut her up. He needed his sleep, after all.

CHAPTER FORTY-ONE

Eleven pounds, six ounces of human flesh-and-bone. Though, as a young teenager, Emmeline had accompanied her mother to visit poor new mothers, she had never seen such a large baby born as Sarah's.

Carefully, Emmeline picked up the infant from its place beside nearly-unconscious Sarah. She marveled in his perfectly-formed fingers, his red-flushed skin, the black hair thatching his domed head.

"Quite a lot of tearing you've got there, Sarah," Doctor Philips commented, his deft hands finishing the sewing. "You'll have pain for quite a while, I should think. And no wonder, with such a baby. Almost twelve pounds."

Sarah didn't reply; she just leaned her head back on her pillow and closed her eyes.

The doctor turned to Emmeline, fatigue draping his body. "Will you be staying here with her? I hate to leave her by herself."

Emmeline nodded. "Yes, I'll stay with her for as long as she needs me." She clasped the warm bundle of baby nearer to her chest and gazed at Sarah, painfully sleeping now.

"I gave her something to make her rest easier," Doctor Philips informed her. "That's the best thing for her right now. She'll feed him when she wakes up."

"Alright." The baby nestled in the crook of Emmeline's arm, as if he belonged there.

"And Sarah usually puts her babies in a bureau drawer, lined with a blanket and maybe a hot water bottle. Oh." He pointed toward a drawer laid next to the far side of the bed, already lined with old blankets. "There it is. She must have prepared it before she went into labor."

Emmeline nodded, her gaze fastened to the baby's tiny flushed face.

"Emmeline." Doctor Philips placed a fatherly hand on Emmeline's shoulder. She looked up to meet his kind eyes. They exuded his concern. "You oughtn't stay here. I know how much you desired your own…" He trailed off, letting her fill in the rest.

She smiled. "The Lord is my strength, Doctor. Don't worry about me."

Doctor Philips sighed, and his hand slid off her shoulder. "Alright."

The doctor left, but Emmeline didn't place the baby in the drawer. Rather, she made certain that Sarah was comfortably asleep and then sat down in the creaky rocking chair next to the bed. Softly humming a hymn, she rocked the baby until dawn touched the windowsill with its golden light.

~ ~ ~

Emmeline had come. Sarah hadn't been able to speak because of the pain last night, but she'd seen her friend arrive, a dark-haired angel, just as Doctor Philips came. And Sarah had been so thankful, so comforted by this woman who had spoken words of compassion and prayed over her for the past few weeks. *I've never known anyone like her. She owes me nothing and yet gives me so much.* Emmeline had stayed through the long hours of grueling labor, holding Sarah's hand, whispering words of encouragement and things from the Bible.

Hovering now between waking and sleeping, Sarah's thoughts whirled to her daughter. Poor Grace! Wherever her daughter was, she surely must have heard Sarah's scream at the very end of the labor, when the baby had torn its way from her body. Everyone must have heard it; even Charlie…

~ ~ ~

He'd waited until late afternoon when Gertrude headed off to do some shopping and he'd seen that lady-friend of Sarah's walk off the property. *His* property. "Don't see why I feel like I have to sneak up to my own house," Charlie grumbled as he scraped his way to the back door.

When he entered the kitchen, he heard the floorboards creak over his head. Relief poured over him. Good; Grace must be doing something upstairs. He couldn't have said why he'd come into to the house anyway; it wasn't mealtime. It couldn't be to see his wife and newborn, yet his feet brought him over to the bedroom that he'd shared with her for nearly twenty years.

Sarah looked like such an shabby thing, couched in that bed that sagged so in the middle. It had been his papa and mama's bed before him, Charlie remembered as he looked down at his wife's plump form. Her arm extended over the quilt; she wore a much-laundered nightgown, thin as a dish rag and not nearly as pretty. Someone must've brushed her hair and tied it back from her face; it climbed over her shoulder in a thin graying rope, the little tassel at the end touching the smooth downy head against her chest. Sarah'd fallen asleep nursing the infant, who nestled close as a squirrel to its mother's body.

It. Whether a boy or yet another girl, the baby certainly looked healthy, not yellow as a banana like Grace and Cliff had been at birth. As Charlie watched, the baby gave a tiny yawn and snuggled even nearer on Sarah's bosom. He leaned against the doorframe and gazed at the woman and her freshly-made child, fighting the emotions twisting his face this way and that in the long seconds before Sarah opened her eyes.

He didn't know what wakened her. She'd always been a light sleeper, so maybe it was just the insignificant movements of the living thing at her breast that did it. Stirring, Sarah didn't see him there at first, leaning back into the shadowy doorway, dark coat still drawn over his body. She blinked away the cobwebs of sleep, pushing one reddened hand over her eyes, tucking a strand of hair behind her ear. Charlie heard the deep sigh Sarah gave as she remembered the little bit of flesh in the crook of her elbow. She shifted her body carefully so that the baby wouldn't wake, raising herself up a little more on the flattened pillows with her free hand. Charlie stuffed down the guilt that rose up inside him as he saw her struggling and knew that he could help her... but wouldn't.

Well. It was now or never. No reason for him to keep standing here in the doorway of his own bedroom, like a visitor, rather than the master of his house. Charlie cleared his throat, hacking up a little wad of mucus so it wouldn't sound like he was trying to be polite for Sarah's sake. He saw her gaze fly up at the sound just as he stepped into the light.

She tensed but didn't drop her eyes. Charlie kept his own as unreadable as he could. *She won't get the best of me.* The bare light bulb created shadows on Sarah's face and neck and shoulders. *She looks old,* he thought, taking in the creases on her forehead, the wrinkles on her chest, the freckled skin on her once-milky upper arms. The contrast between the newly-minted baby and the timeworn bride of his youth brought the bile of revulsion to Charlie's mouth. *I wish Gertrude lay there with my child instead of her.*

But he didn't really; even Charlie knew this. He wished he was a young man again, handsome, dapper, not lacking any women who were eager to hang on his every word. Looking at Sarah made him realize afresh that he was just old Charlie Picoletti, father of seven, strapped by God and law to an aging, offended wife. But – thank the saints! - Gertrude waited for him in the cottage out back, barren of children, yes, but always willing to assure him of his manliness and youth. His eyes fastened on the child at Sarah's bosom. Six children – now seven – Didn't Sarah know when to stop? What did she think she was, a rabbit?

"Did they tell you, Charlie?" Sarah asked in her low voice, the only sound in that ticking silence. "It's a boy." Pride sparkled out of her eyes as she turned the baby toward him a little.

He looked at it, flesh of his flesh, combined with that of Sarah, who'd risked her life once again to deliver that small parcel of humanity. Tightly-wrapped, it lay pink-faced and wrinkled, at peaceful rest. So conflicted between instinct and desire, Charlie didn't move; he knew Sarah wanted him to go over to the bed and pick up the child, hold it against himself. He saw it in Sarah's eyes: It would be her way of claiming him again, her way of triumphing over the woman in the cottage out back.

What right has she to triumph? The thought made him straighten, made the molten emotion in Charlie's heart harden into resolve. *Gertrude lives out in a cottage, hiding away from notice, while I've given Sarah all this – the house, my name, my dough - besides the children. What right does Sarah have to complain about anything?* She wanted him to talk, to compliment her, to return to her arms because of this baby? He thought not. Most certainly he would *not*. He jutted out his jaw and stared at Sarah, wanting to burn holes through her into the headboard for all the trouble she'd caused him. Some women at least had the decency to die off.

"Well, Charlie," she said at last, breaking the silence that had become awkward quickly, "Do you have any names in mind? I-I know we haven't talked about it much…" Her voice trailed off, and she dropped her eyes from his.

Much? They hadn't discussed the baby at all, much less what it would be christened. Charlie snorted. "Name him what you want," he stated, shrugging and turning to go. He'd show Sarah that there'd be no manipulating Charlie Picoletti.

"What do you mean? Don't you want…?"

The thin needy tone coming from the bed annoyed him, and Charlie turned his head just enough so that Sarah could hear him. Why must he repeat himself? Couldn't she hear him the first time? "I don't want nothing, Sarah," he snapped out. "He's not my concern," he added, using one of Gertrude's fancy phrases to intimidate her.

"He's your child," Sarah gasped. "Your own flesh and blood, Charlie!"

The baby started to cry at her slightly raised voice, and Charlie gritted his teeth at the high-pitched mewing. "Is he, Sarah? I didn't want him in the first place, and I don't care what you do with him or what you name him. Just don't name him after me."

Charlie strode out of that confining bedroom and into the cool, dark hall. Glad to breathe freely at last, he paused for just a moment to collect himself. Behind him, he could hear Sarah weeping. She would hide her face in the bedclothes, Charlie knew, so that she didn't further disturb the baby. *Let her cry.* He felt no remorse. She'd had it coming to her, after all.

CHAPTER FORTY-TWO

"Thought I told you to stay away from the house!" Charlie growled through gritted teeth. Why couldn't women ever listen? Gertrude had lived here for, what? More than six months! And she still waltzed around the main residence in broad daylight. If there was anything that would anger Sarah, that would be it!

In the little cove behind the cottage, Gertrude squinched up her nose, peering up at him with narrowed eyes. "I don't like staying down at the cottage all day, Chuckie," she complained. "When are you going to divorce that old woman, anyway, and let me come live at the big house?"

Not over my dead body. "You gotta be patient, Trudy," he evaded. "I'm doing the best I can."

She sneered as only Gertrude could. "Well, *I* don't see you doing nothing. Staying around that wife of yours is all. What, 'cause she cleaned up your face for you when you burned it?"

He would ignore her. Just let her talk on and on; he'd not say anything. Soon enough, Gertrude would run out of words.

"You're a fool, Chuckie, that's what you are. You think I'm gonna stay around and wait for you to get everything straightened out?"

He shrugged. Let her leave. He could always get another girl.

~ ~ ~

Mrs. Kinner stayed at the Picoletti house for a full month

following the birth, going home only to fix up a batch of meals for Mr. Kinner every few days. She bathed Mama, cared for the infant, and helped Grace with the housework and cooking. And Grace knew such gratitude toward the woman; surely the Mother of our Lord must be just like her!

"Grace," Mrs. Kinner said one day as she rocked the baby, "did you keep the geranium plant I gave you for Christmas?"

Startled, Grace nodded. "Of course."

Truth be told, Grace had found herself too busy these past few weeks to pay too much mind to the geranium. Actually, she probably hadn't watered it as much as she should have. What if it had died? "Uh, excuse me, ma'am," she said, hurrying out of the kitchen.

Her bare feet clattered up the staircase, her heart pounding in anticipation. Would she find the plant crumpled and dry from neglect, unable to support itself on its wobbly stalks? Would she never see the red flowers her own plant could produce?

Half-afraid to look, Grace peered into her bedroom. There, in the still stale air, punctuated by the late April sunlight flooding through the windows, the plant held firmly to its place on the sill. She approached it with slow steps and gently lifted up the carved pot.

The soil in the pot was dry; there was no denying that. And a few stems and leaves had grown brittle and brown. Yet, the sight of three bright green shoots flooded Grace's soul with joy.

"Mrs. Kinner! Mrs. Kinner!" Grace forgot all sense of decorum and reserve as she flew down the staircase, pot cradled against her chest.

Mrs. Kinner glanced up, obviously surprised at Grace's unusually boisterous entrance. "What is it?"

Grace took a breath of shuddering joy. "The geranium. It's going to live." She couldn't keep the grin off her face. "I thought... I hadn't taken the time to water it these past few weeks, and so I thought... But it's going to live anyway. See?" She held the plant out for Mrs. Kinner's inspection, and the scent of geraniums filled her nostrils.

Mrs. Kinner gave Grace a smile that reached her eyes. "So it is."

~ ~ ~

The evening light had already dimmed, and Emmeline turned on the lamps when she entered the kitchen, humming a hymn under her breath. Sarah recognized it from the radio minister's broadcasts, but she didn't remember the title.

"You'll have to go home soon," Sarah remarked, hoping her friend – truest in all ways – would protest.

But Emmeline nodded. "Yes, but I'll visit you often. And I wouldn't trade the time that I've spent with you for the world." As the younger woman took a seat at the table, Sarah admired her grace once more.

"What would you name him?" Sarah asked suddenly. Tracing the baby's rounded cheeks with her rough index finger, she felt sorry that he'd gone so long without a name.

Emmeline looked startled. "Oh, Sarah. You have some favorite names, I'm sure." She didn't bring up Charlie's preferences; Sarah had told her already about his reaction to the baby's birth.

"I've used up my favorites on the other kids. Please, what would you name him?"

Sarah watched sadness touch Emmeline's face. "If he was mine," she stated slowly, "I would name him David. It means *beloved.*"

David. It was a good name. Naming her son that... Well, it was the least Sarah could do after all Emmeline had done for her. "Thanks," Sarah offered.

Emmeline smiled and the shadow of sadness disappeared. She leaned forward in her chair. "May I pray for you and your family, Sarah?"

"Yes, please do," Sarah responded immediately, bouncing the baby a little to quiet him. In this past month, a strange working had begun in her heart, a working that she was only just becoming aware of, and the implications of which she was yet unsure. In the compassionate words and hands of Emmeline, Sarah knew she'd experienced something of the love of God, the Savior who gazed down at her from the crucifix on her bedroom wall. As she learned to trust Emmeline, even in her pain, Sarah had begun to believe in Christ in a new and personal way. She couldn't explain it; she was no priest or even a radio minister. But she felt it; she *knew* it.

Their hands clasped in this last evening together, the two women brought the Picoletti household before the throne of God, Emmeline with her sure, steady prayer and Sarah with a halting few sentences. They prayed for Grace; for Ben; for Nancy and Lou; for Cliff; and for Evelyn; for this new baby; and, lastly, Sarah said humbly, "Lord, I could be wrong, but I think it's not right the way our family has been going these last few years. I've... I've not done right by my children. I want to, but I'm not sure how to go about it, what with Charlie and all. Show me. Deliver us."

That last sentence popped out before Sarah knew it. *What did I say?* She peered over at Emmeline, but her friend didn't appear shocked, just a little curious. So Sarah went on, speaking from her heart. "And I will give You whatever You ask to thank You."

It seemed silly. After all, what could she, an impoverished woman, give God?

CHAPTER FORTY-THREE

Gertrude was gone. Sarah was sure of it. A black Roadster had snaked into the driveway around eleven o'clock that morning, while Charlie'd been away. Through the kitchen curtain's veil, Sarah had watched the bottled blond scuttle up the path. A stuffed carpet bag tucked under each arm, Gertrude had hopped into the passenger side with the speed of a mourning dove escaping a hawk.

Maybe he asked her to leave... Maybe the baby's made Charlie think everything over... Her prior experiences with her husband lectured Sarah on the unlikeliness of that, but then, the God whom Sarah was just beginning to know could work miracles, couldn't He? Was this the answer to her prayer?

Hope prickled through her heart, and Sarah couldn't wait for Charlie to come home tonight.

~ ~ ~

The rain pinged on the barn roof as Grace finished milking Bessie that afternoon. Just as she rose from the milking stool, she heard a cough outside the barn door. *Papa.* He'd lain low for several weeks now, not even coming into the house for meals.

Her arm straining under the weight of the milk-pail, Grace peeked between the slats of the barn door. Better to figure out now where Papa lurked so that she could avoid him, if possible.

However, instead of Papa, Paulie stood there, taking cover under

241

the overhang, blowing his nose into his handkerchief! "Why is he here?" she asked aloud. She shrank away from the door. *I thought it was finished for good.*

He kept glancing toward the house, probably figuring she was there. If he went inside the house, Grace would have to talk to him. More so than if she just shooed him away now. Gathering her courage, Grace pulled open the door.

"Hi, Paulie," she forced the words out of her tight throat. Why did seeing him make her want to cry, to weep even, like the sky was weeping now?

He whirled around, handkerchief still to his nose. "Grace!" he gasped and gave a final wipe.

She wouldn't let his dimpled smile soften her. "Why are you here?" she asked, hardening her face, making herself impervious to him, she hoped.

Tucking away his handkerchief, Paulie squared his dripping shoulders and looked at her. To her surprise, he wore a stern expression – gentle but firm, and Grace glimpsed the man he would become – a man who would command her respect.

He took the heavy bucket from her hand and set it down on the ground. "I'm here," he stated, stepping so close to her that she could smell the mint on his breath, "because I care about you, Grace, and I want to help you in whatever way I can."

She raised her chin and met his eyes with only a slight flinch. She mustn't let him break down her barrier; she wouldn't think about the pearl clip earrings hidden away in her desk drawer.

"And what's more," Paulie went on, his throat bobbing as he swallowed, "God cares about you, Grace. Jesus Christ cares about you!"

The bitterness in the laugh she threw at him scared her. "Cares about me? God cares about me? Didn't you hear any of what I told you weeks and weeks ago?"

Again, just like last time, her wild, raw words dug into him; Grace could see that and was glad for it. Let Paulie suffer a little; it was nothing compared to what she had suffered for her whole life! She defied him with hard, tearless eyes.

But gently, Paulie took her cold hand in his warm one. She tensed but couldn't resist. "Grace, I don't pretend to understand the hurt you've undergone. I... I know some of the facts – not all of them.

But even if I knew them all, I would say the same thing to you: What men mean for evil, God uses for good." His eyes held hers with a fervency she'd not seen him display before now. "He is a *good God*, Grace. He gave His Son for you!"

"I know that!" Grace snapped, angry that her vision had begun to blur. "I go to church, same as you! Just because I'm Catholic doesn't make me a heathen," she huffed.

"Sure. But you are a sinner, same as me, same as everyone else. And it's that sin in the world – in us - that causes all this pain, Grace. We're not right on the inside, so how can things go right on the outside?"

She gave him the sourest smile she could muster. "So you're saying that if I become more religious, I'll have a happier life? That you and the Kinners and your dad are more religious than I am, and that's the reason why God gives you all that good stuff, why you all have such great lives?" It sounded ridiculous.

He frowned. "No, Grace. What I'm saying is, it doesn't matter who you are: doctor, teacher, junker, whatever. It matters who you belong to. You know, you're so concerned with the badness of your circumstances that you don't stop to think of who allowed those circumstances to come into your life."

That was where he was wrong. The bitter tang rose in her heart. She knew exactly Who had allowed these circumstances. And she believed what the Bible, what the Church taught: that God was indeed all-powerful. Omnipotent. Mighty to save... *and yet He wouldn't*. So she submitted, not with the love of a daughter, but with the rancor of a slave...

He grasped both of her elbows, drawing her face close to his. "*God* did. God allowed those circumstances *for your good*."

"What good? What possible good could come from my circumstances in life?" Grace burst out, not caring what he thought of her.

Paulie's voice stayed low and earnest. "So you'd seek Him and find Him, even though He's never been far from you, Grace."

"Well, He certainly found a funny way of doing that!"

"What?" Paulie gave her a look of surprise.

Charming. A little boy who'd never felt the knife go into his chest, who'd never had to bite the bullet.

"Of... what would you call it? Bringing me good? Making me find

Him?" Grace snarled. Hearing the anger in her own voice caused a thrill through her bones. "What do you know of it, anyway, Paulie Giorgi? You live in your grand palace. Your papa dotes on you. You have every chance of success in life. You've never known what it is to suffer – to watch all of your dreams die and turn to ash!" She wrenched her arm from his grasp as if he held it tightly.

He stood quietly for a long moment. Only a lone robin broke the silence with its evening serenade. "My mother died," Paulie murmured at last. "When I was eleven, she died from a brain aneurism that we never knew she had. It was… really, really hard."

Paulie met Grace's stare with tear-filled eyes. Her heart broke a little, but she refused to show it. So his mama died? So what? Grace wished her mother could have died so that Mama wouldn't have had to endure this nightmare of a life with Papa.

"So I kinda understand where you're coming from. With the suffering, I mean," he added. "In a small way."

"You don't understand anything at all," Grace ground out from between clenched teeth. "And don't say that you do."

He went on as if he hadn't heard her. "I felt lost. Completely alone, even though I had my dad. He was engrossed in his own grief over Mother. And," he sucked in a deep breath, "that's when I understood the Cross."

"What?" Grace gave him her best glare of disbelief.

"That Jesus came and suffered, just as we do, the effects of sin in this world. The effects of *our sin*, Grace! He suffered *for me. For you.* And He didn't have to. He identified with us – broken humanity - to save us from our sin, to restore us to sit on the Father's knee. Jesus bore the real burden – the sin of the whole world – so that we could be made whole again."

Her ache widened and deepened at his speech. She longed to conquer this unending agony that lashed through her heart. "Go away, Paulie," she commanded. She tucked her unruly hair behind her ears so that she could glower at him good and hard. So that he'd know she really meant it.

And he did. Slowly, Paulie nodded. "Alright, Grace."

But he didn't leave right away. He stood, hesitating, as if waiting for her to regret her words. So Grace picked up the heavy bucket and turned from him, running toward the house through the thick rain, not caring if the milk splashed on the ground.

When she turned again, Paulie had gone.

CHAPTER FORTY-FOUR

The potato skins dropped into a pile on the table. Sarah's hands trembled a bit as she peeled the spuds, and she strictly told them to stop shaking, lest she cut herself good.

Just as she told her heart to stop hoping.

Bang. There he was, with the car. The spring rain came down heavy; Charlie'd want something hot to drink, maybe with a dash of anisette in it. Sarah rose to her feet and hurried to pour a cup of coffee, black and thick as the night that crept around the house.

She had just added the splash of colorless liqueur when the kitchen door scraped open. Breathless with anticipation, Sarah turned from the counter, holding out the steaming cup. "Made you some coffee," she offered.

Charlie stared at her for a long moment. The rainwater dripped off his hat and shoulders onto the floorboards, leaving a dark mark.

"I put anisette in it, the way you like it," Sarah faltered. Why did he stay silent? Had she been wrong to hope that maybe, just maybe...?

Finally, Charlie took off his hat. Looking at him, Sarah could still see the young man whose laughing company had once numbed the memories of Sam Giorgi's betrayal, who had made her his wife, who had given her a few short years of happiness and devotion. Maybe it wasn't too late to start again. Maybe God would give a second chance...

"You didn't have to," he grunted, and he seemed angry as he ripped the mug from her hand. But Charlie had always been a little rough around the edges.

"I wanted to," Sarah replied softly. As he took a satisfied slurp, she picked up the paring knife again and sat down at the table. Should she wait for him to speak? Or was it up to her to broach the subject of Gertrude leaving and what that meant for them?

Charlie drank it up fast, like he always did. Afraid that he would disappear back outside again before they'd talked, Sarah forced herself to open her mouth. "I saw... her leave this morning," she said, stealing glances to see his reaction.

Charlie just looked at her, his face blank.

"Did you ask her to leave, Charlie?" Sarah managed to ask, unnerved by his silence. "Are you... Are you coming back? 'Cause, if you are, I'm glad. We... We don't have to talk about the past, you know. We can just go on from here, like it never happened. We can—"

His explosive curse gagged her. She stared at him, stunned. The paring knife clattered to the tabletop, finding a nest among the potato peels.

The utensil's movement must have caught Charlie's eye. He lurched toward the table and snatched up the knife. The breath whooshed out of Sarah's lungs as her husband towered over her, his face masked in crimson rage. Sweat broke out on her forehead when she felt the blade against her neck.

"You," he growled. "Did you tell her to leave?"

"No. Honest, Charlie, I didn't," Sarah whimpered. She could hear the baby stirring in her bedroom.

He stared down at her for long seconds, and her loud heart kept the time. *There ain't no feeling left in him for me.* And despite the menacing knife at her throat, it was that thought that made Sarah weep.

"You're not worth the trouble it would take to kill you," Charlie snarled finally. He flung the paring knife to the floor and turned away.

The door banged shut behind him.

~ ~ ~

He couldn't believe it. *She took almost everything!* With a forceful sweep of his arm, Charlie threw all the cheap dishware to the cottage floor.

Good thing he'd kept his spare change on him today; Gertrude probably would have had no qualms about snatching that, too. She'd taken the silver teapot, his small hoard of cash, and even Charlie's own cigarettes!

Left him! He – Charlie Picoletti! How *dare* she! Didn't she know a woman should follow through with her promises of love?

"Can't ever trust a woman," he muttered. Just when you thought you had them submissive again, they bucked. Bless all the saints if Charlie could figure out why!

He kicked the table leg savagely. He'd figure out what to do. But first… first he needed a drink.

Shoving his wallet back into his pocket, Charlie headed for Kingpin's Club with a violent thirst.

~ ~ ~

Sarah wept. One hand rubbing at her swollen eyes, the other clutching little David close against her body, she wept and rocked and wept some more. No need to worry about anyone hearing her; Cliff and Grace had escaped upstairs to their bedrooms after a silent supper. No doubt Grace at least had overheard some of her and Charlie's fight.

Fight. Sarah was so tired of it. So very tired of… *everything.* Dully, she glanced up at the small crucifix adorning the wall above the radio. And *He* certainly hadn't helped her, despite her bargaining prayer.

But I meant it. I would have given anything He asked of me, if only He had helped me. If only He had saved me. The tears dripped off the tip of her nose, splashing onto the baby's head. Carefully, she took the corner of the swaddling blanket and wiped away the moisture. Sarah wished for Emmeline's company, for her soothing words, but the woman had returned home for good a day ago.

It was past time for that minister to come on the radio, but Sarah didn't know if she could bear to listen to his airy words of hope tonight. Not when a truer darkness bit at her all around. Yet, perhaps he was done preaching by now; maybe the choir was singing. And anything was better than sitting here, alone and silent with none to comfort her, now that she'd nearly spent all her tears.

She flicked on the dial. The radio crackled. Then the minister's familiar baritone emerged. He was reading Scripture. Sarah recognized the passage vaguely and found herself caught up in the story as the minister told it:

"Now a certain man was sick, named Lazarus, of Bethany, the town of Mary and her sister Martha. (It was that Mary which anointed the Lord with ointment, and wiped his feet with her hair, whose brother Lazarus was sick.) Therefore his sisters sent unto him, saying, Lord, behold, he whom thou lovest is sick.

When Jesus heard that, he said, This sickness is not unto death, but for the glory of God, that the Son of God might be glorified thereby.

Now Jesus loved Martha, and her sister, and Lazarus. When he had heard therefore that he was sick, he abode two days still in the same place where he was. Then after that saith he to his disciples, Let us go into Judaea again.

His disciples say unto him, Master, the Jews of late sought to stone thee; and goest thou thither again?

Jesus answered, Are there not twelve hours in the day? If any man walk in the day, he stumbleth not, because he seeth the light of this world. But if a man walk in the night, he stumbleth, because there is no light in him.

These things said he: and after that he saith unto them, Our friend Lazarus sleepeth; but I go, that I may awake him out of sleep.

Then said his disciples, Lord, if he sleep, he shall do well. Howbeit Jesus spake of his death: but they thought that he had spoken of taking of rest in sleep.

Then said Jesus unto them plainly, Lazarus is dead. And I am glad for your sakes that I was not there, to the intent ye may believe; nevertheless let us go unto him.

Then said Thomas, which is called Didymus, unto his fellow disciples, Let us also go, that we may die with him.

Then when Jesus came, he found that he had lain in the grave four days already. Now Bethany was nigh unto Jerusalem, about fifteen furlongs off: And many of the Jews came to Martha and Mary, to comfort them concerning their brother.

Then Martha, as soon as she heard that Jesus was coming, went and met him: but Mary sat still in the house. Then said Martha unto Jesus, Lord, if thou hadst been here, my brother had not died. But I know, that even now, whatsoever thou wilt ask of God, God will give it thee.

Jesus saith unto her, Thy brother shall rise again.

Martha saith unto him, I know that he shall rise again in the resurrection at the last day.

Jesus said unto her, I am the resurrection, and the life: he that believeth in me, though he were dead, yet shall he live: And whosoever liveth and believeth in me shall never die. Believest thou this?

She saith unto him, Yea, Lord: I believe that thou art the Christ, the Son of God, which should come into the world."

Strange, Sarah had been brought up in the Church but hadn't paid much attention to this story ever before – except perhaps as a proof that God could work miracles if He chose. That He could even raise the dead.

"Jesus asked Martha, *Believest thou this?*" the radio minister stated. "Believest thou that Jesus is the resurrection and the life? And I ask you, my friend: Do you believe? Believest *thou?* Not that Jesus will raise your dead son, your dead wife, your dead father back to *this* life. No, my friend, believest thou *in Him?* Believest thou?"

In Him? Of course Sarah believed that He was real; that He was God! Who didn't believe that? But how did that have anything to do with real life, with the bitter tang of daily living with Charlie?

Didn't the story have more to do with why Jesus had waited to come to Lazarus' aid? Martha made a good point: *If thou hadst been here, my brother would not have died.*

And Jesus had not denied it. He could have come… if He wanted to. He could have given her a happily-ever-after… if He'd wanted to.

"And Martha believes," the radio preacher continued. "She believes that He is the Resurrection and the Life. That the one who believes in Him will not perish but have life forevermore. She believes *in Him.* That *He* is the Christ – the Coming One – who will weep with her – who will wipe all the tears from her eyes."

The clock ticked. *Wipe all the tears from her eyes…* How good that sounded. Sarah rocked slowly, intent on the voice emerging from the radio's speaker.

"There is a larger story here, friends," the minister stated. "A bigger story than the death of one of Jesus' friends. Jesus doesn't take His friend's death lightly; later, we read that He wept. Yet, Jesus knows that there is a bigger story – a great life – beyond the grave. And that sometimes, deep sorrows are permitted by a loving Friend so that the most beautiful story – that of resurrection – can be told."

He paused. "Do you have sorrow, friend? Is there a prayer Jesus seems to have not answered with a yes? Do you weep?"

Sarah nodded, feeling the tears bubble up again, spilling down her cheeks.

"Run like Martha, then. Run to the Savior of the world. Fall at His feet, and reveal to Him your broken heart. He is the Resurrection and the Life. Believe in Him as the One who has taken all your sins, all your griefs upon Himself... and who will exchange them for the crown of life, which He has purchased for you."

Slowly, the notion began to grow within Sarah. Perhaps – perhaps – her current life with Charlie was just a small part of the bigger story – perhaps if this God was good – that if He permitted destruction and bitter disappointment as Sarah'd known in her own life, as Martha had experienced in Lazarus' death – it was only so that He might have the glory of Resurrecting Life – and that she might, in some strange and unfathomable way, share in that life. A life beyond the grave.

"I believe," she whispered into the quiet kitchen. "You and I both know, dear God, that I'm a sinner. And there's no help for me in this life or the next except through You. I... trust You. I believe, like Martha, that You are the Resurrection and the Life. I put my faith in You."

And Sarah knew that, though He'd tarried, Jesus the Christ had come to Chetham, Rhode Island, that day and given new life.

"No matter what happens with Charlie, God," she said tentatively – and anything could happen, after all. "I'm putting my bets on You. You've got me, no matter what comes."

CHAPTER FORTY-FIVE

The rain gave way to an opulent early May sunrise. Waking before Geoff, Emmeline took an enjoyable amble around her gardens before strolling up the pathway to her front door. The sunshine poured over the porch railings, making the wood shine even whiter. Geoff must have given it a fresh coat of paint this week.

She climbed the steps slowly, taking her time, enjoying the feeling of being home for good again. But she wasn't sorry for the time spent with the Picolettis, either. So much good had come out of that. For Sarah and Grace, yes, but also for Emmeline herself.

Winter has passed. There would not be another frost... not until next year, at least. Letting the washed spring air fill her lungs, Emmeline recognized that the time had come.

~ ~ ~

An hour later, she hooked the last basket onto the porch beam. The plants had not flowered yet – she would have to wait for summer for that – but Emmeline knew that they would. *In His time.*

Like His promises. Though she didn't carry a child in her arms, though her womb could never bear again, God would not fail her. He would give good to her, His child.

Lightly, she ran a finger through a ruffle of green leaves. The spicy fragrance, unique to geraniums, wafted on the breeze, and the old hymn rose in Emmeline's mind: *The bud may have a bitter taste, but sweet will be the flower.*

~ ~ ~

"He never knew what hit him, ma'am." Grace entered the kitchen, skirt full of eggs, just in time to hear the man say it to Mama.

Mama's floury hands hung limp by her side. She must have been kneading the lump of dough that sat lonely on the wide table when this visitor arrived with evidently disturbing news. Near the counter, Cliff stood motionless, a soda cracker half-way to his mouth.

Grace stepped over to Cliff as she peered at the man. It was Mick Nelson, one of the town's volunteer firemen. A nice enough man. He used to give Grace and Cliff pennies if they'd carry his love notes to their sister Lou. Now, his fingers twiddled with his cap nervously, and he wouldn't meet Mama's eyes.

"What is it? What's happened?" Grace heard herself asking, as if from far away.

Mick glanced up at Mama, who nodded. "Your papa... He was hit by a truck last night on his way home from..." The man trailed off, obviously feeling awkward.

The blood rushed through her ears, yet Grace felt curiously detached, as if hearing about someone she barely knew. "Is he going to be alright?"

Mick paused. Grace licked her lips.

"Your father's dead, Grace."

She stared blankly at Mick. Papa was dead. Yet, somehow, that knowledge only carved more emptiness into her heart.

CHAPTER FORTY-SIX

Papa will be buried tomorrow. The numb thought paraded through Grace's mind as she passed by the cemetery. The loud lilt of the wren accentuated the loneliness of the place, and she hurried on her way, the scarf tied over her hair blowing a little in the wind.

The stone steps of the church rose before her, and she wondered again why she felt drawn to come, when she would be here tomorrow for Papa's mass. Yet Grace had sensed the constraint tugging at her all day. At last, after supper, she'd given in.

She sat in one of the back rows. Other parishioners had come as well, praying for sick or sinning loved ones or for their heart's desire, no doubt. A man wept in the aisle before the altar; Grace saw Father Frederick move to speak with him.

Why am I here? The question darted into her mind again, and she turned her eyes to the statue of the crucified Christ, that image that had always repelled her with its aloofness.

I'm afraid. There, she had admitted it. But afraid of what? She met the Lord Christ's stony, dolorous gaze, seeking, begging. *Paulie talks as if You are the answer to all of my problems. But then in the same breath, he tells me that You placed me here!*

"*That you would seek Him and find Him, even though He's never far from you...*"

The tears sprang up as she remembered Paulie's words: "*He is a good God, Grace!*"

How could she believe in this good God, how could she trust Him, when Papa — the man upon whom she should have been able to rely – had failed her? When she had to fight for herself against the whims of her earthly father, how could she begin to trust this Man's Father? This Heavenly Father who had given her so much suffering in life?

"He suffered for me. For you."

"You ask too much," she whispered aloud to the statue. Dashing away the moisture on her cheeks, Grace rose to her feet and slipped from the sanctuary.

But her feet took her home the long way, past First Baptist. It looked dark and empty, unlike the church she'd just left. It figured. These people had no worries, nothing for which to beseech God on their knees.

So intent on her acidic thoughts, Grace almost bumped into a waist-high statue near First Baptist's steps. The setting sun gleamed on the three-or-four-foot-high white stone, and she squinted to see it clearly.

It was a portrayal of the Good Shepherd, with a lamb clasped in one arm, his staff gripped in his hand. A full-grown sheep peeked from behind him, closely at his heels. There was writing on the statue's base. Grace leaned close to read it in the fading light.

"Take My yoke upon you, and I will give you rest."

Her thoughts returned to the statue in her own church: the suffering Christ.

Bleeding, dying on a tree. *For me.*

Like the slow dawning of a vernal morning, Grace connected the dots Paulie had pointed out. *He took our sin... He identified with our suffering.*

Grace looked from the words to the Shepherd and back to the words again. *He understands because He underwent the same things that I have.*

She stared at the gentle Shepherd. *But even worse. For me. And yet He has rest...*

Was it really so simple? Her shoulders had felt heavily burdened for so long. *So very long.* Would the Shepherd – that same Man dying on the cross back at her own church – give her His rest?

Is it really so easy?

And yet... so very hard, too. For in this moment, Grace realized that this Jesus was not just part of a phrase in her catechism. He was a real Person; more real than any other person. Though she could not see Him, Grace knew He was present; she heard His knocking at the door of her heart. And she knew that He would demand her loyalty, that there would be no going back to her own way of struggling free.

Was it safe?

Grace knew in a moment that it was not.

But she knew that she would say yes, anyway.

Because she believed that Paulie was right: Despite all the difficulties, all the trouble, all the heartache she had endured, He was a good God. One who had suffered as she had.

And whose plan for her was good.

Paying no mind to anyone who might pass by her, Grace knelt there on the rough pavement.

And she entrusted herself to the Everlasting Arms.

EPILOGUE

Worn from the events of the past few days, yet knowing a deep sense of peace, Sarah took Emmeline aside at the funeral reception. Good thing Sarah's sister Mary had volunteered to arrange everything; Sarah wasn't sure she would have had the energy. As it was, Mary certainly had provided a good spread of food.

Sarah led Emmeline over to two chairs in the corner of the community hall. "I got something I need to tell you," she began, speaking quickly since so many relatives would want to grieve with her today.

Emmeline nodded, that sweet smile gracing her lips. "Alright."

Sarah paused but didn't falter. *I know it's a fitting sacrifice; my thank-offering...* "I want to know if you would take David. As your own, I mean." Her eyes glanced down at the baby cradled in her arms, then back up at her friend.

She'd stunned Emmeline, poor thing. "What?" the younger woman stammered.

"Will you? Take David as your own?"

"You mean, adopt him?" Emmeline shook her head. "Sarah, you can't..."

"Yeah, I can. I... want to," Sarah added quietly, knowing a deep pain coupled with a more triumphant joy.

Emmeline began to weep.

~ ~ ~

257

Across the room, Sam Giorgi sipped his black coffee and tried to pay attention to the conversation of one of the Picoletti relatives. But he had to admit it: His eyes kept roving through this crowded hall that smelled of salami and meatballs and lots and lots of cheese. Ah. There she was.

She sat, talking to Emmeline, cradling her newest baby. Despite the years, regardless of the gray that streaked her hair, Sarah still held the power to captivate Sam. *Utterly* captivate him.

He had dropped her once, to his shame and bitter regret. And she had spurned him by marrying another man.

But Charlie Picoletti was dead now, God rest his soul.

And Sam Giorgi wasn't a man to give up easily. Not this time around.

~ ~ ~

"I'm sorry about your father."

Grace looked up from her uneaten sandwich. Paulie stood quietly before her, hat in his hands.

She opened her mouth to apologize for her harsh words toward him, but he smiled, his dark eyes warm and — she believed — full of forgiveness. "You're wearing the earrings," he commented, and there was pleasure in his voice.

"Yes," she said, glad he'd noticed. She'd taken them out of the desk drawer last night.

"They're beautiful on you, Grace," he said, and, because she knew he really meant it, she blushed.

"Thanks," she said again.

Paulie sat down next to her, and they talked long and deeply. And Grace knew that it was perhaps just the first in many similar conversations she would have with Paulie.

After a time, her thoughts drifted back to the geranium that still sat on her bedroom windowsill, nearly ready to bloom scarlet. She remembered how it had appeared stubby and lifeless during the wintertime, without any buds, its stems cut back. As good as dead, it seemed.

Yet the springtime had come and made it new. God had given it new life, as He had her. And as He was doing in her friendship with Paulie, once almost dead.

She thought of the Good Shepherd with His sheep. Of the Man hanging upon the cross. And the understanding bubbled up in her soul: *He makes all things new.*

A Note to Readers

If you enjoyed this book, I'd love for you to encourage others to read it, too... You can do this simply by leaving your thoughts and/or review on Amazon, Goodreads, or your favorite social media site. Thank you!

I'd love to hear from you personally as well. You can connect with me and learn more about my writing on my website:

http://www.aliciagruggieri.com

Thank you for reading!

Until we meet again,

Grace and peace,

Alicia G. Ruggieri

2 Corinthians 4:7

Made in the USA
Charleston, SC
01 August 2016